MW01152898

COUNT FRONTENAC

AND

NEW FRANCE UNDER LOUIS XIV.

BY

FRANCIS PARKMAN,

AUTHOR OF "THE OREGON TRAIL," "THE CONSPIRACY OF PONTIAC,"
"PIONEERS OF FRANCE IN THE NEW WORLD," "THE
JESUITS IN NORTH AMERICA," "LA SALLE,"
AND "THE OLD RÉGIME IN CANADA."

COPYRIGHT EDITION.

TORONTO:

GEORGE N. MORANG & COMPANY, LIMITED.

1901.

Francis Parkman Jr. (September 16, 1823 – November 8, 1893) was an American historian, best known as author of The Oregon Trail: Sketches of Prairie and Rocky-Mountain Life and his monumental seven-volume France and England in North America. These works are still valued as historical sources and as literature. He was also a leading horticulturist, briefly a professor of Horticulture at Harvard University and author of several books on the topic. Parkman was a trustee of the Boston Athenæum from 1858 until his death in 1893.

Early life:

Parkman was born in Boston, Massachusetts to the Reverend Francis Parkman Sr. (1788–1853), a member of a distinguished Boston family, and Caroline (Hall) Parkman. The senior Parkman was minister of the Unitarian New North Church in Boston from 1813 to 1849. As a young boy,

"Frank" Parkman was found to be of poor health, and was sent to live with his maternal grandfather, who owned a 3,000-acre (12 km²) tract of wilderness in nearby Medford, Massachusetts, in the hopes that a more rustic lifestyle would make him more sturdy. In the four years he stayed there, Parkman developed his love of the forests, which would animate his historical research. Indeed, he would later summarize his books as "the history of the American forest." He learned how to sleep and hunt, and could survive in the wilderness like a true pioneer. He later even learned to ride bareback, a skill that would come in handy when he found himself living with the Sioux.

Education and career:

Parkman enrolled at Harvard College at age 16. In his second year he conceived the plan that would become his life's work. In 1843, at the age of 20, he traveled to Europe for eight months in the fashion of the Grand Tour. Parkman made expeditions through the Alps and the Apennine mountains, climbed Vesuvius, and lived for a time in Rome, where he befriended Passionist monks who tried, unsuccessfully, to convert him to Catholicism.

Upon graduation in 1844, he was persuaded to get a law degree, his father hoping such study would rid Parkman of his desire to write his history of the forests. It did no such thing, and after finishing law school Parkman proceeded to fulfill his great plan. His family was somewhat appalled at Parkman's choice of life work, since at the time writing histories of the American wilderness was considered ungentlemanly. Serious historians would study ancient history, or after the fashion of the time, the Spanish Empire. Parkman's works became so well-received that by the end of his lifetime histories of early America had become the fashion. Theodore Roosevelt dedicated his four-volume history of the frontier, The Winning of the West (1889–1896), to Parkman.

In 1846, Parkman travelled west on a hunting expedition, where he spent a number of weeks living with the Sioux tribe, at a time when they were struggling with some of the effects of contact with Europeans, such as epidemic disease and alcoholism. This experience led Parkman to write about American Indians with a much different tone from earlier, more sympathetic portrayals represented by the "noble savage" stereotype. Writing in the era of manifest destiny, Parkman believed that the conquest and displacement of American Indians represented progress, a triumph of "civilization" over "savagery", a common view at the time. He was elected a fellow of the American Academy of Arts and Sciences in 1855, and in 1865 was elected a member of the American Antiquarian Society.

With the Civil War concluding, Parkman, along with Boston Athenæum librarian William F. Poole and fellow trustees Donald McKay Frost and Raymond Sanger Wilkins, saw the importance of securing, for the benefit of future historians, newspapers, broadsides, books, and pamphlets printed in the Confederate States of America. Thanks to Parkman's foresight, the Boston Athenæum is home to one of the most extensive collections of Confederate imprints in the world.

PREFACE.

THE events recounted in this book group themselves in the main about a single figure, that of Count Frontenac, the most remarkable man who ever represented the crown of France in the New World. From strangely unpromising beginnings, he grew with every emergency, and rose equal to every crisis. His whole career was one oF conflict, sometimes petty and personal, sometimes of momentous consequence, involving the question of national ascendency on this continent.-Now that this question is put at rest for ever, it is hard to conceive the anxiety which it wakened in our forefathers. But for one rooted error of French policy, the future of the English-speaking races in America would have been more than endangered.

Under the rule of Frontenac occurred the first serious collision of the rival powers, and the opening of the grand scheme of military occupation by which France strove to envelop and hold in check the industrial populations of the

PREFACE.

English colonies. It was he who made that scheme possible.

In "The Old Regime in Canada," I tried to show from what inherent causes this wilderness empire of the Great Monarch fell at last before a foe, superior indeed in numbers, but lacking all the forces that belong to a system of civil and military centralization. u!he present volume will show how valiantly, and for a time how successfully, New France battled against a fate which her own organic fault made inevitable?] Her history is a great and significant drama, enacted among untamed forests, with a distant gleam of courtly splendors and the regal pomp of Versailles.

The authorities on which the book rests are drawn chiefly from the manuscript collections of the French government in the Archives Nation-ales, the Bibliotheque Nationale, and, above all, the vast repositories of the Archives of the Marine and Colonies. Others are from Canadian and American sources. I have, besides, availed myself of the collection of French, English, and Dutch documents published by the State of New York, under the excellent editorship of Dr. O'Callaghan, and of the manuscript collections made hi France by the governments of Canada and of Massachusetts. A considerable number of books, contemporary or nearly so with

the events described, also help to throw light upon them; and these have all been examined. The citations in the margins represent but a small part of the authorities consulted.

This mass of material has been studied with extreme care, and peculiar pains have been taken to secure accuracy of statement. In the preface of «The Old Regime," I wrote: " Some of the results here reached are of a character which I regret, since they cannot be agreeable to persons for whom I have a very cordial regard. The conclusions drawn from the facts may be matter of opinion: but it will be remembered that the facts themselves can be overthrown only by overthrowing the evidence on which they rest, or bringing forward counter-evidence of equal or greater strength; and neither task will be found an easy one."

The invitation implied in these words has not been accepted. " The Old Regime " was met by vehement protest in some quarters; but, so far as I know, none of the statements of fact contained in it have been attacked by evidence, or even challenged. The lines just quoted are equally applicable to this volume. Should there be occasion, a collection of documentary proofs will be published more than sufficient to make good the positions taken. Meanwhile, it will, I think, be clear to an impartial reader that the

story is told, not in the interest of any race or nationality, but simply in that of historical truth.

When, at the age of eighteen, I formed the purpose of writing on French-American history, I meant at first to limit myself to the great contest which brought that history to a close. It was by an afterthought that the plan was extended to cover the whole field, so that the part of the work, or series of works, first conceived, would, following the sequence of events, be the last executed. As soon as the original scheme was formed, I began to prepare for executing it by examining localities, journeying in forests, visiting Indian tribes, and collecting materials. I have continued to collect them ever since, so that the accumulation is now rather formidable; and, if it is to be used at all, it had better be used at once. Therefore, passing over for the present an intervening period of less decisive importance, I propose to take, as the next subject of this series, " Montcalm and the Fall of New France."

BOSTON, 1 Jan., 1877.

CONTENTS.

Xll

CONTENTS.

COUNT FRONTENAC AND NEW FRANCE UNDER LOUIS XIY.

CHAPTER I.

1620-1672. COUNT AND COUNTESS FRONTENAC.

MADEMOISELLE DB MONTPENSIER AND MADAME DE FRONIENAC. — ORLEANS. — THE MARECHALE DB CAMP. — COUNT FRONTENAC. — CONJUGAL DISPUTES. — EARLY LIFE OF FRONTENAC. — Hia COURTSHIP AND MARRIAGE. — ESTRANGEMENT. — SCENES AT ST. FARGEAU. — THE LADY OF HONOR DISMISSED. — FRONTENAO AS A SOLDIER. — HE is MADE GOVERNOR OF NEW FRANCE. — LES DIVINES.

AT Versailles there is the portrait of a lady, beautiful and young. She is painted as Minerva, a plumed helmet on her head, and a shield on her arm. In a corner of the canvas is written Anne de La Grange-Trianon, Comtesse de Frontenac* This blooming goddess was the wife of the future governor of Canada.

Madame de Frontenac, at the age of about twenty, was a favorite companion of Mademoiselle de Montpensier, the grand-daughter of Henry IV. and daughter of the weak and dastardly Gaston, Duke of Orleans. Nothing in French annals has found more readers than the story of the exploit of this spirited princess at Orleans during the civil

COUNT AND COUNTESS FRONTENAC. [1662,

war of the Fronde. Her cousin Conde', chief of the revolt, had found favor in her eyes; and she had espoused his cause against her cousin, the king. The royal army threatened Orleans. The duke, her father, dared not leave Paris; but he consented that his daughter should go in his place to hold the city for Cond6 and the Fronde.

The princess entered her carriage and set out on her errand, attended by a small escort. With her were three young married ladies, the Marquise de Br6aut£, the Comtesse de Fiesque, and the Comtesse de Fronteriac. In two days they reached Orleans. The civic authorities were afraid to declare against the king, and hesitated to open the gates to the daughter of their duke, who, standing in the moat with her three companions, tried persuasion and threats in vain. The prospect was not encouraging, when a crowd of boatmen came up from the river and offered the princess their services. " I accepted them gladly," she writes, " and said a thousand fine things, such as one must say to that sort of people to make them do what one wishes." She gave them money as well as fair words, and begged them to burst open one of the gates. They fell at once to the work ; while the guards and officials looked down from the walls, neither aiding nor resisting them. " To animate the boatmen by my presence," she continues, " I mounted a hillock near by. I did not look to see which way I went, but clambered up like a cat, clutching brambles and thorns, and jumping over hedges without hurting myself.

Madame de Br^aute*, who is the most cowardly creature in the world, began to cry out against me and everybody who followed me; in fact, I do not know if she did not swear in her excitement, which amused me very much." At length, a hole was knocked in the gate; and a gentleman of her train, who had directed the attack, beckoned her to come on, " As it was very muddy, a man took me and carried me forward, and thrust me in at this hole, where my head was no sooner through than the drums beat to salute me. I gave my hand to the captain of the guard. The shouts redoubled. Two men took me and put me in a wooden chair. I do not know whether I was seated in it or on their arms, for I was beside myself with joy. Everybody was kissing my hands, and I almost died with laughing to see myself in such an odd position." There was no resisting the enthusiasm of the people and the soldiers. Orleans was won for the Fronde. 1

The young Countesses of Frontenac and Fiesque had constantly followed her, and climbed after her through the hole in the gate. Her father wrote to compliment them on their prowess, and addressed his letter a Mesdames les Comtesses, Marechales de Camp dans Tarmee de ma fille contre le Mazarin. Officers and soldiers took part in the pleasantry; and, as Madame de Frontenac passed on horseback before the troops, they saluted her with the honors paid to a brigadier.

When the king, or Cardinal Mazarin who con-

Mfmoires de Mademoiselle de Montpensier, I. 868-363 (ed. 1869).

trolled him, had triumphed over the revolting princes, Mademoiselle de Montpensier paid the penalty of her exploit by a temporary banishment from the court. She roamed from place to place, with a little court of her own, of which Madame de Frontenac was a conspicuous member. During the war, Count Frontenac had been dangerously ill of a fever in Paris; and his wife had been absent for ;i time, attending him. She soon rejoined the princess, who was at her chateau of St. Fargeau, three days' journey from Paris, when an incident occurred which placed the married life of her fair companion in an unexpected light. " The Duch-esse de Sully came to see me, and brought with her M. d' Herbault and M. de Frontenac. Frontenac had stopped here once before, but it was only for a week, when he still had the fever, and took great care of himself like a man who had been at the door of death. This time he was in high health. His arrival had not been expected, and his wife was so much surprised that everybody observed it, especially as the surprise seemed to be not at all a pleasant one. Instead of going to talk with her husband, she went off and hid herself, crying and screaming because he had said that he would like to have her company that evening. I was very much astonished, especially as I had never before perceived her aversion to him. The elder Com-tesse de Fiesque remonstrated with her; but she only cried the more. Madame de Fiesque then brought books to show her her duty as a wife; but it did no good, and at last she got into such a state

that wie sent for the cure with holy water to exorcise her." l

Count Frontenac came of an ancient and noble race, said to have been of Basque origin. His father held a high post in the household of Louis XIII., who became the child's god-father, and gave him his own name. At the age of fifteen, the young Louis showed an incontrollable passion for the life of a soldier. He was sent to the seat of war in Holland, to serve under the Prince of Orange. At the age of nineteen, he was a volunteer at the siege of Hesdin; m the next year, he was at Arras, where he distinguished himself during a sortie of the garrison; in the next, he took part in the siege of Aire; and, in the next, in those of Callioure and Perpignan. At the age of twenty-three, he was made colonel of the regiment of Normandy, which he commanded in repeated battles and sieges of the Italian campaign. He was several times wounded, and in 1646 he had an arm broken at the siege of Orbitello. In the same year, when twenty-six years old, he was raised to the rank of marechal de camp, equivalent to that of brigadier-general. A year or two later, we find him at Paris, at the house of his father, on the Quai des Celestins. 1

In the same neighborhood lived La Grange-Trianon, Sieur de Neuville, a widower of fifty,

Mfmoires de Mademoiselle de Montpensier, II. 265. The curb's holy water, or his exhortations, were at last successful.

Pinard, Chronologic Historique-militaire, VI.; Table de, la Gazette do France; Jal, Dictionnaire Critique, Biographique, et d'Histoire, art. " tenac; " Goyer, Oraison Funebre du Comte de Frontenac.

with one child, a daughter of sixteen, whom he had placed in the charge of his relative, Madame de Bouthillier. Frontenac fell in love with her. Madame de Bouthillier opposed the match, and told La Grange that he might do better for his daughter than to marry her to a man who, say what he might, had but twenty thousand francs a year. La Grange was weak and vacillating: sometimes he listened to his prudent kinswoman, and sometimes to the eager suitor; treated him as a son-in-law, carried love messages from him to his daughter, and ended by refusing him her hand, and ordering her to renounce him on pain of being immured in a convent. Neither Frontenac nor his mistress was of a pliant temper. In the neighborhood was the little church of St. Pierre aux Bceufs, which had the privilege of uniting couples without the consent of their parents; and here, on a Wednesday in October, 1648, the lovers were married in presence of a number of Frontenac's relatives. La Grange was furious at the discovery; but his anger soon cooled, and complete reconciliar-tion followed. 1

The happiness of the newly wedded pair was short. Love soon changed to aversion, at least on the part of the bride. She was not of a tender nature; her temper was imperious, and she had a restless craving for excitement. Frontenac, on his part, was the most wayward and headstrong of men. She bore him a son; but maternal cares

« HutorietU* de Tallemant de Rdaux, IX, 214 (ed. Monmerqu6); Jal, Dittionnairc Critique, etc.

were not to her liking. The infant, Francois Louis, was placed in the keeping of a nurse at the village of Clion ; and his young mother left her husband, to follow the fortunes of Mademoiselle de Mont-pensier, who for a time pronounced her charming, praised her wit and beauty, and made her one of her ladies of honor. Very curious and amusing are some of the incidents recounted by the princess, in which Madame de Frontenac bore part; but what is more to our purpose are the sketches traced here and there by the same sharp pen, in which one may discern the traits of the destined saviour of New France. Thus, in the following, we see him at St. Fargeau in the same attitude in which we shall often see him at Quebec.

The princess and the duke her father had a dispute touching her property. Frontenac had lately been at Blois, where the duke had possessed him with his own views of the questions at issue. Accordingly, on arriving at St. Fargeau, he seemed disposed to assume the character of mediator. " He wanted," says the princess, " to discuss my affairs with me: I listened to his preaching, and he also spoke about these matters to Prefontaine (her man of business). I returned to the house after our promenade, and we went to dance in the great hall. While we were dancing, I saw Prefontaine walking at the farther end with Frontenac, who was talking and gesticulating. This continued for a long time. Madame de Sully noticed it also, and seemed disturbed by it, as I was myself. I said v * Have we not danced enough ?

Madame de Sully assented, and we went out. I called Pr6fontaine, and asked him, ' What was Frontenac saying to you?' He answered: < He was scolding me. I never saw such an impertinent man in my life. 1 I went to my room, and Madame de Sully and Madame de Fiesque followed. Madame de Sully said to Prefontaine: < I was very much disturbed to see you talking with so much warmth to Monsieur de Frontenac; for he came here in such ill-humor that I was afraid he would quarrel with you. Yesterday, when we were, in the carriage, he was ready to eat us.' The Comtesse de Fiesque said, < This morning he came to see my mother-in-law, and scolded at her/ Prefontaine answered: 'He wanted to throttle me. I never saw a man so crazy and absurd.' We all four began to pity poor Madame de Frontenac for having such a husband, and to think her right in not wanting to go with him." i

Frontenac owned the estate of Isle Savary, on the Indre, not far from Blois; and here, soon after the above scene, the princess made him a visit. "It is a pretty enough place," she says, "for a man like him. The house is well furnished, and he gave me excellent entertainment. He showed me all the plans he had for improving it, and making gardens, fountains, and ponds. It would need the riches of a superintendent of finance to execute his schemes, and how anybody else should venture to think of them I cannot comprehend."

"While Frontenac was at St. Fargeau," she

1 Mtmoire de Mademoiselle de Montoensier, U. 267.

1653-60.] SCENES AT ST. FARGEAU.

continues, " he kept open table, and many of my people went to dine with him; for he affected to hold court, and acted as if everybody owed duty to him. The conversation was always about my affair with his Royal Highness (her father), whose conduct towards me was always praised, while mine was blamed. Frontenac spoke ill of Prefon-taine, and, in fine, said every thing he could to displease me and stir up my own people against me. He praised every thing that belonged to himself, and never came to sup or dine with me without speaking of some ragout or some new sweetmeat which had been served up on his table, ascribing it all to the excellence of the officers of his kitchen. The very meat that he ate, according to him, had a different taste on his board than on any other. As for his silver plate, it was always of good workmanship ; and his dress was always of patterns invented by himself. When he had new clothes, he paraded them like a child. One day he brought me some to look at, and left them on my dressing-table. We were then at Chambord. His Royal Highness came into the room, and must have thought it odd to see breeches and doublets in such a place. Prefontaine and I laughed about it a great deal. Frontenac took everybody who came to St. Fargeau to see his stables; and all who wished to gain his good graces were obliged to admire his horses, which were very indifferent. In short, this is his way in every thing." 1

Though not himself of the highest rank, his

position at court was, from the courtier point of view, an enviable one. The princess, after her banishment had ended, more than once mentions incidentally that she had met him in the cabinet of the queen. Her dislike of him became intense, and her fondness for his wife changed at last to aversion. She charges the countess with ingratitude. She discovered, or thought that she discovered, that in her dispute with her father, and in certain dissensions in her own household, Madame de Frontenac had acted secretly in opposition to her interests and wishes. The imprudent lady of honor received permission to leave her service. It was a woful scene. "She saw me get into my carriage," writes the princess, " and her distress was greater than ever. Her tears flowed abundantly : as for me, my fortitude was perfect, and I looked on with composure while she cried. If any thing could disturb my tranquillity, it was the recollection of the time when she laughed while I waa crying." Mademoiselle de Montpensier had been deeply offended, and apparently with reason. The countess and her husband received an order never again to appear in her presence; but soon after, when the princess was with the king and queen at a comedy in the garden of the Louvre, Frontenac, who had previously arrived, immediately changed his position, and with his usual audacity took a post so conspicuous that she could not help seeing him. " I confess/' she says, " I was so angry that I could find no pleasure in the play; but I said nothing to the king and queen, fearing that

they would not take such a view of the matter as I wished." 1

With the close of her relations with " La Grande Mademoiselle," Madame de Frontenac is lost to sight for a while. In 1669, a Venetian embassy came to France to beg for aid against the Turks, who for more than two years had attacked Candia in overwhelming force. The ambassadors offered to place their own troops under French command, and they asked Turenne to name a general officer equal to the task. Frontenac had the signal honor of being chosen by the first soldier of Europe for this most arduous and difficult position. He went accordingly. The result increased his reputation for ability and courage; but Candia was doomed, and its chief fortress fell into the hands of the infidels, after a protracted struggle, which is said to have cost them a' hundred and eighty thousand men. 9

Three years later, Frontenac received the ap-] pointment of Governor and Lieutenant-General for the king in all New France. " He was," says Saint-Simon, "a man of excellent parts, living much in society, and completely ruined. He found it hard to bear the imperious temper of his wife; and he was given the government of Canada to deliver him from her, and afford him some means of living." 3 Certain scandalous songs of the day

1 Mfmoires de Mademoiselle de Montpensier, III. 270.

2 Oraison funebre du Comte de Frontenac, par le Pere Olivier Goyer. A powerful French contingent, under another command co-operated with the Venetians under Frontenac.

s Mtmoires du£ku:de Saint-Simon, II. 270 ; V. 836.

12 COUNT AND COUNTESS FRONTENAC. [1072

assign a different motive for his appointment, Louis XIV. was enamoured of Madame de Mon-tespan. She had once smiled upon Frontenao ; and it is said that the jealous king gladly embraced the opportunity of removing from his presence, and from hers, a lover who had forestalled him. 1

Frontenac's wife had no thought of following him across the sea. A more congenial life awaited her at home. She had long had a friend of humbler station than herself, Mademoiselle d'Outrelaise, daughter of an obscure gentleman of Poitou, an amiable and accomplished person, who became through life her constant companion. The extensive building called the Arsenal, formerly the residence of Sully, the minister of Henry IV., contained suites of apartments which were granted to persons who had influence enough to obtain

1 Note of M. Brunet, in Correspondance de la Duchesse d* Orleans, I. 200 (ed. 1869).

The following lines, among others, were passed about secretly among the courtiers: —

" Je suis ravi que le roi, notre sire,

Aime la Montespan; Moi, Frontenac, je me creve de rire,

Sachant ce qui lui pend; Et je dirai, sans etre des plus bestes, Tu n'as que mon reste,

Roi, Tu n'as que mon reste."

Mademoiselle de Montpensier had mentioned in her memoirs, some years before, that Frontenac, in taking out his handkerchief, dropped from his pocket a love-letter to Mademoiselle de Mortemart, afterwards Madame de Montespan, which was picked up by one of the attendants of the princess. The king, on the other hand, was at one time attracted by the charms of Madame de Frontenac, against whom, however, no aspersion is cast.

The Comte de Grignan, son-in-law of Madame de S6vign<<, was an unsuccessful competitor with Frontenac for the government of Canada.

them. The Due de Lude, grand master of artillery, had them at his disposal, and gave one of them to Madame de Frontenac. Here she made her abode with her friend; and here at last she died, at the age of seventy-five. The annalist Saint-Simon, who knew the court and all belonging to it better than any other man of his time, says of her: " She had been beautiful and gay, and was always in the best society, where she was greatly in request. Like her husband, she had little property and abundant wit. She and Mademoiselle d'Outrelaise, whom she took to live with her, gave the tone to the best company of Paris and the court, though they never went thither. They were called Les Divines. In fact, they demanded incense like goddesses; and it was lavished upon them all their lives."

Mademoiselle d'Outrelaise died long before the countess, who retained in old age the rare social gifts which to the last made her apartments a resort of, the highest society of that brilliant epoch. It was in her power to be very useful to her absent husband, who often needed her support, and who seems to have often received it.

She was childless. Her son, Francois Louis, was killed, some say in battle, and others in a duel, at an early age. Her husband died nine years before her; and the old countess left what little she had to her friend Beringhen, the king's master of the horse. 1

1 On Frontenac and his family, see Appendix A.

CHAPTER H.

1672-1675.

FRONTENAC AT QUEBEC.

ABRTVAL. — BRIGHT PROSPECTS. — THE THREE ESTATES OP NKW FRANCE. — SPEECH OF THE GOVERNOR. — His INNOVATIONS. — ROYAL DISPLEASURE. — SIGNS OF STORM. — FRONTENAC AND THH PRIESTS. — His ATTEMPTS TO CIVILIZE THE INDIANS. — OPPOSITION. — COMPLAINTS AND HEART-BURNINGS.

FRONTENAC was fifty-two years old when he landed at Quebec. If time had done little to cure his many faults, it had done nothing to weaken the springs of his unconquerable vitality. In his ripe middle age, he was as keen, fiery, and perversely j headstrong as when he quarrelled with Pr£fon-taine in the hall at St. Fargeau.

Had nature disposed him to melancholy, there was much in his position to awaken it. A man of courts and camps, born and bred in the focus of a most gorgeous civilization, he was banished to the ends of the earth, among savage hordes and half-reclaimed forests, to exchange the splendors of St. Germain and the dawning glories of Versailles for a stern gray rock, haunted by sombre priests, rugged merchants and traders, blanketed Indians, and wild bush-rangers. But Frontenac was a man of action. He wasted no time in vain regrets, and

set himself to his work with the elastic vigor of youth. His first impressions had been very favorable. When, as he sailed up the St. Lawrence, the basin of Quebec opened before him, his imagination kindled with the grandeur of the scene. " I never," he wrote, " saw any thing more superb than the position of this town. It could not be better situated as the future capital of a great empire." 1

That Quebec was to become the capital of a great empire there seemed in truth good reason to believe. The young king and his minister Colbert had labored in earnest to build up a new France in the west. For years past, ship-loads of emigrants had landed every summer on the strand beneath the rock. All was life and action, and the air was full of promise. The royal agent Talon had written to his master: " This part of the French monarchy is destined to a grand future. All that I see around me points to it; and the colonies of foreign nations, so long settled on the seaboard, are trembling with fright in view of what his Majesty has accomplished here within the last seven years. The measures we have taken to confine them within narrow limits, and the prior claim we have established against them by formal acts of possession, do not permit them to extend themselves except at peril of having war declared against them as usurpers; and this, in fact, is what they seem greatly to fear." 2

1 Frontenac au Ministre, 2 Nov., 1672.

2 Talon av Afimstre, 2 Nov., 1671.

JO FRONTENAC AT QUEBEC. [1672

Frontenac shared the spirit of the hour. His first step was to survey his government. He talked with traders, colonists, and officials; visited seigniories, farms, fishing-stations, and all the infant industries that Talon had galvanized into life, examined the new ship on the stocks, admired the structure of the new brewery, went to Three Rivers to see the iron mines, and then, having acquired a tolerably exact idea of his charge, returned to Quebec. He was well pleased with what he saw, but not with the ways and means of Canadian travel; for he thought it strangely unbecoming that a lieutenant-general of the king should be forced to crouch on a sheet of bark, at the bottom of a birch canoe, scarcely daring to move his head to the right or left lest he should disturb the balance of the fragile vessel.

At Quebec he convoked the council, made them a speech, and administered the oath of allegiance. 1 This did not satisfy him. He resolved that all Quebec should take the oath together. It was little but a pretext. Like many of his station, Frontenac was not in full sympathy with the centralizing movement of the time, which tended to level ancient rights, privileges, and prescriptions under the ponderous roller of the monarchical administration. He looked back with regret to the day the three orders of the state, clergy, nobles, commons, had a place and a power in the >n of national affairs. The three orders still I, in form, if not in substance, in some of

the provinces of France; and Frontenac conceived the idea of jeproducmg_tEem_in Cana3il Not only did he cherisTrthe tradition of faded liberties, but he loved pomp and circumstance, above all, when he was himself the central figure in it; and the thought of a royal governor of Languedoc or Brittany, presiding over the estates of his province, appears to have fired him with emulation.

He had no difficulty in forming his order of the clergy. The Jesuits and the seminary priests supplied material even more abundant than he wished. For the order of the nobles, he found three or four gentilshommes at Quebec, and these he reinforced with a number of officers. The third estate consisted of the merchants and citizens; and he formed the members of the council and the magistrates into another distinct body, though, properly speaking, they belonged to the third estate, of which by nature and prescription they were the head. The Jesuits, glad no doubt to lay him under some slight obligation, lent him their church for the ceremony that he meditated, and aided in J decorating it for the occasion. Here, on the twenty-third of October, 1672, the three estates of Canada were convoked, with as much pomp and splendor as circumstances would permit. Then Frontenac, with the ease of a man of the world and the loftiness of a grand seigneur, delivered himself of the harangue he had prepared. He wrote exceedingly well; he is said also to have excelled as an orator; certainly he was never averse to the tones of his own eloquence. His

speech was addressed to a double audience : the throng that filled the church, and the king and the minister three thousand miles away. He told his hearers that he had called the assembly, not because he doubted their loyalty, but in order to afford them the delight of making public protestation of devotion to a prince, the terror of whose irresistible arms was matched only by the charms of his person and the benignity of his rule. " The Holy Scriptures," he said, " command us to obey our sovereign, and teach us that no pretext or reason can dispense us from this obedience." And, in a glowing eulogy on Louis XIV., he went on to show that obedience to him was not only a duty, but an inestimable privilege. He dwelt with admiration on the recent victories in Holland, and held forth the hope that a speedy and glorious peace would leave his Majesty free to turn his thoughts to the colony which already owed so much to his fostering care. " The true means," pursued Frontenac, " of gaining his favor and his support, is for us to unite with one heart in laboring for the progress of Canada." Then he addressed, in turn, the clergy, the nobles, the magistrates, and the citi-

Tzens. He exhorted the priests to continue with zeal their labors for the conversion of the Indians,

'[and to make them subjects not only of Christ, but [also of the king; in short, to tame and civilize them, a portion of their_duties in which he plainly gave them to understand that they had not hitherto acquitted themselves to his satisfaction, Next, he appealed to the nobles, commended

their gallantry, and called upon them to be as assiduous in the culture and improvement of the colony as they were valiant in its defence. The magistrates, the merchants, and the colonists in general were each addressed in an appropriate exhortation. "I can assure you, messieurs/* he concluded, " that if you faithfully discharge, your several duties, each in his station, his Majesty will extend to us all the help and all the favor that we can desire. It is needless, then, to urge you to act as I have counselled, since it is for your own interest to do so. As for me, it only remains to protest before you that I shall esteem myself happy in consecrating all my efforts, and, if need be, my life itself, to extending the empire of Jesus Christ throughout all this land, and the supremacy of our king over all the nations that dwell in it."

He administered the oath, and the assembly dissolved. He_now_applied himself to another work ; that of giving a mumclpalr^govefmn^nt to Quebec,

ot the citielTof France

In place of the syndic an official supposed to represent the interests of the citizens, he ordered the public election of three aldermen, of whom the senior shoul(LayoK One of the number was to go out of office every year, his place being filled by a new election ; and the governor, as representing the king, reserved the right of confirmation or rejection. He then, in concert with the chief inhabitants, proceeded to frame a body of regulations for the government of a town destined, as he again and again declares, to become the capi-

tal of a mighty empire; and he farther ordained that the people should hold a meeting every six months to discuss questions involving the welfare of the colony. The boldness of these measures will scarcely be appreciated at the present day. The intendant Talon declined, on pretence of a slight illness, to be present at the meeting of the estates. He knew too well the temper of the king, whose constant policy it was to destroy or paralyze every institution or custom that stood in the way of his autocracy. The despatches in which Frontenac announced to his masters what he had done received in due time their answer. The minister Colbert wrote : " Your assembling of the inhabitants to take the oath of fidelity, and your division of them into three estates, may have had a good effect for the moment; but it is well for you to observe that you are always to follow, in the government of Canada, the forms in use here; and since our kings have long regarded it as good for their service not to convoke the states-general of the kingdom, in order, perhaps, to abolish insensibly this ancient usage, you, on your part, should very rarely, or. to speak more correctly, never, give a corporate form to the inhabitants oi Canada. You should even, as the colony strengthens, suppress gradually the office of the syndic, who presents petitions in the name of the inhabitants ; for it is well that each should speak for himself, and no one for all." 1

» Frontenac au Roi, 2 Nov., 1672; Ibid., 13 Nov., 1678 ; Harangue du Cvnte de Frontenac en I'Assemble a Quebec ; Prestations de Serment, 23 Oct* 1672 ; R4glement de Police fait par Monsieur le Comte de Frontenac ; Colbert ft Frontenac. 18 Juin. 1678.

Here, in brief, is the whole spirit of the French colonial rule in Canada; a government, as I have elsewhere shown, of excellent intentions, but of arbitrary methods. Frontenac, tilled with the traditions of the past, and sincerely desirous of the good of the colony, rashly set himself against the prevailing current. His municipal government, and his meetings of citizens, were, like his three estates, abolished by a word from the court, which, bold and obstinate as he was, he dared not disobey. Had they been allowed to subsist, there can be little doubt that great good would have resulted to Canada.

Frontenac has been called a mere soldier. He was an excellent soldier, and more besides. He was a man of vigorous and cultivated mind, penetrating observation, and ample travel and experience. His zeal for the colony, however, was often counteracted by the violence of his prejudices, and by two other influences. First, he was a ruined man, who meant to mend his fortunes ; and his wish that Canada should prosper was joined with a determination to reap a goodly part of her prosperity for himself. Again, he could not endure a rival; opposition maddened him, and, when crossed or thwarted, he forgot every thing but his passion. Signs of storm quickly showed themselves between him and the intendant Talon; but the danger was averted by the departure of that official for France. A cloud then rose in the direction of the clergy.

" Another thing displeases me," writes Fronte-

nae, " and this is the complete dependence of the grand vicar and the seminary priests on the Jesuits, for they never do the least thing without their order: so that they (the Jesuits) are masters in spiritual matters, which, as you know, is a powerful lever for moving every thing else." And he complains that they have spies in town and country, that they abuse the confessional, intermeddle in families, set husbands against wives, and parents against children, and all, as they say, for the greater glory of God. " I call to mind every day, Mon-seigneur, what you did me the honor to say to me when I took leave of you, and every day I am satisfied more and more of the great importance to the king's service of opposing the slightest of the attempts which are daily made against his authority." He goes on to denounce a certain sermon, preached by a Jesuit, to the great scandal of loyal subjects, wherein the father declared that the king had exceeded his powers in licensing the trade in brandy when the bishop had decided it to be a sin, together with other remarks of a seditious nature. " I was tempted several times," pursues Frontenac, " to leave the church with my guards and interrupt the sermon; but I contented myself with telling the grand vicar and the superior of the Jesuits, after it was over, that I was very much surprised at what I had heard, and demanded justice at their hands. They greatly blamed the preacher, and disavowed him, attributing his language, after their custom, to an excess of zeal, and

Frontenac au Ministry 2 Nov., 1672

making many apologies, with which I pretended to be satisfied; though I told them, nevertheless, that their excuses would not pass current with me another time, and, if the thing happened again, I would put the preacher in a place where he would learn how to speak. Since then they have been a little more careful, though not enough to prevent one from always seeing their intention to persuade the people that, even in secular matters, their authority ought to be respected above any other. As there are many persons here who have no more brains than they need, and who are attached to them by ties of interest or otherwise, it is necessary to have an eye to these matters in this country more than anywhere else." 1

The churchmen, on their part, were not idle. The bishop, who was then in France, contrived by some means to acquaint himself with the contents of the private despatches sent by Colbert in reply to the letters of Frontenac. He wrote to another ecclesiastic to communicate what he had learned, at the same time enjoining great caution; " since, while it is well to acquire all necessary information, and to act upon it, it is of the greatest importance to keep secret our possession of such knowledge." 9

The king and the minister, in their instructions to Frontenac, had dwelt with great emphasis on

1 Frontenac au Ministre, 13 Nov., 1673.

2 Laval a . 1674. The letter is a complete summary of the contents of Colbert's recent despatch to Frontenac. Then follows the injunction to secrecy, " estant de tres-grande consequence que Ton nc sache pas que Ton aye rien appris de tout cela, sur quoi neanmoins il est bon que Ton agisse et que Ton me donne tous les advis qui seroiit necessaires."

the expediency of civilizing the Indians, teaching them the French language, and amalgamating them with the colonists. Frontenac, ignorant as yet of Indian nature and unacquainted with the difficulties of the case, entered into these views with great heartiness. He exercised from the first an extraordinary influence over all the Indians with whom he came in contact; and he persuaded the most savage and refractory of them, the Iroquois, to place eight of their children in his hands. Four of these were girls and four were boys. He took two of the boys into his own household, of which they must have proved most objectionable inmates; and he supported the other two, who were younger, out of his own slender resources, placed them in respectable French families, and required them to go daily to school. The girls were given to the charge of the Ursulines. Frontenac continually urged the Jesuits to co-operate with him in this work of civilization, but the results of his urgency disappointed and exasperated him. He complains that in the village of the Hurons, near Quebec, and under the control of the Jesuits, the French language was scarcely known. In fact, the fathers contented themselves with teaching their converts the doctrines and rites of the Roman Church, while

retaining the food, dress, and habits of their origi-
' nal barbarism.

In defence of the missionaries, it should be said that, when brought in contact with the French, the Indians usually caught the vices of civilization without its virtues ; but Frontenac made no allow-

ances. " The Jesuits he writes, " will not civilize the Indians, because they wish to keep them in perpetual wardship. They think more of beaver skins than of souls, and their missions are pure mockeries." At the same time he assures the minister that, when he is obliged to correct them, he does so with the utmost gentleness. In spite of this somewhat doubtful urbanity, it seems clear that a storm was brewing; and it was fortunate for the peace of the Canadian Church that the attention of the truculent governor was drawn to other quarters.

CHAPTER HI.

1673-1675. FRONTENAC AND PERROT.

LA. BALFJS. — FORT FRONTENAC. — PERROT. — His SPECULATIONS.— His TYRANNY. — THE BUSH-RANGERS. — PERROT REVOLTS. — BECOMES ALARMED.

— DILEMMA OF FRONTENAC. — MEDIATION OB FENELON. — PKRROT IN PRISON. — EXCITEMENT OF THE SULPI-TIANS. — INDIGNATION OF FENELON. — PASSION OF FRONTENAC. — PERROT ON TRIAL. — STRANGE SCENES. — APPEAL TO THE KING. — ANSWERS OF Louis XIV. AND COLBERT. — FENELON REBUKED.

NOT long before Frontenac's arrival, Courcelle, his predecessor, went to Lake Ontario with an armed force, in order to impose respect on the Iroquois, who had of late become insolent. As a means of keeping them in check, and at the same time controlling the fur trade of the upper country, he had recommended, like Talon before him, the building of a fort near the outlet of the lake. Frontenac at once saw the advantages of such a measure, and his desire to execute it was stimulated by the reflection that the proposed fort might be made not only a safeguard to the colony, but also a source of profit to himself.

At Quebec, there was a grave, thoughtful, self-contained young man, who soon found his way into Frontenac's confidence. There was between them the sympathetic attraction of two bold and

energetic spirits; and though Cavelier de Ja Salle had neither the irritable vanity of the count, nor his Gallic vivacity of passion, he had in full measure the same unconquerable pride and hardy resolution. There were but two or three men in Canada who knew the western wilderness so well. He was full of schemes of ambition and of gain; and, from this moment, he and Frontenac seem to have formed an alliance, which ended only with the governor's recall.

In telling the story of La Salle, I have described the execution of the new plan: the muster of the Canadians, at the call of Frontenac ; the consternation of those of the merchants whom he and La Salle had not taken into their counsels, and who saw in the movement the preparation for a gigantic fur trading monopoly; the intrigues set on foot to bar the enterprise; the advance up the St. Lawrence ; the assembly of Iroquois at the destined spot; the ascendency exercised over them by the governor; the building of Fort Frontenac on the ground'where Kingston now stands, and its final transfer into the hands of La Salle, on condition, there can be no doubt, of sharing the expected profits with his patron. 1

On the way to the lake, Frontenac stopped for some time at Montreal, where he had full opportunity to become acquainted with a state of things to which his attention had already been directed. -This state of things was as follows: —

When the intendant, Talon, came for the second

1 Discovery of the Great West, chap. vi.

time to Canada, in 1669, an officer named Perrot, who had married his niece, came with him. Perrot, anxious to turn to account the influence of his wife's relative, looked about him for some post of honor and profit, and quickly discovered that the government of Montreal was vacant. The priests of St. Sulpice, feudal owners of the place, had the right of appointing their own governor. Talon advised them to choose Perrot, who thereupon received the desired commission, which, however, was revocable at the will of those who had granted it. The new governor, therefore, begged another commission from the king, and after a little delay he obtained it. Thus he became, in some measure, independent of the priests, who, if they wished to rid themselves of him, must first gain the royal consent.

Perrot, as he had doubtless foreseen, found himself in an excellent position for making money. The tribes of the upper lakes, and all the neighboring regions, brought down their furs every summer to the annual fair at Montreal. Perrot took his measures accordingly. On the island which still bears his name, lying above Montreal and directly in the route of the descending savages, he built a storehouse, 'and placed it in charge of a retired lieutenant named Brucy, who stopped the Indians on their way, and carried on an active trade with them, to the great profit of himself and his associate, and the great loss of the merchants in the settlements below. This was not all. Perrot connived at the desertion of his own

soldiers, who escaped to the woods, became cow-reurs de bois, or bush-rangers, traded with the Indians in their villages, and shared their gains with their commander. Many others, too, of these forest rovers, outlawed by royal edicts, found in the governor of Montreal a protector, under similar conditions.

The journey from Quebec to Montreal often consumed a fortnight. Perrot thought himself virtually independent; and relying on his commission from the king, the protection of Talon, and his connection with other persons of influence, he felt safe in his position, and began to play the petty tyrant. The judge of Montreal, and several of the chief inhabitants, came to offer a humble remonstrance against disorders committed by some of the ruffians in his interest. Perrot received them with a storm of vituperation, and presently sent the judge to prison. This proceeding was followed by a series of others, closely akin to it, so that the priests of St. Sulpice, who received their full share of official abuse, began to repent bitterly of the governor they had chosen.

Frontenac had received stringent orders from the king to arrest all the bush-rangers, or coureurs de bois ; but, since he had scarcely a soldier at his disposal, except his own body-guard, the order was difficult to execute. As, however, most of these outlaws were in the service of his rival, Perrot, his zeal to capture them rose high against every obstacle. He had, moreover, a plan of his own in regard to them, and had already petitioned the

minister for a galley, to the benches of which the captive bush-rangers were to be chained as rowers, thus supplying the representative of the king with a means of transportation befitting his dignity, and at the same time giving wholesome warning against the infraction of royal edicts. 1 Accordingly, he sent orders to the judge, at Montreal, to seize every coureur de bois on whom he could lay hands.

The judge, hearing that two of the most notorious were lodged in the house of a lieutenant named Carion, sent a constable to arrest them; whereupon Carion threatened and maltreated the officer of justice, and helped the men to escape. Perrot took the part of his lieutenant, and told the judge that he would put him in prison, in spite of Fron-tenac, if he ever dared to attempt such an arrest again. 9

When Frontenac heard what had happened, his ire was doubly kindled. On the one hand, Perrot had violated the authority lodged by the king in the person of his representative; and, on the other, the mutinous official was a rival in trade, who had made great and illicit profits, while his superior had, thus far, made none. As a governor and as a man, Frontenac was deeply moved; yet, helpless as he was, he could do no more than send three of his guardsmen, under a lieutenant named Hizard, with orders to arrest Carion and bring him to Quebec.

The commission was delicate. The arrest was

1 Frontenac au Afinistre, 2 Nov., 1672.

* Memoire des Motifs qni ont oblige* M. h Comte de Frontenac de faire arreter le Sieur Perrot

to be made in the dominions of Perrot, who had the means to prevent it, and the audacity to use them. Bizard acted accordingly. He went to Carion's house, and took him prisoner; then proceeded to the house of the merchant Le Ber, where he left a letter, in which Frontenac, as was the usage on such occasions, gave notice to the local governor of the arrest he had ordered. It was the object of Bizard to escape with his prisoner before Perrot could receive the letter; but, meanwhile, the wife of Carion ran to him with the news, and the governor suddenly arrived, in a frenzy of rage, followed by a sergeant and three or four soldiers. The sergeant held the point of his halberd against the breast of Bizard, while Perrot, choking with passion, demanded, " How dare you arrest an officer in my government without my leave ? " The lieutenant replied that he acted under orders of the governor-general, and gave Frontenac's letter to Perrot, who immediately threw it into his face, exclaiming : " Take it back to your master, and tell him to teach you your business better another time. Meanwhile you are my prisoner." Bizard protested in vain. He was led to jail, whither he was followed a few days after by Le Ber, who had mortally offended Perrot by signing an attestation of the scene he had witnessed. As he was the chief merchant of the place, his arrest produced a great sensation, while his wife presently took to her bed with a nervous fever.

As Perrot's anger cooled, he became somewhat
alarmed. He had resisted the royal authority, and insulted its representative. The consequences might be serious; yet he could not bring himself to retrace his steps. He merely released Bizard, and sullenly permitted him to depart, with a letter to the governor-general, more impertinent than apologetic. 1

Frontenac, as his enemies declare, was accustomed, when enraged, to foam at the mouth. Perhaps he did so when he learned the behavior of Perrot. If he had had at command a few companies of soldiers, there can be little doubt that he would have gone at once to Montreal, seized the offender, and brought him back in irons; but his body-guard of twenty men was not equal to such an enterprise. Nor would a muster of the militia have served his purpose; for the settlers about Quebec were chiefly peaceful peasants, while the denizens of Montreal were disbanded soldiers, fur traders, and forest adventurers, the best fighters in Canada. They were nearly all in the interest of Perrot, who, if attacked, had the temper as well as the ability to make a passionate resistance. Thus civil war would have ensued, and the anger of the king would have fallen on both parties. On the other hand, if Perrot were left unpunished, the coureurs de bois, of whom he was the patron, would set no bounds to their audacity, and Frontenac, who had been ordered to suppress them, would be condemned as negligent or incapable. Among the priests of St. Sulpice at Montreal

1 Mtmoirc de* Motifs etc.

was the Abbe Salignac de Fenelon, half-brother of the celebrated author of Telemaque. He was a zealous missionary, enthusiastic and impulsive, still young, and more ardent than discreet. One of his uncles had been the companion of Frontenac during the Candian war, and hence the count's relations with the missionary had been very friendly. Frontenac now wrote to Perrot, directing him to come to Quebec and give account of his conduct; and he coupled this letter with another to Fenelon, urging him to represent to the offending governor the danger of his position, and advise him to seek an interview with his superior, by which the difficulty might be amicably adjusted. Perrot, dreading the displeasure of the king, soothed by the moderate tone of Frontenac's letter, and moved by the assurances of the enthusiastic abbe, who was delighted to play the part of peace-maker, at length resolved to follow his counsel. It was midwinter. Perrot and Fenelon set out together, walked on snow-shoes a hundred and eighty miles down the frozen St. Lawrence, and made their appearance before the offended count.

Frontenac, there can be little doubt, had never intended that Perrot, once in his power, should return to Montreal as its governor ; but that, beyond this, he meant harm to him, there is not the least proof. Perrot, however, was as choleric and stubborn as the count himself; and his natural disposition had not been improved by several years of petty autocracy at Montreal. Their interview was brief, but stormy. When it ended, Perrot was a

3

prisoner in the chateau, with guards placed over him by day and night. Frontenac made choice of one La Nouguere, a retired officer, whom he knew that he could trust, and sent him to Montreal to command in place of its captive governor. With him he sent also a judge of his own selection. La Nouguere set himself to his work with vigor. Perrot's agent or partner, Brucy, was seized, tried, and imprisoned; and an active .hunt was begun for his coureurs de bois. Among others, the two who had been the occasion of the dispute were captured and sent to Quebec, where one of them was solemnly hanged before the window of Perrot's prison; with the view, no doubt, of producing a chastening effect on the mind of the prisoner. The execution was fully authorized, a royal edict having ordained that bush-ranging was an offence punishable with death. 1 As the result of these proceedings, Frontenac reported to the minister that only five coureurs de bois remained at large; all the rest having returned to the settlements and made their submission, so that farther hanging was needless.

Thus the central power was vindicated, and Montreal brought down from her attitude of partial independence. Other results also followed, if we may believe the enemies of Frontenac, who declare that, by means of the new commandant and other persons in his interest, the governor-general possessed himself of a great part of the trade from which he had ejected Perrot, and tha*

edit et Ordonnances, I. 73.

the coureurs de bois, whom he hanged when breaking laws for his rival, found complete impunity when breaking laws for him.

Meanwhile, there was a deep though subdued excitement among the priests of St. Sulpice. The right. of naming their own governor, which they claimed as seigniors of Montreal, had been violated by the action of Frontenac in placing La Nouguere in command without consulting them. Perrot was j^tad governor; but it was they who had chosen him, and the recollection of his misdeeds did not reconcile them to a successor arbitrarily imposed upon them. Both they and the colonists, their vassals, were intensely jealous of Quebec; and, hi their indignation against Frontenac, they more than half forgave Perrot. None among them all was so angry as the Abb6 Fenelon. He believed that he had been used to lure Perrot into a trap; and his past attachment to the governor-general was turned into wrath. High words had passed between them; and, when Fenelon returned to Montreal, he vented his feelings in a sermon plainly levelled at Frontenac. 1 So sharp and bitter was it, that his brethren of St. Sulpice hastened to disclaim it; and Dollier de Casson, their Superior, strongly reproved the preacher, who protested in return that his words were not meant to apply to Frontenac in particular, but only to bad rulers in general. His offences, however, did not cease with the sermon; for he espoused the cause of

Information faite par nous. Charles le Tardieu, Sieur de Titty. Tilly was a commissioner sent by the council to inquire into the affair.

Perrot with more than zeal, and went about among the colonists to collect attestations in his favor. When these things were reported to Frontenac, his ire was kindled, and he summoned Fenelon before the council at Quebec to answer the charge of instigating sedition.

Fenelon had a relative and friend in the person of the Abbe d'Urfe, his copartner in the work of the missions. D'Urfe, anxious to conjure down the rising storm, went to Quebec to seek an interview with Frontenac ; but, according to his own account, he was very ill received, and threatened with a prison. On another occasion, the count showed him a letter in which D'Urf6 was charged with having used abusive language concerning him. Warm words ensued, till Frontenac, grasping his cane, led the abbe to the door and dismissed him, berating him from the top of the stairs in tones so angry that the sentinel below spread the report that he had turned his visitor out of doors.

Two offenders were now arraigned before the council of Quebec: the first was Perrot, charged with disobeying the royal edicts and resisting the royal authority; the other was the Abbe Fenelon. The councillors were at this time united in the interest of Frontenac, who had the power of appointing and removing them. Perrot, in no way softened by a long captivity, challenged the governor-general, who presided at the council board, as a party to the suit and his personal enemy, and

» Aftmoire de M. d'Urft a Colbert, extracts in Faillon.

took exception to several of the members as being connections of La Nouguere. Frontenac withdrew, and other councillors or judges were appointed provisionally; but these were challenged in turn by the prisoner, on one pretext or another. The exceptions were overruled, and the trial proceeded, though not without signs of doubt and hesitation on the part of some of the councillors.

Meanwhile, other sessions were held for the trial of Fenelon; and a curious scene ensued. Five councillors and the deputy attorney-general were seated at the board, with Frontenac as presiding judge, his hat on his head and his sword at his side, after the established custom. Fenelon, being led in, approached a vacant chair, and was about to seat himself with the rest, when Frontenac interposed, telling him that it was his duty to remain standing while answering the questions of the council. Fenelon at once placed himself in the chair, and replied that priests had the right to speak seated and with heads covered.

" Yes," returned Frontenac, " when they are summoned as witnesses, but not when they are cited to answer charges of crime."

" My crimes exist nowhere but in your head," replied the abbe. And, putting on his hat, he drew it down over his brows, rose, gathered his cassock about him, and walked in a defiant manner

1 All the proceedings in the affair of Perrot will be found in full in the Registre des Jugements et Deliberations du Conseil Supfrieur They extend from the end of January to the beginning of November, 1674.

to and fro. Frontenac told him that his conduct was wanting in respect to the council, and to the governor as its head. Fenelon several times took off his hat, and pushed it on again more angrily than ever, saying at the same time that Frontenac was wanting in respect to his character of priest, in citing him before a civil tribunal. As he persisted in his refusal to take the required attitude, he was at length told that he might leave the room. After being kept for a time in the anteroom in charge of a constable, he was again brought before the council, when he still refused obedience, and was ordered into a sort of honorable imprisonment. 1

This behavior of the effervescent abbe*, which Frontenac justly enough characterizes as unworthy of his birth and his sacred office, was, nevertheless, founded on a claim sustained by many precedents. As an ecclesiastic, Fenelon insisted that the bishop alone, and not the council, had the right to judge him. Like Perrot, too, he challenged his judges as parties to the suit, or otherwise interested against him. On the question of jurisdiction, he had all the priests on his side. Bishop Laval was in France ; and Bernieres, his grand vicar, was far from filling the place of the strenuous and determined prelate. Yet the ecclesiastical storm rose so high that the councillors, discouraged and daunted, were no longer amenable to the will of Frontenac; and it was resolved at last to refer the whole matter to

* Contette entrt le Gouverneur et VAbbtde Ftnelon; Jugements et Dtlibera* tion* du

Conseil Supfrieur, 21 Aout, 1674.

the king. Perrot was taken from the prison, which he had occupied from January to November, and shipped for France, along with Fenelon. An immense mass of papers was sent with them for the instruction of the king; and Frontenac wrote a long despatch, in which he sets forth the offences of Perrot and Fenelon, the pretensions of the ecclesiastics, the calumnies he had incurred in his efforts to serve his Majesty, and the insults heaped upon him, " which no man but me would have endured BO patiently." Indeed, while the suits were pending before the council, he had displayed a calmness and moderation which surprised his opponents. " Knowing as I do," he pursues, " the cabals and intrigues that are rife here, I must expect that every thing will be said against me that the most artful slander can devise. A governor in this country would greatly deserve pity, if he were left without support; and, even should he mak« mistakes, it would surely be very pardonable, seeing that there is no snare that is not spread for him, and that, after avoiding a hundred of them, he will hardly escape being caught at last." 1

In his charges of cabal and intrigue, Frontenac had chiefly in view the clergy, whom he profoundly distrusted, excepting always the Recollet friars, whom he befriended because the bishop and the Jesuits opposed them. The priests on their part declare that he persecuted them, compelled

1 Frontenac au Ministre, 14 Nov., 1674. In a preceding letter, sent by way of Boston, and dated 16 February, he says that he could not suffer Perrot to go unpunished without injury to the regal authority, which "Ue is resolved to defend to the last drop of his blood

them to take passports like laymen when travelling about the colony, and even intercepted their letters. These accusations and many others were carried to the king and the minister by the Abbe d'Urfe, who sailed in the same ship with Fenelon, The moment was singularly auspicious to him. His cousin, the Marquise d'Allegre, was on the point of marrying Seignelay, the son of the minister Colbert, who, therefore, was naturally inclined to listen with favor to him and to Fenelon, his relative. Again, Talon, uncle of Perrot's wife, held a post at court, which brought him into close personal relations with the king. Nor were these the only influences adverse to Frontenac and propitious to his enemies. Yet his enemies were disappointed. The letters written to him both by Colbert and by the king are admirable for calmness and dignity. The following is from that of the king: —

" Though I do not credit all that has been told me concerning various little annoyances which you cause to the ecclesiastics, I nevertheless think it necessary to inform you of it, in order that, if true, you may correct yourself in this particular, giving to all the clergy entire liberty to go and come throughout all Canada without compelling them to take out passports, and at the same time leaving them perfect freedom as regards their letters. I have seen and carefully examined all that you have sent touching M. Perrot; and, after having also seen all the papers given by him in his defence, I have condemned his action in

imprisoning an officer of your guard. To punish him, I have had him placed for a short time in the Bastile, that he may learn to be more circumspect in the discharge of his duty, and that his example may serve as a warning to others. But after having thus vindicated my authority, which has been violated in your person, I will say, in order that you may fully understand my views, that you should not without absolute necessity cause your commands to be executed within the limits of a local government, like that of Montreal, without first informing its governor, and also that the ten months of imprisonment which you have made him undergo seems to me sufficient for his fault. I therefore sent him to the Bastile merely as a public reparation for having violated my authority. After keeping him there a few days, I shall send him back to his government, ordering him first to see you and make apology to you for all that has passed; after which I desire that you retain no resentment against him, and that you treat him in accordance with the powers that I have given him." l

Colbert writes in terms equally measured, and adds: " After having spoken in the name of his Majesty, pray let me add a word in my own. By the marriage which the king has been pleased to make between the heiress of the house of Allegre and my son, the Abbe d'Urfe* has become very closely connected with me, since he is cousin ger-man of my daughter-in-law; and this induces me

1 Le Roi a Frontenac, 22 Avril, 1676.

to request you to show him especial consideration, though, in the exercise of his profession, he will rarely have occasion to see you."

As D'Urfe had lately addressed a memorial to Colbert, in which the conduct of Frontenac is painted in the darkest colors, the almost imperceptible rebuke couched in the above lines does no little credit to the tact and moderation of the stern minister.

Colbert next begs Frontenac to treat with kindness the priests of Montreal, observing that Breton-villiers, their Superior at Paris, is his particular friend. " As to M. Perrot," he continues, " since ten months of imprisonment at Quebec and three weeks in the Bastile may suffice to atone for his fault, and since also he is related or connected with persons for whom I have a great regard, I pray you to accept kindly the apologies which he will make you, and, as it is not at all likely that he will fall again into any offence approaching that which he has committed, you will give me especial pleasure in granting him the honor of your favor and friendship." l

Fenelon, though the recent marriage had allied him also to Colbert, fared worse than either of the other parties to the dispute. He was indeed sustained in his claim to be judged by an ecclesiastical tribunal; but his Superior, Bretonvilliers, forbade him to return to Canada, and the king approved the prohibition. Bretonvilliers wrote to the Sul-pitiaii priests of Montreal: " I exhort you to profit

1 Colbert a Frontenac, 13 Mai, 1676.

by the example of M. de Fenelon. By having busied himself too much in worldly matters, and meddled with what did not concern him, he has ruined his own prospects and injured the friends whom he wished to serve. In matters of this sort, it is well always to stand neutral." l

1 Lettre de Bretonvilliers, 7 Mai, 1675; extract in Faillon. Fenelon, though wanting in prudence and dignity, had been an ardent and devoted missionary. In relation to these disputes, I have received much aid from the research of Abbe" Faillon, and from the valuable paper of Abbe Verreau, Les deux Abb€s de Fdhelon, printed in the Canadian Journal de I'lnstruction Publique, Vol. VHL

CHAPTER IV. 1675-1682.

FRONTENAC AND DUCHESNEAU.

.FHCHTTBNAC RECEIVES A COLLEAGUE. — HE OPPOSES THE CLEKOY.— DISPUTES IN THE COUNCIL. — ROYAL INTERVENTION. — FRONTENAC REBUKED. — FRESH OUTBREAKS. — CHARGES AND COUNTERCHARGES.

— THE DISPUTE GROWS HOT. — DUCHESNEAU CONDEMNED AND FRONTENAC WARNED. — THE QUARREL CONTINUES. — THE KING LOSES PATIENCE. — MORE ACCUSATIONS. — FACTIONS AND FEUDS

— A SIDE QUARREL. — THE KING THREATENS. — FRONTENAC DB NOUNCES THE PRIESTS. — THE GOVERNOR AND THE INTENDANT RECALLED. — QUALITIES OF FRONTENAC.

WHILE writing to Frontenac in terms of studied mildness, the king and Colbert took measures to curb his power. In the absence of the bishop, the appointment and removal of councillors had rested wholly with the governor; and hence the council had been docile under his will. It was now ordained that the councillors should be appointed by the king himself. 1 This was not the only change. Since the departure of the intend ant Talon, his office had been vacant; and Frontenac was left to rule alone. This seems to have been an experiment on the part of his masters at Versailles, who, knowing the peculiarities of his temper, were perhaps willing to try the effect of leaving him without a colleague. The experiment had not

succeeded. An intendant was now, therefore, sent to Quebec, not only to manage the details of administration, but also to watch the governor, keep him, if possible, within prescribed bounds, and report his proceedings to the minister. The change was far from welcome to Frontenac, whose delight it was to hold all the reins of power in his own hands; nor was he better pleased with the return of Bishop Laval, which presently took place. Three preceding governors had quarrelled with that uncompromising prelate; and there was little hope that Frontenac and he would keep the peace. All the signs of the sky foreboded storm.

The storm soon came. The occasion of it was that old vexed question of the sale of brandy, which has been fully treated in another volume/ and on which it is needless to dwell here. Another dispute quickly followed; and here, too, the governor's chief adversaries were the bishop and the ecclesiastics. Duchesneau, the new intendant, took part with them. The bishop and his clergy were, on their side, very glad of a secular ally; for their power had greatly fallen since the days of Mezy, and the rank and imperious character of Frontenac appear to have held them in some awe. They avoided as far as they could a direct collision with him, and waged vicarious war in the person of their friend the intendant. Duchesneau was not of a conciliating spirit, and he felt strong in the support of the clergy; while Frontenac, when his temper was roused, would fight with haughty and

impracticable obstinacy for any position which he had once assumed, however trivial or however mistaken. There was incessant friction between the two colleagues in the exercise of their respective functions, and occasions of difference were rarely wanting.

The question now at issue was that of honors and precedence at church and in religious ceremonies, matters of substantial importance under the Bourbon rule. Colbert interposed, ordered Duchesneau to treat Frontenac with becoming deference, and warned him not to make himself the partisan of the bishop; 1 while, at the same tune, he exhorted Frontenac to live in harmony with the intendant. 2 The dispute continued till the king lost patience.

" Through all my kingdom," he wrote to the governor, " I do not hear of so many difficulties on this matter (of ecclesiastical honors) as I see in the church of Quebec." 3 And he directs him to conform to the practice established in the city of Amiens, and to exact no more ; " since you ought to be satisfied with being the representative of my person in the country where I have placed you in command."

At the same time, Colbert corrects the intendant. " A memorial," he wrote, " has been placed in ray hands, touching various ecclesiastical honors, wherein there continually appears a great preten-

1 Colbert a Duchesneau, 1 Mai, 1677.
2 Ibid., 18 Mai, 1677.

sion on your part, and on that of the bishop of Quebec in your favor, to establish an equality between the governor and you. I think I have already said enough to lead you to know yourself, and to understand the difference between a governor and an intendant; so that it is no longer necessary for me to enter into particulars, which could only serve to show you that you are completely in the wrong.'* 1

Scarcely was this quarrel suppressed, when another sprang up. Since the arrival of the intendant and the return of the bishop, the council had ceased to be in the interest of Frontenac, Several of its members were very obnoxious to him ; and chief among these was Villeray, a former councillor whom the king had lately reinstated. Frontenac admitted him to his seat with reluctance. " I obey your orders," he wrote mournfully to Colbert; " but Villeray is the principal and most dangerous instrument of the bishop and the Jesuits." 2 He says, farther, that many people think him to be a Jesuit in disguise, and that he is an intriguing busybody, who makes trouble everywhere. He also denounces the attorney-general, Auteuil, as an ally of the Jesuits. Another of the reconstructed council, Tilly, meets his cordial approval; but he soon found reason to change his mind concerning him.

The king had recently ordered that the intendant, though holding only the third rank in the

1 Colbert a Duchesneau, 8 Mai, 1679.

2 Frontenac au Ministre, 14 Nov., 1674.

council, should act as its president. 1 The commission of Duchesneau, however, empowered him to preside only in the absence of the governor; a while Frontenac is styled " chief and president of the council" in several of the despatches addressed to him. Here was an inconsistency. (Both parties claimed the right of presiding, and both could rest^their claim on a clear expression of the royal will.

Frontenac rarely began a new quarrel till the autumn vessels had sailed for France ; because a full year must then elapse before his adversaries could send their complaints to the king, and six months more before the king could send back his answer. The governor had been heard to say, on one of these occasions, that he should now be master for eighteen months, subject only to answering with his head for what he might do. It was when the last vessel was gone in the autumn of 1678 that he demanded to be styled chief and president on the records of the council; and he showed a letter from the king in which he was so entitled. 3 In spite of this, Duchesneau resisted, and appealed to precedent to sustain his position. A long series of stormy sessions followed. The councillors in the clerical interest supported the intendant. Frontenac, chafed and angry, refused all compromise. Business was stopped for weeks.

1 Declaration du Roy, 23 Sept., 1676.

2 " Pre'sider au Conseil Souverain en I'absence du dit Sieur de Fron-tenac." — Commission de Duchesneau, 6 Juin, 1676.

8 This letter, still preserved in the Archives de la Marine, is dated 12 Mai, 1678. Several other letters of Louis XIV. give Frontenac the same designation.

Duchesneau lost temper, and became abusive-Auteuil tried to interpose in behalf of the in ten-dant. Frontenac struck the table with his fist, and told him fiercely that he would teach him his duty. Every day embittered the strife. The governor made the declaration usual with him on such occasions, that he would not permit the royal authority to suffer in his person. At length he banished from Quebec his three most strenuous opponents, Villeray, Tilly, and Auteuil, and commanded them to remain in their country houses till they received his farther orders. All. attempts at compromise proved fruitless; and Auteuil, in behalf of the exiles, appealed piteously to the king.

The answer came in the following summer: " Monsieur le Comte de Frontenac," wrote

Louis XIV., " I am surprised to learn all the new troubles and dissensions that have occurred in my country of New France, more especially since I have clearly and strongly given you to understand that your sole care should be to maintain harmony and peace among all my subjects dwelling therein; but what surprises me still more is that in nearly all the disputes which you have caused you have advanced claims which have very little foundation. My edicts, declarations, and ordinances had so plainly made known to you my will, that I have great cause of astonishment that you, whose duty it is to see them faithfully executed, have yourself set up pretensions entirely opposed to them. You have wished to be styled chief and president on the records of the Supreme Council, which is con-

trary to my edict concerning that council; and J am the more surprised at this demand, since I am very sure that you are the only man in my kingdom who, being honored with the title of governor and lieutenant-general, would care to be styled chief and president of such a council as that of Quebec."

He then declares that neither Frontenac nor the intendant is to have the title of president, but that the intendant is to perform the functions of presiding officer, as determined by the edict. He continues: —

" Moreover, your abuse of the authority which I have confided to you in exiling two councillors and the attorney-general for so trivial a cause cannot meet my approval; and, were it not for the distinct assurances given me by your friends that you will act with more moderation in future, and never again fall into offences of this nature, I should have resolved on recalling you." 1

Colbert wrote to him with equal severity: " 1 have communicated to the king the contents of all the despatches which you have written to me during the past year; and as the matters of which they treat are sufficiently ample, including dissensions almost universal among those whose duty it is to preserve harmony in the country under youi command, his Majesty has been pleased to examine all the papers sent by all the parties interested,

1 Le Roy a Frontenac, 29 Avril, 1680. A decree of the council of state soon after determined the question of presidency in accord with this letter. Adits et Ordinances. I. 238.

and more particularly those appended to your letters. He has thereupon ordered me distinctly to make known to you his intentions." The minister then proceeds to reprove him sharply in the name of the king, and concludes: " It is difficult for me to add any thing to what I have just said. Consider well that, if it is any advantage or any satisfaction to you that his Majesty should be satisfied with your services, it is necessary that you change entirely the conduct which you have hitherto pursued." l

This, one would think, might have sufficed to bring the governor to reason, but the violence of his resentments and antipathies overcame the very slender share of prudence with which nature had endowed him. One morning, as he sat at the head of the council board, the bishop on his right hand, and the intendant on his left, a woman made her appearance with a sealed packet of papers. She was the wife of the councillor Amours, whose chair, was vacant at the table. Important business was in hand, the registration of a royal edict of amnesty to the coureurs de bois. The intendant, who well knew what the packet contained, demanded that it should be opened. Frontenac insisted that the business before the council should

1 Colbert a Frontenac, 4 Dec., 1679. This letter seems to have been sent by a special messenger by way of New England. It was too late in the season to send directly to Canada. On the quarrel about the presidency, Duchesneau au Ministre, 10 Nov., 1679; Auteuil au Ministry 10

Aug., 1679 ; Contestations entre le Sieur Comte de Frontenac et M. Dtiches-neau, Chevalier. This last paper consists of voluminous extracts from the records of the council.

proceed. The intendant renewed his demand, the council sustained him, and the packet was opened accordingly. It contained a petition from Amours, stating that Frontenac had put him in prison, because, having obtained in due form a passport to send a canoe to his fishing station of Matane, he had afterwards sent a sail-boat thither without applying for another passport. Frontenac had sent for him, and demanded by what right he did so. Amours replied that he believed that he had acted in accordance with the intentions of the king; whereupon, to borrow the words of the petition, " Monsieur the governor fell into a rage, and said to your petitioner, ' I will teach you the intentions of the king, and you shall stay in prison till you learn them ;' and your petitioner was shut up in a chamber of the chateau, wherein he still remains." He proceeds to pray that a trial may be granted him according to law. 1

Discussions now ensued which lasted for days, and now and then became tempestuous. The governor, who had declared that the council had nothing to do with the matter, and that he could not waste time in talking about it, was not always present at the meetings, and it sometimes became necessary to depute one or more of the members to visit him. Auteuil, the attorney-general, having been employed on this unenviable errand, begged the council to dispense him from such duty in future, " by reason," as he says, " of the abuse, ill treatment, and threats which he received from

Monsieur the governor, when he last had the honor of being deputed to confer with him, the particulars whereof he begs to be excused from reporting, lest the anger of Monsieur the governor should be kindled against him still more/' 1 Frontenac, hearing of this charge, angrily denied it, saying that the attorney-general had slandered and insulted him, and that it was his custom to do so. Auteuil rejoined that the governor had accused him of habitual lying, and told him that he would have his hand cut off. All these charges and countercharges may still be found entered in due form on the old records of the council at Quebec.

It was as usual upon the intendant that the wrath of Frontenac fell most fiercely. He accuses him of creating cabals and intrigues, and causing not only the council, but all the country, to forget the respect due to the representative of his Majesty. Once, when Frontenac was present at the session, a dispute arose about an entry on the record. A draft of it had been made in terms agreeable to the governor, who insisted that the intendant should sigh it. Duchesneau replied that he and the clerk would go into the adjoining room, where they could examine it in peace, and put it into a proper form. Frontenac rejoined that he would then have no security that what he had said in the council would be accurately reported. Duchesneau persisted, and was going out with the draft in his hand, when Frontenac planted himself before the door, and

1 Registre du Conseil Suptrieur, 4 Nov., 1681.

told him that he should not leave the council chamber till he had signed the paper. " Then I will get out of the window, or else stay here all day," returned Duchesneau. A lively debate ensued, and the governor at length yielded the point. 1 The imprisonment of Amours was short, but strife did not cease. The disputes in the council wei-p accompanied throughout with other quarrels which were complicated with them, and which were worse than all the rest, since they involved more important matters and covered a wider field. They related to the fur trade, on which hung the very life of the colony. Merchants, traders, and even habitants, were ranged in two contending factions. Of one of these Frontenac was the chief. With him were La Salle and his lieutenant, La Foret; Du Lhut, the famous leader of coureurs de bois; Boisseau, agent of the farmers of the revenue; Barrois, the governor's secretary; Bizard, lieutenant of his guard ; and various others of greater or less influence. On the other side were the members of the council, with Aubert de la Ches-naye, Le Moyne and all his sons, Louis Joliet, Jacques Le Ber, Sorel, Boucher, Varennes, and many more, all supported by the intendant Duchesneau, and also by his fast allies, the ecclesiastics. The faction under the lead of the governor had every advantage, for it was sustained by all the power of his office. Duchesneau was beside himself with rage. He wrote to the court letters full of bitterness, accused Frontenac of illicit trade,

denounced his followers, and sent huge bundles of proces-verbaux and attestations to prove his charges.

But if Duchesneau wrote letters, so too did Frontenac; and if the intendant sent proofs, so too did the governor. Upon the unfortunate king and the still more unfortunate minister fell the difficult task of composing the quarrels of their servants, three thousand miles away. They treated Duchesneau without ceremony. Colbert wrote to him: " I have examined all the letters, papers, and memorials that you sent me by the return of the vessels last November, and, though it appears by the letters of M. de Frontenac that his conduct leaves something to be desired, there is assuredly far more to blame in yours than in his. As to what you say concerning his violence, his trade with the Indians, and in general all that you allege against him, the king has written to him his intentions ; but since, in the midst of all your complaints, you say many things which are without foundation, or which are no concern of yours, it is difficult to believe that you act in the spirit which the service of the king demands; that is to say, without interest and without passion. If a change does not appear in your conduct before next year, his Majesty will not keep you in your office." 1

At the same time, the king wrote to Frontenac, alluding to the complaints of Duchesneau, and ex-horting the governor to live on good terms with

1 Colbert a Duchesneau, 16 Mai. 1678.

him. The general tone of the letter is moderate, but the following significant warning occurs in it: " Although no gentleman in the position in which I have placed you ought to take part in any trade, directly or indirectly, either by himself or any of his servants, I nevertheless now prohibit you absolutely from doing so. Not only abstain from trade, but act in such a manner that nobody can even suspect you of it; and this will be easy, since the truth will readily come to light." 1

Exhortation and warning were vain alike. The first ships which returned that year from Canada brought a series of despatches from the intendant, renewing all his charges more bitterly than before. The minister, out of patience, replied by berating him without mercy. " You may rest assured," he concludes, " that, did it not appear by your later despatches that the letters you have received have begun to make you understand that you have forgotten yourself, it would not have been possible to prevent the king from recalling you." 2

Duchesneau, in return, protests all manner of deference to the governor, but still insists that he «ets the royal edicts at naught; protects a host of coureurs de bois who are in league with him; corresponds with Du Lhut, their chief; shares his illegal profits, and causes all the disorders which afflict the colony. " As for me, Monseigneur, I have done every thing within the scope of my office to prevent these evils; but all the pains I have taken

1 LeRoya Frontenac, 12 Mai, 1678. 2 Colbert a Duchesneau, 26 Avril, 1679.

have only served to increase the aversion of Monsieur the governor against me, and to bring my ordinances into contempt. This, Monseigneur, is a true account of the disobedience of the coureura de bois, of which I twice had the honor to speak to Monsieur the governor; and I could not help telling him, with all possible deference, that it was shameful to the colony and to us that the king, our master, of whom the whole world stands in awe, who has just given law to all Europe, and whom all his subjects adore, should have the pain of knowing that, in a country which has received so many marks of his paternal tenderness, his orders are violated and scorned; and a governor and an intendant stand by, with folded arms, content with saying that the evil is past remedy. For having made these representations to him, I drew on myself words so full of contempt and insult that I was forced to leave his room to appease his anger. The next morning I went to him again, and did all I could to have my ordinances executed ; but, as Monsieur the governor is interested with many of the coureurs de bois, it is useless to attempt to do any thing. He has gradually made himself master of the trade of Montreal; and, as soon as the Indians arrive, he sets guards in their camp, which would be very well, if these soldiers did their duty and protected the savages from being annoyed and plundered by the French, instead of being employed to discover how many furs they have brought, with a view to future operations. Monsieur the governor then compels

the Indians to pay his guards for protecting them; and he has never allowed them to trade with the inhabitants till they had first given him a certain number of packs of beaver skins, which he calls his presents. His guards trade with them openly at the fair, with their bandoleers on their shoulders."

He says, farther, that Frontenac sends up goods to Montreal, and employs persons to trade in his behalf; and that, what with the beaver skins exacted by him and his guards under the name of presents, and those which he and his favorites obtain in trade, only the smaller part of what the Indians bring to market ever reaches the people of the colony. 1

This despatch, and the proofs accompanying it, drew from the king a sharp reproof to Frontenac.

66 What has passed in regard to the coureurs de bois is entirely contrary to my orders ; and I cannot receive in excuse for it your allegation that it is the intendant who countenances them by the trade he carries on, for I perceive clearly that the fault is your own. As I see that you often turn the orders that I give you against the very object for which they are given, beware not to do so on this occasion. I shall hold you answerable for bringing the disorder of the coureurs de bois to an end throughout Canada; and this you will easily succeed in doing, if you make a proper use of my authority. Take care not to persuade yourself that what I write to you comes from the ill

1 Duchesneau au Afinistre, 10 Nov., 1679.

offices of the intendant. It results from what I fully know from every thing which reaches me from Canada, proving but too well what you are doing there. The bishop, the ecclesiastics, the Jesuit fathers, the Supreme Council, and, in a word, everybody, complain of you; but I am willing to believe that you will change your conduct, and act with the moderation necessary for the good of the colony/' 1

Colbert wrote in a similar strain ; and Frontenac saw that his position was becoming critical. He showed, it is true, no sign of that change of conduct which the king had demanded; but he appealed to his allies at court to use fresh efforts to sustain him. Among the rest, he had a strong friend in the Mare*chal de Bellefonds, to whom he wrote, in the character of an abused and much-suffering man: " You exhort me to have patience, and I agree with you that those placed in a position of command cannot have too much. For this reason, I have given examples of it here such as perhaps • no governor ever gave before; and I have found no great difficulty in doing so, because I felt myself to be the master. Had I been in a private station, I could not have endured such outrageous insults without dishonor. I have always passed over in silence those directed against me personally; and have never given way to anger, except when attacks were made on the authority of which I have the honor to be the guardian. You could not believe all the an-

noyances which the intendant tries to put upon me every day, and which, as you advise me, I scorn or disregard. It would require a virtue like yours to turn them to all the good use of which they are capable; yet, great as the virtue is which has enabled you to possess your soul in tranquillity amid all the troubles of the court, I doubt if you could preserve such complete equanimity among the miserable tumults of Canada." 1 Having given the principal charges of Duches-neau against Frontenac, it is time to give those of Frontenac against Duchesneau. The governor says that all the coureurs de bois would be brought to submission but for the intendant and his allies, who protect them, and carry on trade by their means ; that the seigniorial house of Duchesneau's partner, La Chesnaye, is the constant resort of these outlaws; and that he and his associates have large storehouses at Montreal, Isle St. Paul, and Riviere du Loup, whence they send goods into the Indian country, in contempt of the king's orders. 2 Frontenac also complains of numberless provocations from the intendant. " It is no fault of mine that I am not on good terms with M. Duchesneau; for I have done every thing I could to that end, being too submissive to your Majesty's commands not to suppress my sharpest indignation the moment your will is known to me. But, Sire, it is not so with him; and his desire to excite new disputes, in the hope of making me appear their

1 Frontenac au Marshal de Be/lefonds, 14 Nov., 1680. z M&moire et Preuves du D&ordre des Coureurs de Bois,

principal author, has been so great that the last ships were hardly gone, when, forgetting what your Majesty had enjoined upon us both, he began these dissensions afresh, in spite of all my precautions. If I depart from my usual reserve in regard to him, and make bold to ask justice at the hands of your Majesty for the wrongs and insults I have undergone, it is because nothing but your authority can keep them within bounds. I have never suffered more in my life than when I have been made to appear as a man of violence and a disturber of the officers of justice : for I have always confined myself to what your Majesty has prescribed ; that is, to exhorting them to do their duty when I saw that they failed in it. This has drawn upon me, both from them and from M. Duchesneau, such cutting affronts that your Majesty would hardly credit them." 1

In 1681, Seignelay, the son of Colbert, entered upon the charge of the colonies; and both Fron-tenac and Duchesneau hastened to congratulate him, protest their devotion, and overwhelm him with mutual accusations. The intendant declares that, out of pure zeal for the king's service, he shall tell him every thing. " Disorder," he says, " reigns everywhere ; universal confusion prevails throughout every department of business; the pleasure of the king, the orders of the Supreme Council, and my ordinances remain unexecuted; justice is openly violated, and trade is destroyed; violence, upheld by authority, decides every thing ;

* Frontenac au Roy, 2 Nov. 1681.

and nothing consoles the people, who groan without daring to complain, but the hope, Monseigneur, that you will have the goodness to condescend to be moved by their misfortunes. No position could be more distressing than mine, since, if I conceal the truth from you, I fail in the obedience I owe the king, and in the fidelity that I vowed so long since to Monseigneur, your father, and which I swear anew at your hands; and if I obey, as 1 must, his Majesty's orders and yours, I cannot avoid giving offence, since I cannot render you an account of these disorders without informing you that M. de Frontenac's conduct is the sole cause of them." l

Frontenac had written to Seignelay a few days before : " I have no doubt whatever that M. Du-chesneau will, as usual, overwhelm me with fabrications and falsehoods, to cover his own ill conduct. I send proofs to justify myself, so strong and convincing that I do not see that they can leave any doubt; but, since I fear that their great number might fatigue you, I have thought it better to Bend them to my wife, with a full and exact journal of all that has passed here day by day, in order that she may extract and lay before you the principal portions.

" I send you in person merely the proofs of the conduct of M. Duchesneau, in barricading his house and arming all his servants, and in coming three weeks ago to insult me in my room. You will see thereby to what a pitch of temerity and

lawlessness he lias transported himself, in order to compel me to use violence against him, with the hope of justifying what he has asserted about my pretended outbreaks of anger."

The mutual charges of the two functionaries were much the same; and, so far at least as concerns trade, there can be little doubt that they were well founded on both sides". The strife of the rival factions grew more and more bitter: canes and sticks played an active part in it, and now and then we hear of drawn swords. One is reminded at times of the intestine feuds of some mediaeval city, as, for example, in the following incident, which will explain the charge of Frontenae against the intendant of barricading his house and arming his servants : —

On the afternoon of the twentieth of March, a son of Duchesneau, sixteen years old, followed by a servant named Vautier, was strolling along the picket fence which bordered the descent from the Upper to the Lower Town of Quebec. The boy was amusing' himself by singing a song, when Frontenac's partisan, Boisseau, with one of the guardsmen, approached, and, as young Duchesneau declares, called him foul names, and said that he would give him and his father a thrashing. The boy replied that he would have nothing to say to a fellow like him, and would beat him if he did not keep quiet; while the servant, Yautier, retorted Boisseau's abuse, and taunted him with low birth and disreputable employments. Boisseau made report to

Frontenac au Ministre, 2 Nov., 1681.

f>4 FRONTENAC AND DUCHESNEATJ. [1081.

Frontenac, and Frontenac complained to Duchesneau, who sent his son, with Vautier, to give the governor his version of the affair. The bishop, an ally of the intendant, thus relates what followed. On arriving with a party of friends at the chateau, young Duchesneau was shown into a room in which were the governor and his two secretaries, Barrois'and Chasseur. He had no sooner entered than Frontenac seized him by the arm. shook him, struck him, called him abusive names, and tore the sleeve of his jacket. The secretaries interposed, and, failing to quiet the governor, opened the door and let the boy escape. Vautier, meanwhile, had remained in the guard-room, where Boisseau struck at him with his cane; and one of the guardsmen went for a halberd to run him through the body. After this warm reception, young Duchesneau and his servant took refuge in the house of his father. Frontenac demanded their surrender. The intendant, fearing that he would take them by force, for which he is said to have made preparation, barricaded himself and armed his household. The bishop tried to mediate, and after protracted negotiations young Duchesneau was given up, whereupon Frontenac locked him in a chamber of the chateau, and kept him there a month. 1

The story of Frontenac*s violence to the boy is flatly denied by his friends, who charge

Duches-

1 Mfmoire de I'Evesque de Qntbec, Mars, 1681 (printed in Revue Cana-ttienne, 1878). The bishop is silent about the barricades of which Frontenac and his friends complain in several letters.

neau and his partisans with circulating libels against him, and who say, like Frontenac himself, that the intendant used every means to exasperate him, in order to make material for accusations. 1

The disputes of the rival factions spread through, all Canada. The most heinous offence in the eyes, of the court with which each charged the other was the carrying of furs to the English settlements ; thus' defrauding the revenue, and, as the king believed, preparing the ruin of the colony. The intendant farther declared that the governor's party spread among the Indians the report of a pestilence at Montreal, in order to deter them from their yearly visit to the fair, and thus by means of coureurs de bois obtain all their beaver skins at a low price. The report, according to Duchesneau, had no other foundation than the fate of eighteen or twenty Indians, who had lately drunk themselves to death at La Chine. 2

Montreal, in the mean time, was the scene of a sort of by-play, in which the chief actor was the local governor, Perrot. He and Frontenac appear to have found it for their common interest to come to a mutual understanding; and this was perhaps easier on the part of the count, since his quarrel with Duchesneau gave sufficient employment to his natural pugnacity. Perrot was now left to make a reasonable profit from the illicit trade which had once kindled the wrath of his superior;

1 See, among other instances, the Defense de M. de Frontenac par u« de ses Amis, published by Abbe Verreau in the Revue Canadienne, 1878.

2 Plumitifdu Conseil Souverain, 1681.

6

and, the danger of Frontenac's anger being removed, he completely forgot the lessons of his imprisonment.

The intendant ordered Migeon, bailiff of Montreal, to arrest some of Perrot's coureurs de bois. Perrot at once arrested the bailiff, and sent a sergeant and two soldiers to occupy his house, with orders to annoy the family as much as possible. One of them, accordingly, walked to and fro all night in the bed-chamber of Migeon's wife. On another occasion, the bailiff invited two friends to supper: Le Moyne d'Iberville and one Bouthier, agent of a commercial house at Eochelle. The conversation turned on the trade carried on by Perrot. It was overheard and reported to him, upon which he suddenly appeared at the window, struck Bouthier over the head with his cane, then drew his sword, and chased him while he fled for his life. The seminary was near at hand, and the fugitive clambered over the wall. Dollier de Casson dressed him in the hat and cassock of a priest, and in this disguise he escaped. 1 Perrot's avidity sometimes carried him to singular extremities. " He has been seen," says one of his accusers, " filling barrels of brandy with his own hands, and mixing it with water to sell to the Indians. He bartered with one of them his hat, sword, coat, ribbons, shoes, and stockings, and boasted that he had made thirty pistoles by the bargain, while the Indian walked about town equipped as governor." 2

1 Conduitedu Sieur Perrot, Gouverneur de Montreal en la NouveUe France , 1681 ; Plainte du Sieur Bouthier, 10 Oct., 1680; Proces-verbal des huissiert de Mwdrfal.

* Conduite du Sieur Perrot. La Barre, Frontenac's successor, declares

Every ship from Canada brought to the king fresh complaints of Duchesneau against Frontenac, and of Frontenac against Duchesneau; and the king replied with rebukes, exhortations, and threats to both. At first he had shown a disposition to extenuate and excuse the faults of Frontenac, but every year his letters grew sharper. In 1681 he wrote: " Again I urge you to banish from your mind the difficulties which you have yourself devised against the execution of my orders; to act with mildness and moderation towards all the colonists, and divest yourself entirely of the personal animosities which have thus far been almost your sole motive of action. In conclusion, I exhort you once more to profit well by the directions which this letter contains; since, unless you succeed better herein than formerly, I cannot help recalling you from the command which I have intrusted to you." 1

The dispute still went on. The autumn ships' from Quebec brought back the usual complaints,! and the long-suffering king at length made good his threat. Both Frontenac and Duchesneau re-. ; ceived their recall, and they both deserved it. 2 J

The last official act of the governor, recorded in the register of the council of Quebec, is the formal

that the charges against Perrot were false, including the attestations oi Migeon and his friends; that Dollier de Casson had been imposed upon, and that various persons had been induced to sign unfounded statements without reading them. La Barre au Ministre, 4 Nov., 1683.

1 Le Roy a Frontenac, 30 Avril, 1681.

2 La Barre says that Duchesneau was far more to blame than Frott-tenac. La Barre au Ministre, 1083. This testimony has weight, since Frontenac's friends were La Barrels enemies.

declaration that his rank in that body is superior to that of the intendant. 1

The key to nearly all these disputes lies in the relations between Frontenac and the Church. The fundamental quarrel was generally covered by superficial issues, and it was rarely that the governor fell out with anybody who was not in league with the bishop and the Jesuits. "Nearly all the disorders in New France/' he writes, " spring from the ambition of the ecclesiastics, who want to join to their spiritual authority an absolute power over things temporal, and who persecute all who do not submit entirely to them." He says that the intendant and the councillors are completely under their control, and dare not decide any question against them; that they have spies everywhere, even in his house ; that the bishop told him that he could excommunicate even a governor, if he chose; that the missionaries in Indian villages say that they are equals of Onontio, and tell their converts that all will go wrong till the priests have the government of Canada; that directly or indirectly they meddle in all civil affairs; that they trade even with the English of New York; that, what with Jesuits, Sulpitians, the bishop, and the seminary of Quebec, they hold two-thirds of the good lands of Canada; that, in view of the poverty of the country, their revenues are enormous; that, in short, their object is mastery, and that they use all means to compass it. a The recall of the governor was a tri-

1 Registre du Conseil Supfrieur, 16 F€o., 1682.

* Frontenac, M€mmn adresst a Colbert, 1677. This remarkable

umph to the ecclesiastics, offset but slightly by the recall of their instrument, the intendant, who had done his work, and whom they needed no longer.

Thus far, we have seen Frontenac on his worst side. We shall see him again under an aspect very different. Nor must it be supposed that the years which had passed since his government began, tempestuous as they appear on the record, were wholly given over to quarrelling. They had their periods of uneventful calm, when the wheels of administration ran as smoothly as could be expected in view of the condition of the colony. In one respect at least, Frontenac had shown a remarkable fitness for his office. Few white men have ever equalled_or approached him in the art of dealing with Indians. There seems to have been a sympa-thetic relation between him and them. He conformed to their ways, borrowed their rhetoric, flattered them on occasion with great address, and yet constantly maintained towards them an attitude of paternal superiority. When they were concerned, his native haughtiness always took a form which commanded respect without exciting anger. He would not address them as brothers, but only as children ; and even the Iroquois, arrogant as they were, accepted the new relation. In their eyes Frontenac was by far the greatest of all the " Onontios," or governors of Canada. They ad-

papei will be found in the D&ouvertes et Etablissements des Franfais dans VAmerique Septentrionale; Mfmoires et Documents Originaux edited by M. Margry. The paper is very long, and contains references to attestations and other proofs which accompanied it, especially in regard to the trade of the Jesuits.

70 FEONTENAC AND DUCHESNEAU.

mired the prompt and fiery soldier who played with their children, and gave beads and trinkets to their wives; who read their secret thoughts and never feared them, but smiled on them when their hearts were true, or frowned and threatened them when they did amiss. The other tribes, allies of the French, were of the same mind; and their respect for their Great Father seems not to have been permanently impaired by his occasional practice ot bullying them for purposes of extortion.

Frontenac appears to have had a liking not only for Indians, but also for that roving and lawless class of the Canadian population, the coureurs de bois, provided always that they were not in the service of his rivals. Indeed, as regards the Canadians generally, he refrained from the strictures with which succeeding governors and intendants freely interlarded their despatches. It was not his instinct to clash with the humbler classes, and he generally reserved his anger for those who could retort it.

He had the air of distinction natural to a man familiar all his life with the society of courts, and he was as gracious and winning on some occasions as he was unbearable on others. When in good humor, his ready wit and a certain sympathetic vivacity made him very agreeable. At times he was all sunshine, and his outrageous temper slumbered peacefully till some new offence wakened it again; nor is there much doubt that many of his worst outbreaks were the work of his enemies, who knew his foible, and studied to exasperate him.

He was full of contradictions; and, intolerant and implacable as he often was, there were intervals, even in his bitterest quarrels, in which he displayed a surprising moderation and patience. By fits he could be magnanimous. A woman once brought him a petition in burlesque verse. Frontenac wrote a jocose answer. The woman, to ridicule him, contrived to have both petition and answer slipped among the papers of a suit pending before the council. Frontenac had her fined a few francs, and then caused the money to be given to her children. 1

When he sailed for France, it was a day of rejoicing to more than half the merchants of Canada, and, excepting the K6collets, to all the priests; but he left behind him an impression, very.generall among the people, that, if danger threatened the colony, Count Frontenac was the man for the hour.

1 Note by Abb£ Verreau, in Journal de I'Instruction Publiqm (Canada) VTIL127.

CHAPTER V.

1682-1684 LB FEBVRE DB LA BARBE.

His ARRIVAL AT QUEBEC. — THE GREAT FIRE. — A COMING STOKM, —• IROQUOIS POLICY. — THE DANGER IMMINENT. — INDIAN ALLIES oir FRANCE. — FRONTENAC AND THE IROQUOIS. — BOASTS OF LA BARRE. His PAST LIFE. — His SPECULATIONS. — HE TAKES ALARM. — His DEALINGS WITH THE IROQUOIS. —

His ILLEGAL TRADE. — His COLLEAGUE DENOUNCES HIM. — FRUITS OF HIS SCHEMES. — HlS ANGEB
AND HIS FEARS.

WHEN the new governor, La Barre, and the new intendant, Meules, arrived at Quebec, a dismal greeting waited them. All the Lower Town was in ashes, except the house of the merchant Aubert de la Chesnaye, standing alone amid the wreck. On a Tuesday, the fourth of August, at ten o'clock in the evening, the nuns of the Hotel-Dieu were roused from their early slumbers by shouts, outcries, and the ringing of bells; " and," writes one of them, " what was our terror to find it as light as noonday, the flames burned so fiercely and rose so high." Half an hour before, Chartier de Lot-biniere, judge of the king's court, heard the first alarm, ran down the descent now-called Mountain Street, and found every thing in confusion in the town below. The house of Etienne Planchon was in a blaze; the fire was spreading to those of his

neighbors, and had just leaped the narrow street to the storehouse of the Jesuits. The season was excessively dry ; there were no means of throwing water except kettles an<J buckets, and the crowd was bewildered with excitement and fright. Men were ordered to tear off roofs and pull down houses; but the flames drove them from their work, and at four o'clock in the morning fifty-five buildings were burnt to the ground. They were all of wood, but many of them were storehouses filled with goods; and the property consumed was more in value than all that remained in Canada. 1

Under these gloomy auspices, Le Febvre de la Barre began his reign. He was an old officer who had achieved notable exploits against the English in the West Indies, but who was now to be put to a test far more severe. He made his lodging in the chateau; while his colleague, Meules, could hardly find a shelter. The buildings of the Upper Town were filled with those whom the fire had made roofless, and the intendant was obliged to content himself with a house in the neighboring woods. Here he was ill at ease, for he dreaded an Indian war and the scalping-knives of the Iroquois. 8

So far as his own safety was concerned, his alarm was needless; but not so as regarded the colony with whose affairs he was charged. For those who had eyes to see it, a terror and a woe lowered in the future of Canada. In an evil

1 Chartier de Lotbinifcre, Proces-verbal sur I'Incendie de la Basse ViUe; Meules an Ministre, 6 Oct., 1682; Juchereau, Histoire de I'H&el-Dieu de Quebec, 256.

2 Meules au Ministre, 6 Oct., 1682.

hour for her, the Iroquois had conquered their southern neighbors, the Andastes, who had long held their ground against them, and at one time threatened them with ruin. The hands of the confederates were now free; their arrogance was redoubled by victory, and, having long before destroyed all the adjacent tribes on the north and west, 1 they looked for fresh victims in the wilderness beyond. Their most easterly tribe, the Mohawks, had not forgotten the chastisement they had received from Tracy and Cour-celle. They had learned to fear the French, and were cautious in offending them; but it was not so with the remoter Iroquois. Of these, the Sen-ecas at the western end of the " Long House," as they called their fivefold league, were by far the most powerful, for they could muster as many warriors as all the four remaining tribes together; and they now sought to draw the confederacy into a series of wars, which, though not directed against the French, threatened soon to involve them. Their first movement westward was against the tribes of the Illinois. I have already described their bloody inroad in the summer of 1680. 2 They made the valley of the Illinois a desert, and returned with several hundred prisoners, of whom they burned those that were useless, and incorporated the young and strong into their own tribe.

This movement of the western Iroquois had a double incentive, their love of fighting and their

1 Jesuits in North America. 2 Discovery of the Great West.

love of gain. It was a war of conquest and of trade. All the five tribes of the league had become dependent on the English and Dutch of Albany for guns, powder, lead, brandy, and many other things that they had learned to regard as necessities. Beaver skins alone could buy them, but to the Iroquois the supply of beaver skins was limited. The regions of the west and north-west, the upper Mississippi with its tributaries, and, above all, the forests of the upper lakes, were occupied by tribes in the interest of the French, whose missionaries and explorers had been the first to visit them, and whose traders controlled their immense annual product of furs. La Salle, by his newly built fort of St. Louis, engrossed the trade of the Illinois and Miami tribes; while the Hurons and Ottawas, gathered about the old mission of Michillimackinac, acted as factors for the Sioux, the Winnebagoes, and many other remote hordes. Every summer they brought down their accumulated beaver skins to the fair at Montreal; while French bush-rangers roving through the wilderness, with or without licenses, collected many more. 1

It was the purpose of the Iroquois to master all this traffic, conquer the tribes who had possession of it, and divert the entire supply of furs to themselves, and through themselves to the English and Dutch. That English and Dutch traders urged them on is affirmed by the French, and is very likely. The accomplishment of the scheme would

1 Duchesneau, Memoir on Western Indians in N. Y. Colonial Docs.j IX. 160.

have ruined Canada. Moreover, the Illinois, the Hurons, the Ottawas, and all the other tribes threatened by the Iroquois, were the allies and " children " of the French, who in honor as in interest were bound to protect them. Hence, when the Seneca invasion of the Illinois became known,-there was deep anxiety in the colony, except only among those in whom hatred of the monopolist La Salle had overborne every consideration of the public good. La Salle's new establishment of St. Louis was in the path of the invaders; and, if he could be crushed, there was wherewith to console his enemies for all else that might ensue.

Bad as was the posture of affoirs. it was made far worse by an incident that took place soon after the invasion of the Illinois. A Seneca chief engaged in it, who had left the main body of his countrymen, was captured by a party of Winne-bagoes to serve as a hostage for some of their tribe whom the Senecas had lately seized. They carried him to Michillimackinac, where there chanced to be a number of Illinois, married to Indian women of that neighborhood. A quarrel ensued between them and the Seneca, whom they stabbed to death in a lodge of the Kiskakons, one of the tribes of the Ottawas. Here was a casus belli likely to precipitate a war fatal to all the tribes about Michillimackinac, and equally fatal to the trade of Canada. Frontenac set himself to conjure the rising storm, and sent a messenger to the Iroquois to invite them to a conference.

He found them unusually arrogant. Instead of coming to him, they demanded that he should come to them, and many of the French wished him to comply; but Frontenac refused, on the ground that such a concession would add to their insolence, and he declined to go farther than Montreal, or at the utmost Fort Frontenac, the usual place of meeting with them. Early in August he was at Montreal, expecting the arrival of the Ottawas and Hurons on their yearly descent from the lakes. They soon appeared, and he called them to a solemn council. Terror had seized them all. " Father, take pity on us," said the Ottawa orator, "for we are like dead men." A Huron chief, named the Rat, declared that the world was turned upside down, and implored the protection of

Onon-tio, " who is master of the whole earth." These tribes were far from harmony among themselves. Each was jealous of the other, and the Ottawas charged the Hurons with trying to make favor with the common enemy at their expense. Frontenac told them that they were all his children alike, and advised them to live together as brothers, and make treaties of alliance with all the tribes of the lakes. At the same time, he urged them to make full atonement for the death of the Seneca murdered in' their country, and carefully to refrain from any new offence.

Soon after there was another arrival. La For£t, the officer in command at Fort Frontenac, appeared, bringing with him a famous Iroquois chief called Decanisora or Tegannisorens, attended by a num-

her of warriors. They came to invite Frontenac to meet the deputies of the five tribes at Oswego, within their own limits. Frontenac's reply was characteristic. "It is for the father to tell the children where to hold council, not for the children to tell the father. Fort Frontenac is the proper place, and you should thank me for going so far every summer to meet you." The Iroquois had expressed pacific intentions towards the Hurons and Ottawas. For this Frontenac commended him, but added : " The Illinois also are children of Onon-tio, and hence brethren of the Iroquois. Therefore they, too, should be left in peace; for Onontio wishes that all his family should live together in union." He confirmed his words with a huge belt of wampum. Then, addressing the flattered deputy as a great chief, he desired him to use his influence in behalf of peace, and gave him a jacket and a silk cravat, both trimmed with gold, a hat, a scarlet ribbon, and a gun, with beads for his wife, and red cloth for his daughter. The Iroquois went home delighted.

Perhaps on this occasion Frontenac was too confident of his influence over the savage confederates. Such at least was the opinion of Lamberville, Jesuit missionary at Onondaga, the Iroquois capital. From what he daily saw around him, he thought the peril so imminent that concession on the part of the French was absolutely necessary, since not only the Illinois, but some of the tribes of the lakes, were in danger of speedy and complete destruction,

1 For the papers on this affair, see N. Y Colonial Docs., IX.

" Tegannisorens loves the French," he wrote to Frontenac, " but neither he nor any other of the upper Iroquois fear them in the least. They annihilate our allies, whom by adoption of prisoners they convert into Iroquois; and they do not hesitate to avow that after enriching themselves by our plunder, and strengthening themselves by those who might have aided us> they will pounce all at once upon Canada, and overwhelm it in a single campaign." He adds that within the past two years they have reinforced themselves by more than nine hundred warriors, adopted into their tribes.

Such was the crisis when Frontenac left Canada at the moment when he was needed most, and Le Febvre de la Barre came to supplant him. The new governor introduces himself with a burst of rhodomontade. " The Iroquois," he writes to the king, " have twenty-six hundred warriors. I will attack them with twelve hundred men. They know me before seeing me, for they have been told by'the English how roughly I handled them in the West Indies." This bold note closes rather tamely ; for the governor adds, " I think that if the Iroquois believe that your Majesty would have the goodness to give me some help, they will make peace, and let our allies alone, which would save the trouble and expense of an arduous war." 2 He then begs hard for troops, and in fact there was great need of them, for there were none in Canada;

1 P. Jean de Lamberwlle a Frontenac, 20 Sept., 1682. 8 La Barre au Roy, (4 Oct. ?) 1682.

£0 LE FEBVRE DE LA BARRE, '1682

and even Frontenac had been compelled in the last year of his government to leave unpunished various acts of violence and plunder committed by the Iroquois. La Barre painted the situation in its blackest colors, declared that war was imminent, and wrote to the minister, " We shall lose half our trade and all our reputation, if we do not oppose these haughty conquerors." 1

A vein of gasconade appears in most of his letters, not however accompanied with any conclusive evidence of a real wish to fight. His best fighting days were past, for he was sixty years old ; nor had he always been a man of the sword. His early life was spent in the law ; he had held a judicial post, and had been in tend ant of several French provinces. Even the military and naval employments, in which he afterwards acquitted himself with credit, were due to the part he took in forming a joint-stock company for colonizing Cayenne. 2 In fact, he was but half a soldier; and it was perhaps for this reason that he insisted on being called, not Monsieur le Gouverneur, but Monsieur le General. He was equal to Frontenac neither in vigor nor in rank, but he far surpassed him in avidity. Soon after his arrival, he wrote to the minister that he should not follow the example of

1 La Barre a Seignelay, 1682.

2 He was made governor of Cayenne, and went thither with Tracy in 1664. Two years later, he gained several victories over the English, and recaptured Cayenne, which they had taken in his absence. He wrote a book concerning this colony, called Description de la France Equinoctial*. Another volume, called Journal du Voyage du Sieur de la Barre. en la Terre Ferme et hie de Cayenne, was printed at Paris in 1671.

his predecessors in making money out of his government by trade; and in consideration of these good intentions he asked for an addition to his pay. 1 He then immediately made alliances with certain merchants of Quebec for carrying on an extensive illicit trade, backed by all the power of his office. Now ensued a strange and miserable complication. Questions of war mingled with questions of personal gain. There was a commercial revolution in the colony. The merchants whom Frontenac excluded from his ring now had their turn. It was they who, jointly with the intendant and the ecclesiastics, had procured the removal of the old governor; and it was they who gained the ear of the new one. Aubert de la Chesnaye, Jacques Le Ber, and the rest of their faction, now basked in official favor; and La Salle, La Foret, and the other friends of Frontenac, were cast out. There was one exception. Greysolon Du Lhut, leader of coureurs de bois, was too important to be thus set aside. He was now as usual in the wilderness of the north, the roving chief of a half savage crew, trading, exploring, fighting, and laboring with persistent hardihood to foil the rival English traders of Hudson's Bay. Inducements to gain his adhesion were probably held out to him by La Barre and his allies : be this as it may, it is certain that he acted in harmony with the faction of the new governor. With La For£t it was widely different. He commanded Fort Frontenac, which belonged to La Salle, when La Barre's associates,

* La Barre a Seignelay, 1682. 6

La Chesnaye and Le Ber, armed with an order from the governor, came up from Montreal, and seized upon the place with all that it contained. The pretext for this outrage was the false one that La Salle had not fulfilled the conditions under which the fort had been granted to him. La ForeH was told that he might retain his command, if he would join the faction of La Barre ; but he refused, stood true to his chief, and soon after sailed for France.

La Barre summoned the most able and experienced persons in the colony to discuss the state of affairs. Their conclusion was that the Iroquois would attack and destroy the Illinois, and, this accomplished, turn upon the tribes of the lakes, conquer or destroy them also, and ruin the trade of Canada. 1 Dark as was the prospect, La Barre and his fellow-speculators flattered themselves that the war could be averted for a year at least. The Iroquois owed their triumphs as much to their sagacity and craft as to their extraordinary boldness and ferocity. It had always been their policy to attack their enemies in detail, and while destroying one to cajole the rest. There seemed little doubt that they would leave the tribes of the lakes in peace till they had finished the ruin of the Illinois; so that if these, the allies of the colony, were abandoned to their fate, there would be time for a profitable trade in the direction of Michilli-mackinac.

1 Conference on the State of Affairs with the Iroquois, Oct., 1682, in . Y. Colonial Docs.. IX. 194.

But hopes seemed vain and prognostics illusory, when, early in spring, a report came that the Seneca Iroquois were preparing to attack, in force, "not only the Illinois, but the Hurons and Ottawas of the lakes. La Barre and his confederates were in dismay. They already had large quantities of goods at Michillimackinac, the point immediately threatened ; and an officer was hastily despatched, with men and munitions, to strengthen the defences of the place. 1 A small vessel was sent to France with letters begging for troops. " I will perish at their head," wrote La Barre to the king, " or destroy your enemies; " and he assures the minister that the Senecas must be attacked or the country abandoned. 3 The intendant, Meules, shared something of his alarm, and informed the king that " the Iroquois are the only people on earth who do not know the grandeur of your Majesty."

While thus appealing to the king, La Barre sent Charles le Moyne as envoy to Onondaga. Through his influence, a deputation of forty-three Iroquois chiefs was sent to meet the governor at Montreal. Here a grand council was held in the newly built church. Presents were given the deputies to the value of more than two thousand crowns. Soothing speeches were made them; and they were urged not to attack the tribes of the lakes, nor to plunder French traders, without permission. 3

1 La Barre au Ministre, 4 Nov., 1683.
2 La Barre au Roy, 30 Mai, 1683.
8 La Barre au Ministre, 30 Mai, 1683.
* Meules au Roy, 2 Juin, 1683.
5 Soon after La Barre's arrival, La Chesnaye is said to have induced

They assented; and La Barre then asked, timidly, why they made war on the Illinois. " Because they deserve to die/' haughtily returned the Iroquois orator. La Barre dared not answer. They complained that La Salle had given guns, powder, and lead to the Illinois; or, in other words, that he had helped the allies of the colony to defend themselves. La Barre, who hated La Salle and his monopolies, assured them that he should be punished. 1 It is affirmed, on good authority, that he said more than this, and told them they were welcome to plunder and kill him. a The rapacious old man was playing with a two-edged sword.

Thus the Illinois, with the few Frenchmen who had tried to defend them, were left to perish; and, in return, a brief and doubtful respite was gained for the tribes of the lakes. La Barre and his confederates took heart again. Merchandise, in abundance, was sent to Michillimackinac, and thence to the remoter tribes of the north and west. The governor and his partner, La Chesnaye, sent up a fleet of thirty canoes; 3 and, a

him to urge the Iroquois to plunder all traders who were not provided with passports from the governor. The Iroquois complied so promptly, that they stopped and pillaged, at Niagara, two canoes belonging to La Chesnaye himself, which had gone up the lakes in Frontenac's time, and therefore were without passports. Recueil de ce qui s'est passtf en Canada au Snjet de la Guerre, etc., depuis I'annee 1682. (Published by the Historical Society of Quebec.) This was not the only case in which the weapons of La Barre and his partisans recoiled against themselves.

1 Belmont, Histoiredu Canada (a contemporary chronicle).

8 See Discovery of the Great West. La Barre denies the assertion, and says that he merely told the Iroquois that La Salle should be sent home.

8 Mtmoire adresse a MM les Interests en la Socitfe' de la Ferme ei Commerce du Canada, 1683.

little later, they are reported to have sent more than a hundred. This forest trade robbed the colonists, by forestalling the annual market of Montreal; while a considerable part of the furs acquired by it were secretly sent to the English and Dutch of New York. Thus the heavy duties of the custom-house at Quebec were evaded; and silver coin was received in payment, instead of questionable bills "of exchange. 1 Frontenac had not been faithful to his trust; but, compared to his successor, he was a model of official virtue.

La Barre busied himself with ostentatious preparation for war; built vessels at Fort Frontenac, and sent up fleets of canoes, laden or partly laden with munitions. But his accusers say that the king's canoes were used to transport the governor's goods, and that the men sent to garrison Fort Frontenac were destined, not to fight the Iroquois, but to sell them brandy. " Last year," writes the intendant, " Monsieur de la Barre had a vessel built, for which he made his Majesty pay heavily;" and he proceeds to say that it was built for trade, and was used for no other purpose. "If," he continues, " the two (king's) vessels now at Fort Frontenac had not been used for trading, they would have saved us half the expense we have been forced to incur in transporting munitions and supplies. The pretended necessity of having vessels at this fort, and the consequent employing

1 These statements are made in a memorial of the agents of the custom-house, in letters of Meules, and in several other quarters. La Barre is accused of sending furs to Albany under pretext of official communication with the governor of New York.

of carpenters, and sending up of iron, cordage, sails, and many other things, at his Majesty's charge, was simply in the view of carrying on trade." He says, farther, that in May last, the vessels, canoes, and men being nearly all absent on this errand, the fort was left in so defenceless a state that a party of Senecas, returning from their winter hunt, took from it a quantity of goods, and drank as much brandy as they wanted. " In short/' he concludes, " it is plain that Monsieur de la Barre uses this fort only as a depot for the trade of Lake Ontario." l

In the spring of 1683, La Barre had taken a step as rash as it was lawless and unj ust. He sent the Chevalier de Baugis, lieutenant of his guard, with a considerable number of canoes and men, to seize La Salle's fort of St. Louis on the river Illinois; a measure which, while gratifying the passions and the greed of himself and his allies, would greatly increase the danger of rupture with the Iroquois. Late in the season, he despatched seven canoes and fourteen men, with goods to the value of fifteen or sixteen thousand livres, to trade with the tribes of the Mississippi. As he had sown, so he reaped. The seven canoes passed through the country of the Illinois. A large war party of Senecas and Cayugas invaded it in February. La Barre had told their chiefs that they were welcome to plunder the canoes of La Salle. The Iroquois were not discriminating. They fell upon

1 Meuks a Seignday, 8 July, 1684. This accords perfectly with state jnents made in several memorials of La Salle and his friends.

the governor's canoes, seized all the goods, and captured the men. 1 Then they attacked Bangis at Fort St. Louis. The place, perched on a rock, was strong, and they were beaten off; but the act was one of open war.

When La Barre heard the news, he was furious. 2 He trembled for the vast amount of goods which he and his fellow-speculators had sent to Michilli-mackinac and the lakes. There was but one resource : to call out the militia, muster the Indian allies, advance to Lake Ontario, and dictate peace to the Senecas, at the head of an imposing force; or, failing in this, to attack and crush them. A small vessel lying at Quebec was despatched to France, with urgent appeals for immediate aid, though there was little hope that it could arrive in time. She bore a long letter, half piteous, half bombastic, from La Barre to the king. He declared that extreme necessity and the despair of the people had forced him into war, and protested that he should always think it a privilege to lay down life for his Majesty. " I cannot refuse to your country of Canada, and your faithful subjects, to throw myself, with unequal forces, against

1 There appears no doubt that La Barre brought this upon himself. His successor, Denonville, writes that the Iroquois declared that, in plundering the canoes, they thought they were executing the orders they had received to plunder La Salle's people. Denonville, Mfmoire adresst au Ministre sur les Affaires de la Nouvelle France, 10 Aout. 1688. The Iroquois told Dongan, in 1684, " that they had not don any thing to the French but what Monsr. delaBarr Ordered them, which was that if they mett with any French hunting without his passe to take what they had from them/' Dongan to Denonmlle, 9 Sept., 1687.

a " Ce qui mit M. de la Barre en fureur." Belmont, Bistoire du Canada.

the foe, while at the same time begging your aid for a poor, unhappy people on the point of falling victims to a nation of barbarians." He says that the total number of men in Canada capable of bearing arms is about two thousand; that he received last year a hundred and fifty raw recruits; and that he wants, in addition, seven or eight hundred good soldiers. " Recall me," he concludes," if you will not help me, for I cannot bear to see the country perish in my hands." At the same time, he declares his intention to attack the Senecas, with or without help, about the middle of August. 1 Here we leave him, for a while, scared, excited, and blustering.

1 La Barre au Roy, 6 Juin, 1684.

CHAPTER YL 1684.

LA BARRE AND THE IROQUOIS.

DONGAN. — NEW YORK AND ITS INDIAN NEIGHBORS. — THE RIVAL GOVERNORS. — DONGAN AND THE IROQUOIS. — MISSION TO ONON-DAGA. — AN IROQUOIS POLITICIAN. — WARNINGS OF LAMBERVILLE.

— IROQUOIS BOLDNESS. — LA BARRE TAKES THE FIELD. — His MOTIVES. — THE MARCH. — PESTILENCE. — COUNCIL AT LA FAMINE.

— THE IROQUOIS DEFIANT. — HUMILIATION OF LA BARRE. — THB INDIAN ALLIES. — THEIR RAGE AND DISAPPOINTMENT. — RECALL OF LA BARRE.

THE Dutch Colony of New Netherland had now become the English colony of New York. Its proprietor, the Duke of York, afterwards James II. of England, had appointed Colonel Thomas Dongan its governor. He was a Catholic Irish gentleman of high 'rank, nephew of the famous Earl of Tyr-connel, and presumptive heir to the earldom of Limerick. He had served in France, was familiar with its language, and partial to its king and its nobility; but he nevertheless gave himself with vigor to the duties of his new trust.

The Dutch and English colonists aimed at a share in the western fur trade, hitherto a monopoly of Canada; and it is said that Dutch traders had already ventured among the tribes of the Great Lakes, boldly poaching on the French preserves.

Dongan did his utmost to promote their interests, so far at least as was consistent with his instructions from the Duke of York, enjoining him to give the French governor no just cause of offence. 1

For several years past, the Iroquois had made forays against the borders of Maryland and Virginia, plundering and killing the settlers; and a declared rupture between those colonies and the savage confederates had more than once been imminent. The English believed that these hostilities were instigated by the Jesuits in the Iroquois villages. There is no proof whatever of the accusation ; but it is certain that it was the interest of Canada to provoke a war which might, sooner or later, involve New York. In consequence of a renewal of such attacks, Lord Howard of Effing-ham, governor of Virginia, came to 'Albany in the summer of 1684, to hold a council with the Iroquois.

The Oneidas, Onondagas, and Cayugas were the offending tribes. They all promised friendship for the future. A hole was dug in the court-yard of the council house, each of the three threw a hatchet into it, and Lord Howard and the representative of

1 Sir John Werden to Dongan, 4 Dec., 1684; N. Y. Col. Docs., IIL 363. Werden was the duke's secretary.

Dongan has been chaigrd with instigating the Iroquois to attack the French. The Jesuit Lamberville, writing from Onondaga, says, on the contrary, that he hears that the " governor of New England (New York), when the Mohawk chiefs asked him to continue the sale of powder to them, replied that it should be continued so long as they would not make war on Christians." Lamberville a La Barre, 10 Fe'v., 1684.

The French ambassador at London complained that Dongan excited the Iroquois to war, and Dongan denied the charge. N. Y. Col, Docs. HI. 606, 609.

Maryland added two others; then the hole was filled, the song of peace was sung, and the high contracting parties stood pledged to mutual accord. 1 The Mohawks were also at the council, and the Senecas soon after arrived ; so that all the confederacy was present by its deputies. Not long before, La Barre, then in the heat of his martial preparations, had sent a messenger to Dongan with a letter, informing him that, as the Senecas and Cayugas had plundered French canoes and assaulted a French fort, he was compelled to attack them, and begging that the Dutch and English colonists should be forbidden to supply them with arms. 2 This lotter produced two results, neither of them agreeable to the writer: first, the Iroquois were fully warned of the designs of the French; and, secondly, Dongan gained the opportunity he wanted of asserting the claim of his king to sovereignty over the confederacy, and possession of the whole country south of the Great Lakes. He added that, if the Iroquois had done wrong, he would require them, as British subjects, to make reparation; and he urged La Barre, for the sake of peace between the two colonies, to refrain from his intended invasion of British territory. 3

Dongan next laid before the assembled sachems the complaints made against them in the letter of La Barre. They replied by accusing the French of carrying arms to their enemies, the Illinois and

1 Report of Conferences at Albany, in Colden, History of the Fivt Nations, 50 (ed. 1727, Shea's reprint).

2 La Barre a Dongan, 16 Juin, 1684. * Dongan a La Barre, 24 Juin, 1684

the Miamis. " Onontio," said their orator, " calls us his children, and then helps our enemies to knock us in the head." They were somewhat disturbed at the prospect of La Barre's threatened attack; and Dongan seized the occasion to draw from them an acknowledgment of subjection to the Duke of York, promising in return that they should be protected from the French. They did not hesitate. "We put ourselves/* said the Iroquois speaker, "under the great sachem Charles, who lives over the Great Lake, and under the protection of the great Duke of York, brother of your great sachem." But he added a moment after, " Let your friend (King Charles) who lives over the Great Lake know that we are a free people, though united to the English." \'7d They consented that the arms of the Duke of York should be planted in their villages, being told that this would prevent the French from destroying them. Dongan now insisted that they should make no treaty with Onontio without his consent; and he promised that, if their country should be invaded, he would send four hundred horsemen and as many foot soldiers to their aid.

As for the acknowledgment of subjection to the king and the Duke of York, the Iroquois neither understood its full meaning nor meant to abide by it. What they did clearly understand was that, while they recognized Onontio, the governor of Canada, as their father, they recognized Cor-

1 Speech of the Onondagas and Cayugas, in Colden, Five A" men*, 68 11727).

laer, the governor of New York, only as their brother. 1 Dongan, it seems, could not, or dared not, change this mark of equality. He did his best, however, to make good his claims, and sent Arnold Viele, a Dutch interpreter, as his envoy to Onon-daga. Viele set out for the Iroquois capital, and thither we will follow him.

He mounted his horse, and in the heats of August rode westward along the valley of the Mohawk. On a hill a bow-shot from the river, he saw the first Mohawk town, Kaghnawaga, encircled by a strong palisade. Next he stopped for a time at Gandagaro, on a meadow near the bank; and next, at Canajora, on a plain two miles away. Tionondogue', the last and strongest of these fortified villages, stood like the first on a hill that overlooked the river, and all the rich meadows around were covered with Indian corn. The largest of the four contained but thirty houses, and all together could furnish scarcely more than three hundred warriors. 2

When the last Mohawk town was passed, a ride of four or five days still lay before the envoy. He held his way along the old Indian trail, now traced through the grass of sunny meadows, and now tunnelled through the dense green of shady forests, till it led him to the town of the Oneidas, contain-

1 Except the small tribe of the Oneidas, who addressed Corlaer as Father. Corlaer was the official Iroquois name of the governor of New York ; Onas (the Feather, or Pen), that of the governor of Pennsylvania; and Assarigoa (the Big Knife, or Sword), that of the governor of Virginia. Corlaer, or Cuyler, was the name of a Dutchman whom the Iroquois held in great respect.

2 Journal of Wentworth Greenhalgh, 1677, in 2V. Y. Col, Docs- ITJ. 250,

ing about a hundred bark houses, with twice as many fighting men. the entire force of the tribe. Here, as in the four Mohawk villages, he planted the scutcheon of the Duke of York, and, still advancing, came at length to a vast open space where the rugged fields, patched with growing corn, sloped upwards into a broad, low hill, crowned with the clustered lodges of Onondaga. There were from one to two hundred of these large bark dwellings, most of them holding several families. The capital of the confederacy was not fortified at this time, and its only defence was the valor of some four hundred warriors. 1

In this focus of trained and organized savagery, where ferocity was cultivated as a virtue, and every emotion of pity stifled as unworthy of a man ; where ancient rites, customs, and traditions were held with the tenacity of a people who joined the extreme of wildness with the extreme of conservatism, — here burned the council fire of the five confederate tribes ; and here, in time of need, were gathered their bravest and their wisest to debate high questions of policy and war.

The object of Viele was to confirm the Iroquois in their very questionable attitude of subjection to the British crown, and persuade them to make no treaty or agreement with the French, except through the intervention of Dongan, or at least

1 Journal of Greenhalgh. The site of Onondaga, like that of all the Iroquois towns, was changed from time to time, as the soil of the neighborhood became impoverished, and the supply of wood exhausted. Greenhalgh, in 1677, estimated the warriors at three hundred and fifty ; but the number had increased of late by the adoption of prisoners.

with his consent. The envoy found two Frenchmen in the town, whose presence boded ill to his errand. The first was the veteran colonist of Montreal, Charles le Moyne, sent by La Barre to invite the Onondagas to a conference. They had known him, in peace or war, for a quarter of a century; and they greatly respected him. The other wan the Jesuit Jean de Lamberville, who had long lived among them, and knew them better than they knew themselves. Here, too, was another personage who cannot pass unnoticed. He was a famous Onondaga orator named Otre'ouati, and called also Big Mouth, whether by reason of the dimensions of that feature or the greatness of the wisdom that issued from it. His contemporary, Baron La Hontan, thinking perhaps that his French name of La Grande Gueule was wanting in dignity, Latinized it into Grangula; and the Scotchman, Golden, afterwards improved it into Garangula, under which high-sounding appellation Big Mouth has descended to posterity. He was an astute old savage, well trained in the arts of Iroquois rhetoric, and gifted with the power of strong and caustic sarcasm, which has marked more than one of the chief orators of the confederacy. He shared with most of his countrymen the conviction that the earth had nothing so great as the league of the Iroquois; but, if he could be proud and patriotic, so too he could be selfish and mean. He valued gifts, attentions,' and a good ineal, and would pay for them abundantly in promises, which he kept or not, as his own interests

or those of his people might require. He could use bold and loud words in public, and then secretly make his peace with those he had denounced. He was so given to rough jokes that the intendant, Meules, calls him a buffoon ; but his buffoonery seems to have been often a cover to his craft. He had taken a prominent part in the council of the preceding summer at Montreal; and, doubtless, as he stood in full dress before the governor and the officers, his head plumed, his face painted, his figure draped in a colored blanket, and his feet decked with embroidered moccasins, he was a picturesque and striking object. He was less so as he sqiiatted almost naked by his lodge fire, with a piece of board laid across his lap, chopping rank tobacco with a scalping-knife to fill his pipe, and entertaining the grinning circle with grotesque stories and obscene jests. Though not one of the hereditary chiefs, his influence was great. " He has the strongest head and the loudest voice among the Iroquois," wrote Lamberville to La Barre. "He calls himself your best friend. . . . He is a venal creature, whom you do well to keep in pay. I assured him I would send him the jerkin you promised." 1 Well as the Jesuit knew the Iroquois, he was deceived if he thought that Big Mouth was securely won.

Lamberville's constant effort was to prevent a rupture. He wrote with every opportunity to the governor, painting the calamities that war would

1 Letters of Lamberville in N. Y. Col. Docs., IX. For specimens of Big Mouth's skill in drawing, see ibid., IX. 386.

bring, and warning him that it was vain to hope that the league could be divided, and its three eastern tribes kept neutral, while the Senecas were attacked. He assured him, on the contrary, that they would all unite to fall upon Canada ? ravaging, burning, and butchering along the whole range of defenceless settlements. " You cannot believe, Monsieur, with what joy the Senecas learned that you might possibly resolve on war. When they heard of the preparations at Fort Frontenac, they said that the French had a great mind to be stripped, roasted, and eaten; and that they will see if their flesh, which they suppose to have a salt taste, by reason of the salt which we use with our food, be as good as that of their other enemies." 1 Lamberville also informs the governor that the Senecas have made ready for any emergency, buried their last year's corn, prepared a hiding place in the depth of the forest for their old men, women, and children, and stripped their towns of every thing that they value ; and that their fifteen hundred warriors will not shut themselves up in forts, but tight under cover, among trees and in the tall grass, with little risk to themselves and extreme danger to the invader. " There is no profit," he says, " in fighting with this sort of banditti, whom you cannot catch, but who will catch many of your people. The Onon-dagas wish to bring about an agreement. Must the father and the children, they ask, cut each other's throats?"

1 Lambervilk , T.a Barre, 11 July, 1684, in N. Y. Cd. Docs., IX. 258.

7

The Onondagas, moved by the influence of the Jesuit and the gifts of La Barre, did in fact wish to act as mediators between their Seneca confederates and the French; and to this end they invited the Seneca elders to a council. The meeting took place before the arrival of Yiele, and lasted two days. The Senecas were at first refractory, and hot for war, but at length consented that the Onondagas might make peace for them, if they could; a conclusion which was largely due to the eloquence of Big Mouth.

The first act of Yiele was a blunder. He told the Onondagas that the English governor was master of their country; and that, as they were subjects of the king of England, they must hold no council with the French without permission. The pride of Big Mouth was touched. " You say," he exclaimed to the envoy, " that we are subjects of the king of England and the Duke of York; but we say that we are brothers. We must take care of ourselves. The coat of arms which you have fastened to that post cannot defend us against Onontio. We tell you that we shall bind a covenant chain to our arm and to his. We shall take the Senecas by one hand and Onontio by the other, and their hatchet and his sword shall be thrown into deep water." l

Thus well and manfully did Big Mouth assert the independence of his tribe, and proclaim it the arbiter of peace. He told the warriors, moreover, to close their ears to the words of the Dutch-

1 Golden, Five Nations ,80 (1727).

man, who spoke as if he were drunk ; l and it was resolved at last that he, Big Mouth, with an em-"bassy of chiefs and elders, should go with Le Moyne to meet the French governor.

While these things were passing at Onondaga, La Barre had finished his preparations, and was now in full campaign. Before setting out, he had written to the minister that he was about to advance on the enemy, with seven hundred Canadians, a hundred and thirty regulars, and two hundred mission Indians; that more Indians were to join him on the way; that Du Lhut and La Duran-taye were to meet him at Niagara with a body of coureurs de bois and Indians from the interior; and that, " when we are all united, we will perish or destroy the enemy." 2 On the same day, he wrote to the king: " My purpose is to exterminate the Senecas; for otherwise your Majesty need take no farther account of this country, since there is no hope of peace with them, except when they are driven to it by force. I pray you do not abandon me ; and be assured that I shall do my duty at the head of your faithful colonists." 3

A few days after writing these curiously incoherent epistles, La Barre received a letter from his colleague, Meules, who had no belief that he meant to fight, and was determined to compel him to do BO, if possible. " There is a report," wrote the intendant, " that you mean to make peace. It is doing great harm. Our Indian allies will despise

1 Lamberville to La Barre, 28 Aug., 1684, in N. Y. Col. Docs , IX 267-

2 La Barre au Ministre, 9 July, 1684. 8 La Barre au Roy, meme dot*.

us. I trust the story is untrue, and that you will listen to no overtures. The expense has been enormous. The whole population is roused." Not satisfied with this, Meules sent the general a second letter, meant, like the first, as a tonic and a stimulant. " If we come to terms with the Iroquois, without first making them feel the strength of our arms, we may expect that, in future, they will do every thing they can to humiliate us, because we drew the sword against them, and showed them our teeth. I do not think that any course is now left for us but to carry the war to their very doors, and do our utmost to reduce them to such a point that they shall never again be heard of as a nation, but only as our subjects and slaves. If, after having gone so far, we do not fight them, we shall lose all our trade, and bring this country to the brink of ruin. The Iroquois, and especially the Senecas, pass for great cowards. The Reverend Father Jesuit, who is at Prairie de la Madeleine, told me as much yesterday ; and, though he has never been among them, he assured me that he has heard everybody say so. But, even if they were brave, we ought to be very glad of it; since then we could hope that they would wait our attack, and give us a chance to beat them. If we do not destroy them, they will destroy us. I think you see but too well that your honor and the safety of the country are involved in the results of this war." 9

1 Meules a La Barre, 16 July, 1684.

* Meules a La Barre, 14 Aout, 1684. This and the preceding lettei gtand, by a copyist's error, in the name of La Barre. They are certainly written by Meules.

While Meules thus wrote to the governor, he wrote also to the minister, Seignelay, and expressed his views with great distinctness. " I feel bound in conscience to tell you that nothing was ever heard of so extraordinary as what we see done in this country every day. One would think that there was a divided empire here between the king and the governor; and, if things should go on long in this way, the governor would have a far greater share than his Majesty. The persons whom Monsieur, la Barre has sent this year to trade at Fort Frontenac have already shared with him from ten to twelve thousand crowns." He then recounts numerous abuses and malversations on the part of the governor. "In a word, Monseigneur, this war has been decided upon in the cabinet of Monsieur the general, along with six of the chief merchants of the country. If it had not served their plans, he would have found means to settle every thing; but the merchants made him understand that they were in danger of being plundered, and that, having an immense amount of merchandise in the woods in nearly two hundred canoes fitted out last year, it was better to make use of the people of the country to carry on war against the Senecas. This being done, he hopes to make extraordinary profits without any risk, because one of two things will happen : either we shall gain some considerable advantage over the savages, as there is reason to hope, if Monsieur the general will but attack them in their villages; or else we shall make a peace which will keep every thing

safe for a time. These are assuredly the sole motives of this war, which has for principle and end nothing but mere interest. He says himself that there is good fishing in troubled waters. 1

" With all our preparations for war, and all the expense in which Monsieur the general is involving his Majesty, I will take the liberty to tell you, Monseigneur, though I am no prophet, that J discover no disposition on the part of Monsieur the general to make war against the aforesaid savages. In my belief, he will content himself with going in a canoe as far as Fort Frontenac, and then send for the Senecas to treat of peace with them, and deceive the people, the intendant, and, if I may be allowed with all possible respect to say so, hia Majesty himself.

" P. S. — I will finish this letter, Monseigneur, by telling you that he set out yesterday, July 10th, with a detachment of two hundred men. All Quebec was filled with grief to see him embark on an expedition of war tete-a-tete with the man named La Chesnaye. Everybody says that the war is a sham, that these two will arrange every

1 The famous voyageur, Nicolas Perrot, agrees with the intendant. w Us (La Barre et ses associfs) s'imaginerent que sitost que le Fra^ois viendroit a paroistre, rirroquois luy demanderoit mise'ricorde, qu'il seroit facile d'establir des magasins, construire des barques dans le lac Ontario, Dt que c'estoit un moyen de trouver des richesses." Mtmaire sur las Maeurs, Coustumes, et Relligion des Sauvages, chap. xxi.

The Sulpitian, Abbe* Belmont, says that the avarice of the merchants was the cause of the war; that they and La Barre wished to prevent the Iroquois from interrupting trade ; and that La Barre aimed at an indemnity for the sixteen hundred livres in merchandise which the Senecas had taken from his canoes early in the year. Belmont adds that he wanted to brine them to terms without fighting.

thing between them, and, in a word, do whatever will help their trade. The whole country is in despair to see how matters are managed."

After a long stay at Montreal, La Barre embarked his little army at La Chine, crossed Lake St. Louis, and began the ascent of the upper St. Lawrence. In one of the three companies of regulars which formed a part of the force was a young subaltern, the Baron la Hontan, who has left a lively account of the expedition. Some of the men were in flat boats, and some were in birch canoes. Of the latter was La Hontan, whose craft was paddled by three Canadians. Several times they shouldered it through the forest to escape the turmoil of the rapids. The flat boats could not be so handled, and were dragged or pushed up in the shallow water close to the bank, by gangs of militia men, toiling and struggling among the rocks and foam. The regulars, unskilled in such matters, were spared these fatigues, though tormented night and day by swarms of gnats- and mosquitoes, objects of La Hontan's bitterest invective. At length the last rapid was passed, and they moved serenely on their way, threaded the mazes of the Thousand Islands, entered what is now the harbor of Kingston, and landed under the palisades of Fort Frontenac.

Here the whole force was soon assembled, the regulars in their tents, the Canadian* militia and the Indians in huts and under sheds of bark. Of these red allies there were several hundred ; Abe-

1 Meules au Ministry 8-11 Juillet, 1684.

nakis and Algonquins from Sillery, Hurons from Lorette, and converted Iroquois from the Jesuit mission of Saut St. Louis, near Montreal. The camp of the French was on a low, damp plain near the fort; and here a malarious fever presently attacked them, killing many and disabling many more. La Hontan says that La Barre himself was brought by it to the brink of the grave. If he had ever entertained any other purpose than that of inducing the Senecas to agree to a temporary peace, he now completely abandoned it. He dared not even insist that the offending tribe should meet him in council, but hastened to ask the mediation of the Onondagas, which the letters of Lamberville had assured him that they were disposed to offer. He sent Le Moyne to persuade them to meet him on their own side of the lake, and, with such of his men as were able to move, crossed to the mouth of Salmon River, then called La Famine.

The name proved prophetic. Provisions fell short from bad management in transportation, and the men grew hungry and discontented. September had begun ; the place was unwholesome, and the malarious fever of Fort Frontenac infected the new encampment. The soldiers sickened rapidly. La Barre, racked with suspense, waited impatiently the return of Le Moyne. We have seen already the result of his mission, and how he and Lamberville, in spite of the envoy of the English governor, gained from the Onondaga chiefs the promise to meet Onontio in council. Le Moyne appeared at La Famine on the third of the month, bringing

with him Big Mouth and thirteen other deputies. La Barre gave them a feast of bread, wine, and salmon trout, and on the morning of the fourth the council began.

Before the deputies arrived, the governor had sent the sick men homeward in order to conceal his helpless condition; and he now told the Iro-quois that he had left his army at Fort Frontenac, and had come to meet them attended only by an escort. The Onondaga politician was not to be so deceived. He, or one of his party, spoke a little French; and during the night, roaming noiselessly among the tents, he contrived to learn the true state of the case from the soldiers.

The council was held on an open spot near the French encampment. La Barre was seated in an arm-chair. The Jesuit Bruyas stood by him as interpreter, and the officers were ranged on his right and left. The Indians sat on the ground in a row opposite the governor; and two lines of soldiers ? forming two sides of a square, closed the intervening space. Among the officers was La Hontan, a spectator of the whole proceeding. He may be called a man in advance of his time ; for he had the caustic, sceptical, and mocking spirit which a century later marked the approach of the great revolution, but which was not a characteristic of the reign of Louis XIV. He usually told the truth when he had no motive to do otherwise, and yet was capable at times of prodigious mendacity. 1

1 La Hontan attempted to impose on his readers a marvellous story of pretended

discoveries beyond the Mississippi; and his ill repute in the

There is no reason to believe that he indulged in it on the present occasion, and his account of what he now saw and heard may probably be taken as substantially correct. According to him, La Barre opened the council as follows : —

"The king my master, being informed that the Five Nations of the Iroquois have long acted in a manner adverse to peace, has ordered me to come with an escort to this place, and to send Akouessan (Le Moyne) to Onondaga to invite the principal chiefs to meet me. It is the wish of this great king that you and I should smoke the calumet of peace together, provided that you promise, in the name of the Mohawks, Oneidas, Onondagas, Cayugas, and Senecas, to give entire satisfaction and indemnity to his subjects, and do nothing in future which may occasion rupture."

Then he recounted the offences of the Iroquois. First, they had maltreated and robbed French traders in the country of the Illinois; " wherefore," said the governor, " I am ordered to demand reparation, and in case of refusal to declare war against you."

Next, " the warriors of the Five Nations have introduced the English into the lakes which belong to the king my master, and among the tribes who are his children, in order to destroy the trade of his subjects, and seduce these people from the obedience they owe him. I am willing to forget this ; but, should it happen again, I am expressly . ordered to declare war against you."

matter of veracity is due chiefly to this fabrication. On the other hand, his account of what he saw in the colony is commonly in accord with the best com.enipor rt r> evidence.

Thirdly, " the warriors of the Five Nations have made sundry barbarous inroads into the country of the Illinois and Miamis, seizing, binding, and leading into captivity an infinite number of these savages in time of peace. They are the children of my king, and are not to remain your slaves. They must at once be set free and sent home. If you refuse to do this, I am expressly ordered to declare war against you."

La Barre concluded by assuring Big Mouth, as representing the Five Nations of the Iroquois, that the French would leave them in peace if they made atonement for the past, and promised good conduct for the future; but that, if they did not heed his words, their villages should be burned, and they themselves destroyed. He added, though he knew the contrary, that the governor of New York would join him in war against them.

During the delivery of this martial harangue, Big Mouth sat silent and attentive, his eyes fixed on the bowl of his pipe. When the interpreter had ceased, he rose, walked gravely two or three times around the lines of the assembly, then stopped before the governor, looked steadily at him, stretched his tawny arm, opened his capacious jaws, and uttered himself as follows: —

" Onontio, I honor you, and all the warriors who are with me honor you. Your interpreter has ended his speech, and now I begin inline. Listen to my words.

" Onontio, when you left Quebec, you must have thought that the heat of the sun had burned the

forests that make our country inaccessible to the French, or that the lake had overflowed them so that we could not escape from our villages. You must have thought so, Onontio; and curiosity to see such a fire or such a flood must have brought you to this place. Now your eyes are opened ; for I and my warriors have come to tell you that the Senecas, Cayugas, Onondagas, Oneidas, and Mohawks are all alive. I thank you in their name for bringing back the calumet of peace which they gave to your predecessors ; and I give you joy that you have not dug up the hatchet which has been so often red with the blood of your countrymen.

" Listen, Onontio. I am not asleep. My eyes are open; and by the sun that gives me light I see a great captain at the head of a band of soldiers, who talks like a man in a dream. He says that he has come to smoke the pipe of peace with the Onondagas; but I see that he came to knock them in the head, if so many of his Frenchmen were not too weak to fight. I see Onontio raving in a camp of sick men, whose lives the Great Spirit has saved by smiting them with disease. Our wornen had snatched war-clubs, and our children and old men seized bows and arrows to attack your camp, if our warriors had not restrained them, when your messenger, Akouessan, appeared in our village/'

He next justified the pillage of French traders on the ground, very doubtful in this case, that they were carrying arms to the Illinois, enemies of the confederacy; and he flatly refused to make reparation, telling La Barre that even the old men

of his tribe had no fear of the French. He also avowed boldly that the Iroquois had conducted English traders to the lakes. " We are born-free/' he exclaimed, " we depend neither on Onontio nor on Corlaer. We have the right to go whithersoever we please, to take with us whomever we please, and buy and sell of whomever we please. If your allies are your slaves or your children, treat them like slaves or children, and forbid them to deal with anybody but your Frenchmen.

" We have knocked the Illinois in the head, because they cut down the tree of peace and hunted the beaver on our lands. We have done less than the English and the French, who have seized upon the lands of many tribes, driven them away, and built towns, villages, and forts in their country.

" Listen, Onontio. My voice is the voice of the Five Tribes of the Iroquois. When they buried the hatchet at Cataraqui (Fort Frontenac] in presence of your predecessor, they planted the tree of peace in the middle of the fort, that it might be a post of traders and not of soldiers. Take care that all the soldiers you have brought with you, shut up in so small a fort, do not choke this tree of peace. I assure you in the name of the Five Tribes that our warriors will dance the dance of the calumet under its branches; and that they will sit quiet on their mats and never dig up the hatchet, till their brothers, Onontio and Corlaer, separately or together, make ready to attack the country that the Great Spirit has given to our ancestors."

The session presently closed; and La Barre with-

drew to his tent, where, according to La Hontan, he vented his feelings in invective, till reminded that good manners were not to be expected from an Iroquois. Big Mouth, on his part, entertained some of the French at a feast which he opened in person by a dance. There was another session in the afternoon, and the terms of peace were settled in the evening. The tree of peace was planted anew; La Barre promised not to attack the Senecas; and Big Mouth, in spite of his former declaration, consented that they should make amends for the pillage of the traders. On the other hand, he declared that the Iroquois would fight the Illinois to the death; and La Barre dared not utter a word in behalf of his allies. The Onondaga next demanded that the council fire should be removed from Fort Frontenac to La Famine, in the Iroquois country. This point was yielded without resistance ; and La Barre promised to decamp and set out for home on the following morning. 1

Such was the futile and miserable end of the grand expedition. Even the promise to pay for the plundered goods was contemptuously broken. 9 The honor rested with the Iroquois. They had spurned the French, repelled the claims of the English, and by act and word asserted their independence of both.

La Barre embarked and hastened home in ad-

1 The articles of peace will be found in N. Y. Col. Docs., IX. 236. Compare Memoir of M. de la Barre regarding the War against the Senecas, ibid., 239. These two documents do not agree as to date, one placing the council on the 4th and the other on the 5th.

* This appears from the letters of Denonville, La Barre's successor

vance of his men. His camp was again full of the sick. Their comrades placed them, shivering with ague fits, on board the flat-boats and canoes; and the whole force, scattered and disordered, floated down the current to Montreal. Nothing had been gained but a thin and flimsy truce, with new troubles and dangers plainly visible behind it. The better to understand their nature, let us look for a moment at an episode of the campaign.

When La Barre sent messengers with gifts and wampum belts to summon the Indians of the Upper Lakes to join in the war, his appeal found a cold response. La Durantaye and Du Lhut, French commanders in that region, vainly urged the surrounding tribes to lift the hatchet. None but the Hurons would consent, when, fortunately, Nicolas Perrot arrived at Michillimackinac on an errand of trade. This famous coureur de bois — a very different person from Perrot, governor of Montreal — was well skilled in dealing with Indians. Through his influence, their scruples were overcome; and some five hundred warriors, Hurons, Ottawas, Ojibwas, Pottawatamies, and Foxes, were persuaded to embark for the rendezvous at Niagara, along with a hundred or more Frenchmen. The fleet of canoes ; numerous as a flock of blackbirds in autumn, began the long and weary voyage. The two commanders had a heavy task. Discipline was impossible. The French were scarcely less wild than the savages. Many of them were painted and feathered like their red companions, whose ways they imitated with perfect success. The Indians, on their part, were but half-hearted for the work in hand, for they had already discovered that the English would pay twice as much for a beaver skin as the French ; and they asked nothing better than the appearance of English traders on the lakes, and a safe peace with the Iroquois, which should open to them the market of New York. But they were like children with the passions of men, inconsequent, fickle, and wayward. They stopped to hunt on the shore of Michigan, where a Frenchman accidentally shot himself with his own gun. Here was an evil omen. But for the efforts of Perrot, half the party would have given up the enterprise, and paddled home. In the Strait of Detroit there was another hunt, and another accident. In firing at a deer, an Indian wounded his own brother. On this the tribesmen of the wounded man proposed to kill the French, as being the occasion of the mischance. Once more the skill of Perrot prevailed; but when they reached the Long Point of Lake Erie, the Foxes, about a hundred in number, were on the point of deserting in a body. As persuasion failed, Perrot tried the effect of taunts. " You are cowards," he said to the naked crew, as they crowded about him with their wild eyes and long lank hair. " You do not know what war is : you never killed a man and you never ate one, except those that were given you tied hand and foot." They broke out against him in a storm of abuse. " You shall see whether we are men. We are going to fight the Iroquois; and, unless you do your part, we will knock you in the head." " You will never have to give yourselves the trouble," retorted Perrot, " for at the first war-whoop you will all run off." He gained his point. Their pride was roused, and for the moment they were full of fight. 1

Immediately after, there was trouble with the Ottawas, who became turbulent and threatening, and refused to proceed. With much ado, they were persuaded to go as far as Niagara, being lured by the rash assurance of La Durantaye that three vessels were there, loaded with a present of guns for them. They carried their canoes by the cataract, launched them again, paddled to the mouth of the river, and looked for the vessels in vain. At length a solitary sail appeared on the lake. She brought no guns, but instead a letter from La Barre, telling them that peace was made, and that they might all go home. Some of them had paddled already a thousand miles, in the hope of seeing the Senecas humbled. They turned back in disgust, filled with wrath and scorn against the governor and all the French. Canada had incurred the contempt, not only of enemies, but of allies. There was danger that these tribes would repudiate the French alliance, welcome the English traders, make peace at any price with the Iroquois, and carry their beaver skins to Albany instead of Montreal.

The treaty made at La Famine was greeted with contumely through all the colony. The governor found, however, a comforter in the Jesuit Lamber-

1 La Potherie, II. 159 (ed. 1722). Perrot himself, in his Moeurs des Salvages, briefly mentions the incident.

8

ville, who stood fast in the position which he had held from the beginning. He wrote to La Barre : " You deserve the title of saviour of the country for making peace at so critical a time. In the condition in which your army was, you could not have advanced into the Seneca country without utter defeat. The Senecas had double palisades, which could not have been forced without great loss. Their plan was to keep three hundred men inside, and to perpetually harass you with twelve hundred others. All the Iroquois were to collect together, and fire only at the legs of your people, so as to master them, and burn them at their leisure, and then, after having thinned their numbers by a hundred ambuscades in the woods and grass, to pursue you in your retreat even to Montreal, and spread desolation around it." 1

La Barre was greatly pleased with this letter, and made use of it to justify himself to the king. His colleague, Meules, on the other hand, declared that Lainberville, anxious to make favor with the governor, had written only what La Barre wished to hear. The intendant also informs the minister that La Barrels excuses are a mere pretence; that everybody is astonished and disgusted with him; that the sickness of the troops was his own fault, because he kept them encamped on wet ground for an unconscionable length of time; that Big Mouth shamefully befooled and bullied him; that, after the council at La Famine, he lost liis wits, and went off in a fright; that,

1 Lamberville to La Barre, 9 Oct., 1684, in N. Y. Col. Dec*., IX. 260.

since the return of the troops, the officers have openly expressed their contempt for him; and that the people would have risen against him, if he, Meules, had not taken measures to quiet them. 1 These, with many other charges, flew across the sea from the pen of the intendant.

The next ship from France brought the following tetter from the king: —

MONSIEUR DE LA BARRE, — Having been informed that your years do not permit you to support the fatigues inseparable from your office of governor and lieutenant-general in Canada, I send you this letter to acquaint you that I have selected Monsieur de Denonville to serve in your place; and my intention is that, on his arrival, after resigning to him the command, with all instructions concerning it, you embark for your return to France. Louis.

La Barre sailed for home; and the Marquis de Denonville, a pious colonel ^ of dragoons, assumed the vacant office.

1 Mevlea au Ministre, 10 Oct., 1684.

CHAPTEK VH.

1685-1687. DENONVILLE AND DONGAN.

TfiOUBLES OP THE NEW GOVERNOR. — HlS CHARACTER. — ENGLISH RIVALRY. — INTRIGUES OF DONGAN. — ENGLISH CLAIMS. — A DIPLOMATIC DUEL. — OVERT ACTS. — ANGER OP DENONVILLE. — JAMES II.

CHUCKS DONGAN. — DENONVILLE EMBOLDENED. — STRIFE IN THE NORTH. — HUDSON'S BAT. — ATTEMPTED PACIFICATION. — ARTIFICE OF DENONVILLE. — HE PREPARES FOR WAR.

DENONVILLE embarked at Rochelle in June, with his wife and a part of his family. Saint-Vallier, the destined Bishop, was in the same vessel ; and the squadron carried five hundred soldiers, of whom a hundred and fifty died of fever and scurvy on the way. Saint-Yallier speaks in glowing terms of the new governor. " He spent nearly all his time in prayer and the reading of good books. The Psalms of David were always in hia hands. In all the voyage, I never saw him do any thing wrong; and there was nothing in his words or acts which did not show a solid virtue and a consummate prudence, as well in the duties of the Christian life as in the wisdom of this world." 1

When they landed, the nuns of the Hotel-Dieu
were overwhelmed with the sick. " Not only our halls, but our church, our granary, our hen-yard, and every corner of the hospital where we could make room, were filled with them." 1

Much was expected of Denonville. He was to repair the mischief wrought by his predecessor, and restore the colony to peace, strength, and security. The king had stigmatized La Barre's treaty with the Iroquois as disgraceful, and expressed indignation at his abandonment of the Illinois allies. All this was now to be changed; but it was easier to give the order at Versailles than to execute it in Canada. Denonville's difficulties were great; and his means of overcoming them were small. What he most needed was more troops and more money. The Senecas, insolent and defiant, were still attacking the Illinois; the tribes of the north-west were angry, contemptuous, and disaffected; the English of New York were urging claims to the whole country south of the Great Lakes, and to a controlling share in all the western fur trade; while the English of Hudson's Bay were competing for the traffic of the northern tribes, and the English of New England were seizing upon the fisheries of Acadia, and now and then making piratical descents upon its coast. The great question lay between New York and Canada. Which of these two should gain mastery in the west ?

Denonville, like Frontenac, was a man of the army and the court. As a soldier, he had the experience of thirty years of service; and he was in

1 Juchereau, Hdtel-Dieu, 283.

high repute, not only for piety, but for probity and honor. He was devoted to the Jesuits, an ardent servant of the king, a lover of authority, filled with the instinct of subordination and order, and, in short, a type of the ideas, religious, political, and 8QciaI,then dominant mJFrance. He was greatly distressed at the disturbed condition of the colony; while the state of the settlements, scattered in broken lines for two or three hundred miles along the St. Lawrence, seemed to him an invitation to destruction. " If we have a war," he wrote, " nothing can save the country but a miracle of God."

Nothing was more likely than war. Intrigues were on foot between the Senecas and the tribes of the lakes, which threatened to render the appeal to arms a necessity to the French. Some of the Hurons of Michillimackinac were bent on allying themselves with the English. " They like the manners of the French," wrote Denonville ; " but they like the cheap goods of the English better/' The Senecas, in collusion with several Huron chiefs, had captured a considerable number of that tribe and of the Ottawas. The scheme was that these prisoners should be released, on condition that the lake tribes should join the Senecas and repudiate their alliance with the French. 1 The governor of New York favored this intrigue to the utmost.

Denonville was quick to see that the peril of the colony rose, not from the Iroquois alone, but from the English of New York, who prompted them.

1 Denonville au Ministre, 12 Juin, 1686.

Dongan understood the situation. He saw that the French armed at mastering the whole interior of the continent. They had established themselves in the valley of the Illinois, had built a fort on the lower Mississippi, and were striving to entrench themselves at its mouth. They occupied the Great Lakes ; and it was already evident that, as soon as their resources should permit, they would seize the avenues of communication throughout the west. In short, the grand scheme of French colonization had begun to declare itself. Dongan entered the lists against them. If his policy should prevail, New France would dwindle to a feeble province on the St. Lawrence : if the French policy should prevail, the English colonies would remain a narrow strip along the sea. Dongan' s cause was that of all these colonies ; but they all stood aloof, and left him to wage the strife alone. Canada was matched against New York, or rather against the governor of New York. The population of the English colony was larger than that of its rival ; but, except the fur traders, few of the settlers cared much for the questions at issue. 1 Dongan' s chief difficulty, however, rose from the relations of the French and English kings. Louis XIV. gave Denonville an unhesitating support. James II., on the other hand, was for a time cautious to timidity. The two monarchs were closely united. Both hated constitutional liberty, and both held the same principles j)f supr^^oy in rhur^h nnd ptntfi ; but

' New York had about 18,000 inhabitants (Brodhead, Hist. N. Y. (II. 468). Canada, by the census of 1685, had 12,263.

Louis was triumphant and powerful, while James, in conflict with his subjects, was in constant need of his great ally, and dared not offend him.

The royal instructions to Denonville enjoined him to humble the Iroquois, sustain the allies of the colony, oppose the schemes of Dongan, and treat him as an enemy, if he encroached on French territory. At the same time, the French ambassador at the English court was directed to demand from James II. precise orders to the governor of New York for a complete change of conduct in regard to Canada and the Iroquois. 1 But Dongan, like the French governors, was not easily controlled. In the absence of money and troops, he intrigued busily with his Indian neighbors. " The artifices of the English," wrote Denonville, " have reached such a point that it would be better if they attacked us openly and burned our settlements, instead of instigating the Iroquois against us for our destruction. I know beyond a particle of doubt that M. Dongan caused all the five Iroquois nations to be assembled last spring at Orange (Albany), in order to excite them against us, by telling them publicly that I meant to declare war against them." He says, further, that Dongan supplies them with arms and ammunition, incites them to attack the colony, and urges them to deliver Lamberville, the priest at Onondaga, into his hands. " He has sent people, at the same time, to our Montreal Indians to entice them over to

1 Seignday to Barillon, French Ambassador at London, in N Y. CoU Docs., IX. 269.

him, promising them missionaries to instruct them, and assuring them that he would prevent the introduction of brandy into their villages. All these intrigues have given me not a little trouble throughout the summer. M. Dongan has written to me, and I have answered him as a man may do who wishes to dissimulate and does not feel strong enough to get angry." 1

Denonville, accordingly, while biding his time, made use of counter intrigues, and, by means of the useful Lamberville, freely distributed secret or " underground" presents among the Iroquois chiefs; while the Jesuit Engelran was busy at Michillimackinac in adroit and vigorous efforts to prevent the alienation of the Hurons,.0ttawas, and other lake tribes. The task was difficult; and, filled with anxiety, the father came down to Montreal to see the governor, " and communicate to me," writes Denonville, "the deplorable state of affairs with our allies, whom we can no longer trust, qwing to the discredit into which we have fallen among them, and from which we cannot recover, except by gaining some considerable advantage over the Iroquois; who, as I have had the honor to inform you, have labored incessantly since last autumn to rob us of all our allies, by using every means to make treaties with them independently of us. You may be assured, Mon-seigneur, that the English are the chief cause of the arrogance and insolence of the Iroquois, adroitly using them to extend the limits of their dominion,

i DenonviUe a Seignelay, 8 Nov., 1686-

and uniting with them as one nation, insomuch that the English claims include no less than the Lakes Ontario and Erie, the region of Saginaw (Michigan), the country of the Hurons, and all the country in the direction of the Mississippi." 1

The most pressing danger was the defection of the lake tribes. " In spite of the king's edicts/' pursues Denonville, " the coureurs de bois have carried a hundred barrels of brandy to Michilli-mackinac in a single year; and their libertinism and debauchery have gone to such an extremity that it is a wonder the Indians have not massacred them all to save themselves from their violence and recover their wives and daughters from them.. This, Monseigneur, joined to our failure in the kst war, has drawn upon us such contempt among all the tribes that there is but one way to regain our credit, which is to humble the Iroquois by our unaided strength, without asking the help of our Indian allies." 2 And he begs hard for a strong reinforcement of troops.

Without doubt, Denonville was right in thinking that the chastising of the Iroquois, or at least the Senecas, the head and front of mischief, was a matter of the last necessity. A crushing blow dealt against them would restore French prestige, paralvze English intrigue, save the Illinois from destruction, and confirm the wavering allies of Canada. Meanwhile, matters grew from bad to worse. In the north and in the west, there was

1 Derwnville a Seignelay, 12 Juin, 1686.

2 Ibid.

scarcely a tribe in the French interest which was not either attacked by the Senecas or cajoled by them into alliances hostile to the colony. " We may set down Canada as lost," again writes Denonville, " if we do not make war next year ; and yet, in our present disordered state, war is the most dangerous thing in the world. Nothing can save us but the sending out of troops and the building of forts and blockhouses. Yet I dare not begin to build them ; for, if I do, it will bring down all the Iroquois upon us before we are in a condition to fight them."

Nevertheless, he made what preparations he could, begging all the while for more soldiers, and carrying on at the same time a correspondence with his rival, Dongan. At first, it was courteous on both sides; but it soon grew pungent, and at last acrid. Denonville wrote to announce his arrival, and Dongan replied in French: " Sir, I have had the honor of receiving your letter, and greatly rejoice at having so good a neighbor, whose reputation is so widely spread that it has anticipated your arrival. I have a very high respect for the king of France, of whose bread I have eaten so much that I feel under an obligation to prevent whatever can give the least umbrage to our masters. M. de la Barre is a very worthy gentleman, but he has not written to me in a civil and befitting style." 1

Denonville replied with many compliments : " I know not what reason you may have had to be

1 Dongan to Denonville, 13 Oct., 1685, in N. Y. Col. Docs., IX. 292.

dissatisfied with M. de la Barre; but I know very well that I should reproach myself all my life if I could fail to render to you all the civility and attention due to a person of so great rank and merit. In regard to the affair in which M. de la Barre interfered, as you write me, I presume you refer to his quarrel with the Senecas. As to that, Monsieur, I believe you understand the character of that nation well enough to perceive that it is not easy to live in friendship with a people who have neither religion, nor honor, nor subordination. The king, my master, entertains affection and friendship for this country solely through zeal for the establishment of religion here, and the support and protection of the missionaries whose ardor in preaching the faith leads them to expose themselves to the brutalities and persecutions of the most ferocious of tribes. You know better than I what fatigues and torments they have suffered for the sake of Jesus Christ. I know your heart is penetrated with the glory of that name which makes Hell tremble, and at the mention of which all the powers of Heaven fall prostrate. Shall we be so unhappy as to refuse them our master's protection ? You are a man of rank and abounding in merit. You love our holy religion. Can we not then come to an understanding to sustain our missionaries by keeping those fierce tribes in respect and fear ? " 1

This specious appeal for maintaining French Jesuits on English territory, or what was claimed

1 Denonville to Dongan, 6 Juin, 1686, N. Y. Col. Does., III. 466.

as such, was lost on Dongan, Catholic as he was, He regarded them as dangerous political enemies, and did his best to expel them, and put English priests in their place. Another of his plans was to build a fort at Niagara, to exclude the French from Lake Erie. Denonville entertained the same purpose, in order to exclude the English; and he watched eagerly the moment to execute it. A rumor of the scheme was brought to Dongan by one of the French coureurs de bois, who often deserted to Albany, where they were welcomed and encouraged. The English governor was exceedingly wroth. He had written before in French out of complaisance. He now dispensed with ceremony, and wrote in his own peculiar English: " I am informed that you intend to build a fort at Ohniagero (Niagara) on this side of the lake, within my Master's territoryes without question. I cannot beleev that a person that has your reputation in the world would follow the steps of Monsr. Labarr, and be ill advized by some interested persons in your Govert. to make disturbance between our Masters subjects in those parts of the world for a little pelttree (peltry). I hear one of the Fathers (the Jesuit Jean de Lamberville) is gone to you, and th'other that stayed (Jacques de Lamberville) I have sent for him here lest the Indians should insult over him, tho' it's a thousand pittys that those that have made such progress in the service of God should be disturbed, and that by the fault of those that laid the foundation of Christianity amongst these barbarous people;

setting apart the station I am in, I am as much Monsr. Des Nevilles (Denonville s) humble servant as any friend he has, and will ommit no opportunity of manifesting the same. Sir, your humble servant, Thomas Dongan." *

Denonville in reply denied that he meant to build a fort at Niagara, and warned Dongan not to believe the stories told him by French deserters. " In order," he wrote, " that we may live on a good understanding, it would be well that a gentleman of your character should not give protection to all the rogues, vagabonds, and thieves who desert us and seek refuge with you, and who, to gain your favor, think they cannot do better than tell nonsensical stories about us, which they will continue to do so long as you Us ten to them." 3

The rest of the letter was in terms of civility, to which Dongan returned: " Beleive me it is much joy to have soe good a neighbour of soe excellent qualifications and temper, and of a humour altogether differing from Monsieur de la Barre, your predecessor, who was so furious and hasty and very much addicted to great words, as if I had bin to have bin frighted by them. For my part, I shall take all immaginable care that the Fathers who preach the Holy Gospell to those Indians over whom I have power bee not in the least ill treated, and upon that very accompt have sent for one of each nation to come to me, and then those beastly crimes you reproove shall be checked severely,

l Dongan to Denonville, 22 May, 1686. in N, Y. Col. Docs., HI. 465. * DenowiUe a Dongan, 20 Juin, 1686

and all my endevours used to suppress their filthy drunkennesse, disorders, debauches, warring, and quarrels, and whatsoever doth obstruct the growth and enlargement of the Christian faith amongst those people." He then, in reply to an application of Denonville, promised to give up " runawayes."

Promise was not followed by performance ; and he still favored to the utmost the truant Frenchmen who made Albany their resort, and often brought with them most valuable information. This drew an angry letter from Denonville. " You were so good, Monsieur, as to tell me that you would give up all the deserters who have fled to you to escape chastisement for their knavery. As most of them are bankrupts and thieves, I hope that they will give you reason to repent having harbored them, and that your merchants who employ them will be punished for trusting such rascals." 2 To the great wrath of the French governor, Dongan persisted in warning the IroquoJs that he.meant to attack them. "You proposed, Monsieur," writes Denonville, " to submit every thing to the decision of our masters. Nevertheless, your emissary to the Onondagas told all the Five Nations in your name to pillage and make war on us." Next, he berates his rival for furnishing the Indians with rum. " Think you that religion will make any progress, while your traders supply the savages in abundance with the liquor which, as you ought to know, converts them into demons and their lodges into counterparts of Hell? "

1 Donyan to Denonwlle, 26 July, 1686, in N. Y. Col. Docs., HI. 460.

2 Denonville a Dongan, 1 Oct., 1686.

" Certainly," retorts Dongan, " our Rum doth as little hurt as your Brandy, and, in the opinion of Christians, is much more wholesome." 1

Each tried incessantly to out-general the other. Denonville, steadfast in his plan of controlling the passes of the western country, had projected forts, not only at Niagara, but also at Toronto, on Lake Erie, and on the Strait of Detroit. He thought that a time had come when he could, without rashness, secure this last important passage; and he sent an order to Du Lhut, who was then at Michil-limackinac, to occupy it with fifty coureurs de bois* That enterprising chief accordingly repaired to Detroit, and built a stockade at the outlet of Lake Huron on the western side of the strait. It was not a moment too soon. The year before, Dongan had sent a party of armed traders in eleven canoes, commanded by Johannes Rooseboom, a Dutchman of Albany, to carry English goods to tHe upper lakes. They traded successfully, winning golden opinions from the Indians, who begged them to come every year ; and, though Denonville Bent an officer to stop them at Niagara, they returned in triumph, after an absence of three months. 3 A larger expedition was organized in the autumn of 1686. Rooseboom again set out for the lakes with twenty or more canoes. He was to winter among the Senecas, and wait the arrival of Major Mc-Gregory, a Scotch officer, who was to leave Albany

1 Dongan to Denonville, 1 Dec., 1686, in N. Y. Col. Docs., III. 462. 8 Denonville a Du Lhut, 6 Juin, 1686.

8 Brodhead, Hist, of New York, II. 429 ; Denonville au Ministre, 8 Mai, 1686.

in the spring with fifty men, take command of the united parties, and advance to Lake

Huron, accompanied by a band of Iroquois, to form a general treaty of trade and alliance with the tribes claimed by France as her subjects. 1

Denonville was beside himself at the news. He had already urged upon Louis XIV. the policy of buying the colony of New York, which he thought might easily be done, and which, as he said, " would make us masters of the Iroquois without a war." This time he wrote in a less pacific mood: " I have a mind to go straight to Albany, storm their fort, and burn every thing." 2 And he begged for soldiers more earnestly than ever. " Things grow worse and worse. The English stir up the Iroquois against us, and send parties to Michilli-mackinac to rob us of our trade. It would be better to declare war against them than to perish by their intrigues." 3

He complained bitterly to Dongan, and Dongan replied: " I beleeve it is as lawfull for the English as the French to trade amongst the remotest Indians. I desire you to send me word who it was that pretended to have my orders for the Indians to plunder and fight you. That is as false as 'tis true that God is in heaven. I have desired you to send for the deserters. I know not who they are but had rather such Rascalls and Bankrouts,

1 Brodhead, Hist, of New York, II. 443 ; Commission of Me Gregory, in . Y. Cot. Does., IX. 318. 3 Denonville an Ministre, 16 Nov., 1686. 8 Ibid., 16 Oct., 1686.

9

as you call them, were amongst their own countrymen."

He had, nevertheless, turned them to good account; for, as the English knew nothing of western geography, they employed these French bush-rangers to guide their trading parties. Denonville sent orders to Du Lhut to shoot as many of them as he could catch.

Dongan presently received despatches from the English court, which showed him the necessity of caution; and, when next he wrote to his rival, it was with a chastened pen: " I hope your Excellency will be so kinde as not desire or seeke any correspondence with our Indians of this side of the Great lake (Ontario): if they doe amisse to any of your Governmt. and you make it known to me, you shall have all justice done." He complained mildly that the Jesuits were luring their Iroquois converts to Canada; " and you must pardon me if I tell you that is not the right way to keepe fair correspondence. I am daily expecting Keligious men from England, which I intend to put amongst those five nations. I desire you would order Monsr. de Lamberville that soe long as he stayes amongst those people he would meddle only with the affairs belonging to his function Sir, I send you some Oranges, hearing that they are a rarity in your partes." 2

" Monsieur," replies Denonville, " I thank you

1 Dongan to Denonville, 1 Dec., 1686; Ibid., 20 June, 1687, in N. Y. Col. Docs., III. 462, 466.

2 Dongan to Denonvilte, 20 Juin, 1687, in N. Y. Col. Docs., III. 465.

for your oranges. It is a great pity that they were all rotten."

The French governor, unlike his rival, felt strong in the support of his king, who had responded amply to his appeals for aid ; and the temper of his letters answered to his improved position. " I was led, Monsieur, to believe, by your civil language in the letter you took the trouble to write me on my arrival, that we should live in the greatest harmony in the world ; but the result has plainly shown that your intentions did not at all answer to your fine words." And he upbraids him without measure for his various misdeeds: " Take my word for it. Let us devote ourselves to the accomplishment of our masters' will; let us seek, as they do, to serve and promote religion; let us live together in harmony, as they desire. I repeat and protest, Monsieur, that it rests with you alone; but do not imagine that I am a man to suffer others to play tricks on me. I willingly believe that you have not ordered the Iroquois to plunder our Frenchmen; but, whilst I have the honor to write to you, you know that Salvaye, Gedeon Petit, and many other rogues and bank rupts like them, are with you, and boast of sharing your table. I should not be surprised that you tolerate them in your country; but I am astonished that you should promise me not to tolerate them, that you so promise me again, and that you perform nothing of what you promise. Trust me, Monsieur, make no promise that you are not willing to keep." 1

1 Denonville a Donqan, 21 Aug., 1687; Ibid., no date (1687).

Denonville, vexed and perturbed by his long strife with Dongan and the Iroquois, presently found a moment of comfort in tidings that reached him from the north. Here, as in the west, there was violent rivalry between the subjects of the two crowns. With the help of two French renegades, named Radisson and Groseilliers, the English Company of Hudson's Bay, then in its infancy, had established a post near the mouth of Nelson Kiver, on the western shore of that dreary inland sea. The company had also three other posts, called Fort Albany, Fort Hayes, and Fort Rupert, at the southern end of the bay. A rival French company had been formed in Canada, under the name of the Company of the North ; and it resolved on an effort to expel its English competitors. Though it was a time of profound peace between the two kings, Denonville warmly espoused the plan ; and, in the early spring of 1686, he sent the Chevalier de Troyes from Montreal, with eighty or more Canadians, to execute it. 1 With Troyes went Iberville, Sainte-Helene, and Maricourt, three of the sons of Charles Le Moyne; and the Jesuit Silvy joined the party as chaplain.

They ascended the Ottawa, and thence, from stream to stream and lake to lake, toiled painfully towards their goal. At length, they neared Fort

1 The Compagnie du Nord had a grant of the trade of Hudson's Bay from Louis XIV. The bay was discovered by the English, under Hudson ; but the French had carried on some trade there before the establishment of Fort Nelson. Denonville's commission to Troyes merely directs him to build forts, and " se saisir des voleurs coureurs de bois et autrea que nous savons avoir pris et arretd plusieurs de nos Francis commer-caiita avec les sauvages."

Hayes. It was a stockade with four bastions, mounted with cannon. There was a strong blockhouse within, in which the sixteen occupants of the place were lodged, unsuspicious of danger. Troyes approached at night. Iberville and Sainte-Helene with a few followers climbed the palisade on one side, while the rest of the party burst the main gate with a sort of battering ram, and rushed in, yelling the war-whoop. In a moment, the door of the blockhouse was dashed open, and its astonished inmates captured in their shirts.

The victors now embarked for Fort Rupert, distant forty leagues along the shore. In construction, it resembled Fort Hayes. The fifteen traders who held the place were all asleep at night in their blockhouse, when the Canadians burst the gate of the stockade and swarmed into the area. One of them mounted by a ladder to the roof of the building, and dropped lighted hand-grenades down the chimney, which, exploding among the occupants, told them unmistakably that something was wrong. At the same time, the assailants fired briskly on them through the loopholes, and, placing a petard under the walls, threatened to blow them into the air. Five, including a woman, were killed or wounded; and the rest cried for quarter. Meanwhile, Iberville with another party attacked a vessel anchored near the fort, and, climbing silently over her side, found the man on the watch asleep in his blanket. He sprang up and made fight, but they killed him, then stamped on the deck to rouse those below, sabred two of them as they came up the hatchway, and captured the rest. Among them was Bridger, governor for the company of all its stations on the bay.

They next turned their attention to Fort Albany, thirty leagues from Fort Hayes, in a direction opposite to that of Fort Rupert. Here there were about thirty men, under Henry Sargent, an agent of the company. Surprise was this time impossible ; for news of their proceedings had gone before them, and Sargent, though no soldier, stood on his defence. The Canadians arrived, some in canoes, some in the captured vessel, bringing ten captured pieces of cannon, which they planted in battery on a neighboring hill, well covered by intrench-ments from the English shot. Here they presently opened fire; and, in an hour, the stockade with the houses that it enclosed was completely riddled. The English took shelter in a cellar, nor was it till.the fire slackened that they ventured out to show a white flag and ask for a parley. Troyes and Sargent had an interview. The Englishman regaled his conqueror with a bottle of Spanish wine ; and, after drinking the health of King Louis and King James, they settled the terms of capitular tion The prisoners were sent home in an English vessel which soon after arrived; and Maricourt remained to command at the bay, while Troyes returned to report his success to Denonville. 1

1 On the capture of the forts at Hudson's Bay, see La Potherie, 1.147-163; the letter of Father Silvy, chaplain of the expedition, in Saint-Val-lier, Etat Present,, 43; and Oldmixon, British Empire in America, I. 661-664 (ed. 1741). An account of the preceding events will be found in La Potherie and Oldmixon ; in Jere*mie, Relation de la Bate de Hudson; and in

This buccaneer exploit exasperated the English public, and it became doubly apparent that the state of affairs in America could not be allowed to continue. A conference had been arranged between the two powers, even before the news came from Hudson's Bay; and Count d'Avaux appeared at London as special envoy of Louis XIV. to settle the questions at issue. A treaty of neutrality was signed at Whitehall, and commissioners were appointed on both sides. 1 Pending the discussion, each party was to refrain from acts of hostility or encroachment; and, said the declaration of the commissioners, " to the end the said agreement may have the better effect, we do likewise agree that the said serene kings shall immediately send necessary orders in that behalf to their respective governors in America." 2 Dongan accordingly was directed to keep a friendly correspondence with his rival, and take good care to give him no cause of complaint. 3

It was this missive which had dashed the ardor of the English governor, and softened his epistolary style. More than four months after, Louis XIV. sent corresponding instructions to Denonville; 4 but,

N. Y. Col. Docs., IX. 796-802. Various embellishments have been added to the original narratives by recent writers, such as an imaginary hand-to-hand fight of Iberville and several Englishmen in the blockhouse of Fort Hayes.

1 Traitfde Neutrality pour I'Am&ique, conclu a Londres le 16 Nov., 1686, in M&moires des Commissaires, II. 86.

2 Instrument for preventing Acts of Hostility in America in N. Y, Col, Docs., III. 505.

» Order to Gov. Dongan, 22 Jan., 1687, in N. Y. Col. Docs., III. 504.

4 Louis XIV. a Denonville, 17 Juin, 1687. At the end of March, the king had written that " he did not think it expedient to make any attack on the English."

meantime, he had sent him troops, money, and munitions in abundance, and ordered him to attack the Iroquois towns. Whether such a step was consistent with the recent treaty of neutrality may well be doubted ; for, though James II. had not yet formally claimed the Iroquois as British subjects, his representative had done so for years with his tacit approval, and out of this claim had risen the principal differences which it was the object of the treaty to settle.

Eight hundred regulars were already in the colony, and eight hundred more were sent in the spring, with a hundred and sixty-eight thousand livres in money and supplies. 1 Denonville was prepared to strike. He had pushed his preparations actively, yet with extreme secrecy ; for he meant to fall on the Senecas unawares, and shatter at a blow the mainspring of English intrigue. Harmony reigned among the chiefs of the colony, military, civil, and religious. The intendant Meules had been recalled on the complaints of the governor, who had quarrelled with him; and a new intendant, Champigny, had been sent in his place. He was as pious as Denonville himself, and, like him, was in perfect accord with the bishop and the Jesuits. All wrought together to promote the new crusade.

It was not yet time to preach it, or at least Denonville thought so. He dissembled his purpose to the last moment, even with his best friends. Of all the Jesuits among the Iroquois, the two

1 Abstract of Letters, in N. Y. Col. Does., IX. 314. This answers exactly to the statement of the Me'moire adresstau Regent, which places the number of troops in Canada at this time at thirty-two companies of fifty men each

brothers Lamberville had alone held their post. • Denonville, in order to deceive the enemy, had directed these priests to urge the Iroquois chiefs to meet him in council at Fort Frontenac, whither, as he pretended, he was about to go with an escort of troops, for the purpose of conferring with them. The two brothers received no hint whatever of his real intention, and tried in good faith to accomplish his wishes; but the Iroquois were distrustful, and hesitated to comply. On this, the elder Lamberville sent the younger with letters to Denonville to explain the position of affairs, saying at the same time that he himself would not leave Onon-daga except "to accompany the chiefs to the proposed council. " The poor father," wrote the governor, " knows nothing of our designs. I am sorry to see him exposed to danger; but, should I recall him, his withdrawal would certainly betray our plans to the Iroquois." This unpardonable reticence placed the Jesuit in extreme peril; for the moment the Iroquois discovered the intended treachery they would probably burn him as its instrument. No man in Canada had done so much as the elder Lamberville to counteract the influence of England and serve the interests of France, and in return the governor exposed him recklessly to the most terrible of deaths. 1

1 Denonville au Mmistre, 9 Nov., 1686; Ibid., 8 Juin, 1687. Denon-ville at last seems to have been seized with some compunction, and writes: " Tout cela me fait craindre que le pauvre pere n'ayt de la peine ti, se retirer d'entre les mains de ces barbares ce qui m'inquiete fort." Dongan, though regarding the Jesuit as an insidious enemy, had treated him much better, and protected him on several occasions, for which he received the emphatic thanks of Dablon, superior of the missions. Dablon to Donaan (1685?). in N. Y. Col. Docs., III. 454.

In spite of all his pains, it was whispered abroad that there was to be war; and the rumor was brought to the ears of Dongan by some of the Canadian deserters. He lost no time in warning the Iroquois, and their deputies came to beg his help. Danger humbled them for the moment; and they not only recognized King James as their sovereign, but consented at last to call his representative Father Corlaer instead of Brother. Their father, however, dared not promise them soldiers; though, in spite of the recent treaty, he caused gunpowder and lead to be given them, and urged them to recall the powerful war-parties which they had lately sent against the Illinois. 1

Denonville at length broke silence, and ordered the militia to muster. They grumbled and hesitated, for they remembered the failures of La Barre. The governor issued a proclamation, and the bishop a pastoral_mandate. There were sermons, prayers, and exhortations in all the churches. A revulsion of popular feeling followed; and the people, says Denonville, " made ready for the march with extraordinary animation." The church showered blessings on them as they went, and daily masses were ordained for the downfall of the foes of Heaven and of France. 3

1 Golden, 97 (1727), Denonville au Ministre, 8 Juin, 1687.

2 Saint-Vallier, Atat Present. Even to the moment of marching, Denonville pretended that he meant only to hold a peace council at Fort Frontenac. " J'ai toujours public* que je n'allois qu'a l'assemblee ge'ne'-rale projete'e a Cataracouy (Fort Frontenac). J'ai toujours tenu ce dig-courg jusqu'au temps de la marche." Denonville au Ministre, 8 Juin, 1687.

CHAPTER

1687. DENONVILLE AND THE SENEGAS.

THEACHEBY OF DENONVILLE. — IROQUOIS GENEROSITY. — THE INVADING ARMY. — THE WESTERN ALLIES. — PLUNDER OP ENGLISH TRADERS. — ARRIVAL OF THE ALLIES. — SCENE AT THE FRENCH CAMP. — MARCH OP DENONVILLE. — AMBUSCADE. — BATTLE. — VICTORY. — THE SENECA BABYLON. — IMPERFECT SUCCESS.

A HOST of flat-boats filled with soldiers, and a host of Indian canoes, struggled against the rapids of the St. Lawrence, and slowly made their way to Fort Fi-ontenac. Among the troops was La Hon-tan. When on his arrival he entered the gate of the fort, he saw a strange sight. A row of posts was planted across the area within, and to each post an Iroquois was tied hy the neck, hands, and feet, " in such a way," says the indignant witness, " that he could neither sleep nor drive off the mosquitoes." A number of Indians attached to the expedition, all of whom were Christian converts from the mission villages, were amusing themselves by burning the fingers of these unfortunates in the bowls of their pipes, while the sufferers sang their death songs. La Hontan recognized one of them who, during his campaign with La Barre, had often feasted him in his wigwam; and the

sight so exasperated the young officer that he could scarcely refrain from thrashing the tormentors with his walking stick. 1

Though the prisoners were Iroquois, they were not those against whom the expedition was directed; nor had they, so far as appears, ever given the French any cause of complaint. They belonged to two neutral villages, called Kente* and Gannei-ous, on the north shore of Lake Ontario, forming a sort of colony, where the Sulpitians of Montreal had established a mission. 2 They hunted and fished for the garrison of the fort, and had been on excellent terms with it. Denonville, however, feared that they would report his movements to their relations across the lake; but this was not his chief motive for seizing them. Like La Barre before him, he had received orders from the court that, as the Iroquois were robust and strong, he should capture as many of them as possible, and send them to France as galley slaves. 3 The order, without doubt, referred to prisoners taken in war; but Denonville, aware that the hostile Iroquois were not easily caught, resolved to entrap their unsuspecting relatives.

The intendant Champigny accordingly proceeded to the fort in advance of the troops, and invited the neighboring Iroquois to a feast. They

1 La Hontan,!. 93-05 (1709).

2 Ganneious or Ganeyout was on an arm of the lake a little west of the present town of Fredericksburg. Rente' or Quinte was on Quinte Bay.

1 Le Roy a La Barre, 21 Juillet, 1684 ; Le Roy a DenonviUe et Champigny, SO Mars, 1687.

came to the number of thirty men and about ninety women and children, whereupon they were surrounded and captured by the intendant's escort and the two hundred men of the garrison. The inhabitants of the village of Ganneious were not present; and one Perre, with a strong party of Canadians and Christian Indians, went to secure them. He acquitted himself of his errand with great address, and returned with eighteen warriors and abo.ut sixty women and children. Champigny's exertions did not end here. Learning that a party of Iroquois were peaceably fishing on an island in the St. Lawrence, he offered them also the hospitalities of Fort Frontenac; but they were too wary to be entrapped. Four or five Iroquois were however caught by the troops on their way up the river. They were in two or more parties, and they all had with them their women and children, which was never the case with Iroquois on the war-path. Hence the assertion of Denonville, that they came with hostile designs, is very improbable. As for the last six months he had constantly urged them, by the lips of Lamberville, to visit him and smoke the pipe of peace, it is not unreasonable to suppose that these Indian families were on their way to the colony in consequence of his invitations. Among them were the son and brother of Big Mouth, who of late had been an advocate of peace; and, in order not to alienate him, these two were eventually set free. The other warriors were tied like the rest to stakes at the fort.

The whole number of prisoners thus secured

was fifty-one, sustained by such food as their wives were able to get for them. Of more than a hundred and fifty women and children captured with them, many died at the fort, partly from excitement and distress, and partly from a pestilential disease. The survivors were all baptized, and then distributed among the mission villages in the colony. The men were sent to Quebec, where some of them were given up to their Christian relatives in the missions who -had claimed them, and whom it was not expedient to offend; and the rest, after being baptized, were sent to France, to share with convicts and Huguenots the horrible slavery of the royal galleys. 1

Before reaching Fort Frontenac, Denonville, to his great relief, was joined by Lamberville, delivered from the peril to which the governor had exposed him. He owed his life to an act of njagnanimity

1 The authorities for the above are Denonville, Champigny, Abbe* Belmont, Bishop Saint-Vallier, and the author of Recueil de ce qui s'est passfen Canada au Sujet dela Guerre, etc., depuis I'anne'e 1682.

Belmont, who accompanied the expedition, speaks of the affair with indignation, which was shared by many French officers. The bishop, on the other hand, mentions the success of the stratagem as a reward accorded by Heaven to the piety of Denonville. titat Present de l'£glise, 91,92 (reprint, 1856).

Denonville's account, which is sufficiently explicit, is contained in the long journal of the expedition which he sent to the court, and in several letters to the minister. Both Belmont and the author of the Recueil speak of the prisoners as having been " pris par I'appat d'un festin."

Mr. Shea, usually so exact, has been led into some error by confounding the different acts of this affair. By Denonville's official journal, it appears that, on the 10th June, Perre', by his order, captured several Indians on the St. Lawrence ; that, on the 25th June, the governor, then at Rapide Plat on his way up the river, received a letter from Champigny, informing him that he had seized all the Iroquois near Fort Frontenac; and that, on the 3d July, Perre', whom Denonville had sent several days before to attack Ganneious, arrived with his prisoners.

on the part of the Iroquois, which does them signal honor. One of the prisoners at Fort Frontenac had contrived to escape, and, leaping sixteen feet to the ground from the window of a blockhouse, crossed the lake, and gave the alarm to his countrymen. Apparently, it was from him that the Onondagas learned that the invitations of Onontio were a snare ; that he had entrapped their relatives, and -was about to fall on their Seneca brethren with all the force of Canada. The Jesuit, whom they trusted and esteemed, but who had been used as an instrument to beguile them, was summoned before a council of the chiefs. They were in a fury at the news; and Lamberville, as much astonished by it as they, expected instant death, when one of them is said to have addressed him to the following effect: " We know you too well to believe that you meant to betray us. We think that you have been deceived as well as we; and we are not unjust enough to punish you for the crime of others. But you are not safe here. When once our young men have sung the war-song, they will listen to nothing but their fury; and we shall not be able to save you." They gave him guides, and sent him by secret paths to meet the advancing army. 1

1 I have ventured to give this story on the sole authority of Charlo voix, for the contemporary writers are silent concerning it. Mr. Shea thinks that it involves a contradiction of date; but this is entirely due to confounding the capture of prisoners by Perre' at Ganneious on July 8d with the capture by Champigny at Fort Frontenac about June 20th. Lamberville reached Denonville's camp, one day's journey from the fort, on the evening of the 29th. (Journal of Denonville) This would

Again the fields about Fort Frontenac were covered with tents, camp-sheds, and wigwams. Regulars, militia, and Indians, there were about two thousand men; and, besides these, eight hundred regulars just arrived from France had been left at Montreal to protect the settlers. 1 Fortune thus far had smiled on the enterprise, and she now gave Denonville a fresh proof of her favor. On the very day of his arrival, a canoe came from Niagara with news that a large body of allies from the west had reached that place three days before, and were waiting his commands. It was more than he had dared to hope. In the preceding autumn, he had ordered Tonty, commanding at the Illinois, and La Durantaye, commanding at Michillimackinac, to muster as many coureurs de bois and Indians as possible, and join him early in July at Niagara. The distances were vast, and the difficulties incalculable. In the eyes of the pious governor, their timely arrival was a manifest sign of the favor of Heaven. At Fort St. Louis, of the Illinois, Tonty had mustered sixteen Frenchmen and about two hundred Indians, whom he led across the country to Detroit; and here he found Du Lhut, La Foret, and La Durantaye, with a large body of French

give four and a half days for news of the treachery to reach Onondaga, and four and a half days for the Jesuit to rejoin his countrymen.

Charlevoix, with his usual carelessness, says that the Jesuit Milet had also been used to lure the Iroquois into the snare, and that he was soon after captured by the Oneidas, and delivered by an Indian matron. Milet's captivity did not take place till 1689-90.

1 Denonville. Champigny says 832 regulars, 930 militia, and 300 Indians. This was when the army left Montreal. More Indians afterwards joined it. Belmont says 1,800 French and Canadians and about 300 Indians.

and Indians from the upper lakes. 1 It had been the work of the whole winter to induce these savages to move. Presents, persuasion, and promises had not been spared; and while La Durantaye, aided by the Jesuit Engelran, labored to gain over the tribes of Michillimackinac, the indefatigable Nicolas Perrot was at work among those of the Mississippi and Lake Michigan. They were of a race unsteady as aspens and fierce as wild-cats, full of mutual jealousies, without rulers, and without laws; for each was a law to himself. It was difficult to persuade them, and, when persuaded, scarcely possible to keep them so. Perrot, however, induced some of them to follow him to Michillimackinac, where many hundreds of Algonquin savages were presently gathered : a perilous crew, who changed their minds every day, and whose dancing, singing, and yelping might turn at any moment into war-whoops against each other or against their hosts, the French. The Hurons showed more stability; and La Durantaye was reasonably sure that some of them would follow him to the war, though it was clear that others were bent on allying themselves with the Senecas and the English. As for the Pottawatamies, Sacs, Ojibwas, Ottawas, and other Algonquin hordes, no man could foresee what they would do. 2

Suddenly a canoe arrived with news that a party of English traders was approaching. It will be re-

1 Tonty, Mfmoire in Margry, Relations Intfdites.

2 The name of Ottawas, here used specifically, was often employed by the French as a generic term for the Algonquin tribes of the Great Lakes.

10

membered that two bands of Dutch and English, under Rooseboom and McGregorj, had prepared to set out together for Michillimackinac, armed with commissions from Dongan. They had rashly changed their plan, and parted company. Rooseboom took the lead, and Me Gregory followed some time after. Their hope was that, on reaching Michillimackinac, the Indians of the place, attracted by their cheap goods and their abundant supplies of rum, would declare for them and drive off the French; and this would probably have happened, but for the prompt action of La Durantaye. The canoes of Rooseboom, bearing twenty-nine whites and five Mohawks and Mohicans, were not far distant, when, amid a prodigious hubbub, the French commander embarked to meet him with a hundred and twenty coureurs de bois. 1 Behind them followed a swarm of Indian canoes, whose occupants scarcely knew which side to take, but for the most part inclined to the English. Rooseboom and his men, however, naturally thought that they came to support the French; and, when La Durantaye bore down upon them with threats of instant death if they made the least resistance, they surrendered at once. The captors carried them in triumph to Michillimackinac, and gave their goods to the delighted Indians.

"It is certain," wrote Denonville, "that, if the English had not been stopped and pillaged, the Hurons and Ottawas would have revolted and cut

1 Attestation of N. Harmentse and others of Rooseboom's party N. Y. Col. Docs., III. 436. La Potherie says, three hundred.

the throats of all our Frenchmen." 1 As it was, La Durantaye's exploit produced a revulsion of feeling, and many of the Indians consented to follow him. He lost no time in leading them down the lake to join Du Lhut at Detroit; and, when Tonty arrived, they all paddled for Niagara. On the way, they met McGregory with a party about equal to that of Rooseboom. He had with him a considerable number of Ottawa and Huron prisoners whom the Iroquois had captured, and whom he meant to return to their countrymen as a means of concluding the long projected triple alliance between the English, the Iroquois, and the tribes of the lakes. This bold scheme was now completely crushed. All the English were captured and carried to Niagara, whence they and their luckless precursors were sent prisoners to Quebec.

La Durantaye and his companions, with a hundred and eighty coureurs de bois and four hundred Indians, waited impatiently at Niagara for orders from the governor. A canoe despatched in haste from Fort Frontenac soon appeared; and they were directed to repair at once to the rendezvous at Irondequoit Bay, on the borders of the Seneca country. 2

Denonville was already on his way thither. On the fourth of July, he had embarked at Fort Frontenac with four hundred bateaux and canoes,

1 Denonville au Ministre, 25 Ao&t, 1687.

2 The above is drawn from papers in 2V. Y. Col. Docs., HI. 436, DL 324, 336, 346, 405; Saint-Vallier, Etat Present, 92; Denonrille, Journal Belmont, Histoire du Canada; La Potherie, II. chap. xvi.; La Hontan I. 96. Colden's account is confused and incorrect.

crossed the foot of Lake Ontario, and moved westward along the southern shore. The weather was rough, and six days passed before he descried the low headlands of Irondequoit Bay. Far off on the glimmering water, he saw a multitude of canoes advancing to meet him. It was the flotilla of La Durantaye. Good management and good luck had so disposed it that the allied bands, concentring from points more than a thousand miles distant, reached the rendezvous on the same day. This was not all. The Ottawas of Michillimackinac, who refused to follow La Durantaye, had changed their minds the next morning, embarked in a body, paddled up the Georgian Bay of Lake Huron, crossed to Toronto, and joined the allies at Niagara. White and red, Denonville now had nearly three thousand men under his command. 1

All were gathered on the low point of land that separates Irondequoit Bay from Lake Ontario. " Never," says an eye-witness, " had Canada seen such a sight; and never, perhaps, will she see such a sight again. Here was the camp of the regulars from France, with the general's head-quarters; the camp of the four battalions of Canadian militia, commanded by the noblesse of the country; the camp of the Christian Indians; and, farther on, a swarm of savages of every nation. Their features were different, and so were their manners, their weapons, their decorations, and their dances. They sang and whooped and harangued in every accent

1 Recueil de ce qui Jest paste" en Canada depuis 1682; Captain Duplessis's Plan for the Defence of Canada, in N. Y. Col Docs., IX. 447.

and tongue. Most of them wore nothing but horns on their heads, and the tails of beasts behind their backs. Their faces were painted red or green, with black or white spots ; their ears and noses were hung with ornaments of iron ; and their naked bodies were daubed with figures of various sorts of animals." *

These were the allies from the upper lakes. The enemy, meanwhile, had taken alarm. Just after the army arrived, three Seneca scouts called from the edge of the woods, and demanded what they meant to do. " To fight you, you blockheads/' answered a Mohawk Christian attached to the French. A volley of bullets was fired at the scouts; but they escaped, and carried the news to their villages. 2 Many of the best warriors were absent. Those that remained, four hundred or four hundred and fifty by their own accounts, and eight hundred by that of the French, mustered in haste ; and, though many of them were mere boys, they sent off the women and children, hid their most valued possessions, burned their chief town, and prepared to meet the invaders.

On the twelfth, at three o'clock in the afternoon, Denonville began his march, leaving four hundred men in a hastily built fort to guard the bateaux and canoes. Troops, officers, and Indians, all carried their provisions at their backs. Some of the Christian Mohawks guided them ; but guides were scarcely needed, for a broad Indian trail led

1 The first part of the extract is from Belmont; the second, from 8aint-Vallier.

2 Information Deceived from several Indians, in N. Y Col. Docs., Ill 44.4.

from the bay to the great Seneca town, twenty-two miles southward. They marched three leagues through the open forests of oak, and encamped for the night. In the morning, the heat was intense. The men gasped in the dead and sultry air of the woods, or grew faint in the pitiless sun, as they waded waist-deep through the rank grass of the narrow intervales. They passed safely through two dangerous defiles, and, about two in the afternoon, began to enter a third. Dense forests covered the hills on either hand. La Du-rantaye with Tonty and his cousin Du Lhut led the advance, nor could all Canada have supplied three men better for the work. Each led his band of coureurs de bois, white Indians, without discipline, and scarcely capable of it, but brave and accustomed to the woods. On their left were the Iro-quois converts from the missions of Saut St. Louis and the Mountain of Montreal, fighting under the influence of their ghostly prompters against their own countrymen. On the right were the pagan Indians from the west. The woods were full of these painted spectres, grotesquely horrible in horns and tail; and among them flitted the black robe of Father Engelran, the Jesuit of Michilli-mackinac. Nicolas Perrot and two other bush-ranging Frenchmen were assigned to command them, but in fact they obeyed no man. These formed the vanguard, eight or nine hundred in all, under an excellent officer, Callieres, governor of Montreal. Behind came the main body under Denonville, each of the four battalions of regulars

alternating with a battalion of Canadians. Some of the regulars wore light armor, while the Canadians were in plain attire of coarse cloth or buckskin. Denonville, oppressed by the heat, marched in his shirt. " It is a rougl\'7d life," wrote the marquis, " to tramp afoot through the woods, carrying one's own provisions in a haversack, devoured by mosquitoes, and faring no better than a mere soldier." l With him was the Chevalier de Vau-dreuil, who had just arrived from France in command of the eight hundred men left to guard the colony, and who, eager to take part in the campaign, had pushed forward alone to join the army. Here, too, were the Canadian seigniors at the head of their vassals, Berthier, La Valterie, Granville, Longueuil, and many more. A guard of rangers and Indians brought up the rear.

Scouts thrown out in front ran back with the report that they had reached the Seneca clearings, and had seen no more dangerous enemy than three or four women in the cornfields. This was a device of the Senecas to cheat the French into the belief that the inhabitants were still in the town. It had the desired effect. The vanguard pushed rapidly forward, hoping to surprise the place, and ignorant that, behind the ridge of thick forests on their right, among a tangled growth of beech-trees in the gorge of a brook, three hundred ambushed warriors lay biding their time.

Hurrying forward through the forest, they left the main body behind, and soon reached the end

1 Denonville au Ministre, 8 Juin, 1687

of the defile. The woods were still dense on their left and front; but on their right lay a great marsh, covered with alder thickets and rank grass. Suddenly the air was filled with yells, and a rapid thoiigh distant fire was opened from the thickets and the forest. Scores of painted savages, stark naked, some armed with swords and some with hatchets, leaped screeching from their ambuscade, and rushed against the van. Almost at the same moment a burst of whoops and firing sounded in the defile behind. It was the ambushed three hundred supporting the onset of their countrymen in front; but they had made a fatal mistake. Deceived by the numbers of the vanguard, they supposed it to be the whole army, never suspecting that Denonville was close behind with sixteen hundred men. It was a surprise on both sides. So dense was the forest that the advancing battalions could see neither the enemy nor each other. Appalled by the din of whoops and firing, redoubled by the echoes of the narrow valley, the whole army was seized with something like a panic. Some of the officers, it is said, threw themselves on the ground in their fright. There were a few moments of intense bewilderment. The various corps became broken and confused, and moved hither and thither without knowing why. Denonville behaved with great courage. He ran, sword in hand, to where the uproar was greatest, ordered the drums to beat the charge, turned back the militia of Berthier who were trying to escape, and commanded them and all others whom he met to fire on whatever looked like an enemy. He was bravely seconded by Callieres, La Valterie, and several other officers. The Christian Iroquois fought well from the first, leaping from tree to tree, and exchanging shots and defiance w'^h their heathen countrymen; till the Senecas, seeing themselves confronted by numbers that seemed endless, abandoned the field, after heavy loss, carrying with them many of their dead and all of their wounded. 1

Denonville made no attempt to pursue. He had learned the dangers of this blind warfare of the woods; and he feared that the Senecas would waylay him again in the labyrinth of bushes that lay between him and the town. " Our troops," he says, " were all so overcome by the extreme heat and the long march that we were forced to remain where we were till morning. We had the pain of 4 witnessing the usual cruelties of the Indians, who cut the dead bodies into quarters, like butchers \ meat, to put into their kettles, and opened most of* them while still warm to drink the blood. Our rascally Ottawas particularly distinguished themselves by these barbarities, as well as by cowardice; for they made off in the fight. We had five or six men killed on the spot, and about twenty wounded, among whom was Father Engelran, who was badly hurt by a gun-shot. Some prisoners who escaped from the Senecas tell us that they lost forty men killed outright, twenty-five of whom we saw butch-

1 For authorities, see note at the end of the chapter. The account of Charlevoix is contradicted at several points by the contemporary writers

ered. One of the escaped prisoners saw the rest buried, and he saw also more than sixty very dangerously wounded." 1

In the morning, the troops advanced in order of battle through a marsh covered with alders and tall grass, whence they had no sooner emerged than, says Abbe* Belmont, " we began to see the famous Babylon of the Senecas, where so many crimes have been committed, so much blood spilled, and so many men burned. It was a village or town of bark, on the top of a hill. They had burned it a week before. We found nothing in it but the graveyard and the graves, full of snakes and other creatures; a great mask, with teeth and eyes of brass, and a bearskin drawn over it, with which they performed their conjurations." 2 The fire had also spared a number of huge receptacles of bark, still filled with the last season's corn; while the fields around were covered with the growing crop, ripening in the July sun. There were.hogs, too, in great number; for the Iroquois did not share the antipathy with which Indians are apt to regard that unsavory animal, and from which certain philosophers have argued their descent from the Jews.

The soldiers killed the hogs, burned the old corn, and hacked down the new with their swords. Next they advanced to an abandoned Seneca fort on a hill half a league distant, and burned it, with

1 Denonville au Ministre, 25 Aout, 1687. In his journal, written afterwards, he says that the Senecas left twenty-seven dead on the field, and carried off twenty more, besides upwards of sixty mortally wounded

2 Belmout. A few words are added from Saint-Vallier.

all that it contained. Ten days were passed in the work of havoc. Three neighboring villages were levelled, and all their fields laid waste. The amount of corn destroyed was prodigious. De-nonville reckons it at the absurdly exaggerated amount of twelve hundred thousand bushels.

The Senecas, laden with such of their possessions as they could carry off, had fled to their confederates in the east; and Denonville did not venture to pursue them. His men, feasting without stint on green corn and fresh pork, were sickening rapidly, and his Indian allies were deserting him. " It is a miserable business," he wrote, " to command savages, who, as soon as they have knocked an enemy in the head, ask for nothing but to go home and carry with them the scalp, which they take off like a skull-cap. You cannot believe what trouble I had to keep them till the corn was cut."

On the twenty-fourth, he withdrew, with all his army, to the fortified post at Irondequoit Bay, whence, he proceeded to Niagara, in order to accomplish his favorite purpose of building a fort there. The troops were set at work, and a stockade was planted on the point of land at the eastern angle between the River Niagara and Lake Ontario, the site of the ruined fort built by La Salle nine years before. 1 Here he left a hundred men, under the Chevalier de Troyes, and, embarking with the rest of the army, descended to Montreal.

The campaign was but half a success. Joined

1 Proces-verbal de la Prise de Possession de Niagara, 31 Juillet, 1687 There are curious errors of date in this document regarding the proceedings of La Salle.

to the capture of the English traders on the lakes, it had, indeed, prevented the defection of the western Indians, and in some slight measure restored their respect for the French, of whom, nevertheless, one of them was heard to say that they were good for nothing but to make war on hogs and corn. As for the Senecas, they were more enraged than hurt. They could rebuild their bark villages in a few weeks; and, though they had lost their harvest,, their confederates would not let them starve. 1 A converted Iroquois had told the governor before his departure that, if he overset a wasps' nest, he must crush the wasps, or they would sting him. Denonville left the wasps alive.

DENONVILLE'S CAMPAIGN AGAINST THE SENECAS. — The chief authorities on this matter are the journal of Denonville, of which there is a translation in the Colonial Documents of New York, IX. ; the letters of Denonville to the Minister ; the £tat Present de VlZglise de la Colonie Franqaise, by Bishop Saint-Vallier; the Recueil dc ce qui s'est passe en Canada au Sujet de la Guerre, tant des Anglais que des Iroquois, depuis Vannee 1682; and the excellent account by Abbe Belmont in his chronicle called Histoire du Canada. To these may be added La Hontan, Tonty, Nicolas Perrot, La Potherie, and the Senecas examined before the authorities of Albany, whose statements are printed in the Colonial Documents, [II. These are the original sources. Charlevoix drew his account from a portion of them. It is inexact, and needs the correction of his learned annotator, Mr. Shea. Golden, Smith, and other English writers follow La Hoiitan.

The researches of Mr. O. H. Marshall, of Buffalo, have lett no reasonable doubt as to the scene of the battle, and the site of the neighboring town. The Seneca ambuscade was on the marsh and

1 The statement of some later writers, that many of the Senecas died during the following winter in consequence of the loss of their corn, is extremely doubtful. Captain Duplessis, in his Plan for the Defence of Canada, 1690, declares that not one of them perished of hunger.

the hills immediately north and west of the present village of Victor; and their chief town, called Gannagaro by Denonville, was on the top of Boughton's Hill, about a mile and a quarter distant. Immense quantities of Indian remains were formerly found here, and many are found to this day. Charred corn has been turned up in abundance by the plough, showing that the place was destroyed by fire. The -emaina of the fort burned by the French are still plainly visible on a hill a mile and a quarter from the ancient town. A plan of it will be found in Squier's Aboriginal Monuments of New York. The site of the three other Seneca towns destroyed by Denonville, and called Totiakton, Gannondata, and Gannongarae, can also be identified. See Marshall, in Collections N. Y. Hist. Soc., 2d Series, II. Indian traditions of historical events are usually almost worthless ; but the old Seneca chief Dyunehogawah, or "John Blacksmith," who was living a few years ago at the Tonawanda reservation, recounted to Mr. Marshall with remarkable accuracy the story of the battle as handed down from his ancestors who lived at Gannagaro, close to the scene of action. Gannagaro was the Canagorah of Wentworth Greenalgh's Journal. The old Seneca, on being shown a map of the locality, placed his finger on the spot where the fight took place, and which was long known to the Senecas by the name of Dyagodiyu, or " The Place of a Battle." It answers in the most perfect manner to the French contemporary descriptions.

The Chevalier de Baugy, aide-de-camp to Denonville, kept a journal of the expedition, which has lately been discovered among the papers of his descendant, Madame de Vaveray. His account of the battle is confused and adds little to what is known from other sources.

CHAPTER IX.

1687-1689. THE IROQUOIS INVASION.

ALTERCATIONS. — ATTITUDE OP DONGAN. — MARTIAL PREPARATION. — PERPLEXITY OP DENONVILLE. — AWGRY CORRESPONDENCE. — RECALL OF DONGAN. — SIR EDMUND ANDROS. — HUMILIATION OF DENONVILLE. — DISTRESS OP CANADA. — APPEALS FOR HELP. — IROQUOIS DIPLOMACY. — A HURON MACCHIAVEL. — THE CATASTROPHE.—FEROCITY OP THE VICTORS. — WAR WITH ENGLAND.— RECALL or DENONVILLE.

WHEN Dongan heard that the French had invaded the Senecas, seized English traders on the lakes, and built a fort at Niagara, his wrath was kindled anew. He sent to the Iroquois, and summoned them to meet him at Albany; told the assembled chiefs that the late calamity had fallen upon them because they had held councils with the French without asking his leave ; forbade them to do so again, and informed them that, as subjects of King James, they must make no treaty, except by the consent of his representative, the governor of New York. He declared that the Ottawas and other remote tribes were also British subjects ; that the Iroquois should unite with them, to expel the French from the west; and that all alike should bring down their beaver skins to the English at Albany. Moreover, he enjoined them to

receive no more French Jesuits into their towns, and to call home their countrymen whom these fathers had converted and enticed to Canada. " Obey my commands/' added the governor, " for that is the only way to eat well and sleep well, without fear or disturbance." The Iroquois, who wanted his help, seemed to assent to all he said. " We will fight the French," exclaimed their orator, " as long as we have a man left." [1]

At the same time, Dongan wrote to Denonville demanding the immediate surrender of the Dutch and English captured on the lakes. Denonville angrily replied that he would keep the prisoners, since Dongan had broken the treaty of neutrality by " giving aid and comfort to the savages." The English governor, in return, upbraided his correspondent for invading British territory. " I will endevour to protect his Majesty's subjects here from your unjust invasions, till I hear from the King, my Master, who is the greatest and most glorious Monarch that ever set on a Throne, and would do as much to propagate the Christian faith as any prince that lives. He did not send me here to suffer you to give laws to his subjects. I hope, notwithstanding all your trained souldiers and greate Officers come from Europe, that our masters at home will suffer us to do ourselves justice on you for the injuries and spoyle you have committed on us; and I assure you, Sir, if my Master gives leave, I will be as soon at Quebeck as

[1] Dongan'a Propositions to the Five Nations; Answer of the Five Nations N. Y. Col. Docs., m. 438, 441.

you shall be att Albany. What you alleage concerning my assisting the Sinnakees

(Senecas) with arms and ammunition to warr against you was never given by mee untill the sixt of August last, when understanding of your unjust proceedings in invading the King my Master's territorys in a hostill manner, I then gave them powder, lead, and armes, and united the five nations together to defend that part of our King's dominions from your jnjurious invasion. And as for offering them men, in that you doe me wrong, our men being all buisy then at their harvest, and I leave itt to your judgment whether there was any occasion when only foure hundred of them engaged with your whole army. I advise you to send home all the Christian and Indian prisoners the King of England's subjects you unjustly do deteine. This is what I have thought fitt to answer to your reflecting and provoking letter." 1

As for the French claims to the Iroquois country and the upper lakes, he turned them to ridicule. They were founded, in part, on the missions established there by the Jesuits. " The King of China," observes Dongan, "never goes anywhere without two Jessuits with him. I wonder you make not the like pretense to that Kingdome." He speaks with equal irony of the claim based on discovery: " Pardon me if I say itt is a mistake, except you will affirme that a few loose fellowes rambling amongst Indians to keep themselves from starving gives the French a right to the Countrey." And of the claim

i Dongan to Denonville, 9 Sept., 1687, in N. Y. Col. Docs., HI. 472.

based on geographical divisions : " Your reason is that some rivers or rivoletts of this country run out into the great river of Canada. 0 just God! what new, farr-fetched, and unheard-of pretense is this for a title to a country. The French King may have as good a pretence to all those Countrys that drink clarett and Brandy." In spite of his sarcasms, it is clear that the claim of prior discovery and occupation was on the side of the French.

The dispute now assumed a new phase. James II. at length consented to own the Iroquois as his subjects, ordering Dongan to protect them, and repel the French by force of arms, should they attack them again. 2 At the same time, conferences were opened at London between the French ambassador and the English commissioners appointed to settle the questions at issue. Both disputants claimed the Iroquois as subjects, and the contest wore an aspect more serious than before.

The royal declaration was a great relief to Dongan. Thus far he had acted at his own risk; now he was sustained by the orders of his king. He instantly assumed a warlike attitude; and, in the next spring, wrote to the Earl of Sunderland that he had been at Albany all winter, with four hundred infantry, fifty horsemen, and eight hundred Indians. This was not without cause, for a report had come from Canada that the French

1 Dongan's Fourth Paper to the French Agents, N. Y. Col Docs., III. 628. a Warrant authorizing Governor Dongan to protect the Five Nations, 10 Nov., 1687, 2V. Y. Col. Docs., III. 603.

11

were about to march on Albany to destroy it. " And now, my Lord/' continues Dongan, " we must build forts in y e countrey upon y e great Lakes, as y e French doe, otherwise we lose y fl Countrey, y 6 Bever trade, and our Indians." 4 Denonville, meanwhile, had begun to yield, and promised to send back McGregory and the men captured with him. 2 Dongan, not satisfied, insisted on payment for all the captured merchandise, and on the immediate demolition of Fort Niagara. He added another demand, which must have been singularly galling to his rival. It was to the effect that the Iroquois prisoners seized at Fort Frontenac, and sent to the galleys in France, should be surrendered as British subjects to the English ambassador at Paris or the secretary of state in London. 3 Denonville was sorely perplexed. He was hard pressed, and eager for peace with the Iroquois at any price; but Dongan was using every means to prevent their treating of peace with the French governor until he had complied with all the English demands. In this extremity, Denonville sent Father Vaillant to Albany, in the hope of bringing his intractable rival to conditions less humiliating. The Jesuit played his part with ability, and proved more than a match for his adversary in dialectics ; but Dongan held fast to all his demands. Vaillant

1 Dongan to Sunderland, Feb., 1688, N. Y. Col. Docs., III. 510.

2 Denonville a Dongan, 2 Oct., 1687. McGregory soon arrived, and Dongan sent him back to Canada as an emissary with a civil message to Denonville. Dongan to Denonville, 10 Nov., 1687.

8 Dongan to Denonville, 31 Oct., 1687; Dongan's First Demand of th& French Agents, N. Y. Col. Docs., HI. 615, 620.

tried to temporize, and asked for a truce, with a view to a final settlement by reference to the two kings. 1 Dongan referred the question to a meeting of Jroquois chiefs, who declared in reply that they would make neither peace nor truce till Fort Niagara was demolished and all the prisoners restored. Dongan, well pleased, commended their spirit, and assured them that King James," who is the greatest man the sunn shines uppon, and never told a ly in his life, has given you his Eoyall word to protect you." 2 Yaillant returned from his bootless errand; and a stormy correspondence followed between the two governors. Dongan renewed his demands, then protested his wish for peace, extolled King James for his pious zeal, and declared that he was sending over missionaries of his own to convert the Iroquois. 3 What Denonville wanted was not their conversion by Englishmen, but their conversion by Frenchmen, and the presence in their towns of those most useful political agents, the Jesuits. 4 He replied angrily, charging Dongan with preventing the conversion of the Iroquois by driving off the French missionaries, and accusing him, farther, of instigating the tribes of New York to attack

1 The papers of this discussion will be found in N. Y. Col. Docs., ILL

2 Dongan's Reply to the Five Nations, Ibid., III. 535.

8 Dongan to Denonville, 17 Feb., 1688, Ibid., III. 619.

* " II y a une necessite indispensable pour les inte'rais de la Religion et de la Colonie de restablir les inissionaires Jesuites dans tous les villages Iroquois : si vous ne trouves rnoyen de faire retourner ces Peres dans leurs anciennes missions, vous deves en attendre beaucoup de raalheur pour cette Coionie ; car je dois vous dire que jusqu'icy c'est leur habilitd qui a soutenu les affaires du pays par leur scavoir-faire a gouverner lea esprits de ces barbares, qui ne sont Sauvages que de noni." Denonvilla M&noire actresse* au Ministre, 9 Nov., 1688.

Canada. 1 Suddenly there was a change in the temper of his letters. He wrote to his rival in terms of studied civility; declared that he wished he could meet him, and consult with him on the best means of advancing the cause of true religion; begged that he would not refuse him his friendship ; and thanked him in warm terms for befriending some French prisoners whom he had saved from the Iroquois, and treated with great kindness. 2

This change was due to despatches from Versailles, in which Denonville was informed that the matters in dispute would soon be amicably settled by the commissioners; that he was to keep on good terms with the English commanders, and, what pleased him still more, that the king of England was about to recall Dongan. 8 In fact, James II. had resolved on remodelling his American colonies. New York, New Jersey, and New England had been formed into one government under Sir Edmund Andros; and Dongan was summoned home, where a regiment was given him, with the rank of major-general of artillery. Denonville says that, in his efforts to extend English trade to the Great

1 Denonville a Dongan, 24 Avril, 1688; Ibid., 12 Mai, 1688. Whether the charge is true is questionable. Dongan had just written that, if the Iroquois did harm to the French, he was ordered to offer satisfaction, and had already done so.

* Denonville a Dongan, 18 Juin, 1688; Ibid., 5 Juilkt, 1688; Ibid., 20 Aug., 1688. " Je n'ai done qu'a vous asseurer que toute la Colonie a une tres-parfaite reconnoissance des bons offices que ces pauvres malheureux ont recu de vous et de vos peuples."

* Me'moire pour servir d" Instruction au Sr. Marquis de Denonvitte, 8 Mars, 1688; Le Roy a Denonville, meme date; Seignelay a Denonville, meme date. Louis XIV. had demanded Dongan's recall. How far this had influenced the action of James II. it is difficult to say.

Lakes and tile Mississippi, his late rival had been influenced by motives of personal gain. Be this as it may, he was a bold and vigorous defender of the claims of the British crown.

Sir Edmund Andros now reigned over New York; and, by the terms of his commission, his rule stretched westward to the Pacific. - The usual official courtesies passed between him and Denon-ville; but Andros renewed all the demands of his predecessor, claimed the Iroquois as subjects, and forbade the French to attack them. 1 The new governor was worse than the old. Denonville wrote to the minister : " I send you copies of his letters, by which you will see that the spirit of Dongan has entered into the heart of his successor, who may be less passionate and less interested, but who is, to say the least, quite as much opposed to us, and perhaps more dangerous by his suppleness and smoothness than the other was by his violence. What he has just done among the Iroquois, whom he pretends to be under his government, and whom he prevents from coming to meet me, is a certain proof that neither he nor the other English governors, nor their people, will refrain from doing this colony all the harm they can." 2

While these things were passing, the state of Canada was deplorable, and the position of its

1 Andros to Denonvuic, 21 Aug., 1688 ; Ibid., 29 Sept., 1688.

2 Memoire de I'Estat Present des Affaires de ce Pays depuis le IQme Aoust, 1688, jusqu'au dernier Octobrede la mesme anne'e. He declares that the English are always " itching for the western trade/' that their favorite plan is to establish a post on the Ohio, and that they have made the attempt three times already

4

governor as mortifying as it was painful. He thought with good reason that the maintenance of the new fort at Niagara was of great importance to the colony, and he had repeatedly refused the demands of Dongan and the Iroquois for its demolition. But a power greater than sachems and governors presently intervened. The provisions left at Niagara, though abundant, were atrociously bad. Scurvy and other malignant diseases soon broke out among the soldiers. The Senecas prowled about the place, and no man dared venture out for hunting, fishing, or firewood. 1 The fort was first a prison, then a hospital, then a charnel-house, till before spring the garrison of a hundred men was reduced to ten or twelve. In this condition, they were found towards the end of April by a large war-party of friendly Miamis, who entered the place and held it till a French detachment at length arrived for its relief. 2 The garrison of Fort Frontenac had suffered from the same causes, though not to the same degree. Denonville feared that he should be forced to abandon them both. The way was so long and so dangerous, and the governor had grown of late so cautious, that he dreaded the risk of maintaining such remote communications. On second thought, he resolved to keep Frontenac and sacrifice Niagara. He promised Dongan that he would demolish it, and he kept his word. 3

1 Denonville, Mfmoire du 10 Aoust, 1688.

3 Recueil de ce qui s'est passe' en Canada depuis I'annte 1682. The writer was an officer of the detachment, and describes what he saw. Compare La Pothwie.IL 210; and La Hontan, I. 131 (1709).

* Denonville a Dongan, 20 Aoust, 1688; Frocks-verbal of the Condition of

He was forced to another and a deeper humiliation. At the imperious demand of Dongan and the Iroquois, he begged the king to send back the prisoners entrapped at Fort Fronteriac, and he wrote to the minister : " Be pleased, Monseigneur, to remember that I had the honor to tell you that, in order to attain the peace necessary to the country, I was obliged to promise that I would beg you to send back to us the prisoners I sent you last year. I know you gave orders that they should be well treated, but I am informed that, though they were well enough treated at first, your orders were not afterwards executed with the same fidelity. If ill treatment has caused them all to die, — for they are people who easily fall into dejection, and who die of it, — and if none of them come back, I do not know at all whether we can persuade these barbarians not to attack us again."

What had brought the marquis to this pass ? Famine, destitution, disease, and the Iroquois were making. Canada their prey. The fur trade had been stopped for two years ; and the people, bereft of their only means of subsistence, could contribute nothing to their own defence. Above Three Rivers, the whole population was imprisoned in stockade forts hastily built in every seigniory. 9

Fort Niagara, 1688 ; N. Y. Col. Docs., IX. 386. The palisades were torn down by Denonville's order on the 15th of September. The rude dwellings and storehouses which they enclosed, together with a large wooden cross, were left standing. The commandant De Troyes had died, and Captain Desbergeres had been sent to succeed him.

1 Denonville, Memoire du 10 Aoust, 1688.

2 In the Depot des Cartes de la Marine, there is a contemporary manuscript map, on which all these forts are laid down.

Here they were safe, provided that they never ventured out; but their fields were left untilled, and the governor was already compelled to feed many of them at the expense of the king. The Iroquois roamed among the deserted settlements or prowled like lynxes about the forts, waylaying convoys and killing or capturing stragglers. Their war-parties were usually small; but their movements were so mysterious and their attacks so sudden, that they spread a universal panic through the upper half of the colony. They were the wasps which Denonville had failed to kill.

" We should succumb," wrote the distressed governor, " if our cause were not the cause of God. Your Majesty's zeal for religion, and the great things you have done for the destruction of heresy, encourage me to hope that you will be the bulwark of the Faith in the new world as you are in the old. I cannot give you a truer idea of the war we have to wage with the Iroquois than by comparing them to a great number of wolves or other ferocious beasts, issuing out of a vast forest to ravage the neighboring settlements. The people gather to hunt them down; but nobody can find their lair, for they are always in motion. An abler man than I would be greatly at a loss to manage the affairs of this country. It is for the interest of the colony to have peace at any cost whatever. For the glory of the king and the good of religion, we should be glad to have it an advantageous one; and so it would have been, but for the malice of the English and the protection they have given our enemies." 1

And yet he had, one would think, a reasonable force at his disposal. His thirty-two companies of regulars were reduced by this time to about fourteen hundred men, but he had also three or four hundred Indian converts, besides the militia of the colony, of whom he had stationed a large body under Vaudreuil at the head of the Island of Montreal. All told, they were several times more numerous than the agile warriors who held the colony in terror. He asked for eight hundred more regulars. The king sent him three hundred. Affairs grew worse, and he grew desperate. Rightly judging that the best means of defence was to take the offensive, he conceived the plan of a double attack on the Iroquois, one army to assail the Onondagas and Cayugas, another the Mohawks and Oneidas. 2 Since to reach the Mohawks as he proposed, by the way of Lake Champlain, he must pass through territory indisputably British, the attempt would be a flagrant violation of the treaty of neutrality. Nevertheless, he implored the king to send him four thousand soldiers to accomplish it. 3 His fast friend, the bishop, warmly seconded his appeal. "The glory of God is involved," wrote the head of the church, " for the Iroquois are the only tribe who oppose the progress of the gospel. The glory of the king is involved,

1 Denonville au Roy, 1688; Ibid., Mfmoire du 10 Aoust, 1688; TWrf, Mfmoire du 9 Nov., 1688.

2 Plan for the Termination of the Iroquois War, N. Y. Col. Docs., IX. 876

3 "Denonyille, Mtmoire du 8 Aoust, 1688.

for they are the only tribe who refuse to recognize his grandeur and his might. They hold the French in the deepest contempt; and, unless they are completely humbled within two years, his Majesty will have no colony left in Canada/' l And the prelate proceeds to tell the minister how, in his opinion, the war ought to be conducted. The appeal was vain. " His Majesty agrees with you," wrote Seignelay, " that three or four thousand men would be the best means of making peace, but he cannot spare them now. If the enemy breaks out again, raise the inhabitants, and fight as well as you can till his Majesty-is prepared to send you troops." 2

A hope had dawned on the governor. He had been more active of late in negotiating than in fighting, and his diplomacy had prospered more than his arms. It may be remembered that some of the Iroquois entrapped at Fort Frontenac had been given to their Christian relatives in the mission villages. Here they had since remained. Denonville thought that he might use them as messengers to their heathen countrymen, and he sent one or more of them to Onondaga with gifts and overtures of peace. That shrewd old politician, Big Mouth, was still strong in influence at the Iroquois capital, and his name was great to the farthest bounds of the confederacy. He knew by personal experience the advantages of a neutral

1 Saint-Vallier, Mfmoire sur les Affaires du Canada pour Monseigneuf U Marquis de Seignelay.

* Memoir* dn Ministre adres»€a Denonville, 1 Mai, 1689.

position between the rival European powers, from both of whom he received gifts and attentions; and he saw that what was good for him was good for the confederacy, since, if it gave itself to neither party, both would court its alliance. • In his opinion, it had now leaned long enough towards the English; and a change of attitude had become expedient. Therefore, as Denonville promised the return of the prisoners, and was plainly ready to make other concessions, Big Mouth, setting at naught the prohibitions of Andros, consented to a conference with the French. He set out at his leisure for Montreal, with six Onondaga, Cayuga, and Oneida chiefs; and, as no diplomatist ever understood better the advantage of negotiating at the head of an imposing force, a body of Iroquois warriors, to the number, it is said, of twelve hundred, set out before him, and silently took path to Canada.

The ambassadors paddled across the lake 'and presented themselves before the commandant of Fort Frontenac, who received them with distinction, and ordered Lieutenant Perelle to escort them to Montreal. Scarcely had the officer conducted his august charge five leagues on their way, when, to his amazement, he found himself in the midst of six hundred Iroquois warriors, who amused themselves for a time with his terror, and then accompanied him as far as Lake St. Francis, where he found another body of savages nearly equal in number. Here the warriors halted, and the am-

bassadors with their escort gravely pursued their way to meet Denonville at Montreal. 1

Big Mouth spoke haughtily, like a man who knew his power. He told the governor that he and his people were subjects neither of the French nor of the English; that they wished to be friends of both; that they held their country of the Great Spirit; and that they had never been conquered in war. He declared that the Iroquois knew the weakness of the French, and could easily exterminate them ; that they had formed a plan of burning all the houses and barns of Canada, killing the cattle, setting fire to the ripe grain, and then, when the people were starving, attacking the forts; but that he, Big Mouth, had prevented its execution. He concluded by saying that he was allowed but four days to bring back the governor's reply; and that, if he were kept waiting longer, he would not answer for what might happen. 2 Though it appeared by some expressions in his speech that he was ready to make peace only with the French, leaving the Iroquois free to attack the Indian allies of the colony, and though, while the ambassadors were at Montreal, their warriors on the river above actually killed several of the Indian converts, Denonville felt himself compelled to pretend ignorance of the outrage. 3 A declaration of neutrality was drawn up, and Big Mouth

1 Relation des Evtnements de la Guerre, 30 Oct., 1688.

3 Declaration of the Iroquois in presence of M. de Denonville, N, Y. Col Docs., IX. 384; Relation des Evfnements de la Guen t, 30 Oct.. 1688; Bel-mont, Htstoire du Canada.

8 Callieres a Seignelay, Jan., 1689-

affixed to it the figures of sundry birds and beasts as the signatures of himself and his fellow-chiefs. 1 He promised, too, that within a certain time deputies from the whole confederacy should come to Montreal and conclude a general peace.

The time arrived, and they did not appear. It became known, however, that a number of chiefs were coming from Onondaga to explain the delay, and to promise that the deputies should soon follow. Th.e chiefs in fact were on their way. They reached La Famine, the scene of La Barre's meeting with Big Mouth; but here an unexpected incident arrested them, and completely changed the aspect of affairs.

Among the Hurons of Michillimackinac there was a chief of high renown named Kondiaronk, or the Rat. He was in the prime of life, a redoubted warrior, and a sage counsellor. The French seem to have admired him greatly. " He is a gallant man," says La Hontan, " if ever there was one;" while Charlevoix declares that he was the ablest Indian the French ever knew in America, and that he had nothing of the savage but the name and the dress. In spite of the father's eulogy, the moral condition of the Rat savored strongly of the wigwam. He had given Denonville great trouble by his constant intrigues with the Iroquois, with whom he had once made a plot for the massacre of his neighbors, the Ottawas, under cover of a pretended treaty. 2 The French had spared no pains to gain

1 See the signatures in N Y. Col. Docs., IK. 386, 386.

2 Nicolas Perrot, 148.

him; and he had at length been induced to declare for them, under a pledge from the governor that the war should never cease till the Iroquois were destroyed. During the summer, he raised a party of forty warriors, and came down the lakes in quest of Iroquois scalps. 1 On the way, he stopped at Fort Frontenac to hear the news, when, to his amazement, the commandant told him that deputies from Onondaga were coming in a few days to conclude peace, and that he had better go home at once.

" It is well," replied the Rat.

He knew that for the Hurons it was not well. He and his tribe stood fully committed to the war, and for them peace between the French and the Iroquois would be a signal of destruction, since Denonville could not or would not protect his allies. The Rat paddled off with his warriors. He had secretly learned the route of the expected deputies; and he shaped his course, not, as he had pretended, for Michillimackinac, but for La Famine, where he knew that they would land. Having reached his destination, he watched and waited four or five days, till canoes at length appeared, approaching from the direction of Onondaga. On this, the Rat and his friends hid themselves in the bushes.

The new comers were the messengers sent as precursors of the embassy. At their head was a famous personage named Decanisora, or Tegan-nisorens, with whom were three other chiefs, and, it seems, a number of warriors. They had scarcely

1 Denonville a Seignday, 9 Nov., 1688. La Hontan saw the party set out, and says that there were about a hundred of them

landed when the ambushed Hurons gave them a volley of bullets, killed one of the chiefs, wounded all the rest, and then, rushing upon them, seized the whole party except a warrior who escaped with a broken arm. Having secured his prisoners, the Rat told them that he had acted on the suggestion of Denonville, who had informed him that an Iroquois war-party was to pass that way. The astonished captives protested that they were envoys of peace. The Eat put on a look of amazement, then of horror and fury, and presently burst into invectives against Denonville for having made him the instrument of such atrocious perfidy. " Go, my brothers," he exclaimed, " go home to your people. Though there is war between us, I give you your liberty. Onon-tio has made me do so black a deed that I shall never be happy again till your five tribes take a just vengeance upon him." After giving them guns, powder, and ball, he sent them on their way, well pleased with him and filled with rage against the governor.

In accordance with Indian usage, he, however, kept one of them to be adopted, as he declared, in place of one of his followers whom he had lost in the skirmish; then, recrossing the lake, he went alone to Fort Frontenac, and, as he left the gate to rejoin his party, he said coolly, " I have killed the peace: we shall see how the governor will get out of this

1 " Il dit, J'ai tud la paix." Belmont, Histoire du Canada. " Le Rat passa ensuite seul a Catarakouy (Fart Frontenac) sans vouloir dire le tour qu'il aroit fait, dit eeulement estant hors de la porte, en s'en allant, Nous verrons comme le gouverneur se tirera d'att'aire." Penonviile

business." l Then, without loss of time, he repaired to Michillimackinac, and gave his Iroquois prisoner to the officer in command. No news of the intended peace had yet reached that distant outpost; anil, though the unfortunate Iroquois told the story of his mission and his capture, the Eat declared that it was a crazy invention inspired by the fear of death, and the prisoner was immediately shot by a file of soldiers. The Rat now sent for an old Iroquois who had long been a prisoner at the Huron village, telling him with a mournful air that he was free to return to his people, and recount the cruelty of the French, who, had put their countryman to death. The liberated Iroquois faithfully acquitted himself of his mission. 1

One incident seemed for a moment likely to rob the intriguer of the fruits of his ingenuity. The Iroquois who had escaped in the skirmish contrived to reach Fort Frontenac some time after the last visit of the Rat. He told what had happened ; and, after being treated with the utmost attention, he was sent to Onondaga, charged with -explanations and regrets. The Iroquois dignitaries seemed satisfied, and Denonville wrote to the minister that

1 La Hontan,!. 189 (1709). Most of the details of the story are drawn from this writer, whose statement I have compared with that of Denonville, in his letter dated Nov. 9, 1688 ; of Callieres, Jan., 1689 ; of the Abstract of Letters from Canada, in AT. Y. Col. Docs., IX. 393 ; and of the writer of Relation des Evfnements de la Guerre, 30 Oct., 1688. Belmont notices the affair with his usual conciseness. La Hontan's account is sustained by the others in most, though not in all of its essential points. He calls the Huron chief Adario, ou le Rat. He is elsewhere mentioned as Kondiaronk, Kondiaront, Soiioias, and Soiia'iti. La Hontan says that the scene of the treachery was one of the rapids of the St. Lawrence, but more authentic accounts place it at La Famine.

there was still good hope of peace. He little knew his enemy. They could dissemble and wait; but they neither believed the governor nor forgave him. His supposed treachery at La Famine, and his real treachery at Fort Frontenac, filled them with a patient but unextinguishable rage. They sent him word that they were ready to renew the negotiation; then they sent again, to say that Andros forbade them. Without doubt they used his prohibition as a pretext. Months passed, and Denonville remained in suspense. He did not trust his Indian allies, nor did they trust him. Like the Bat and his Hurons, they dreaded the conclusion of peace, and wished the war to continue, that the French might bear the brunt of it, and stand between them and the wrath of the Iroquois. 1

In the direction of the Iroquois, there was a long and ominous silence. It was broken at last by the crash of a thunderbolt. On the night between the fourth and fifth of August, a violent hail-storm burst over Lake St. Louis, an expansion of the St. Lawrence a little above Montreal. Concealed by the tempest and the darkness, fifteen hundred warriors landed at La Chine, and silently posted themselves about the houses of the sleeping settlers, then screeched the war-whoop, and began the most frightful massacre in Canadian history. The houses were burned, and men, women, and children indiscriminately butchered. In the neighborhood were three stockade forts, called Remy, Roland, and La Presentation; and they all had

1 Denonville au Ministre, 9 Nov., 1(588. 12

garrisons. There was also an encampment of two hundred regulars about three miles distant, under an officer named Subercase, then absent at Montreal on a visit to Denonville, who had lately arrived with his wife and family. At four o'clock in the morning, the troops in this encampment heard a cannon-shot from one of the forts. They were at once ordered under arms. Soon after, they saw a man running towards them, just escaped from the butchery. He told his story, and passed on with the news to Montreal, six miles distant. Then several fugitives appeared, chased by a band of Iroquois, who gave over the pursuit at sight of the soldiers, but pillaged several houses before their eyes. The day was well advanced before Suber-case arrived. He ordered the troops to march. About a hundred armed inhabitants had joined them, and they moved together towards La Chine. Here they found the houses still burning, and the bodies of their inmates strewn among them or hanging from the stakes where they had been tortured. They learned from a French surgeon, escaped from the enemy, that the Iroquois were all encamped a mile and a half farther on, behind a tract of forest. Subercase, whose force had been strengthened by troops from the forts, resolved to attack them; and, had he been allowed to do so, he would probably have punished them severely, for most of them were helplessly drunk with brandy taken from the houses of the traders. Sword in hand, at the head of his men, the daring officer entered the forest; but, at that moment, a voice from the rear

commanded a halt. It was that of the Chevalier de Vaudreuil, just come from Montreal, with positive orders from Denonville to run no risks and stand solely on the defensive. Subercase was furious. High words passed between him and Vaudreuil, "but he was forced to obey.

The troops were led back to Fort Roland, where about five hundred regulars and militia were now collected under command of Yaudreuil. On the next day, eighty men from Fort Remy attempted to join them; but the Iroquois had slept off the effect of their orgies, and were again on the alert. The unfortunate detachment was set upon by a host of savages, and cut to pieces in full sight of Fort Roland. All were killed or captured, except Le Moyne de Longueuil, and a few others, who escaped within the gate of Fort Remy. 1

Montreal was wild with terror. It had been fortified with palisades since the war began; but, though there were troops in the town under the governor himself, the people were in mortal dread. No attack was made either on the town or on any of the forts, and such of the inhabitants as could reach them were safe; while the Iroquois held undisputed possession of the open country, burned all the houses and barns over an extent of nine miles, and roamed in small parties, pillaging and scalping, over more than twenty miles. There is

1 Recueil de ce qui s'est passe 1 en Canada depuis l'anne"e 1682; Observations on the State of Affairs in Canada, 1689,2V. Y. Col. Docs., IX. 431; Belmont, Histoire du Canada ;

Frontenac au Ministre, 16 Nov., 1689. This detachment was commanded by Lieutenant de la Rabeyre, and consisted of fifty French and thirty Indian converts.

no mention of their having encountered opposition; nor do they seem to have met with any loss but that of some warriors killed in the attack on the detachment from Fort Re'my, and that of three drunken stragglers who were caught and thrown into a cellar in Fort La Presentation. When they came to their senses, they defied their captors, and fought with such ferocity that it was necessary to shoot them. Charlevoix says that the invaders remained in the neighborhood of Montreal till the middle of October, or more than two months ; but this seems incredible, since troops and militia enough to drive them all into the St. Lawrence might easily have been collected in less than a week. It is certain, however, that their stay was strangely long. Troops and inhabitants seem to have been paralyzed with fear.

At length, most of them took to their canoes, and recrossed Lake St. Louis in a body, giving ninety yells to show that they had ninety prisoners in their clutches. This was not all; for the whole number carried off was more than a hundred arid twenty, besides about two hundred who had the good fortune to be killed on the spot. As the Iroquois passed the forts, they shouted, " Onontio, you deceived us, and now we have deceived you." Towards evening, they encamped on the farther side of the lake, and began to torture and devour their prisoners. On that miserable night, stupefied and speechless groups stood gazing from the strand of La Chine at the lights that gleamed along the distant shore of Ch&teaugay, where their

friends, wives, parents, or children agonized in the fires of the Iroquois, and scenes were enacted of indescribable and nameless horror. The greater part of the prisoners were, however, reserved to be distributed among the towns of the confederacy, and there tortured for the diversion of the inhabitants. While some of the invaders went home to celebrate their triumph, others roamed in small parties through all the upper parts of the colony, spreading universal terror. 1

Canada lay bewildered and benumbed under the shock of this calamity; but the cup of her misery was not full. There was revolution in

1 The best account of the descent of the Iroquois at La Chine is that of the Recueil de ce qui s'est pass? en Canada, 1682-1712. The writer was an officer under Subercase, and was on the spot. Belmont, superior of the mission of Montreal, also gives a trustworthy account in his Histoire du Canada. Compare La Hontan, I. 193 (1709), and La Potherie, II. 229, Farther particulars are given in the letters of Callieres, 8 Nov.; Cham-pigny, 16 Nov.; and Frontenac, 15 Nov. Frontenac, after visiting the scene of the catastrophe a few weeks after it occurred, writes: " Us (les Iroquois) avoient brusM plus de trois lieues de pays, saccage toutes les maisons jusqu'aux portes de la ville, enleve' plus de six vingt personnes,-tant hommes, femmes, qu'enfants, apres avoir massacre' plus de deux cents dont ils avoient casse* la teste aux uns, brusle', rosty, et mange" les autres, ouvert le ventre des femmes grosses pour en arracher les enfants, et fait des cruautez inou'ies et sans exemple." The details given by Belmont, and by the author of Histoire de I'lfau de Vie en Canada, are no less revolting. The last-mentioned writer thinks that the massacre was a judgment of God upon the sale of brandy at La Chine.

Some Canadian writers have charged the English with instigating the massacre. I find nothing in contemporary documents to support the accusation. Denonville wrote to the minister, after the Rat's treachery came to light, that Andros had forbidden the Iroquois to attack the colony. Immediately after the attack at La Chine, the Iroquois sachems, in a conference with the agents of New England, declared that " we did not make war on the French at the persuasion of our brethren at Albany; for we did not so much as acquaint them of our intention till fourteen days after our army had begun their march." Report of Conference in Colden, 103

England. James II., the friend and ally of France, had been driven from his kingdom, and William of Orange had seized his vacant throne. Soon there came news of war between the two crowns. The Iroq uois alone had brought the colony to the brink of ruin; and now they would be supported by the neighboring British colonies, rich, strong, and populous, compared to impoverished and depleted Canada.

A letter of recall for Denonville was already on its way. 1 His successor arrived in October, and the marquis sailed for France. He was a good soldier in a regular war, and a subordinate command; and he had some of the qualities of a good governor, while lacking others quite as essential. He had more activity than vigor, more personal bravery than firmness, and more clearness of perception than executive power. He filled his despatches with excellent recommendations, but was not the man to carry them into effect. He was sensitive, fastidious, critical, and conventional, and plumed himself on his honor, which was not always able to bear a strain; though as regards illegal trade, the besetting sin of Canadian governors, his hands were undoubtedly clean. 2 It is said that he had an

1 If. Roy a Denonville, 31 Mai, 1689.

2 " I shall only add one article, on which possibly you will find it strange that I have said nothing; namely, whether the governor carries on any trade. I shall answer, no; but my Lady the Governess (Madame la Gouvernante), who is disposed not to neglect any opportunity for making a profit, had a room, not to say a shop, full of goods, till the close of last winter, in the chateau of Quebec, and found means afterwards to make a lottery to get rid of the rubbish that remained, which produced her more than her good merchandise." Relation of the State of Affairs in Canada, 1688, in N. Y. Col. Docs., IX. 388. This paper was written at Quebec.

instinctive antipathy for Indians, such as some persons have for certain animals ; and the coureurs de bois, and other lawless classes of the Canadian population, appeared to please him no better. Their license and insubordination distressed him, and he constantly- complain3d of them to the king. For the Church and its hierarchy his devotion was unbounded; and his government was a season of unwonted sunshine for the ecclesiastics, like the balmy days of the Indian summer amid the gusts of November. They exhausted themselves in eulogies of his piety; and, in proof of its depth and solidity, Mother Juchereau tells us that he did not regard station and rank as very useful aids to salvation. While other governors complained of too many priests, Denonville begged for more. All was harmony between him and Bishop Saint-Vallier; and the prelate was constantly his friend, even to the point of justifying his worst act, the treacherous seizure of the Iroquois neutrals,. 1 When he left Canada, the only mourner besides the churchmen was his colleague, the in-tendant Champigny; for the two chiefs of the colony, joined in a common union with the Jesuits, lived together in unexampled concord. On his arrival at court, the good offices of his clerical allies gained for him the highly honorable post of governor of the royal children, the young Dukes of Burgundy, Anjou, and Berri.

i Saint-Vallier, Etat Prfsent, 91,92 (Quebec, 1868).

CHAPTER X.

1689, 1690. RETURN OF FRONTENAC.

VERSAILLES. — FRONTBNAO AND THE KING. — FRONTENAC SAILS FOR QUEBEC. — PROJECTED CONQUEST OP NEW YORK. — DESIGNS OF THE KING. — FAILURE. — ENERGY OF FRONTENAC. — FORT FRON. TENAC. — PANIC. — NEGOTIATIONS. — THE IROQUOIS IN COUNCIL. — CHEVALIER o'Aux.— TAUNTS OF THE INDIAN ALLIES. — BOLDNESS OF FRONTENAC. — AN IROQUOIS DEFEAT.

THE sun of Louis XIV. had reached its zenith. From a morning of unexampled brilliancy it had mounted to the glare of a cloudless noon; but the hour of its decline was near. The mortal enemy of France was on the throne of England, turning against her from that new point of vantage all the energies of his unconquerable genius. An invalid built the Bourbon monarchy, and another invalid battered and defaced the imposing structure: two potent and daring spirits in two frail bodies, Richelieu and William of Orange.

Versailles gave no sign of waning glories. On three evenings of the week, it was the pleasure of the king that the whole court should assemble in the vast suite of apartments now known as the Halls of Abundance, of Venus, of Diana, of Mars, of Mercury, and of Apollo. The magnificence of their decorations, pictures of the great Italian masters, sculptures, frescoes, mosaics, tapestries, vases and statues of silver and gold; the vista of light and splendor that opened through the wide portals ; the courtly throngs, feasting, dancing, gaming, promenading, conversing, formed a scene which no palace of Europe could rival or approach. Here were all the great historic names of France, princes, warriors, statesmen, and all that was highest in rank and place; the flower, in short, of that brilliant society, so dazzling, captivating, and illusory. In former years, the king was usually present, affable and gracious, mingling with his courtiers and sharing their amusements; but he had grown graver of late, and was more often in his cabinet, laboring with his ministers on the task of administration, which his extravagance and ambition made every day more burdensome. 1

There was one corner of the world where his emblem, the sun, would not shine on him. He had done his best for Canada, and had got nothing for his pains but news of mishaps and troubles. He was growing tired of the colony which he had nursed with paternal fondness, and he was more than half angry with it because it did not prosper. Denon-ville's letters had grown worse and worse; and,

1 Saint-Simon speaks of these assemblies. The halls in question were finished in 1682; and a minute account of them, and of the particular use to which each was destined, was printed in the Mercure Fran-fais of that year. See also Soulie, Notice du Muste imperial de VersaiUea y where copious extracts from the Mercure are given. The grands apparte-ments are now entirely changed in appearance, and turned into an historic picture gallery.

though he had not heard as yet of tlie last great calamity, he was sated with ill tidings already.

Count Frontenac stood before him. Since his recall, he had lived at court, needy and no longer hi favor; but he had influential friends, and an intriguing wife, always ready to serve him. The king knew his merits as well as his faults; and, in the desperate state of his Canadian affairs, he had been led to the resolution of restoring him to the command from which, for excellent reasons, he had removed him seven years before. He now told him that, in his belief, the charges brought against him were without foundation. 1 " I send you back to Canada/' he is reported to have said, " where I am sure that you will serve me as well as you did before; and I ask nothing more of you." * The post was not a tempting one to a man in his seventieth year. Alone and unsupported, — for the king, with Europe rising against him, would give him no more troops, — he was to restore the prostrate colony to hope and courage, and fight two enemies with a force that had proved no match for one of them alone. The audacious count trusted himself, and undertook the task; received the royal instructions, and took his last leave of the master whom even he after a fashion honored and admired.

He repaired to Rochelle, where two ships of the royal navy were waiting his arrival, embarked in

* Journal de Dangean, II. 390. Frontenac, since his recall, had not been wholly without marks of royal favor. In 1685, the king gave him a " gratification " of 3,600 francs. Ibid., I. 205.

2 Goyer, Oraison Funebre du Comte de Frontenac.

one of them, and sailed for the New World. An heroic remedy had been prepared for the sickness of Canada, and Frontenac was to be the surgeon, The cure, however, was not of his contriving. Denonville had sent Callieres, his second in command, to represent the state of the colony to the court, and beg for help. Callieres saw that there was little hope of more troops or any considerable supply of money; and he laid before the king a plan, which had at least the recommendations of boldness and cheapness. This was to conquer New York with the forces already in Canada, aided only by two ships of war. The blow, he argued, should be struck at once, and the English taken by surprise. A thousand regulars and six hundred Canadian militia should pass Lake Champlain and Lake George in canoes and bateaux, cross to the Hudson and capture Albany, where they would seize all the river craft and descend the Hudson to the town of New York, which, as Callieres stated, had then about two hundred houses and four hundred lighting men. The two ships were to cruise at the mouth of the harbor, and wait the arrival of the troops, which was to be made known to them by concerted signals, whereupon they were to enter and aid in the attack. The whole expedition, he thought, might be accomplished in a month; so that by the end of October the king would be master of all the country. The advantages were manifold. The Iroquois, deprived of English arms and ammunition, would be at the mercy of the French; the question of English rivalry in the

west would be settled for ever; the king would acquire a means of access to his colony incomparably better than the St. Lawrence, and one that remained open all the year; and, finally, New England would be isolated, and prepared for a possible conquest in the future.

The king accepted the plan with modifications, which complicated and did not improve it. Extreme precautions were taken to insure secrecy; but the vast distances, the difficult navigation, and the accidents of weather appear to have been forgotten in this amended scheme of operation. There was, moreover, a long delay in fitting the two ships for sea. The wind was ahead, and they were fifty-two days in reaching Chedabucto, at the eastern end of Nova Scotia. Thence Frontenac and Callieres had orders to proceed in a merchant ship to Quebec, which might require a month more; and, on arriving, they were to prepare for the expedition, while at the same time Frontenac was to send back a letter to the naval commander at Chedabucto, revealing the plan to him, and ordering him to sail to New York to co-operate in it. It was the twelfth of September when Chedabucto was reached, and the enterprise was ruined by the delay. Frontenac's first step in his new government was a failure, though one for which he was in no way answerable. 1

1 Projet du Chevalier de Callieres de fanner une Expedition pour otter attaquer Orange, Manatte, etc.; Re"sum£ du Ministre sur la Proposition de M. de Callieres; Autre Me'moire de M. de Callieres sur ton Projet d'attaquer la Nouvelle York; Me'moire des Armes, Munitions, et Ustensiles ne'cessairet pour CEntreprise proposes par M de Callieres; Observations du Ministre BUT

It will be well to observe what were the intentions of the king towards the colony which he proposed to conquer. They were as follows: If any Catholics were found in New York, they might be left undisturbed, provided that they took an oath of allegiance to the king. Officers, and other persons who had the means of paying ransoms, were to be thrown into prison. All lands in the colony, except those of Catholics swearing allegiance, were to be taken from their owners, and granted under a feudal tenure to the French officers and soldiers. All property, public or private, was to be seized, a portion of it given to the grantees of the land, and the rest sold on account of the king. Mechanics and other workmen might, at the discretion of the commanding officer, be kept as prisoners to work at fortifications and do other labor. The rest of the English and Dutch inhabitants, men, women, and children, were to be carried out of the colony and dispersed in New England, Pennsylvania, or other places, in such a manner that they could not combine in any attempt to recover their property and their country. And, that the conquest might be perfectly secure, the nearest settlements of New England were to be destroyed, and those more remote laid under contribution. 1

le Projet et le Me'moire ci-dessus; Observations du Ministre sur le Projel d'Attaque de la Nouvelle York; Autre Me'moire de M. de Callieres au Sujet de I'Entreprise proposte; Autre Me'moire de M. de Callieres sur le meme Sujet.

1 Me'moire pour servir d*'Instruction a Monsieur le Comte de Frontenae sur I'Entrf.prise de la Nouvelle York, 7 Juin, 1689. " Si panny les habitans de la Nouvelle York il se trouve des Catholiques de la fidelite desquels il croye se pouvoir asseurer, il pourra les laisser dans leurs habitations apres .eur avoir fait prester serment de fidelite* a sa Majeste'. . . . H

In the next century, some of the people ot Acadia were torn from their homes by order of a British commander. The act was harsh and violent, and the innocent were involved with the guilty; but many of the sufferers had provoked their fate, and deserved it.

Louis XIV. commanded that eighteen thousand unoffending persons should be stripped of all that they possessed, and cast out to the mercy of the wilderness. The atrocity of the plan is matched by its folly. The king gave explicit orders, but he gave neither ships nor men enough to accomplish them; and the Dutch farmers, goaded to desperation, would have cut his sixteen hundred soldiers to pieces. It was the scheme of a man blinded by a long course of success. Though perverted by flattery and hardened by unbridled power, he was not cruel by nature; and here, as in the burning of the Palatinate and the persecution of the Huguenots, he would have stood aghast, if his dull imagination could have pictured to him the miseries he was preparing to inflict. 9

pourra aussi garder, s'il le juge a propos, des artisans et autres gens de service necessaires pour la culture des terres ou pour travailler aux fortifications en qualite de prisonniers. ... II faut retenir en prison les officiers et les principaux habitans desquels on pourra retirer des ran-£ons. A l'esgard de tous les autres estrangers (cenx qui ne sont pas Fran-fais) hommes, femmes, et enfans, sa Majeste* trouve a propos qu ils soient mis hors <le la Colonie et envoyez a la Nouvelle Angleterre, a la Pennsyl-vanie, ou en d'autres endroits qu'il jugera a propos, par mer ou par terre, ensemble ou separe'ment, le tout suivant qu'il trouvera plus seur pour les dissiper et empescher qn'en se re'unissant ils ne puissent donner occasion a des entreprises de la part des ennemis contre cette Colonie. II envoy-era en France les Fran^ais fugitifs qu'il y pourra trouver, et particuliere-ment ceux de la Religion Pre'tendue-Reformee (Huguenots)." A translation of the entire document will be found in N. Y. Col Docs., IX. 422. 8 On the details of the projected attack of New York, Le Roy h

With little hope left that the grand enterprise against New York could succeed, Frontenac made sail for Quebec, and, stopping by the way at Isle Perc(3e, learned from Eecollet missionaries the irruption of the Iroquois at Montreal. He hastened on ; but the wind was still against him, and the autumn woods were turning brown before he reached his destination. It was evening when he landed, amid fireworks, illuminations, and the firing of cannon. All Quebec came to meet him by torchlight; the members of the council offered their respects, and the Jesuits made him an harangue of welcome. 1 It was but a welcome of words. They and the councillors had done their best to have him recalled, and hoped that they were rid of him for ever; but ttDw he was among them again, rasped by the memory of real or fancied wrongs. The count, however, had no time for quarrelling. The king had told him to bury old animosities and forget the past, and for the present he was too busy to break the royal injunction. 2 He caused boats to be made ready, and in spite of incessant rains pushed up the river to Montreal. Here he found Denonville and his frightened wife. Every thing was in confusion. The Iroquois were gone, leaving dejection and terror behind them. Frontenac reviewed the troops. There were seven or eight hundred of them in the town, the rest being in garrison at the

Denonville, 7 Juin, 1689; Le Ministre a Denonville, meme date; Le Ministre a Frontenac, meme date; Ordre du Roy a Vaudreuil, meme date; Le Roy au Sieur dela Caffiniere, meme date; Champigny au Ministre, 16 Nov., 1689

1 La Hontan, I. 199.

2 instruction pour h Sieur Comte de Frontenac, 7 Juin, 1689-

various forts. Then he repaired to what was once La Chine, and surveyed the miserable waste of ashes and desolation that spread for miles around. To his extreme disgust, he learned that Denon-ville had sent a Canadian officer by secret paths to Fort Frontenac, with orders to Valrenne, the commandant, to blow it up, and return with his garrison to Montreal. Frontenac had built the fort, had given it his own name, and had cherished it with a paternal fondness, reinforced by strong hopes of making money out of it. For its sake he had become the butt of scandal and opprobrium; but not the less had he always stood its strenuous and passionate champion. An Iroquois envoy had lately with great insolence demanded its destruction of Denonville; and this alone, in the eyes of Frontenac, was ample reason for maintaining it at any cost. 1 He still had hope that it might be saved, and with all the energy of youth he proceeded to collect canoes, men, provisions, and arms; battled against dejection, insubordination, and fear, and in a few days despatched a convoy of three hundred men to relieve the place, and stop the execution of Denonville's orders. His orders had been but too promptly obeyed. The convoy was scarcely gone an hour, when, to Frontenac's unutterable wrath, Valrenne appeared with his garrison. He reported that he had set fire to every thing in the fort that would burn, sunk the three vessels belonging to it, thrown the cannon into the lake, mined the walls and bastions, and left matches burning

1 Frontenac au Ministre, 16 Nov., 1689.

in the powder magazine; and, further, that when he and his men were five leagues on their way to Montreal a dull and distant explosion told them that the mines had sprung. It proved afterwards that the destruction was not complete ; and the Iroquois took possession of the abandoned fort, with a large quantity of stores and munitions left by the garrison in their too hasty retreat. 1

There was one ray of light through the clouds. The unwonted news of a victory came to Montreal. It was small, but decisive, and might be an earnest of greater things to come. Before Frontenac's arrival, Denonville had sent a reconnoitring party up the Ottawa. They had gone no farther than the Lake of Two Mountains, when they met twenty-two Iroquois in two large canoes, who immediately bore down upon them, yelling furiously. The French party consisted of twenty-eight coureurs de bois under Du Lhut and Mantet, excellent partisan chiefs, who manoeuvred so well that the rising sun blazed full in the eyes of the advancing enemy, and spoiled their aim. The French received their fire, which wounded one man; then, closing with them while their guns were empty, gave them a volley, which killed and wounded eighteen of their number. One swam ashore. The remaining three were captured, and given to the Indian allies to be burned. 2

1 Frontenac au Ministre, 15 Nov., 1689; Recueil de ce qui s'est passt en Canada depuis Vannte 1682.

2 Frontenac au Ministre, 15 Nov., 1689; Champigny au Ministre, 16 Nov., 1689. Compare Belmont, whose account is a little different; also N. T. Col. Docs., IX. 435.

13 :

This gleam of sunshine passed, and all grew black again. On a snowy November day, a troop of Iroquois fell on the settlement of La Chesnaye, burned the houses, and vanished with a troop of prisoners, leaving twenty mangled corpses on the snow. 1 " The terror/' wrote the bishop, " is in describable." The appearance of a few savages would put a whole neighborhood to flight. 9 So desperate, wrote Frontenac, were the needs of the colony, and so great the contempt with which the Iroquois regarded it, that it almost needed a miracle either to carry on war or make peace. What he most earnestly wished was to keep the Iroquois quiet, and so leave his hands free to deal with the English. This was not easy, to such a pitch of audacity had late events raised them. Neither his temper nor his convictions would allow him to beg peace of them, like his predecessor; but he had inordinate trust in the influence of his name, and he now took a course which he hoped might answer his purpose without increasing their insolence. The perfidious folly of Denonville in seizing their countrymen at Fort Frontenac had been a prime cause of their hostility; and, at the request of the late governor, the surviving captives, thirteen in all, had been taken from the galleys, gorgeously clad in French attire, and sent back to Canada in the ship which carried Frontenac. Among them was a famous Cayuga war-chief called

1 Belmont, Histoire du Canada; Frontenac a , 17 Nov., 1689;

Champigny au Ministre, 16 Nov., 1689. This letter is not the one just cited. Champigny wrote twice on the same day.

2 N. Y. Col. Doct.. IX. 436.

Ourehaoue*, whose loss had infuriated the Iroquois. 1 Frontenac gained his good-will on the voyage ; and, when they reached Quebec, he lodged him in the chateau, and treated him with such kindness that the chief became his devoted admirer and. friend. As his influence was great among his people, Frontenac hoped that he might use him with success to bring about an accommodation. He placed three of the captives at the disposal of the Cayuga, who forthwith sent them to Onondaga with a message which the governor had dictated, and which was to the following effect: " The great Onontio, whom you all know, has come back again. He does not blame you for what you have done; for he looks upon you as foolish children, and blames only the English, who are the cause of your folly, and have made you forget your obedience to a father who has always loved and never deceived you. He will permit me, Ourehaoue, to return to you as soon as you will come to ask for me, not as you have spoken of late, but like children speaking to a father." 9 Frontenac hoped that they would send an embassy to reclaim their chief, and thus give him an opportunity to use his personal influence over them. With the three released captives, he sent an Iroquois convert named Cut Nose with a wampum belt to announce his return.

When the deputation arrived at Onondaga and made known their errand, the Iroquois

1 Ourehaoue was not one of the neutrals entrapped at Fort Frontenac, but was seized about the same time by the troops on their way up the St. Lawrence.

2 Frontenac au Ministre, 30 Avril, 1690.

magnates, with their usual deliberation, deferred answering till a general council of the confederacy should have tune to assemble; and, meanwhile, they sent messengers to ask the mayor of Albany, and others of their Dutch and English friends, to come to the meeting. They did not comply, merely sending the government interpreter, with a few Mohawk Indians, to represent their interests. On the other hand, the Jesuit Milet, who had been captured a few months before, adopted, and made an Oneida chief, used every effort to second the designs of Frontenac. The authorities of Albany tried in vain to induce the Iroquois to place him in their hands. They understood their interests too well, and held fast to the Jesuit. 1

The grand council took place at Onondaga on the twenty-second of January. Eighty chiefs and sachems, seated gravely on mats around the council fire, smoked their pipes in silence for a while; till at length an Onondaga orator rose, and announced that Frontenac, the old Onontio, had returned with Ourehaoue and twelve more of their captive friends, that he meant to rekindle the council fire at Fort Frontenac, and that he invited them to meet him there. 9

1 Milet was taken in 1689, not, as has been supposed, in 1690. Lettre du Pere Milet, 1691, printed by Shea.

2 Frontenac declares that he sent no such message, and intimates that Cut Nose had been tampered with by persons over-anxious to conciliate the Iroquois, and who had even gone so far as to send them messages on their own account These persons were Lamberville, Frai^ois Hertel, and one of the Le Moynes. Frontenac was very angry at this interference, to which he ascribes the most mischievous conse-

" Ho, ho, ho," returned the eighty senators, from the bottom of their throats. It was the unfailing Iroquois response to a speech. Then Cut Nose, the governor's messenger, addressed the council: "I advise you to meet Onontio as he desires. Do so, if you wish to live." He presented a wampum belt to confirm his words, and the conclave again returned the same guttural ejaculation,

" Ourehaoue* sends you this," continued Cut Nose, presenting another belt of wampum : " by it he advises you to listen to Onontio, if you wish to live."

When the messenger from Canada had ceased, the messenger from Albany, a Mohawk Indian, rose and repeated word for word a speech confided to him by the mayor of that town, urging the Iroquois to close their ears against the invitations of Onontio.

Next rose one Cannehoot,.a sachem of the Sene-cas, charged with matters of grave import; for they involved no less than the revival of that scheme,- so perilous to the French, of the union of the tribes of the Great Lakes in a triple alliance with the Iroquois and the English. These lake tribes, disgusted with the French, who, under Denonville, had left them to the mercy of the Iroquois, had been impelled, both by their fears and their interests, to make new advances to the confederacy,' and had first addressed themselves to the Senecas, whom they had most cause to dread. They had given up some of the Iroquois prisoners

quences. Cut Nose, or Nez Coupe, is called Adarahta by Golden and Gagniegaton, or Red Bird, by some French writers.

in their hands, and promised soon to give up the rest. A treaty had been made; and it was this event which the Seneca sachem now announced to the council. Having told the story to his assembled colleagues, he exhibited and explained the wampum belts and other tokens brought by the envoys from the lakes, who represented nine distinct tribes or bands from the region of Michilli-mackinac. By these tokens, the nine tribes declared that they came to learn wisdom of the Iroquois and the English; to wash off the warpaint, throw down the tomahawk, smoke the pipe of peace, and unite with them as one body. " On-ontio is drunk," such was the interpretation of the fourth wampum belt; " but we, the tribes of Michillimackinac, wash our hands of all his actions. Neither we nor you must defile ourselves by listening to him." When the Seneca sachem had ended, and when the ejaculations that echoed his words had ceased, the belts were hung up before all the assembly, then taken down again, and distributed among the sachems of the five Iroquois tribes, excepting one, which was given to the messengers from Albany. Thus was concluded the triple alliance, which to Canada meant no less than ruin.

" Brethren," said an Onondaga sachem, " we must hold fast to our brother Quider (Peter Schuy-ler, mayor of Albany), and look on Onontio as our enemy, for he is a cheat."

Then they invited the interpreter from Albany to address the council, which he did, advising them

not to listen to the envoys from Canada. When he had ended, they spent some time in consultation among themselves, and at length agreed on the following message, addressed to Corlaer, or New York, and to Kinshon, the Fish, by which they meant New England, the authorities of which had sent them the image of a fish as a token of alliance: 1 —

" Brethren, our council fire burns at Albany. We will not go to meet Onontio at Fort Frontenac. We will hold fast to the old chain of peace with Corlaer, and we will fight with Onontio. Brethren, we are glad to hear from you that you are preparing to make war on Canada, but tell us no lies.

" Brother Kinshon, we hear that you mean to send soldiers against the Indians to the eastward; but we advise you, now that we are all united against the French, to fall upon them at once. Strike at the root: when the trunk is cut down, all the'branches fall with it.

" Courage, Corlaer! courage, Kinshon ! Go to Quebec in the spring; take it, and you will have your feet on the necks of the French and all their friends."

Then they consulted together again, and agreed on the following answer to Ourehaoue and Frontenac : —

" Ourehaoue', the whole council is glad to hear that you have come back.

1 The wooden image of a codfish still hangs in the State House at Boston, the emblem of a colony which lived chiefly by the fisheries.

" Onontio, you have told us that you have come back again, and brought with you thirteen of our people who were carried prisoners to France. We are glad of it. You wish to speak with us at Cata-raqui (Fort Frontenac). Don't you know that your council fire there is put out ? It is quenched in blood. You must first send home the prisoners. When our brother Ourehaoue' is returned to us, then we will talk with you of peace. You must send him and the others home this very winter. We now let you know that we have made peace with the tribes of Michillimackinac. You are not to think, because we return you an answer, that we have laid down the tomahawk. Our warriors will continue the war till you send our countrymen back to us/' 1

The messengers from Canada returned with this reply. Unsatisfactory as it was, such a quantity of wampum was sent with it as showed plainly the importance attached by the Iroquois to the matters in question. Encouraged by a recent success against the English, and still possessed with an overweening confidence in his own influence over the confederates, Frontenac resolved that Ourehaou6 should send them another message. The chief, whose devotion to the count never wavered, ac-

1 The account of this council is given, with condensation and the omission of parts not essential, from Colden (105-112, ed. 1747). It will serve as an example of the Iroquois method of conducting political business, the habitual regularity and decorum of which has drawn from several contemporary French writers the remark that in such matters the five tribes were savages only in name. The reply to Frontenac is also given by Monseignat (N. Y. Col. Docs., IX. 465),

and, after him, by La Potherie. Compare Le Clercq, Jftablissement de la Foy, II. 403. Ourehaoue' is the Tawerahet of Colden.

cordingly despatched four envoys, with a load of wampum belts, expressing his astonishment that his countrymen had not seen fit to send a deputation of chiefs to receive him from the hands of On-ontio, and calling upon them to do so without delay, lest he should think that they had forgotten him. Along with the messengers, Frontenac ventured to send the Chevalier d'Aux, a half-pay officer, with orders to observe the disposition of the Iroquois, and impress them in private talk with a sense of the count's power, of his good-will to them, and of the wisdom of coming to terms with him, lest, like an angry father, he should be forced at last to use the rod. The chevalier's reception was a warm one. They burned two of his attendants, forced him to run the gauntlet, and, after a vigorous thrashing, sent him prisoner to Albany. The last; failure was worse than the first. The count's name was great among the Iroquois, but he had trusted its power too far. 1

The-worst of news had come from Michillimack-inac. La Durantaye, the commander of the post, and Carheil, the Jesuit, had sent a messenger to Montreal in the depth of winter to say that the tribes around them were on the point of revolt. Carheil wrote that they threatened openly to throw themselves into the arms of the Iroquois and the English; that they declared that the protection of Oiiontio was an illusion and a snare ; that they

1 Message of Ourehaonf, in N. Y. Col Docs., III. 735; Instructions to Chevalier d'Eau, Ibid., 733; Chevalier d'Aux au Ministry 15 Mai, 1693. The chevalier's name is also written d'O. He himself wrote it as in the

text.

once mistook the French for warriors, but saw now that they were no match for the Iroquois, whom they had tamely allowed to butcher them at Montreal, without even daring to defend themselves; that when the French invaded the Senecas they did nothing but cut down corn and break canoes, and since that time they had done nothing but beg peace for themselves, forgetful of their allies, whom they expected to bear the brunt of the war, and then left to their fate; that they had surrendered through cowardice the prisoners they had caught by treachery, and this, too, at a time when the Iroquois were burning French captives in all their towns; and, finally, that, as the French would not or could not make peace for them, they would make peace for themselves. " These," pursued Carheil, " are the reasons they give us to prove the necessity of their late embassy to the Senecas; and by this one can see that our Indians are a great deal more clear-sighted than they are thought to be, and that it is hard to conceal from their penetration any thing that can help or harm their interests. What is certain is that, if the Iroquois are not stopped, they will not fail to come and make themselves masters here." l

Charlevoix thinks that Frontenac was not displeased at this bitter arraignment of his predecessor's administration. At the same time, his position was very embarrassing. He had no men

1 Carheil a Frontenac, 1690. Frontenac did not receive this letter till September, and acted on the information previously sent him, Charlevoix 's version of the letter does not conform with the original.

to spare; but such was the necessity of saving Michillimackinac, and breaking off the treaty with the Senecas, that when spring opened he sent Captain Louvigny with a hundred and forty-three Canadians and six Indians to reinforce the post and replace its commander, La Durantaye. Two other officers with an additional force were ordered to accompany him through the most dangerous part of the journey. With them went Nicolas Perrot, bearing a message from the count to his rebellious children of Michillimackinac. The following was the pith of this characteristic document : —

" I am astonished to learn that you have forgotten the protection that I always gave you. Do you think that I am no longer alive ; or that I have a mind to stand idle, like those who have been here in my place ? Or do you think that, if eight or ten hairs have been torn from my children's heads when I was absent, I cannot put ten hand-fuls of hair in the place of every one that was pulled out? You know that before I protected you the ravenous Iroquois dog was biting everybody. I tamed him and tied him up; but, when he no longer saw me, he behaved worse than ever. If he persists, he shall feel my power. The English have tried to win him by flatteries, but I will kill all wlio encourage him. The English have deceived and devoured their children, but I am a good father who loves you. I loved the Iroquois once, because they obeyed me. When I knew that they had been treacherously captured and carried

to France, I set them free; and, when I restore them to their country, it will not be through fear, but through pity, for I hate treachery. I am strong enough to kill the English, destroy the Iro-quois, and whip you, if you fail in your duty to me. The Iroquois have killed and captured you in time of peace. Do to them as they have done to you, do to the English as they would like to do to you, but hold fast to your true father, who will never abandon you. Will you let the English brandy that has killed you in your wigwams lure you into the kettles of the Iroquois ? Is not mine better, which has never killed you, but always made you strong ? " l

Charged with this haughty missive, Perrot set out for Michillimackinac along with Louvigny and his men. On their way up the Ottawa, they met a large band of Iroquois hunters, whom they routed with heavy loss. Nothing could have been more auspicious for Perrot' s errand. When towards midsummer they reached their destination, they ranged their canoes in a triumphal procession, placed in the foremost an Iroquois captured in the fight, forced him to dance and sing, hung out the fleur-de-lis, shouted Vive le Roi, whooped, yelled, and fired their guns. As they neared the village of the Ottawas, all the naked population ran down to the shore, leaping, yelping, and firing, in refurn. Louvigny and his men passed on, and landed at the

1 Parole (de M. de Frontenac) qui doit elre dite a l'Outaouais pour le di&-suader de VAlliance qu'il veut faire avec l'Iroquois et l'Anglais. The mes sage is long. Only the principal points are given above.

neighboring village of the French settlers, who, drawn up in battle array on the shore, added more yells and firing to the general uproar; though, amid this joyous fusillade of harmless gunpowder, they all kept their bullets ready for instant use, for they distrusted the savage multitude. The story of the late victory, however, confirmed as it was by an imposing display of scalps, produced an effect which averted the danger of an immediate outbreak.

The fate of the Iroquois prisoner now became the point at issue. The French hoped that the Indians in their excitement could be induced to put him to death, and thus break their late treaty ; with his countrymen. Besides the Ottawas, there was at Michillimackinac a village of Hurons under their crafty chief, the Rat. They had pretended to stand fast for the French, who nevertheless believed them to be at the bottom of all the mischief. They now begged for the prisoner, promising to burn him. On the faith of this pledge, he was given, to them; but they broke their word, and kept him alive, in order to curry favor with the Iroquois. The Ottawas, intensely jealous of the preference shown to the Hurons, declared in their anger that the prisoner ought to be killed and eaten. This was precisely what the interests of the French demanded; but the Hurons still persisted in protecting him. Their Jesuit missionary now interposed, and told them that, unless they "put the Iroquois into the kettle," the French would take him from them.

After much discussion, this argument prevailed. They planted a stake, tied him to it, and began to torture him; bat, as he did not show the usual fortitude of his countrymen, they declared him unworthy to die the death of a warrior, and accordingly shot him. 1

Here was a point gained for the French, but the danger was not passed. The Ottawas could disavow the killing of the Iroquois; and, in. fact, though there was a great division of opinion among them, they were preparing at this very time to send a secret embassy to the Seneca country to ratify the fatal treaty. The French commanders called a council of all the tribes. It met at the house of the Jesuits. Presents in abundance were distributed. The message of Frontenac was reinforced by persuasion and threats; and the assembly was told that the five tribes of the Iroquois were like five nests of muskrats in a marsh, which the French would drain dry, and then burn with all its inhabitants. Perrot took the disaffected chiefs aside, and with his usual bold adroitness diverted them for the moment from their purpose. The projected embassy was stopped, but any day might revive it. There was no safety for the French,

1 "Le Pere Missionnaire des Hurons, pre>oyant que cette affaire auroit peut-£tre une suite qui pourrait e"tre pre'judiciable aux soins qu'il prenoit de leur instruction, demanda qu'il lui fut permis d'aller a leur village pour les obliger de trouver quelque moyen qui fut capable d'appaiser le ressentiment des Francois. II leur dit que ceux-ci vouloient absolument que Ton mit l'froquois a la chaudiere, et que si on ne le faisoit, on devoit venir le leur enlever." La Potherie, II. 237 (1722). By the " result prejudicial to his cares for their instruction " he seems to mean their possible transfer from French to English influences. The expression mettre a la chaudiere, though derived from cannibal practices, is often used figuratively for torturing and killing. The missionary in question was either Carheil or another Jesuit, who must have acted with his sanction.

and the ground of Michillimackinac was hollow under their feet. Every thing depended on the success of their arms. A few victories would confirm their wavering allies; but the breath of another defeat would blow the fickle crew over to the enemy like a drift of dry leaves.

CHAPTER XL

1690. THE THREE WAR-PARTIES.

MEASURES OF FRONTENAC. — EXPEDITION AGAINST SCHENECTADT. — THE MARCH. —THE DUTCH VILLAGE.— THE SURPRISE. — THB MASSACRE. — PRISONERS SPARED. — RETREAT. — THE ENGLISH AND THEIR IROQUOIS FRIENDS. — THE ABENAKI WAR. — REVOLUTION AT BOSTON. — CAPTURE OF PEMAQUID. — CAPTURE OF SALMON FALLS. — CAPTURE OF FORT LOYAL. — FRONTENAC AND HIS PRISONER. — THE CANADIANS ENCOURAGED.

WHILE striving to reclaim his allies, Frontenac had not forgotten his enemies. It was of the last necessity to revive the dashed spirits of the Canadians and the troops; and action, prompt and bold, was the only means of doing so. He resolved, therefore, to take the offensive, not against the Iroquois, who seemed invulnerable as ghosts, but against the English; and by striking a few sharp and rapid blows to teach both friends and foes that Onontio was still alive. The effect of his return had already begun to appear, and the energy and fire of the undaunted veteran had shot new life into the dejected population." He formed three war-parties of picked men, one at Montreal, one at Three Rivers, and one at Quebec; the first to strike at Albany, the second at the border settlements of New Hampshire, and the third at those of Maine. That of Montreal was ready first. It consisted of two hundred and ten men, of whom ninety-six were Indian converts, chiefly from the two mission villages of Saut St. Louis and the Mountain of Montreal.

They were Christian Iroquois whom the priests had persuaded to leave their homes and settle in Canada, to the great indignation of their heathen countrymen, and the great annoyance of the English colonists, to whom they were a constant menace. When Denonville attacked the Senecas, they had joined him; but of late they had shown reluctance to fight their heathen kinsmen, with whom the French even suspected them of collusion. Against the English, however, they willingly took up the hatchet. The French of the party were for the most part coureurs de bois. As the sea is the sailor's element, so the forest was theirs. Their merits were hardihood and skill in woodcraft; their chief faults were insubordination and lawlessness. They had shared the general demoralization that followed the inroad of the Iroquois, and under Denonville had proved mutinous and unmanageable. In the best times, it was a hard task to command them, and one that needed, not bravery alone, but tact, address, and experience. Under a chief of such a stamp, they were admirable bush-fighters, and such were those now chosen to lead them. D'Aillebout de Mantet and Le Moyne de Sainte-Helene, the brave son of Charles Le Moyne, had the chief command, supported by the brothers

14

Le Moyne d'Iberville and Le Moyne de Bienville, with Repentigny de Montesson, Le Ber du Chesne, and others of the sturdy Canadian noblesse, nerved by adventure and trained in Indian warfare. 1

It was the depth of winter when they began their march, striding on snow-shoes over the vast white field of the frozen St. Lawrence, each with the hood of his blanket coat drawn over his head, a gun in his mittened hand, a knife, a hatchet, a tobacco pouch, and a bullet pouch at his belt, a pack on his shoulders, and his inseparable pipe hung at his neck in a leather case. They dragged their blankets and provisions over the snow on Indian sledges. Crossing the forest to Chambly. they advanced four or five days up the frozen Richelieu and the frozen Lake Champlain, and then stopped to hold a council. Frontenac had left the precise point of attack at the discretion of the leaders, and thus far the men had been ignorant of their destination. The Indians demanded to know it. Mantet and Sainte-Helene replied that they were going to Albany. The Indians demurred. " How long is it," asked one of them, " since the French grew so bold ?" The commanders answered that, to regain the honor of which their late misfortunes had robbed them, the French would take Albany or die in the attempt. The

1 Relation de Monseignat, 1689-90. There is a translation of this valuable paper in N. Y. Col. Docs., IX. 462. The party, according to three of their number, consisted at first of 160 French and 110 Christian Indians, but was reduced by sickness and desertion to 250 in all. Examination of three French prisoners taken by y* Maquas (Mohawks), and brought to Skinnectady, who were examined by Peter Schuyler, Mayor of Albany, Domine Godevridus Dellius, and some of y* Gentle? that went from

Indians listened sullenly; the decision was postponed, and the party moved forward again. When after eight days they reached the Hudson, and found the place where two paths diverged, the one for Albany and the other for Schenectady, they all without farther words took the latter. Indeed, to attempt Albany would have been an act of desperation. The march was horrible. There was a partial thaw, and they waded knee-deep through the half melted snow, and the mingled ice, mud, and water of the gloomy swamps. So painful and so slow was their progress, that it was nine days more before they reached a point two leagues from Schenectady. The weather had changed again, and a cold, gusty snow-storm pelted them. It was one of those days when the trees stand white as spectres in the sheltered hollows of the forest, and bare and gray on the wind-swept ridges. The men were half dead with cold, fatigue, and hunger. It was four in the afternoon of the eighth of February. The scouts found an Indian hut, and in it were four Iroquois squaws, whom they captured. There was a fire in the wigwam; and the shivering Canadians crowded about it, stamping their chilled feet and warming their benumbed hands over the blaze. The Christian chief of the Saut St. Louis, known as Le Grand Agnie, or the Great Mohawk, by the French, and by the Dutch called Kryn, harangued his followers, and exhorted them to wash out their wrongs in blood. Then they all advanced again, and about dark reached the river Mohawk, a little above the village. A

Canadian named Gigni&res, who had gone with nine Indians to reconnoitre, now returned to say that he had been within sight of Schenectady, and hai seen nobody. Their purpose had been to postpone the attack till two o'clock in the morning ; but the situation was intolerable, and the limit of human endurance was reached. They could not make fires, and they must move on or perish. Guided by the frightened squaws, they crossed the Mohawk on the ice, toiling through the drifts amid the whirling snow that swept down the valley of the darkened stream, till about eleven o'clock they descried through the storm the snow-beplastered palisades of the devoted village. Such was their plight that some of them afterwards declared that they would all have surrendered if an enemy had appeared to summon them. 1

Schenectady was the farthest outpost of the colony of New York. Westward lay the Mohawk forests ; and Orange, or Albany, was fifteen miles or more towards the south-east. The village was oblong in form, and enclosed by a palisade which had two gates, one towards Albany and the other towards the Mohawks. There was a blockhouse near the eastern gate, occupied by eight or nine Connecticut militia men under Lieutenant Talmage. There were also about thirty friendly Mohawks in the place, on a visit. The inhabitants, who were all Dutch, were in a state of discord and confusion. The revolution in England had produced a revolution in New York. The demagogue Jacob Leisler had got pos-

* Golden, 114 (ed. 1747).

session of Fort William, and was endeavoring to master the whole colony. Albany was in the hands of the anti-Leisler or conservative party, represented by a convention of which Peter Schuyler was the chief. The Dutch of Schenectady for the most part favored Leisler, whose emissaries had been busily at work among them; but their chief magistrate, John Sander Glen, a man of courage and worth, stood fast for the Albany convention, and in consequence the villagers had threatened to kill him. Talmage and his Connecticut militia were under orders from Albany; and therefore, like Glen, they were under the popular ban. In vain the magistrate and the officer entreated the people to stand on their guard. They turned the advice to ridicule, laughed at the idea of danger, left both their gates wide open, and placed there, it is said, two snow images as mock sentinels. A French account declares that the village contained $jghty houses, which is certainly an exaggeration. There had been some festivity during the evening, but it was now over ; and the primitive villagers, fathers, mothers, children, and infants, lay buried in unconscious sleep. They were simple peasants and rude woodsmen, but with human affections and capable of human woe.

The French and Indians stood before the open gate, with its blind and dumb warder, the mock sentinel of snow. Iberville went with a detachment to find the Albany gate, and bar it against the escape of fugitives; but he missed it in the gloom, and hastened back. The assailants were

now formed into two bands, Sainte-Helene leading the one and Mantet the other. They passed through the gate together in dead silence: one turned to the right and the other to the left, and they filed around the village between the palisades and the houses till the two leaders met at the farther end. Thus the place was completely sur-roumled. The signal was then given: they all screeched the war-whoop together, burst in the doors with hatchets, and fell to their work. Roused by the infernal din, the villagers leaped from their beds. For some it was but a momentary nightmare of fright and horror, ended by the blow of the tomahawk. Others were less fortunate. Neither women nor children were spared. " No pen can write, and no tongue express," wrote Schuyler, " the cruelties that were committed." 1 There was little resistance, except at the blockhouse^ where Talmage and his men made a stubborn fight; but the doors were at length forced open, the defenders killed or taken, and the building set on fire. Adam Vrooman, one of the villagers, saw his wife shot and his child brained against the door-post; but he fought so desperately that the assailants promised him his life, Orders had been given to spare Peter Tassemaker, the domine or minister, from whom it was thought that valuable information might be obtained; but

1 " The women bigg with Childe rip'd up, and the Children alive throwne into the flames, and their heads dashed to pieces against the Doors and windows." Schnyler to the Council of Connecticut, 16 Feb., 1690. Similar statements are made by Leisler. 'See Doc. Hist. N. Y. t I. 307, 810.

he was hacked to pieces, and his house burned. Some, more agile or more fortunate than the rest, escaped at the eastern gate, and fled through the storra to seek shelter at Albany or at houses along the way. Sixty persons were killed outright, of whom thirty-eight were men and boys, ten were women, and twelve were children. 1 The number captured appears to have been between eighty and ninety. The thirty Mohawks in the town were treated with studied kindness by the victors, who declared that they had no quarrel with them, but only with the Dutch and English.

The massacre and pillage continued two hours; then the prisoners were secured, sentinels posted, and the men told to rest and refresh themselves. In the morning, a small party crossed the river to the house of Glen, which stood on a rising ground half a mile distant. It was loopholed and palisaded; and Glen had mustered his servants and tenants, closed his gates, and prepared to defend himself. The French told him to fear nothing, for they had orders not to hurt a chicken of his; whereupon, after requiring them to lay down their arms, he allowed them to enter. They urged him to go with them to the village, and he complied; they on their part leaving one of their number as a hostage in the hands of his followers. Iberville appeared at the gate with the Great Mohawk, and, drawing his commission from the breast of his coat, told

1 List of y* People kild and destroyed by y e . French of Canida and there Indians at Skinnechtady. in Doc. Hist, N. Y., I. 304

Glen that he was specially charged to pay a debt which the French owed him. On several occasions, he had saved the lives of French prisoners in the hands of the Mohawks; and he, with his family, and, above all, his wife, had shown them the greatest kindness. He was now led before the crowd of wretched prisoners, and told that not only were his own life and property safe,, but that all his kindred should be spared. Glen stretched his privilege to the utmost, till the French Indians, disgusted at his multiplied demands for clemency, observed that everybody seemed to be his relation.

Some of the houses had already been burned. Fire was now set to the rest, excepting one, in which a French officer lay wounded, another belonging to Glen, and three or four more which he begged the victors to spare. At noon Schenectady was in ashes. Then the French and Indians withdrew, laden with booty. Thirty or forty captured horses dragged their sledges; and a troop of twenty-seven men and boys were driven prisoners into the forest. About sixty old men, women, and children were left behind, without farther injury, in order, it is said, to conciliate the Mohawks in the place, who had joined with Glen in begging that they might be spared. Of the victors, only two had been killed. 1

1 Many of the authorities on the burning of Schenectady will be found in the Documentary History of New York, I. 297-312. One of the most important is a portion of the long letter of M. de Monseignat, comptroller-general of the marine in Canada, to a lady of rank, said to be Madame de Maintenon. Others are contemporary documents pro-

At the outset of the attack, Simon Schermer-horn threw himself on a horse, and galloped through the eastern gate. The French shot at and wounded him; but he escaped, reached Albany at daybreak, and gave the alarm. The soldiers and inhabitants were called to arms, cannon were fired to rouse the country, and a party of horsemen, followed by some friendly Mohawks, set out for Schenectady. The Mohawks had promised to carry the news to their three towns on the river above ; but, when they reached the ruined village, they were so frightened at the scene of havoc that they would not go farther. Two days passed before the alarm reached the Mohawk towns. Then troops of warriors came down on

served at Albany, including, among others, the lists of killed and cap tured, letters of Leisler to the governor of Maryland, the governor of Massachusetts, the governor of Barbadoes, and the Bishop of Salisbury J of Robert Livingston to Sir Edmund Andros and to Captain Nicholson; and of Mr. Van Cortlandt to Sir Edmund Andros. One of the best contemporary authorities is a letter of Schuyler and his colleagues to the governor and council of Massachusetts, 15 February, 1690, preserved in the Massachusetts archives, and printed in the third volume of Mr. Whitmore's Andros Tracts. La Potherie, Charlevoix, Golden, Smith, and many others, give accounts at second-hand.

Johannes Sander, or Alexander, Glen, was the son of a Scotchman of good family. He was usually known as Captain Sander. The French wrote the name Cendre, which became transformed into Condre, and then into Coudre. In the old family Bible of the Glens, still preserved at the placed named by them Scotia, near Schenectady, is an entry in Dutch recording the "murders " committed by the French, and the exemption accorded to Alexander Glen on account of services rendered by him and his family to French prisoners. See Proceedings of N. Y. Hist. Soc. t 1846, 118.

The French called Schenectady Corlaer or Corlar, from Van Curler, its founder. Its treatment at their hands was ill deserved, as its inhabitants, and notably Van Curler himself, had from the earliest times been the protectors of French captives among the Mohawks. Leisler says that only one-sixth of the inhabitants escaped unhurt.

snow-shoes, equipped with tomahawk and gun, to chase the retiring French. Fifty young men from Albany joined them; and they followed the trail of the enemy, who, with the help of their horses, made such speed over the ice of Lake Champlain that it seemed impossible to overtake them. They thought the pursuit abandoned ; and, having killed and eaten most of their horses, and being spent with fatigue, they moved more slowly as they neared home, when a band of Mohawks, who had followed stanchly on their track, fell upon a party of stragglers, and killed or captured fifteen or more, almost within sight of Montreal.

Three of these prisoners, examined by Schuyler, declared that Frontenac was preparing for a grand attack on Albany in the spring. In the political confusion of the time, the place was not in fighting condition; and Schuyler appealed for help to the authorities of Massachusetts. " Dear neighbours and friends, we must acquaint you that nevir poor People in the world was in a worse Condition than we are at Present, no Governour nor Command, no money to forward any expedition, and scarce Men enough to maintain the Citty. We have here plainly laid the case before you, and doubt not but you will so much take it to heart, and make all Readinesse in the Spring to invade Canida by water." l The Mohawks were of the same mind. Their elders came down to Albany to condole with their Dutch and English

l Schuyler, Wessell, and Van Rensselaer to the Governor and Council of Massachusetts, 15 Feb., 1690, in Andros Tracts, III. 114.

friends on the late disaster. " We are oome," said their orator, " with tears in our eyes, to lament the murders committed at Schenectady by the perfidious French. Onontio comes to our country to speak of peace, but war is at his heart. He has broken into our house at both ends, once among the Senecas and once here; but we hope to be revenged. Brethren, our covenant with you is a silver chain that cannot rust or break. We are of the race of the bear; and the bear does not yield, so long as there is a drop of blood in his body. Let us all be bears. We will go together with an army to ruin the country of the French. Therefore, send in all haste to New England. Let them be ready with ships and great guns to attack by water, while we attack by land/' l Schuyler did not trust his red allies, who, however, seem on this occasion to have meant what they said. He lost no time in sending commissioners to urge the several governments of New England to a combined attack on the French.

New England needed no prompting to take up arms; for she presently learned to her cost that, though feeble and prostrate, Canada could sting, The war-party which attacked Schenectady was, as we have seen, but one of three which Frontenac had sent against the English borders. The second, aimed at New Hampshire, left Three Rivers on the twenty-eighth of January, commanded by Francois

* Propositions made by the Sachems of y* Maquase (Mohawk) Castles to y* Mayor, Aldermen, and Commonality of y* Citty of Albany, y* 25 day of , 1690 in Doc. Hist. N. Y., II. 164-169.

Hertel. It consisted of twenty-four Frenchmen, twenty Abenakis or the Sokoki band, and five Algonquins. After three months of excessive hardship in the vast and rugged wilderness that intervened, they approached the little settlement of Salmon Falls on the stream which separates New Hampshire from Maine ; and here for a moment we leave them, to observe the state of this unhappy frontier.

It was twelve years and more since the great Indian outbreak, called King Philip's War, had carried havoc through all the borders of New England. After months of stubborn fighting, the fire was quenched in Massachusetts, Plymouth, and Connecticut; but in New Hampshire and Maine it continued to burn fiercely till the treaty of Casco, in 1678. The principal Indians of this region were the tribes known collectively as the Abenakis. The French had established relations with them through the missionaries; and now, seizing the opportunity, they persuaded many of these distressed aiid exasperated savages to leave the neighborhood of the English, migrate to Canada, and settle first at Sillery near Quebec and then at the falls of the Chaudiere. Here the two Jesuits, Jacques and Vincent Bigot, prime agents in their removal, took them in charge; and the missions of St. Francis became villages of Abenaki Christians, like the village of Iroquois Christians at Saut St. Louis. In both cases, the emigrants were -sheltered under the wing of Canada; and they and their tomahawks were always at her service. The two Bigots spared

no pains to induce more of the Abenakis to join these mission colonies. They were in good measure successful, though the great body of the tribe still clung to their ancient homes on the Saco, the Ken-nebec, and the Penobscot. 1

There were ten years of critical and dubious peace along ;the English border, and then the war broke out again.- The occasion of this new uprising is not very clear, and it is hardly worth while to look for it. Between the harsh and reckless borderer on the one side, and the fierce savage on the other, a single spark might at any moment set the frontier in a blaze. The English, however, believed firmly that their French rivals had a hand in the new outbreak; and, in fact, the Abenakis told some of their English captives that Saint-Castin, a French adventurer on the Penobscot, gave every Indian who would go to the war a pound of gunpowder, two pounds of lead, and a supply of tobacco. 2 The trading house of Saint-Castin, which stood on ground claimed by England, had lately been plundered by Sir Edmund Andros, and some of the English had foretold that an Indian war would be the consequence; but none of them seem at this time to have suspected that the governor of Canada and his Jesuit friends had any part in their woes. Yet there is proof that this was the case;

1 The Abenaki migration to Canada began as early as the autumn of 1676 (Relation, 1676-77). On the mission of St. Francis on the Chau-diere, see Bigot, Relation, 1684; Ibid., 1685. It was afterwards removed to the river St. Francis.

a Hutchinson, Hist. Mass., I. 326. Compare N. Y. Col. Docs., IV. 282, 176.

for Denonville himself wrote to the minister at Versailles that the successes of the Abenakis on this occasion were due to the " good understanding which he had with them," by means of the two brothers Bigot and other Jesuits. 1

Whatever were the influences that kindled and maintained the war, it spread dismay and havoc through the English settlements. Andros at first made light of it, and complained of the authorities of Boston, because in his absence they had sent troops to protect the settlers; but he soon changed his mind, and in the winter went himself to the scene of action with seven hundred men. Not an Indian did he find. They had all withdrawn into

1 " En partant de Canada, j'ay laisse* une tres grande disposition & attirer au Christianisme la plus grande partie des sauvages Abenakia qui abitent les bois du voisinage de Baston. Pour cela il faut les attirer k la mission nouvellement 6tablie pres Quebec sous le nom de S. Fran-9ois de Sale. Je l'ai vue en peu de temps au nombre de six cents ames venues du voisinage de Baston. Je l'ay laissee en estat d'augmenter beaucoup si elle est protegee ; j'y ai fait quelque depense qui n'est pa§ inutile. La bonne intelligence que fai eue avec ces sauvages par les soins des J&uites, et surtout des deux peres Bigot freres a fait le succes de toutes les at-toques qu'ils ont faites stir les Anglois cet este", aux quels ils ont enleve' 16 forts, outre celuy de Pemcuit (Pemaquid) ou il y avoit 20 pieces de canon, et leur ont tu£ plus de 200 hommes." Denonville au Ministre, Jan., 1690.

It is to be observed that this Indian outbreak began in the summer of 1688, when there was peace between France and England. News of the declaration of war did not reach Canada till July, 1689. (Belmont.) Dover and other places were attacked in June of the same year.

The intendant Champigny says that most of the Indians who attacked the English were from the mission villages near Quebec. Champigny au Ministre, 16 Nov., 1689. He says also that he supplied them with gunpowder for the war.

The " forts " taken by the Indians on the Kennebec at this time were nothing but houses protected by palisades. They were taken by treachery and surprise. Lettre du Pere Thury, 1689. Thury says that 142 men, women, and children were killed.

the depths of the frozen forest. Andros did what he could, and left more than five hundred men in garrison on the Kennebec and the Saco, at Casco Bay, Pemaquid, and various other exposed points. He then returned to Boston, where surprising events awaited him. Early in April, news came that the Prince of Orange had landed in England. There was great excitement. The people of the town rose against Andros, whom they detested as the agent of the despotic policy of James II. They captured his two forts with their garrisons of regulars, seized his frigate in the harbor, placed him and his chief adherents in custody, elected a council of safety, and set at its head their former governor, Brad street, an old man of eighty-seven. The change was disastrous to the eastern frontier. Of the garrisons left for its protection the winter before, some were partially withdrawn by the new council; while others, at the first news of the revolution, mutinied, seized their officers, and returned home. 1 These garrisons were withdrawn or reduced,

1 Andros, Account of Forces in Maine, in 3 Mass. Hist. Coll., I. 86. Compare Andros Tracts, I. 177; Ibid., II. 181, 193, 207, 213, 217; Ibid., III. 232; Report of Andros in N. Y. Col. Docs., III. 722. The order for the reduction of the garrisons and the return of the suspected officers was passed at the first session of the council of safety, 20 April. The agents of Massachusetts at London endeavored to justify it. See Andros Tracts, in. 34. The only regular troops in New England were two companies brought by Andros. Most of them were kept at Boston, though a few men and officers were sent to the eastern garrison. These regulars were regarded with great jealousy, and denounced as " a crew that began to teach New England to Drab, Drink, Blaspheme, Curse, and Damm." Ibid., II. 50.

In their hatred of Andros, many of the people of New England held the groundless and foolish belief that he was in secret collusion with the French and Indians. Their most dangerous domestic enemies were some of their own traders, who covertly sold arms and ammunition to the Indians.

partly perhaps because the hated governor had established them, partly through distrust of his officers, some of whom were taken from the regulars, and partly because the men were wanted at Boston. The order of withdrawal cannot be too strongly condemned. It was a part of the bungling inefficiency which marked the military management of the New England governments from the close of Philip's war to the peace of Utrecht.

When spring opened, the Indians turned with redoubled fury against the defenceless frontier, seized the abandoned stockades, and butchered the helpless settlers. Now occurred the memorable catastrophe at Cocheco, or Dover. Two squaws came at evening and begged lodging in the palisaded house of Major Waldron. At night, when all was still, they opened the gates and let in their savage countrymen. Waldron was eighty years old. He leaped from his bed, seized his sword, and drove back the assailants through two rooms; but, as he turned to snatch his pistols, they stunned him by the blow of a hatchet, bound him in an arm-chair, and placed him on a table, where after torturing him they killed him with his own sword.

The crowning event of the war was the capture of Pemaquid, a stockade work, mounted with seven or eight cannon. Andros had placed in it a garrison of a hundred and fifty-six men, under an officer devoted to him. Most of them had been withdrawn by the council of safety; and the entire force of the defenders consisted of Lieutenant James Weems and thirty soldiers, nearly half of whom

appear to have been absent at the time of the attack. 1 The Indian assailants were about a hundred in number, all Christian converts from mission villages. By a sudden rush, they got possession of a number of houses behind the fort, occupied only by women and children, the men being at their work. 2 Some ensconced themselves in the cellars, and others behind a rock on the seashore, whence they kept up a close and galling fire. On the next day, Weems surrendered, under a promise of life, and, as the English say, of liberty to himself and all his followers. The fourteen men who had survived the fire, along with a number of women and children, issued from the gate, upon which some were butchered on the spot, and the rest, excepting Weems and a few others, were made prisoners. In other respects, the behavior of the victors is said to have been creditable. They tortured nobody, and their chiefs broke the rum barrels in the fort, to prevent disorder. Father Thury, a priest of the seminary of Quebec, was present at the attack.; and the assailants were a part of his Abenaki flock. Religion was one of the impelling forces of the war. In the eyes of the Indian converts, it

1 Andros in 3 Mass. Hist. Coll., I. 85. The original commanding officer, Brockholes, was reputed a " papist." Hence his removal. Andros Tracts, III. 35. Andros says that but eighteen men were left in the fort. A list of them in the archives of Massachusetts, certified by Weems himself, shows that there were thirty. Doubt is thrown on this certificate by the fact that the object of it was to obtain a grant of money in return for advances of pay made by Weems to his soldiers. Weems was a regular officer. A number of letters from him, showing his condition before the attack, will be found in Johnston, History of Bristol, Bremen, and Pemaquid.

2 Captivity of John Gyles. Gyles was one of the inhabitants.

15

was a crusade against the enemies of God. They made their vows to the Virgin before the fight; and the squaws, in their distant villages on the Penobscot, told unceasing beads, and offered unceasing prayers for victory. 1

The war now ran like wildfire through the settlements of Maine and New Hampshire. Sixteen fortified houses, with or without defenders, are said to have fallen into the hands of the enemy; and the extensive district then called the county of Cornwall was turned to desolation. Massachusetts and Plymouth sent hasty levies of raw men, ill-armed and ill-officered, to the scene of action. At Casco Bay, they met a large body of Indians, whom they routed after a desultory fight of six hours; and then, as the approaching winter seemed to promise a respite from attack, most of them were withdrawn and disbanded.

1 Thiiiy, Relation du Combat des Canibas. Compare Hutchinson, Hist Mass., I. 352, and Mather, Magnalia, II. 690 (ed. 1853). The murder of prisoners after the capitulation has been denied. Thury incidentally confirms the statement, when, after saying that he exhorted the Indians to refrain from drunkenness and cruelty, he adds that, in consequence, they did not take a single scalp, and " tuerent sur le champ ceux qu'ils voulurent tver."

English accounts place the number of Indians at from two to three hundred. Besides the persons taken in the fort, a considerable number were previously killed, or captured in the houses and fields. Those who were spared were carried to the Indian towns on the Penobscot, the seat of Thury's mission. La Motte-Cadillac, in his Mtmoire sur I'Acadie, 1692, Bays that 80 persons in all were killed; an evident exaggeration. He adds that Weems and six men were spared at the request of the chief, Madockawando. The taking of Pemaquid is remarkable as one of the very rare instances in which Indians have captured a fortified place otherwise than by treachery or surprise. The exploit was undoubtedly due to French prompting. We shall see hereafter with what energy and success Thury incited his flock to war.

It was a false and fatal security. Through snow and ice and storm, Hertel and his band were moving on their prey. On the night of the twenty-seventh of March, they lay hidden in the forest that bordered the farms and clearings of Salmon Falls. Their scouts reconnoitred the place, and found a fortified house with two stockade forts-built as a refuge for the settlers in case of alarm. Towards daybreak, Hertel, dividing his followers into three parties, made a sudden and simultaneous attack. The settlers, unconscious of danger, were in their beds. No watch was kept even in the so-called forts; and, when the French and Indians burst in, there was no time for their few tenants to gather for defence. The surprise was complete; and, after a short struggle, the assailants were successful at every point. They next turned upon the scattered farms of the neighborhood, burned houses, barns, and cattle, and laid the entire settlement in ashes. About thirty persons of both sexes and all ages were tomahawked or shot ;• and fifty-four, chiefly women and children, were made prisoners. Two Indian scouts now brought word that a party of English was advancing to the scene of havoc from Piscataqua, or Portsmouth, not many miles distant. Hertel called his men together, and began his retreat. The pursuers, a hundred and forty in number, overtook him about sunset at Wooster River, where the swollen stream was crossed by a narrow bridge. Hertel and his followers made a stand on the farther bank, killed and wounded a number of the Eng-

lish as they attempted to cross, kept up a brisk fire on the rest, held them in check till night, and then continued their retreat. The prisoners, or some of them, were given to the Indians, who tortured one or more of the men, and killed and tormented children und infants with a cruelty not always equalled by their heathen countrymen. 1

Hertel continued his retreat to one of the Abenaki villages on the Kennebec. Here he learned that a band of French and Indians had lately passed southward on their way to attack the English fort at Casco Bay, on the site of Portland. Leaving at the village his eldest son, who had been badly wounded at Wooster River, he set out to join them with thirty-six of his followers. The band in question was Frontenac's third war-party. It consisted of fifty French and sixty Abenakis from the mission of St. Francis; and it had left Quebec in January, under a Canadian officer named

1 The archives of Massachusetts contain various papers on the disaster at Salmon Falls. Among them is the report of the authorities of Portsmouth to the governor and council at Boston, giving many particulars, and asking aid. They estimate the killed and captured at upwards of eighty, of whom about one fourth were men. They say that about twenty houses were burnt, aud mention but one fort. The other, mentioned in the French accounts, was probably a palisaded house. Speaking of the combat at the bridge, they say, " We fought as long as we could distinguish friend from foe. We lost two killed and six or seven wounded, one mortally." The French accounts say fourteen. This letter is accompanied by the examination of a French prisoner, taken the same day. Compare Mather, Magnolia, II. 695; Belknap, Hist. New Hampshire, I. 207 ; Journal of Rev. John Pike (Proceedings of Mass. Hist. Soc. 1875); and the French accounts of Monseignat and La Potherie. Charlevoix adds various embellishments, not to be found in the original sources. Later writers copy and improve upon him, until Hertel is pictured as charging the pursuers sword in hand, while the English fly in disorder before him.

Portneuf and his lieutenant, Courtemanche. They advanced at their leisure, often stopping to hunt, till in May they were joined on the Kennebec by a large body of Indian warriors. On the twenty-fifth, Portneuf encamped in the forest near the English forts, with a force which, including Hertel's party, the Indians of the Kennebec, and another band led by Saint-Castin from the Penobscot, amounted to between four and five hundred men. 1 Fort Loyal was a palisade work with eight cannon, standing on rising ground by the shore of the bay, at what is now the foot of India Street in the city of Portland. Not far distant were four blockhouses and a village which they were designed to protect. These with the fort were occupied by about a hundred men, chiefly settlers of the neighborhood, under Captain Sylvanus Davis, a prominent trader. Around lay rough and broken fields stretching to the skirts of the forest half a mile distant. Some of Portneuf s scouts met a straggling Scotchman, and could not resist the temptation of killing him. Their scalp-yells alarmed the garrison, and thus the advantage of surprise was lost. Davis resolved to keep his men within their defences, and to stand on his guard; but there was little or no discipline in the yeoman garrison, and thirty young volunteers under Lieutenant Thad-deus Clark sallied out to find the enemy. They were too successful; for, as they approached the top of a hill near the woods, they observed a number of cattle staring with a scared look at some

1 Declaration of Sylvanus Davis ; Mather Magnolia, II. 603.

object on the farther side of a fence; and, rightly judging that those they sought were hidden there, they raised a cheer, and ran to the spot. They were met by a fire .so close and deadly that half their number were shot down. A crowd of Indians leaped the fence and rushed upon the survivors, who ran for the fort; but only four, all of whom were wounded, succeeded in reaching it. 1

The men in the blockhouses withdrew under cover of night to Fort Loyal, where the whole force of the English was now gathered along with their frightened families. Portneuf determined to besiege the place in form; and, after burning the village, and collecting tools from the abandoned blockhouses, he opened his trenches in a deep gully within fifty yards of the fort, where his men were completely protected. They worked so well that in three days they had wormed their way close to the palisade; and, covered as they were in their burrows, they lost scarcely a man, while their enemies suffered severely. They now summoned the fort to surrender. Davis asked for a delay of six days, which was refused; and in the morning the fight began again. For a time the fire was sharp and heavy. The English wasted much powder in vain efforts to dislodge the besiegers from their trenches; till at length, seeing a machine loaded with a tar-barrel and other combustibles shoved against their palisades, they asked for a parley. Up to this time, Davis had supposed that his assailants were all Indians, the French being probably

1 Relation de Monseignat, La Potherie, in. 79.

dressed and painted like their red allies. " We demanded/' he says, " if there were any French among them, and if they would give us quarter. They answered that they were Frenchmen, and that they would give us good quarter. Upon this, we sent out to them again to know from whence they came, and if they would give us good quarter for our men, women, and children, both wounded and sound, and (to demand) that we should have liberty to march to the next English town, and have a guard for our defence and safety; then we would surrender; and also that the governour of the French should hold up his hand and swear by the great and ever living God that the several articles should be performed: all which he did solemnly swear."

The survivors of the garrison now filed through the gate, and laid down their arms. They with their women and children were thereupon abandoned to the Indians, who murdered many of them, and carried off the rest. When Davis protested against this breach of faith, he was told that he and his countrymen were rebels against their lawful king, James II. After spiking the cannon, burning the fort, and destroying all the neighboring settlements, the triumphant aUies departed for their respective homes, leaving the slain unburied where they had fallen. 1

1 Their remains were buried by Captain Church, three years later.

On the capture of Fort Loyal, compare Monseignat and La Potherie with Mather, Magnalia, II. 603, and the Declaration of Sylvanus Davis, in 3 Mass. Hist. Coll., I. 101. Davis makes curious mistakes in regard to French names, his rustic ear not being accustomed to the accents of the Gallic tongue. He calls Courtemanche, Monsieur Corte de March, and

Davis with three or four others, more fortunate than their companions, was kept by the French, and carried to Canada. " They were kind to ine," he says, " on my travels through the country. I arrived at Quebeck the 14th of June, where I was civilly treated by the gentry, and soon carried to the fort before the governour, the Earl of Fron-tenack." Frontenac told him that the governor and people of New York were the cause of the war, since they had stirred up the Iroquois against Canada, and prompted them to torture French prisoners. 1 Davis replied that New York and New England were distinct and separate governments, each of which must answer for its own deeds; and that New England would gladly have remained at peace with the French, if they had not set on the Indians to attack her peaceful settlers. Frontenac admitted that the people of New England were not to be regarded in the same light with those who had stirred up the Indians against Canada; but he added that they were all rebels to their king, and that if they had been good subjects there would have been no war. " I do believe,"

Portneuf, Monsieur Burniffe or Burneffe. To these contemporary authorities may be added the account given by Le Clercq, titablissement de, la Foy, II. 393, and a letter from Governor Bradstreet of Massachusetts to Jacob Leisler in Doc. Hist. N. Y., II. 259. The French writers of course say nothing of any violation of faith on the part of the victors, but they admit that the Indians kept most of the prisoners. Scarcely was the fort taken, when four English vessels appeared in the harbor, too late to save it. Willis, in his History of Portland (ed. 1865), gives a map of Fort Loyal and the neighboring country. In the Massachusetts archives is a letter from Davis, written a few days before the attack, complaining that his fort is in wretched condition.

observes the captive Puritan, " that there was a popish design against the Protestant interest in New England as in other parts of the world/' He told Frontenac of the pledge given by his conqueror, and the violation of it. " We were promised good quarter," he reports himself to have said, " and a guard to conduct us to our English ; but now we are made captives and slaves in the hands of the heathen. I thought I had to do with Christians that would have been careful of their engagements, and not to violate and break their oaths. Whereupon the governour shaked his head, and, as I was told, was very angry with Burniffe (Port-neuf)."

Frontenac was pleased with his prisoner, whom he calls a bonhomme. He told him in broken English to take courage, and promised him good treatment; to which Davis replied that his chief con-.cern was not for himself, but for the captives in the hands of the Indians. Some of these were afterwards ransomed by the French, and treated with much kindness, as was also Davis himself, to whom the count gave lodging in the chateau.

The triumphant success of his three war-parties produced on the Canadian people all the effect that Frontenac had expected. This effect was very apparent, even before the last two victories had become known. " You cannot believe, Mon-seigneur," wrote the governor, speaking of the capture of Schenectady, " the joy that this slight success has caused, and how much it contributes to raise the people from their dejection and terror."

One untoward accident damped the general joy for a moment. A party of Iroquois Christians from the Saut St. Louis had made a raid against the English borders, and were returning with prisoners. One evening, as they were praying at their camp near Lake Champlain, they were discovered by a band of Algonquins and Abenakis who were out on a similar errand, and who, mistaking them for enemies, set upon them and killed several of their number, among whom was Kryn, the great Mohawk, chief of the mission of the Saut. This mishap was near causing a rupture between the best Indian allies of the colony; but the difference was at length happily adjusted, and the relatives of the slain propitiated by gifts. 1

1 The attacking party consisted of some of the Abenakis and Algonquins who had been with Hertel, and who had left the main body after the destruction of Salmon Falls. Several of - hem were killed in the skirmish, and among the ,re8t their chief, Hope hood, or Wohawa, " that memorable tygre." as Cotton Mather calls him.

CHAPTER XH.

1690.

MASSACHUSETTS ATTACKS QUEBEC.

ENGLISH SCHEMES. — CAPTURE OP PORT ROYAL. — ACADIA SEDUCED. — CONDUCT OF PHIPS. — His HISTORY AND CHARACTER. — BOSTON IN ARMS. — A PURITAN CRUSADE. — THE MARCH FROM ALBANY. — FRONTENAC AND THE COUNCIL. — FRONTENAC AT MONTREAL. — His WAR DANCE. — AN ABORTIVE 'EXPEDITION. — AN ENGLISH RAID. — FRONTENAC AT QUEBEC. — DEFENCES OF THE TOWN. — THE ENEMY ARRIVES. «

WHEN Frontenac sent his war-parties against New York and New England, it was in the hope not only of reanimating the Canadians, but also of teaching the Iroquois that they could not safely rely on English aid, and of inciting the Abenakis to renew their attacks on the border settlements. He imagined, too, that the British colonies could be chastised into prudence and taught a policy of conciliation towards their Canadian neighbors; but he mistook the character of these bold and vigorous though not martial communities. The plan of a combined attack on Canada seems to have been first proposed by the Iroquois ; and New York and the several governments of New England, smarting under French and Indian attacks, hastened to embrace it. Early in May, a congress of their delegates was held in the city of New York. It

was agreed that the colony of that name should furnish four hundred men, and Massachusetts, Plymouth, and Connecticut three hundred and fifty-five jointly; while the Iroquois afterwards added their worthless pledge to join the expedition with nearly all their warriors. The colonial militia were to rendezvous at Albany, and thence advance upon Montreal by way of Lake Champlain, Mutual jealousies made it difficult to agree upon a commander; but Fitz-John Winthrop of Connecticut was at length placed at the head of the feeble and discordant band.

While Montreal wa"s thus assailed by land, Massa-chusettg and the other New England colonies were invited to attack Quebec by sea; .a task formidable in difficulty and in cost, and one that imposed on them an inordinate share in the burden of the war. Massachusetts hesitated. She had no money, and she was already engaged in a less remote and less critical enterprise. During the winter, her commerce had suffered from French cruisers, which found convenient harborage at Port Royal, whence also the hostile Indians were believed to draw supplies. Seven vessels, with two hundred and eighty-eight sailors, were impressed, and from four to five hundred militia-men were drafted for the service. 1 That rugged son of New England, Sir William Phips, was appointed to the command. He sailed from Nantasket at the end of April, reached Port Royal

1 Summary of Muster Roll, appended to A Journal of the Expedition from Boston against Port Royal, among the papers of George Chalmers In the Library of Harvard College.

on the eleventh of May, landed his militia, and summoned Meneval, the governor, to surrender. The fort, though garrisoned by about seventy soldiers, was scarcely in condition to repel an assault; and Meneval yielded without resistance, first stipulating, according to French accounts, that private property should be respected, the church left untouched, and the troops sent to Quebec or to France. 1 It was found, however, that during the parley a quantity of goods, belonging partly to the king and partly to merchants of the place, had been carried off and hidden in the woods. 2 Phips thought this a sufficient pretext for plundering the merchants, imprisoning the troops, and desecrating the church. " We cut down the cross," writes one of his followers, " rifled their church, pulled down their high altar, and broke their images." 3 The houses of the two priests were also pillaged. The people were promised security to life, liberty, and property, on condition of swearing allegiance to King William and Queen Mary; " which," says the journalist, " they did with great acclamation," and thereupon they were left unmolested. 4 The lawful portion

1 Relation de la Prise du Port Royal par les Anglois de Hasten, pile* anonyme, 27 Mai, 1690.

2 Journal of the Expedition from Boston against Port Royal. 8 Ibid.

4 Relation de Monseignat. Nevertheless, a considerable number seem to have refused the oath, and to have been pillaged. The Relation de la Prise du Port Royal par les Anglois de Baston, written on the spot immediately after the event, says that, except that nobody was killed, the place was treated as if taken by assault. Meneval also says that the inhabitants were pillaged. Meneval au Ministre, 29 Mai, 1690; also Rapport de Champigny, Oct., 1690. Meneval describes the New England men

of the booty included twenty-one pieces of cannon, with a considerable sum of money belonging to the king. The smaller articles, many of which were taken from the merchants and from such of the settlers as refused the oath, were packed in hogsheads and sent on board the ships. Phips took no measures to secure his conquest, though he commissioned a president and BIX councillors, chosen from the inhabitants, to govern the settlement till farther orders from the crown or from the authorities of Massachusetts. The president was directed to constrain nobody in the matter of religion; and he was assured of protection and support so long as he remained " faithful to our government," that is, the government of Massachusetts. 1 The little Puritan commonwealth already gave itself airs of sovereignty.

Phips now sent Captain Alden, who had already taken possession of Saint-Castin's post at Penob-scot, to seize upon La Heve, Chedabucto, and other stations on the southern coast. Then, after providing for the reduction of the settlements at the head of the Bay of Fundy, he sailed, with the rest of the fleet, for Boston, where he arrived triumphant on the thirtieth of May, bringing with him, as prisoners, the French governor, fifty-nine soldiers, and the two priests, Petit and Trouve. Massachusetts had made an easy conquest of all Acadia; a conquest, however, which she had neither

as excessively irritated at the late slaughter of settlers at Salmon Falls and elsewhere.

1 Journal of the Expedition, etc.

the men nor the money to secure by sufficient garrisons.

The conduct of the New England commander in this affair does him no credit. It is true that no blood was spilt, and no revenge taken for the repeated butcheries of unoffending and defenceless settlers. It is true, also, that the French appear to have acted in bad faith. But Phips, on the other hand, displayed a scandalous rapacity. Charle-voix says that he robbed Meneval of all his money; but Meneval himself affirms that he gave it to the •English commander for safe keeping, and that Phips and his wife would return neither the money nor various other articles belonging to the captive governor, whereof the following are specified: " Six silver spoons, six silver forks, one silver cup in the shape of a gondola, a pair of pistols, three new wigs, a gray vest, four pair of silk garters, two dozen of shirts, six vests of dimity, four nightcaps with lace edgings, all my table service of fine tin, all my kitchen linen," and many other items which give an amusing insight into MenevaTis housekeeping. 1

1 An Account of the Silver and Effects which Mr. Phips keeps back from Mr. Meneval, in 3 Mass. Hist. Coll., I. 115.

Monseignat and La Potherie describe briefly this expedition against Port Royal. In the archives of Massachusetts are various papers concerning it, among which are Governor Bradstreet's instructions to Phips, and a complete invoice of the plunder. Extracts will be found in Professor Bo wen's Life of Phips, in Sparks's American Biography, VIL There is also an order of council, " Whereas the French soldiers lately brought to this place from Port Royal did surrender on capitulation," they shall be set at liberty. Meneval, Lettre au Ministre, 29 Mai, 1690, says that there was a capitulation, and that Phips broke it. Perrot, former governor of Acadia, accuses both Meneval and the priest Petit of being

240 MASSACHUSETTS ATTACKS QUEBEC.

Meneval, with the two priests, was confined in a house at Boston, under guard. He says that he petitioned the governor and council for redress; " but, as they have little authority and stand in fear of Phips, who is supported by the rabble, to which he himself once belonged, and of which he is now the chief, they would do nothing for me." This statement of Meneval is not quite correct: for an order of the council is on record, requiring Phips to restore his chest and clothes; and, as the order received no attention, Governor Bradstreet wrote to the refractory commander a note, enjoining him to obey it at once. 2 Phips thereupon gave up some of the money and the worst part of the clothing, stiU keeping the rest. 3 After long-delay, the council released Meneval: upon which, Phips and the populace whom he controlled demanded that he should be again imprisoned; but the " honest people 5 ' of the town took his part, his persecutor was forced to desist, and he set sail covertly for France. 4 This, at least, is his own account of the affair.

As Phips was to play a conspicuous part in the events that immediately followed, some notice of

in collusion with the English. Perrot a de Chevry, 2 Juin, 1690. The same charge is made as regards Petit in Me'moire sur I'Acadie, 1691.

Charlevoix's account of this affair is inaccurate. He ascribes to Phips acts which took place weeks after his return, such as the capture of Chedabucto.

1 Me'moire pr€sent(a M. de Ponchartrain par M. de Meneval, 6 Avril, 1691.

2 This note, dated 7 Jan., 1691, is cited by Bowen in his Lift ofPfiips, Sparks's American Biography, VII.

* Me'moire de Menevdi. « Ibid.

him will not be amiss. He is said to have been one of twenty-six children, all of the same mother, and was born in 1650 at a rude border settlement, since called Woolwich, on the Kennebec. His parents were ignorant and poor; and till eighteen years of age he was employed in keeping sheep. Such a life ill suited his active and ambitious nature. To better his condition, he learned the trade of ship-carpenter, and, in the exercise of it, came to' Boston, where he married a widow with some property, beyond him in years, and much above him in station. About this time, he learned to read and write, though not too well, for his signature is like that of a peasant. Still aspiring to greater things, he promised his wife that he would one day command a king's ship and own a " fair brick house in the Green Lane of North Boston," a quarter then occupied by citizens of the better class. He kept his word at both points. Fortune was inauspicious to him for several years; till at length, under the pressure of reverses, he conceived the idea of conquering fame and wealth at one stroke, by fishing up the treasure said to be stored in a Spanish galleon wrecked fifty years before somewhere in the West Indian seas. Full of this project, he went to England, where, through influences which do not plainly appear, he gained a hearing from persons in high places, and induced the admiralty to adopt his scheme. A frigate was given him, and he sailed for the West Indies; whence, after a long search, he returned unsuccessful, though not without adventures which proved his mettle. It was the epoch of the buccaneers ; and his crew, tired of a vain and toilsome search, came to the quarterdeck, armed with cutlasses, and demanded of their captain that he should turn pirate with them. Phips, a tall and powerful man, instantly fell upon them with his fists, knocked down the ringleaders, and awed them all into submission. Not long after, there was a more formidable mutiny; but, with great courage and address, he quelled it for a time, and held his crew to their duty till he had brought the ship into Jamaica, and exchanged them for better men.

Though the leaky condition of the frigate compelled him to abandon the search, it was not till he had gained information which he thought would lead to success; and, on his return, he inspired such confidence that the Duke of Albemarle, with other noblemen and gentlemen, gave him a fresh outfit, and despatched him again on his Quixotic errand. This time he succeeded, found the wreck, and took from it gold, silver, and jewels to the value of three hundred thousand pounds sterling. The crew now leagued together to seize the ship and divide the prize; and Phips, pushed to extremity, was compelled to promise that every man of them should have a share in the treasure, even if he paid it himself. On reaching England, he kept his pledge so well that, after redeeming it, only sixteen thousand pounds was left as his portion, which, however, was an ample fortune in the New England of that day. He gained, too, what he valued almost as much, the honor of knight-

hood. Tempting offers were made him of employment in the royal service; but he had an ardent love for his own country, and thither he presently returned.

Phips was a rude sailor, bluff, prompt, and choleric. He never gave proof of intellectual capacity; and such of his success in life as he did not owe to good luck was due probably to an energetic and adventurous spirit, aided by a blunt frankness of address that pleased the great, and commended him to their favor. Two years after the expedition to Port Royal, the king, under the new charter, made him governor of Massachusetts, a post for which, though totally unfit, he had been recommended by the elder Mather, who, like his son Cotton, expected to make use of him. He carried his old habits into his new office, cudgelled Brinton, the collector of the port, and belabored Captain Short of the royal navy with his cane. Far from trying to hide the obscurity of his origin, he leaned to the opposite foible, and was apt to boast of it, delighting to exhibit himself as a self-made man. New England writers describe him as honest in private dealings; but, in accordance with his coarse nature, he seems to have thought that any thing is fair in war. On the other hand, he was warmly patriotic, and was almost as ready to serve New England as to serve himself. 1

When he returned from Port Royal, he found

1 An excellent account of Phips will be found in Professor Bowen's biographical notice, already cited. His Life by Cotton Mather is excessively eulogistic.

Boston alive with martial preparation. A bold enterprise was afoot. Massachusetts of her own motion had resolved to attempt the conquest of Quebec. She and her sister colonies had not yet recovered from the exhaustion of Philip's war, and still less from the disorders that attended the expulsion of the royal governor and his adherents. The public treasury was empty, and the recent expeditions against the eastern Indians had been supported by private subscription. Worse yet, New England had no competent military commander. The Puritan-gentlemen of the original emigration, some of whom were as well fitted for military as for civil leadership, had passed from the stage; and, by a tendency which circumstances made inevitable, they had left none behind them equally qualified. The great Indian conflict of fifteen years before had, it is true, formed good partisan chiefs, and proved that the New England yeoman, defending his family and his hearth, was not to be surpassed in stubborn fighting ; but, since Andros and his soldiers had been driven out, there was scarcely a. single man in the colony of the slightest training or experience in regular war. Up to this moment, New England had never asked help of the mother country. When thousands of savages burst on her defenceless settlements, she had conquered safety and peace with her own blood and her own slender resources; but now, as the proposed capture of Quebec would inure to the profit of the British crown, Bradstreet and his council thought it not unfitting to ask for a supply

of arms and ammunition, of which they were in great need. 1 The request was refused, and no aid of any kind came from the English government, whose resources were engrossed by the Irish war. While waiting for the reply, the colonial authorities urged on their preparations, in the hope that the plunder of Quebec would pay the expenses of its conquest. Humility was not among the New England virtues, and it was thought a sin to doubt that God would give his chosen people the victory over papists and idolaters; yet no pains were spared to ensure the divine favor. A proclamation was issued, calling the people to repentance; a day of fasting was ordained; and, as Mather expresses it, "the wheel of prayer was kept in continual motion/' 2 The chief difficulty was to provide funds. An attempt was made to collect a part of the money by private subscription; 3 but, as this plan failed, the provisional government, already in debt, strained its credit yet farther, and borrowed the needful sums. Thirty-two trading and fishing vesse.ls, great and small, were impressed for the service. The largest was a ship called the " Six Friends," engaged in the dangerous West India trade, and carrying forty-four guns. A call was made for volunteers, and many enrolled themselves; but, as more were wanted, a press was ordered to complete the number. So rigorously was it applied

1 Bradstreet and Council to the Earl of Shrewsbury, 29 Mar., 1690; Dan-forth to Sir H. Ashurst, 1 April, 1690.

2 Mass. Colonial Records, 12 Mar., 1690 ; Mather, Life of Phips.

8 Proposals for an Expedition against Canada, in 3 Mass. Hist. Coll, X. 119.

24 f) MASSACHUSETTS ATTACKS QUEBEC. f!690.

that, what with voluntary and enforced enlistment, one town, that of Gloucester, was deprived of two-thirds of its fencible men. 1 There was not a moment of doubt as to the choice of a commander, for Phips was imagined to be the very man for the work. One John Walley, a respectable citizen of Barristable, was made second in command with the modest rank of major; and a sufficient number of ship-masters, merchants, master mechanics, and substantial farmers, were commissioned as subordinate officers. About the middle of July, the, committee charged with the preparations reported that all was ready. Still there was a long delay. The vessel sent early in spring to ask aid from England had not returned. Phips waited for her as long as he dared, and the best of the season was over when he resolved to put to sea. The rustic warriors, duly formed into companies, were sent on board; and the fleet sailed from Nantasket on the ninth of August. Including sailors, it carried twenty-two hundred men, with provisions for four months, but insufficient ammunition and no pilot for the St. Lawrence. 9

While Massachusetts was making ready to conquer Quebec by sea, the militia of the land expedition against Montreal had mustered at Albany.

1 RPV. John Emerson to Wait Winthrop, 26 July, 1690. Emerson was the minister of Gloucester. He begs for the release of the impressed men.

* Mather, Life of Phips, gives an account of the outfit. Compare the Humble Address of Divers of the Gentry, Merchants and others inhabiting in Boston, to the King's Most Excellent Majesty. Two officers of the expedition, Walley and Savage, have left accounts of it, as Phips

would probably have done, had his literary acquirements been equal to the task.

Their strength was even less than was at first proposed; for, after the disaster at Casco, Massachusetts and Plymouth had recalled their contingents to defend their frontiers. The rest, decimated by dysentery and small-pox, began their march to Lake Champlain, with bands of Mohawk, Oneida, and Mohegan allies. The western Iroquois were to join them at the lake, and the combined force was then to attack the head of the colony, while Phips struck at its heart.

Frontenac was at Quebec during most of the winter and the early spring. When he had despatched the three war-parties, whose hardy but murderous exploits were to bring this double storm upon him, he had an interval of leisure, of which he made a characteristic use. The English and the Iroquois were not his only enemies. He had opponents within as well as without, and he counted as among them most of the members of the supreme council. Here was the bishop, representing that clerical power which had clashed so often with the civil rule ; here was that ally of the Jesuits, the intendant Champigny, who, when Frontenac arrived, had written mournfully to Versailles that he would do his best to live at peace with him; here were Villeray and Auteuil, whom the governor had once banished, Damours, whom he had imprisoned, and others scarcely more agreeable to him. They and their clerical friends had conspired for his recall seven or eight years before; they had clung to Denonville, that faithful son of the Church, in spite of all his failures ; and they had

seen with troubled minds the return of King Stork in the person of the haughty and irascible count. He on his part felt his power. The country was in deadly need of him, and looked to him for salvation ; while the king had shown him such marks of favor, that, for the moment at least, his enemies must hold their peace. Now, therefore, was the time to teach them that he was their master. Whether trivial or important the occasion mattered little. What he wanted was a conflict and a victory, or submission without a conflict.

The supreme council had held its usual weekly meetings since Frontenac's arrival; but as yet he had not taken his place at the board, though his presence was needed. Auteuil, the attorney-general, was thereupon deputed to invite him. He visited the count at his apartment in the chateau, but could get from him no answer, except that the council was able to manage its own business, and that he would come when the king's service should require it. The councillors divined that he was waiting for some assurance that they would receive him with befitting ceremony; and, after debating the question, they voted to send four of their number to repeat the invitation, and beg the governor to say what form of reception would be agreeable to him. Frontenac answered that it was for them to propose the form, and that, when they did so, he would take the subject into consideration. The deputies returned, and there was another debate. A ceremony was devised, which it was thought must needs be acceptable to the count; and the

first councillor, Villeray, repaired to the chateau to submit it to him. After making him an harangue of compliment, and protesting the anxiety of himself and his colleagues to receive him with all possible honor, he explained the plan, and assured Frontenac that, if not wholly satisfactory, it should be changed to suit his pleasure. " To which," says the record, " Monsieur the governor only answered that the council could consult the bishop and other persons acquainted with such matters." The bishop was consulted, but pleaded ignorance. Another debate followed; and the first councillor was again despatched to the chateau, with proposals still more deferential than the last, and full power to yield, in addition, whatever the governor might desire. Frontenac replied that, though they had made proposals for his reception when he should present himself at the council for the first time, they had not informed him what ceremony they meant to observe when he should come to the subsequent sessions. This point also having been thoroughly debated, Yilleray went again to the count, and with great deference laid before him the following plan : That, whenever it should be his pleasure to make his first visit to the council, four of its number should repair to the chateau, and accompany him, with every mark of honor, to the palace of the intendant, where the sessions were held; and that, on his subsequent visits, two councillors should meet him at the head of the stairs, and conduct him to his seat. The envoy farther protested that, if this failed to meet his approval, the council would conform itself to

all his wishes on the subject. Frontenac now demanded to see the register in which the proceedings on the question at issue were recorded. Villeray was directed to carry it to him. The records had been cautiously made; and, after studying them carefully, he could find nothing at which to cavil.

- He received the next deputation with great affability, told them that he was glad to find that the council had not forgotten the consideration due to his office and his person, and assured them, with urbane irony, that, had they offered to accord him marks of distinction greater than they felt were due, he would not have permitted them thus to compromise their dignity, having too much regard for the honor of a body of which he himself waa the head. Then, after thanking them collectively and severally, he graciously dismissed them, saying that he would come to the council after Easter, or in about two months. 1 During four successive Mondays, he had forced the chief dignitaries of the colony to march in deputations up and down the rugged road from the intendant's palace to the

1 " M. le Gouverneur luy a repondu qu'il avoit reconnu avec plaisir que la Compagnie (lc Conseil) conservoit la consideration qu'elle avoit pour son caractere et pour sa personne, et qu'elle pouvoit bien s'assurer qu'en-core qu'elle luy eust fait des propositions au dela de ce qu'elle auroit cru devoir faire pour sa reception au Conseil, il ne les auroit pas acceptees, 1'honneur de la Compagnie luy estant d'autant plus considerable, qu'en estant le chef, il n'auroit rien voulu souffrir qui peust estre contraire k sa digniteV' Registre du Conseil Souverain, stance du 13 Mars, 1690. The affair had occupied the preceding sessions of 20 and 27 February and 6 March. The submission of the councillors did not prevent them from complaining to the minister. Champiyny au Ministre, 10 Mai, 1691; Me'moire instructif sur le Canada, 1691.

chamber of the chateau where he sat in solitary state. A disinterested spectator might see the humor of the situation ; but the council felt only its vexations. Frontenac had gained his point: the enemy had surrendered unconditionally.

Having settled this important matter to his satisfaction, he again addressed himself to saving the country. During the winter, he had employed gangs of men in cutting timber in the forests, hewing it into palisades, and dragging it to Quebec. Nature had fortified the Upper Town on two sides by cliffs almost inaccessible, but it was open to attack in the rear; and Frontenac, with a happy prevision of approaching danger, gave his first thoughts to strengthening this, its only weak side. The work began as soon as the frost was out of the ground, and before midsummer it was well advanced. At the same time, he took every precaution for the safety of the settlements in the upper parts of the colony, stationed detachments of regulars at the stockade forts, which Denonville had built in all the parishes above Three Rivers, and kept strong scouting parties in continual movement in all the quarters most exposed to attack. Troops were detailed to guard the settlers at their work in the fields, and officers and men were enjoined to use the utmost vigilance. Nevertheless, the Iroquois war-parties broke in at various points, burning and butchering, and spreading such terror that in some districts the fields were left untilled and the prospects of the harvest ruined.

Towards the end of July, Frontenac left Major

Provost to finish the fortifications, and, with the intendant Champigny, went up to Montreal, the chief point of danger. Here he arrived on the thirty-first; and, a few days after, the officer commanding the fort at La Chine sent him a messenger in hot haste with the startling news that Lake St. Louis was " all covered with canoes." J Nobody doubted that the Iroquois were upon them again. Cannon were fired to call in the troops from the detached posts; when alarm was suddenly turned to joy by the arrival of other messengers to announce that the new comers were not enemies, but friends. They were the Indians of the upper lakes descending from Michillimackinac to trade at Montreal. Nothing so auspicious had happened since Frontenac's return. The messages he had sent them in the spring by Louvigny and Perrot, reinforced by the news of the victory on the Ottawa and the capture of Schenectady, had had the desired effect; and the Iroquois prisoner whom their missionary had persuaded them to torture had not been sacrificed in vain. Despairing of an English market for their beaver skins, they had come as of old to seek one from the French.

On the next day, they all came down the rapids, and landed near the town. There were fully five hundred of them, Hurons, Ottawas, Ojibwas, Potta-watamies, Crees, and Nipissings, with a hundred and ten canoes laden with beaver skins to the value of nearly a hundred thousand crowns. Nor was

1 " Que le lac estoit tout couvert de canote " Frontenac CM Mlnistt-p, 9 et 12 Nov., 1690.

this all; for, a few days after, La Durantaye, late commander at Michillimackinac, arrived with fifty-five more canoes, manned by French traders, and filled with valuable furs. The stream of wealth dammed back so long was flowing upon the colony at the moment when it was most needed. Never had Canada known a more prosperous trade than now in the midst of her danger and tribulation. It was a triumph for Frontenac. If his policy had failed with the Iroquois, it had found a crowning success among the tribes of the lakes.

Having painted, greased, and befeathered themselves, the Indians mustered for the grand council which always preceded the opening of the market. The Ottawa orator spoke of nothing but trade, and, with a regretful memory of the cheapness of English goods, begged that the French would sell them at the same rate. The Huron touched upon politics and war, declaring that he and his people had come to visit their old father and listen to his voice, being well assured that he would never abandon them, as others had done, nor fool away his time, like Denonville, in shameful negotiations for peace ; and he exhorted Frontenac to fight, not the English only, but the Iroquois also, till they were brought to reason. " If this is not done," he said, " my father and I shall both perish; but, come what may, we will perish together." i " I answered," writes Frontenac, " that I would fight the Iroquois till they came to beg for peace,

1 La Potherie, III. 94; Monseignat, Relation ; Frontenac au Ministre 9 et 12 Nov.. 1690.

and that I would grant them no peace that did not include all my children, both white and red, for I was the father of both alike."

Now ensued a curious scene. Frontenac took a hatchet, brandished it in the air and sang the war-song. The principal Frenchmen present followed his example. The Christian Iroquois of the two neighboring missions rose and joined them, and so also did the Hurons and the Algonquins of Lake Ni-pissing, stamping and screeching like a troop of madmen; while the governor led the dance, whooping like the rest. His predecessor would have perished rather than play such a part in such company ; but the punctilious old courtier was himself half Indian at heart, as much at home in a wigwam as in the halls of princes. Another man would have lost respect in Indian eyes by such a performance. In Frontenac, it roused his audience to enthusiasm. They snatched the proffered hatchet and promised war to the death. 1

Then came a solemn war-feast. Two oxen and six large dogs had been chopped to pieces for the occasion, and boiled with a quantity of prunes. Two

1 " Je leur mis moy-mesme la hache a la main en chantant la chanson de guerre pour m'accommoder a leurs fa9ons de faire " Frontenac au Mi-nittre, 9 et 12 Nov., 1690.

" Monsieur de Frontenac commensa la Chanson de guerre, la Hache a la main, les principaux Chefs des Francois se joignant a luy avec de pareilles armes, la chanterent ensemble. Les Iroquois du Saut et de la Montagne, les Hurons et les Nipisiriniens donnerent encore le branle: Ton cut dit, Monsieur, que ces Acteurs etoient des possedez par lei gestes et les contorsions qu'ils faisoient. Les Sussakouez, oil les cris et les hurlemens que M* de Frontenac e'toit oblig£ de faire pour se confer mer a leur maniere, augmentoit encore la fureur bachique." La Po-therie, ill. 97

barrels of wine with abundant tobacco were also served out to the guests, who devoured the meal in a species of frenzy. 1 All seemed eager for war except the Ottawas, who had not forgotten their late dalliance with the Iroquois. A Christian Mohawk of the Saut St. Louis called them to another council, and demanded that they should explain clearly their position. Thus pushed to the wall, they no longer hesitated, but promised like the rest to do all that their father should ask.

Their sincerity was soon put to the test. An Iroquois convert called La Plaque, a notorious reprobate though a good warrior, had gone out as a scout in the direction of Albany. On the day when the market opened and trade was in full activity, the buyers and sellers were suddenly startled by the sound of the death-yell. They snatched their weapons, and for a moment all was confusion; when La Plaque, who had probably meant to amuse himself at their expense, made his appearance, and explained that the yells proceeded from him. The news that he brought was, however, sufficiently alarming. He declared that he had been at Lake St. Sacrement, or Lake George, and had seen there a great number of men making canoes as if about to advance on Montreal. Frontenac, thereupon, sent the Chevalier de Clermont to scout as far as Lake Champlain. Clermont soon sent back one of his followers to announce that he had discovered a party of the enemy, and that they were already on their way down the Richelieu. Frontenac ordered

* La Potherie, III. 96, 98.

MASSACHUSETTS ATTACKS QUEBEC- [1690.

cannon to be fired to call in the troops, crossed the St. Lawrence followed by all the Indians, and encamped with twelve hundred men at La Prairie to meet the expected attack. He waited in vain. All was quiet, and the Ottawa scouts reported that they could find no enemy. Three days passed. The Indians grew impatient, and wished to go home. Neither English nor Iroquois had shown themselves; and Frontenac, satisfied that their strength had been exaggerated, left a small force at La Prairie, recrossed the river, and distributed the troops again among the neighboring parishes to protect the harvesters. He now gave ample presents to his departing allies, whose chiefs he had entertained at his own table, and to whom, says Charlevoix, he bade farewell " with those engaging manners which he knew so well how to assume when he wanted to gain anybody to his interest." Scarcely were they gone, when the distant cannon of La Prairie boomed a sudden alarm.

The men whom La Plaque had seen near Lake George were a part of the combined force of Connecticut and New York, destined to attack Montreal. They had made their way along Wood Creek to the point where it widens into Lake Champlain, and here they had stopped. Disputes between the men of the two colonies, intestine quarrels in the New York militia, who were divided between the two factions engendered by the late revolution, the want of provisions, the want of canoes, and the ravages of small-pox, had ruined an enterprise which had been mismanaged from the first. There

was no birch bark to make more canoes, and owing to the lateness of the season the bark of the elms would not peel. Such of the Iroquois as had joined them were cold and sullen; and news came that the three western tribes of the confederacy, terrified by the small-pox, had refused to move. It was impossible to advance ; and Winthrop, the commander, gave orders to return to Albany, leaving Phips to conquer Canada alone. 1 But first, that the campaign might not seem wholly futile, he permitted Captain John Schuyler to make a raid into Canada with a band of volunteers. Schuyler left the camp at Wood Creek with twenty-nine whites and a hundred and twenty Indians, passed Lake Champlain, descended the Eichelieu to Cham-bly, and fell suddenly on the settlement of La Prairie, whence Frontenac had just withdrawn with his forces. Soldiers and inhabitants were reaping in the wheat-fields. Schuyler and his followers killed or captured twenty-five, including several

1 On this expedition see the Journal of Major General Winthrop, in N. Y. Col. Docs., IV. 193; Publick Occurrences, 1690, in Historical Magazine, I. 228; and various documents in N. Y. Col. Docs., III. 727, 762, and in Doc. Hist. N. Y., II. 266,288. Compare La Potherie, III. 126, and N. Y. Col. Docs., IX. 513. These last are French statements. A Sokoki Indian brought to Canada a greatly exaggerated account of the English forces, and said that disease had been spread among them by boxes of infected clothing, which they themselves had provided in order to poison the Canadians. Bishop Laval, Lettre du 20 Nov., 1690, says that there was a quarrel between the English and their Iroquois allies, who, having plundered a magazine of spoiled provisions, fell ill, and thought that they were poisoned. Golden and other English writers seem to have been strangely ignorant of this expedition. The Jesuit Michel Germain declares that the force of the English alone amounted to four thousand men (Relation de la Dffaite des Anglois, 1690). About one tenth of this number seem actually to have taken the field.

17

MASSACHUSETTS ATTACKS QUEBEC. [1690.

women. He wished to attack the neighboring fort, but his Indians refused; and after burning houses, barns, and hay-ricks, and killing a great number of cattle, he seated himself with his party at dinner in the adjacent woods, while cannon answered cannon from Chambly, La Prairie, and Montreal, and the whole country was astir. " We thanked the Governor of Canada," writes Schuyler, "for his salute of heavy artillery during our meal."

The English had little to boast in this affair, the paltry termination of an enterprise from which great things had been expected. Nor was it for their honor to adopt the savage and cowardly mode of warfare in which their enemies had led the way. The blow that had been struck was less an injury to the French than an insult; but, as such, it galled Frontenac excessively, and he made no mention of it in his despatches to the court. A few more Iro-quois attacks and a few more murders kept Montreal in alarm till the tenth of October, when matters of deeper import engaged the governor's thoughts.

A messenger arrived in haste at three o'clock in the afternoon, and gave him a letter from Provost, town major of Quebec. It was to the effect that an Abenaki Indian had just come over land from Acadia, with news that some of his tribe had captured an English woman near Portsmouth, who told them that a great fleet had sailed from Boston to attack Quebec. Frontenac, not easily alarmed, doubted the report. Nevertheless, he embarked

1 Journal of Captain John Schuyler, in Doc. Hist. N. Y., II. 285. Compare La Potherie,

at once with the intendant in a small vessel, which proved to be leaky, and was near foundering with all on board. He then took a canoe, and towards evening set out again for Quebec, ordering some two hundred men to follow him. On the next day, he met another canoe, bearing a fresh message from Provost, who announced.that the English fleet had been seen in the river, and that it was already above Tadoussac. Frontenac now sent back Captain de Ramsay with orders to Cal-lieres, governor of Montreal, to descend immediately to Quebec with all the force at his disposal, and to muster the inhabitants on the way. Then he pushed on with the utmost speed. The autumnal storms had begun, and the rain pelted him without ceasing; but on the morning of the fourteenth he neared the town. The rocks of Cape Diamond towered before him; the St. Lawrence lay beneath them, lonely and still; and the Basin of Quebec outspread its broad bosom, a solitude without a sail. Frontenac had arrived in time.

He landed at the Lower Town, and the troops and the armed inhabitants came crowding to meet him. He was delighted at their ardor. 1 Shouts, cheers, and the waving of hats greeted the old man as he climbed the steep ascent of Mountain Street. Fear and doubt seemed banished by his presence. Even those who hated him rejoiced at his coming, and hailed him as a deliverer. He went at once to inspect the fortifications. Since the alarm a week before, PreVost had accomplished wonders, and

1 Frontenac au Ministre, 9 et 12 Nov., 1690.

not only completed the works begun in the spring, but added others to secure a place which was a natural fortress in itself. On two sides, the Upper Town scarcely needed defence. The cliffs along the St. Lawrence and those along the tributary river St. Charles had three accessible points, guarded at the present day by the Prescott Gate, the Hope Gate, and the Palace Gate. Prevost had secured them by barricades of heavy beams and casks filled with earth. A continuous line of palisades ran along the strand of the St. Charles, from the great cliff called the Saut au Matelot to the palace of the intendant. At this latter point began the line of works constructed by Frontenac to protect the rear of the town. They consisted of palisades, strengthened by a ditch and an embankment, and flanked at frequent intervals by square towers of stone. Passing behind the garden of the Ursulines, they extended to a windmill on a hillock called Mt. Carmel, and thence to the brink of the cliffs in front. Here there was a battery of eight guns near the present Public Garden; two more, each of three guns, were planted at the top of the Saut au Matelot; another at the barricade of the Palace Gate ; and another near the windmill of Mt. Carmel; while a number of light pieces were held in reserve for such use as occasion might require. The Lower Town had no defensive works; but two batteries, each of three guns, eighteen and twenty-four pounders, were placed here at the edge of the river. 1

1 Relation de Monseignat; Plan de Quebec, par Villeneuve, 1690; Relation du Mercure Galant, 1691. The summit of Cape Diamond, which

Two days passed in completing these defences under the eye of the governor. Men were flocking in from the parishes far and near; and on the evening of the fifteenth about twenty-seven hundred, regulars and militia, were gathered within the fortifications, besides the armed peasantry of Beau-port and Beaupre, who were ordered to watch the river below the town, and resist the English, should they attempt to land. 1 At length, before dawn on the morning of the sixteenth, the sentinels on the Saut au Matelot could descry the slowly moving lights of distant vessels. At daybreak the fleet was in sight. Sail after sail passed the Point of Orleans and glided into the Basin of Quebec. The excited spectators on the rock counted thirty-four of them. Four were large ships, several others were of considerable size, and the rest were brigs, schooners, and fishing craft, all thronged with men.

commanded the town, was not fortified till three years later, nor were any guns placed here during the English attack.

1 l>iary of Sylvanus Davis, prisoner in Quebec, in Mass. Hist. CoL. 8,1.101. There is a difference of ten days in the French and English dates, th° New Style having been adopted by the former and not by the latter.

CHAPTER XTTT.

1690.

DEFENCE OF QUEBEC.

PHIPS OH THE ST. LAWRENCE. — PHIPB AT QUEBEC. — A FLAG Of TBUCB. — SCENE AT THB CHATEAU. — THE SUMMONS AND THB Aw-SWER. — PLAN OP ATTACK. — LANDING OP THE ENGLISH. — THB CANNONADE. — THE SHIPS REPULSED. — THE LAND ATTACK. — RETREAT OP PHIPS. — CONDITION OP QUEBEC. — REJOICINGS OF THB FRENCH. — DISTRESS AT BOSTON.

THE delay at Boston, waiting aid from England that never came, was not propitious to Phips; nor were the wind and the waves. The voyage to the St. Lawrence was a long one ; and when he began, without a pilot, to grope his way up the unknown river, the weather seemed in league with his enemies. He appears, moreover, to have wasted time. What was most vital to his success was rapidity of movement; yet, whether by his fault or his misfortune, he remained three weeks within three days' sail of Quebec. 1 While anchored off Tadoussac, with the wind ahead, he passed the idle hours in holding councils of war and framing rules for the government of his men; and, when at length the wind veered to the east, it is doubtful if he made the best use of his opportunity. 9

* Journal of Major Walley, in Hutchinson, Hist. Mass., I. 470.

* " Us ne profiterent pas du vent favorable pour nous surprendre eomme ils auroieut pu faire." Juchereau, 320.

He presently captured a small vessel, commanded by Granville, an officer whom Prevost had sent to watch his movements. He had already captured, near Tadoussac, another vessel, having on board Madame Lalande and Madame Joliet, the wife and the mother-in-law of the discoverer of the Mississippi. 1 When questioned as to the condition of Quebec, they tol(J him that it was imperfectly fortified, that its cannon were dismounted, and that it had not two hundred men to defend it. Phips was greatly elated, thinking that, like Port Royal, the capital of Canada would fall without a blow. The statement of the two prisoners was true, for the most part, when it was made; but the energy of Prevost soon wrought a change.

Phips imagined that the Canadians would offer little resistance to the Puritan invasion;

for some of the Acadians had felt the influence of their New England neighbors, and shown an inclination to them. It was far otherwise in Canada, where the English heretics were regarded with abhorrence. Whenever the invaders tried to land at the settlements along the shore, they were met by a rebuff. At the river Ouelle, Francheville. the cur£ put on a cap and capote, took a musket, led his parishioners to the river, and hid with them in the bushes. As the English boats approached their ambuscade, they gave the foremost a volley, which killed nearly every man on board; upon which the rest sheared off. It was the same when the

1 " Les Demoiselles Lalande et Joliet." The title of madame was at this time restricted to married women of rank. The wives of the bourgeois, and even of the lesser nobles, were called demoiselles.

fleet neared Quebec. Bands of militia, vigilant, agile, and well commanded, followed it along the shore, and repelled with showers of bullets every attempt of the enemy to touch Canadian soil.

When, after his protracted voyage, Phips sailed into the Basin of Quebec, one of the grandest scenes on the western continent opened upon his sight: the wide expanse of waters, the lofty promontory beyond, and the opposing heights of Levi; the cataract of Montmorenci, the distant range of the Laurentian Mountains, the warlike rock with its diadem of walls and towers, the roofs of the Lower Town clustering on the strand beneath, the Chateau St. Louis perched at the brink of the cliff, and over it the white banner, spangled with fleurs-de-lis, flaunting defiance in the clear autumnal air. Perhaps, as he gazed, a suspicion seized him that the task he had undertaken was less easy than he had thought; but he had conquered once by a simple summons to surrender, and he resolved to try its virtue again.

The fleet anchored a little below Quebec; and towards ten o'clock the French saw a boat put out from the admiral's ship, bearing a flag of truce. Four canoes went from the Lower Town, and met it midway. It brought a subaltern officer, who announced himself as the bearer of a letter from Sir William Phips to the French commander. He was taken into one of the canoes and paddled to the quay, after being completely blindfolded by a bandage which covered half his face. Prevost received him as he landed, and ordered two sergeants

to take him by the arms and lead him to the governor. His progress was neither rapid nor direct. They drew him hither and thither, delighting to make him clamber in the dark over every possible obstruction; while a noisy crowd hustled him, and laughing women called him Colin Mail-lard, the name of the chief player in blindman's buff.Amid a prodigious hubbub, intended to bewilder him and impress him with a sense of immense warlike preparation, they dragged him over the three barricades of Mountain Street, and brought him at last into a large room of the chateau. Here they took the bandage from his eyes. He stood for a moment with an air of astonishment and some confusion. The governor stood before him, haughty and stern, surrounded by French and Canadian officers, Maricourt, Sainte-H61ene, Longueuil, Villebon, Valrenne, Bienville, and many more, bedecked with gold lace and silver lace, perukes and powder, plumes and ribbons, and all the martial foppery in which they took delight, and regarding the envoy with keen, defiant eyes. 8 After a moment, he recovered his breath and his composure, saluted Frontenac, and, expressing a wish that the duty assigned him had been of a more agreeable nature, handed him the letter of Phips. Frontenac gave it to an interpreter, who read it aloud in French that all might hear. It ran thus : —

1 Juchereau, 823.

a " Tous cea Officiers s'&oient habilMs le plug proprement qu'ils pOrerit, les galong d'or et d'argent, les rubans, les plumete, la poudre et la frigure, rien ne nwn<juoit," etc. Ibid

" Sir William Phips, Knight, General and Commander in-chief in and over their Majesties' Forces of New England, by Sea and Land, to Count Frontenac, Lieutenant-General and Governour for the French Kiny at Canada; or, in his absence, to his Deputy, or him or them in chief command at Quebeck:

" The war between the crowns of England and France doth not only sufficiently warrant, but the destruction made by the French and Indians, under your command and encouragement, upon the persons and estates of their Majesties' subjects of New England, without provocation on their part, hath put them under the necessity of this expedition for their own security and satisfaction. And although the cruelties and barbarities used against them by the French and Indians might, upon the present opportunity, prompt unto a severe revenge, yet, being desirous to avoid all inhumane and unchristian-like actions, and to prevent shedding of blood as much as may be,

" I, the aforesaid William Phips, Knight, do hereby, in the name and in the behalf of their most excellent Majesties, William and Mary, King and Queen of England, Scotland, France, and Ireland, Defenders of the Faith, and by order of their said Majesties' government of the Massachuset-colony in New England, demand a present surrender of your forts and castles, undemolished, and the King's and other stores, unimbezzled, with a seasonable delivery of all captives; together with a surrender of all your persons and estates to my dispose: upon the doing whereof, you may expect mercy from me, as a Christian, according to what shall be found for their Majesties' service and the subjects' security. Which, if you refuse forthwith to do, I am come provided, and am resolved, by the help of God, in whom I trust, by force of arms to revenge all wrongs and injuries offered, and bring you under subjection to the Crown of England, and, when too late, make you wish you had accepted of the favour tendered.

" Your answer positive in an hour returned by your own trumpet, with the return of mine, is required upon the peril that will ensue." 1

1 See the Letter in Mather, Magnolia, I. 186. The French kept a copy of it, which, with an accurate translation, in parallel columns, was sent to Versailles, and is still preserved in the Archives de la Maime. The text answers perfectly to that given by Mather.

Entry of Phips into the Quebec Basin

When the reading was finished, the Englishman pulled his watch from his pocket, and handed it to the governor. Frontenac could not, or pretended that he could not, see the hour. The messenger thereupon told him that it was ten o'clock, and that he must have his answer before eleven. A general cry of indignation arose; and Valrenne called out that Phips was nothing but a pirate, and that his man ought to be hanged. Frontenac contained himself for a moment, and then said to the envoy:—

" I will not keep you waiting so long. Tell your general that I do not recognize King William; and that the Prince of Orange, who so styles himself, is a usurper, who has violated the most sacred laws of blood in attempting to dethrone his father-in-law. I know no king of England but King James. Your general ought not to be surprised at the hostilities which he says that the

French have carried on in the colony of Massachusetts; for, as the king my master has taken the king of England under his protection, and is about to replace him on his throne by force of arms, he might have expected that his Majesty would order me to make war on a people who have rebelled against their lawful prince." Then, turning with a smile to the officers about him: " Even if your general offered me conditions a little more gracious, and if I had a mind to accept them, does he suppose that these brave gentlemen would give their consent, and advise me to trust a man who broke his agreement with the governor of Port Eoyal, or a rebel

who has failed in his duty to his king, and forgotten all the favors he had received from him, to follow a prince who pretends to be the liberator of England and the defender of the faith, and yet destroys the laws and privileges of the kingdom and overthrows its religion ? The divine justice which your general invokes in his letter will not fail to punish such acts severely."

The messenger seemed astonished and startled; but he presently asked if the governor would give him his answer in writing.

" No," returned Frontenac, " I will answer your general only by the mouths of my cannon, that he may learn that a man like me is not to be summoned after this fashion. Let him do his best, and I will do mine;" and he dismissed the Englishman abruptly. He was again blindfolded, led over the barricades, and sent back to the fleet by the boat that brought him. 1

Phips had often given proof of personal courage, but for the past three weeks his conduct seems that of a man conscious that he is charged with a work too large for his capacity. He had spent a good part of his time in holding councils of war; and now, when he heard the answer of Frontenac, he called another to consider what should be done. A plan of attack was at length arranged. The militia were to be landed on the shore of Beauport, which was just below Quebec, though separated

1 Lettre de Sir William Phips a M. de Frontenac, avec *(i Rfponse ver-bale; delation de ce qui s'est pass€ a la Descente des Anglois a Quebec au mots d'Octobre.lQQQ. Compare Monseignat, Relation. The English accounts, though more brief, confirm those of the French.

from it by the St. Charles. They were then to cross this river by a ford practicable at low water, climb the heights of St. Genevieve, and gain the rear of the town. The small vessels of the fleet were to aid the movement by ascending the St. Charles as far as the ford, holding the enemy in check by their fire, and carrying provisions, ammunition, and intrenching tools, for the use of the land troops. When these had crossed and were ready to attack Quebec in the rear, Phips was to cannonade it in front, and land two hundred men under cover of his guns to effect a diversion by storming the barricades. Some of the French prisoners, from whom their captors appear to have received a great deal of correct information, told the admiral that there was a place a mile or two above the town where the heights might be scaled and the rear of the fortifications reached from a direction opposite to that proposed. This was precisely the movement by which Wolfe afterwards gained his memorable victory; but Phips chose to abide -by the original plan.

While the plan was debated, the opportunity for accomplishing it ebbed away. It was still early when the messenger returned from Quebec; but, before Phips was ready to act, the day was on the wane and the tide was against him. He lay quietly at his moorings when, in the evening, a great shouting, mingled with the roll of drums and the sound of fifes, was heard from the Upper Town. The

Journal of Major Walley; Savage, Account of the Late Action of thi New Englanders (Lond. 1691).

English officers asked their prisoner Granville, what it meant. " Ma foi, Messieurs," he replied, " you have lost the game. It is the governor of Montreal with the people frctn the country above. There is nothing for you now but to pack and go home." In fact, Callieres had arrived with seven or eight hundred men, many of them regulars. With these were bands of coureurs de bois and other young Canadians, all full of fight, singing and whooping with martial glee as they passed the western gate and trooped down St. Louis Street.

The next day was gusty and blustering; and still Phips lay quiet, waiting on the winds and the waves. A small vessel, with sixty men on board, under Captain Ephraim Savage, ran in towards the shore of Beauport to examine the landing, and stuck fast in the mud. The Canadians plied her with bullets, and brought a cannon to bear on her. They might have waded out and boarded her, but Savage and his men kept up so hot a fire that they forbore the attempt; and, when the tide rose, she floated again.

There was another night of tranquillity; but at about eleven on Wednesday morning the French heard the English fifes and drums in full action, while repealed shouts of " God save King William!" rose from all the vessels. This lasted an hour or more; after which a great number of boats, loaded with men, put out from the fleet and rowed rapidly towards the shore of Beauport. The tide was low, and the boats grounded before reaching the land-

1 Juchereau, 325. 326.

ing-place. The French on the rock could see the troops through telescopes, looking in the distance like a swarm of black ants, as they waded through mud and water, and formed in companies along the strand. They were some thirteen hundred in number, and were commanded by Major Walley. 1 Fron-tenac had sent three hundred sharpshooters, under Sainte-Helene, to meet them and hold them in check. A battalion of troops followed; but, long before they could reach the spot, Sainte-Helene's men, with a few militia from the neighboring parishes, and a band of Huron warriors from Lorette, threw themselves into the thickets along the front of the English, and opened a distant but galling fire upon the compact bodies of the enemy. Walley ordered a charge. The New England men rushed, in a disorderly manner, but with great impetuosity, up the rising ground; received two volleys, which failed to check them; and drove back the assailants in some confusion. They turned, however, and fought in Indian fashion with courage and address, leaping and dodging among trees, rocks, and bushes, firing as they retreated, and inflicting more harm than they received. Towards evening they disappeared; and Walley, whose men had been much scattered in the desultory fight, drew them together as well as he could, and advanced towards the St. Charles, in order to meet the vessels which were to aid him in passing the ford.

1 "Between 12 and 1,300 men." Waliey, Journal. " About 1,200men/' Savage, Account of the Late Action. Savage was second in command of the militia. Mather says, 1,400. Most of the French accounts say, 1,500. Some say, 2,000; and La Hontan raises the number to 3,000.

Here he posted sentinels, and encamped for the night. He had lost four killed and about sixty wounded, and imagined that he had killed twenty or thirty of the enemy. In fact, however, their loss was much less, though among the killed was a valuable officer, the Chevalier de Clermont, and among the wounded the veteran captain of Beau-port, Juchereau de Saint-Denis, more than sixty-four years of age. In the evening, a deserter came to the English camp, and brought the unwelcome intelligence that there were three thousand armed men in Quebec. 1

Meanwhile, Phips, whose fault hitherto had not been an excess of promptitude, grew impatient, and made a premature movement inconsistent with the preconcerted plan. He left his moorings, anchored his largest ships before the town, and prepared to cannonade it; but the fiery veteran, who watched him from the Chateau St. Louis, anticipated him, and gave him the first shot. Phips replied furiously, opening fire with every gun that he could bring to bear; while the rock paid him back in kind,

1 On this affair, Walley, Journal; Savage, Account of the Late Action (in a letter to his brother); Monseignat, Relation; Relation de la Descents des Anglois; Relation de 1682-1712; La Hontan, I. 213. " M. le comte de Frontenac se trouva avec 3,000 hommes." Belmont, Histoire du Canada, A.D. 1690. The prisoner Captain Sylvanus Davis, in his diary, says, as already mentioned, that on the day before Phips's arrival so many regulars and militia arrived that, with those who came with Frontenac, there were about 2,700. This was before the arrival of Callieres, who, according to Davis, brought but 300. Thus the three accounts of the deserter, Belmont, and Davis, tally exactly as to the sum total.

An enemy of Frontenac writes, " Ce n'est pas sa presence qui fit prendre la fuite aux Anglois, mais le grand nombre de Francois aux-quels ils virent bien que celuy de leurs guerriers n'e'toit pas capable de faire tete." Remarques sur VOraison Funebre de feu M. de Frontenac.

and belched flame and smoke from all its batteries. So fierce and rapid was the firing, that La Hon-tan compares it to volleys of musketry; and old officers, who had seen many sieges, declared that they had never known the like. 1 The din was prodigious, reverberated from the surrounding heights, and rolled back from the distant mountains in one continuous roar. On the part of the English, however, surprisingly little was accomplished beside noise and smoke. The practice of their gunners was so bad that many of their shot struck harmlessly against the face of the cliff. Their guns, too, were very light, and appear to have been charged with a view to the most rigid economy of gunpowder; for the balls failed to pierce the stone walls of the buildings, and did so little damage that, as the French boasted, twenty crowns would have repaired it all. 2 Night came at length, and the turmoil ceased.

Phips lay quiet till daybreak, when Frontenac sent a shot to waken him, and the cannonade began again. Sainte-Helene had returned from Beauport; and he, with his brother Maricourt, took charge of the two batteries of the Lower Town, aiming the guns in person, and throwing balls of eighteen and twenty-four pounds with excellent precision against the four largest ships of the fleet. One of their shots cut the flagstaff of the admiral, and the cross of St. George fell into the river. It drifted with the tide towards the north shore; whereupon sev-

La Hontan, I. 216; Juchereau, 326. 3 Pfcre Germain, Relation de la Dtfaite des Anglois.

18

eral Canadians paddled out in a birch canoe, secured it, and brought it back in triumph. On the spire of the cathedral in the Upper Town had been hung a picture of the Holy Family, as an invocation of divine aid. The Puritan gunners wasted their ammunition in vain attempts to knock it down. That it escaped their malice was ascribed to miracle, but the miracle would have been greater if they had hit it.

At length, one of the ships, which had suffered most, hauled off and abandoned the fight. That of the admiral had fared little better, and now her condition grew desperate. With her rigging torn, her mainmast half cut through, her mizzen-mast splintered, her cabin pierced, and her hull riddled with shot, another volley seemed likely to sink her, when Phips ordered her to be cut loose from her moorings, and she drifted out of fire, leaving cable and anchor behind. The remaining ships soon gave over the conflict, and withdrew to stations where they could neither do harm nor suffer it. 1

Phips had thrown away nearly all his ammunition in this futile and disastrous attack, which should have been deferred till the moment when Walley, with his land force, had gained the rear of the town. Walley lay in his camp, his men wet, shivering with cold, famished, and sickening with the small-pox. Food, and all other supplies, were to have been brought him by the small vessels, which

1 Besides authorities before cited, Le Clercq, fitaf>hsse*nent ete la Foy,U. 434; La Potherie, IIL 118; Rapport de Champigny, Oct., 1690; Laval, Lettre a , 20 Nov., 1690.

should have entered the mouth of the St. Charles and aided him to cross it. But he waited for them in vain. Every vessel that carried a gun had busied itself in cannonading, and the rest did not move. There appears to have been insubordination among the masters of these small craft, some of whom, being owners or part-owners of the vessels they commanded, were probably unwilling to run them into danger. Walley was no soldier; but he saw that to attempt the passage of the river without aid, under the batteries of the town and in the face of forces twice as numerous as his own, was not an easy task. Frontenac, on his part, says that he wished him to do so, knowing that the attempt would ruin him. 1 The New England men were eager to push on; but the night of Thursday, the day of Phips's repulse, was so cold that ice formed more than an inch in thickness, and the half-starved militia suffered intensely. Six field-pieces, with their ammunition, had been sent ashore; but they were nearly useless, as there were no means of moving them. Half a barrel of musket powder, and one biscuit for each man, were also landed; and with this meagre aid Walley was left to capture Quebec. He might, had he dared, have made a dash across the ford on the morning of Thursday, and assaulted the town in the rear while Phips was cannonading it in front; but his courage was not equal to so desperate a venture. The firing ceased, and the possible opportunity was lost. The citizen soldier despaired of success; and, on the morning of Friday, he went

1 Frontenac au Ministre, 12 et 19 Nov., 1690.

on board the admiral's ship to explain his situation. While he was gone, his men put themselves in motion, and advanced along the borders of the St. Charles towards the ford. Frontenac, with three battalions of regular troops, went to receive them at the crossing; while Sainte-Hel&ne, with his brother Lon-gueuil, passed the ford with a body of Canadians, and opened fire on them from the neighboring thickets. Their advance parties were driven in, and there was a hot skirmish, the chief loss falling on the New England men, who were fully exposed. On the side of the French, Sainte-Helene was mortally wounded, and his brother was hurt by a spent ball. Towards evening, the Canadians withdrew, and the English encamped for the night. Their commander presently rejoined them. The admiral had given him leave to withdraw them to the fleet, and boats were accordingly sent to bring them off; but, as these did not arrive till about daybreak, it was necessary to defer the embarkation till the next night.

At dawn, Quebec was all astir with the beating of drums and the ringing of bells. The New England drums replied; and Walley drew up his men under arms, expecting an attack, for the town was so near that the hubbub of voices from within could plainly be heard. The noise gradually died away; and, except a few shots from the ramparts, the invaders were left undisturbed. Walley sent two or three companies to beat up the neighboring thickets, where he suspected that the enemy was lurking. On the way, they had the good luck to

find and kill a number of cattle, which they cooked and ate on the spot; whereupon, being greatly refreshed and invigorated, they dashed forward in complete disorder, and were soon met by the fire of the ambushed Canadians. Several more companies were sent to their support, and the skirmishing became lively. Three detachments from Quebec had crossed the river; and the militia of Beauport and Beaupre* had hastened to join them. They fought like Indians, hiding behind trees or throwing themselves flat among the bushes, and laying repeated ambuscades as they slowly fell back. At length, they all made a stand on a hill behind the buildings and fences of a farm; and here they held their ground till night, while the New England men taunted them as cowards who would never fight except under cover. 1

Walley, who with his main body had stood in arms all day, now called in the skirmishers, and fell back to the landing-place, where, as soon as it grew dark, the boats arrived from the fleet. The sick men, of whom there were many, were sent on board, and then, amid floods of rain, the whole force embarked in noisy confusion, leaving behind them in the mud five of their cannon. Hasty as was their parting, their conduct on the whole had been creditable ; and La Hontan, who was in Quebec at the time, says of them, u They fought vigorously, though as ill-disciplined as men gathered together at random could be; for they did not lack courage, and, if the\'7d T failed, it was by reason

1 Relation de la Descente des Anqlois.

of their entire ignorance of discipline, and because they were exhausted by the fatigues of the voyage." Of Phips he speaks with contempt, and says that he could not have served the French better if they had bribed him to stand all the while with his arms folded. Some allowance should, nevertheless, be made him for the unmanageable character of the force under his command, the constitution of which was fatal to military subordination.

On Sunday, the morning after the re-embarkation, Phips called a council of officers, and it was resolved that the men should rest for a day or two, that there should be a meeting for prayer, and that, if ammunition enough could be found, another landing should be attempted; but the rough weather prevented the prayer-meeting, and the plan of a new attack was fortunately abandoned.

Quebec remained in agitation and alarm till Tuesday, when Phips weighed anchor and disappeared, with all his fleet, behind the Island of Orleans. He did not go far, as indeed he could not, but stopped four leagues below to mend rigging, fortify wounded masts, and stop shot-holes. Subercase had gone with a detachment to watch the retiring enemy; and Phips was repeatedly seen among his men, on a scaffold at the side of his ship, exercising his old trade of carpenter. This delay was turned to good use by an exchange of prisoners. Chief among those in the hands of the French was Captain Davis, late commander at Casco Bay; and there were also two ycung daugh-

ters of Lieutenant Clark, who had been killed at the same place. Frontenac himself had humanely ransomed these children from the Indians ; and Madame de Champigny, wife of the intendanfc, had, with equal kindness, bought from them a little girl named Sarah Gerrish, and placed her in charge of the nuns at the H6tel-Dieu, who had become greatly attached to her, while she, on her part, left them with reluctance. The French had the better in these exchanges, receiving able-bodied men, and returning, with the exception of Davis, only women and children.

The heretics were gone, and Quebec breathed freely again. Her escape had been a narrow one; not that three thousand men, in part regular troops, defending one of the strongest positions on the continent, and commanded by Frontenac, could not defy the attacks of two thousand raw fishermen and farmers, led by an ignorant civilian, but the numbers which were a source of strength were at the same time a source of weakness. 1 Nearly all the adult males of Canada were gathered at Quebec, and there was imminent danger of starvation. Cattle from the neighboring parishes had been hastily driven into the town; but there was little other provision, and before Phips retreated the pinch of famine had begun. Had he come a week earlier or stayed a week later, the French them-

1 The small-pox had left probably less than 2,000 effective men in the fleet when it arrived before Quebec. The number of regular troops in Canada by the roll of 1689 was 1,418. Nothing had since occurred to greatly diminish the number. Callieres left about fifty in Montreal,

and perhaps also a few in the neighboring forts The rest were in Quebec-

selves believed that Quebec would have fallen, in the one case for want of men, and in the other for want of food.

The Lower Town had been abandoned by its inhabitants, who bestowed their families and their furniture within the solid walls of the seminary. The cellars of the Ursuline convent were filled with women and children, and many more took refuge at the H6tel-Dieu. The beans and cabbages in the garden of the nuns were all stolen by the soldiers; and their wood-pile was turned into bivouac fires. " We were more dead than alive when we heard the cannon," writes Mother Juchereau ; but the Jesuit Fremin came to console them, and their prayers and their labors never ceased. On the day when the firing was heaviest, twenty-six balls fell into their yard and garden, and were sent to the gunners at the batteries, who returned them to their English owners. At the convent of the Ursulines, the corner of a nun's apron was carried off by a cannon-shot as she passed through her chamber. The sisterhood began a novena, or nine days' devotion, to St. Joseph, St. Ann, the angels, and the souls in purgatory; and one of their number remained day and night in prayer before the images of the Holy Family. The bishop came to encourage them; and his prayers and his chants were so fervent that they thought their last hour was come. 1

The superior of the Jesuits, with some of the elder members of the Order, remained at their col-

1 Ifccit d'une Religieuse Ursuline, in Let Ursulines de Quebec, I. 470-

lege during the attack, ready, should the heretics prevail, to repair to their chapel, and die before the altar. Eumor exaggerated the numbers of the enemy, and a general alarm pervaded the town. It was still greater at Lorette, nine miles distant. The warriors of that mission were in the first skirmish at Beauport; and two of them, running off in a fright, reported at the village that the enemy were carrying every thing before them. On this, the villagers fled to the woods, followed by Father Germain, their missionary, to whom this hasty exodus suggested the flight of the Holy Family into Egypt. 1 The Jesuits were thought to have special reason to fear the Puritan soldiery, who, it was reported, meant to kill them all, after cutting off their ears to make necklaces. 2

When news first came of the approach of Phips, the bishop was absent on a pastoral tour. Hastening back, he entered Quebec at night, by torchlight, to the great joy of its inmates, who felt that his presence brought a benediction. He issued a pastoral address, exhorting his flock to frequent and full confession and constant attendance at mass, as the means of insuring the success of their arms. 3 Laval, the former bishop, aided his efforts. " We appealed," he writes, " to God, his Holy Mother, to all the Angels, and to all the Saints/' 4 Nor was

1 " n nous ressouvint alors de la fuite de Nostre Seigneur en Egypte." Pfere Germain, Relation.

a Ibid.

8 Lettre pastorale pour disposer les Peuples de ce Diocese a e bten deffendrt centre les Anglois (Reg. de 1'Eveche de Que'bec). m

* Laval a Nov. 20, 1690

the appeal in vain: for each day seemed to bring some new token of celestial favor; and it is not surprising that the head-winds which delayed the approach of the enemy, the cold and the storms which hastened his departure, and, above all, his singularly innocent cannonade, which killed but two or three persons, should have been accepted as proof of divine intervention. It was to the Holy Virgin that Quebec had been most lavish of its vows, and to her the victory was ascribed.

One great anxiety still troubled the minds of the victors. Three ships, bringing large sums of money and the yearly supplies for the colony, were on their way to Quebec ; and nothing was more likely than that the retiring fleet would meet and capture them. Messengers had been sent down the river, who passed the English in the dark, found the ships at St. Paul's Bay, and warned them of the danger. They turned back, and hid themselves within the mouth of the Saguenay; but not soon enough to prevent Phips from discovering their retreat. He tried to follow them; but thick fogs arose, with a persistent tempest of snow, which completely baffled him, and, after waiting five days, he gave over the attempt. When he was gone, the three ships emerged from their hiding-place, and sailed again for Quebec, where they were greeted with a universal jubilee. Their deliverance was ascribed to Saint Ann, the mother of the Virgin, and also to St. Francis Xavier, whose name one of them bore.

Quebec was divided between thanksgiving and

rejoicing. The captured flag of Phips's ship was borne to the cathedral in triumph ; the bishop sang Te Deum; and, amid the firing of cannon, the image of the Virgin was carried to each church and chapel in the place by a procession, in which priests, people, and troops all took part. The day closed with a grand bonfire in honor of Fron-tenac.

One of the three ships carried back the news of the victory, which was hailed with joy at Versailles ; and a medal was struck to commemorate it. The ship carried also a despatch from Fron-tenac. " Now that the king has triumphed by land and sea," wrote the old soldier, "will he think that a few squadrons of his navy would be ill employed in punishing the insolence of these genuine old parliamentarians of Boston, and crushing them in their den and the English of New York as well ? By mastering these two towns, we shall secure the whole sea-coast, besides the fisheries of the Grand Bank, which is no slight matter: and this would be the true, and perhaps the only, way of bringing the wars of Canada to an end; for, when the English are conquered, we can easily reduce the Iroquois to complete submission." *

Phips returned crestfallen to Boston late in November; and one by one the rest of the fleet came straggling after him, battered and weather-beaten. Some did not appear till February, and three or four never came at all. The autumn and early winter were unusually stormy. Captain Rainsford, with sixty men, was wrecked on the

1 Frontenac an Ministre, 9 et 12 Nov., 1690.

Island of Anticosti, where more than half their number died of cold and misery. 1 In the other vessels, some were drowned, some frost-bitten, and above two hundred killed by small-pox and fever. At Boston, all was dismay and gloom. The Puritan bowed before " this awful frown of God," and searched his conscience for the sin that had brought upon him so stern a chastisement. 9 Massachusetts, already impoverished, found herself in extremity. The war, instead of paying for itself, had burdened her with an additional debt of fifty thousand -pounds. 3 The sailors and soldiers were clamorous for their pay; and, to satisfy them, the colony was forced for the first time in its history to issue a paper currency. It was made receivable at a premium for all public debts, and was also fortified by a provision for its early redemption by taxation ; a provision which was carried into effect in spite of poverty and distress. 4

1 Mather, Magnolia, I. 192.

2 The Governor and Council to the Agents of Massachusetts, in Andros Tracts, III. 53.

1 Address of the Gentry, Merchants, and others, Ibid., II. 236. 4 The following is a literal copy of a specimen of this paper money, which varied in value from two shillings to ten pounds :
—

No. (2161) 10«
This Indented Bill of Ten Shillings, due from the Massachusetts Colony to the Possessor,

shall be in value equal to Money, and shall be accordingly accepted by the Treasurer and Receivers subordinate to him in all Publick Payments, and for any Stock at any time in the Treasury Boston in New England, December the lO* 1690. By Order of the General Court.

PKTER TOWNSKND ^ ADAM WINTHROP TIM. THORNTON)

When this paper came into the hands of the treasurer, it was burned. Nevertheless, owing to the temporary character of the provisional gov-

Massachusetts had made her usual mistake. She had confidently believed that ignorance and inexperience could match the skill of a tried veteran, and that the rude courage of her fishermen and farmers could triumph without discipline or leadership. The conditions of her material prosperity were adverse to efficiency in war. A trading republic, without trained officers, may win victories; but it wins them either by accident or by an extravagant outlay in money and life.

ernment, it fell for a time to the value of from fourteen to sixteen shillings in the pound.

In the Bibliotheque Nationale is the original draft of a remarkable map, by the engineer Villeneuve, of which a fac-simile is before me. It represents in detail the town and fortifications of Quebec, the surrounding country, and the positions of the English fleet and land forces, and is entitled PLAN DE QU&BEC, et de ses Enuirons, EN LA NOU-VELLE FRANCE, ASSltfGtf PAR LES ANGLOIS, le 16 d>Oc-tobre 1690 jusqu'au 22 dud. mois qu'ils s'en allerent, appres auoir est€ bien battus PAR M r . LE COMTE DE FRONTENAC, gouuerneur general du Pays.

CHAPTER XIV.

1690-1694. THE SCOURGE OF CANADA.

IBOQUOIB INROADS. — DEATH OP BIBNVILLB. — ENGLISH ATTACK. — A DBSPERATE FIGHT. — MISERIES OF THE COLONY. — ALARMS. — A WINTER EXPEDITION. — LA CHESNATE BURNED. — THE HEROINE OF VERCHERES. — MISSION INDIANS. — THE MOHAWK EXPEDITION. — RETREAT AND PURSUIT. — RELIEF ARRIVES. — FRONTENAC TRIUMPHANT.

ONE of Phips's officers, charged with the exchange of prisoners at Quebec, said as he took his leave, " We shall make you another visit in the spring; " and a French officer returned, with martial courtesy, " "We shall have the honor of meeting you before that time." Neither side made good its threat, for both were too weak and too poor. No more war-parties were sent that winter to ravage the English border; for neither blankets, clothing, ammunition, nor food could be spared. The fields had lain un-tilled over half Canada; and, though four ships had arrived with supplies, twice as many had been captured or driven back by English cruisers in the Gulf. The troops could not be kept together; and they were quartered for subsistence upon the settlers, themselves half famished.

Spring came at length, and brought with it the

swallows, the bluebirds, and the Iroquois. They rarely came in winter, when the trees and bushes had no leaves to hide them, and their movements were betrayed by the track of their snow-shoes; but they were always to be expected at the time of sowing and of harvest, when they could do most mischief. During April, about eight hundred of them, gathering from their winter hunting-grounds, encamped at the mouth of the Ottawa, whence they detached parties to ravage the settlements. A large band fell upon Point aux Trembles, below Montreal, burned some thirty houses, and killed such of the inmates as could not escape. Another band attacked the Mission of the Mountain, just behind the town, and captured thirty-five of the Indian converts in broad daylight. Others prowled among the deserted farms on both shores of the St. Lawrence; while the inhabitants remained pent in their stockade forts, with misery in the present and starvation in the future.

Troops and militia were not wanting. The difficulty was to find provisions enough to enable them to keep thejfreld. By begging from house to house, getting here a biscuit and there a morsel of bacon, enough was collected to supply a considerable party for a number of days; and a hundred and twenty soldiers and Canadians went out under Vaudreuil to hunt the hunters of men. Long impunity had made the Iroquois so careless that they were easily found. A band of about forty had made their quarters at a house near the fort at Repentigny, and here the French scouts discovered them early

in the night. Yaudreuil and his men were in canoes. They lay quiet till one o'clock, then landed, and noiselessly approached the spot. Some of the Iroquois were in the house, the rest lay asleep on the ground before it. The French crept towards them, and by one close volley killed them all. Their comrades within sprang up in dismay. Three rushed out, and were shot: the others stood on their defence, fired from windows and loopholes, and killed six or seven of the French, who presently succeeded in setting fire to the house, which was thatched with straw. Young Fra^ois de Bienville, one of the sons of Charles Le Moyne, rushed up to a window, shouted his name like an Indian warrior, fired on the savages within, and was instantly shot dead. The flames rose till surrounding objects were bright as day. The Iroquois, driven to desperation, burst out like tigers, and tried to break through their assailants. Only one succeeded. Of his companions, some were shot, five were knocked down and captured, and the rest driven back into the house, where they perished in the fire. Three of the prisoners were given to the inhabitants of Repentigny, Point aux Trembles, and Boucherville, who, in their fury, burned them alive.

For weeks, the upper parts of the colony were infested by wolfish bands howling around the forts, which they rarely ventured to attack. At length, help came. A squadron from France, strong enough

1 Relation de Be'nac, 1691; Relation de ce qui s'est passe" de plus conside'-rable en Canada, 1690, 1691; La Potherie, III. 134; Relation de 1682-1712, Champigny au Ministre, 12 May, 1691. The name of Bienville was taken, after his death, by one of his brothers, the founder of New Orleans.

to beat off the New England privateers which blockaded the St. Lawrence, arrived at Quebec with men and supplies; and a strong force was despatched to break up the Iroquois camp at the Ottawa. The enemy vanished at its approach; and the suffering farmers had a brief respite, which enabled them to sow their crops, when suddenly a fresh alarm was sounded from Sorel to Montreal, and again the settlers ran to their forts for refuge.

Since the futile effort of the year before, the English of New York, still distracted by the political disorders that followed the usurpation of Leis-ler, had fought only by deputy, and contented themselves with hounding on the Iroquois against the common enemy. These savage allies at length lost patience, and charged their white neighbors with laziness and fear. " You say to us, ' Keep the French in perpetual alarm.' Why don't you say, ' We will keep the French in perpetual alarm' ? " 1 It was clear that something must be done, or New York would be left to fight her battles alone. A war-party was therefore formed at Albany, and the Indians were invited to join it. Major Peter Schuy-ier took command; and his force consisted of two hundred and sixty-six men, of whom a hundred and twenty were English and Dutch, and the rest Mohawks and Wolves, or Mohegans. 2 He advanced to a point on the Richelieu ten miles above Fort Chambly, and, leaving his canoes under a strong guard, marched towards La Prairie de la Madeleine, opposite Montreal.

i Golden, 125, 140.

Scouts had brought warning of his approach; and Callieres, the local governor, crossed the St. Lawrence, and encamped at La Prairie with seven or eight hundred men. 1 Here he remained for a week, attacked by fever and helpless in bed. The fort stood a few rods from the river. Two battalions of regulars lay on a field at the right; and the Canadians and Indians were bivouacked on the left, between the fort and a small stream, near which was a windmill. On the evening of the tenth of August, a drizzling rain began to fall; and the Canadians thought more of seeking shelter than of keeping watch. They were, moreover, well supplied with brandy, and used it freely. 2 At an hour before dawn, the sentry at the mill descried objects like the shadows of men silently advancing along the borders of the stream. They were Schuyler's vanguard. The soldier cried, " Qui vive ? " There was no answer. He fired his musket, and ran into the mill. Schuyler's men rushed in a body upon the Canadian camp, drove its occupants into the fort, and killed some of the Indian allies, who lay under their canoes on the adjacent strand.

The regulars on the other side of the fort, roused by the noise, sprang to arms and hastened to the spot. They were met by a volley, which laid some fifty of them on the ground, and drove back the rest in disorder. They rallied and attacked again; on which, Schuyler, greatly outnumbered, withdrew his men to a neighboring ravine, where he once

Relation de Bthac; Relation de 1682-1712.

" La bauche fut extreme en toute mantere." Belmont

more repulsed his assailants, and, as he declares, drove them into the fort with great loss. By this time it was daylight. The English, having struck their blow, slowly fell back, hacking down the corn in the fields, as it was still too green for burning, and pausing at the edge of the woods, where their Indians were heard for some time uttering frightful howls, and shouting to the French that they were not men, but dogs. Why the invaders were left to retreat unmolested, before a force more than double their own, does not appear. The helpless condition of Callieres and the death of Saint-Cirque, his second in command, scarcely suffice to explain it. Schuyler retreated towards his canoes, moving, at his leisure, along the forest path that led to Chambly. Tried by the standard of partisan war, his raid had been a success. He had inflicted great harm and suffered little; but the affair was not yet ended.

A day or two before, Valrenne, an officer of birth and ability, had been sent to Chambly, with about a hundred and sixty troops and Canadians, a body of Huron and Iroquois converts, and a band of Algonquins from the Ottawa. His orders were to let the English pass, and then place himself in their rear to cut them off from their canoes. His scouts had discovered their advance; and, on the morning of the attack, he set his force in motion, and advanced six or seven miles towards La Prairie, on the path by which Schuyler was retreating. The country was buried in forests. At about nine o'clock, the scouts of the hostile

parties met each other, and their war-whoops gave the alarm. Valrenne instantly took possession of a ridge of ground that crossed the way of the approaching English. Two large trees had fallen along the crest of the acclivity; and behind these the French crouched, in a triple row, well hidden by bushes and thick standing trunks. The English, underrating the strength of their enemy, and ignorant of his exact position, charged impetuously, and were sent reeling back by a close and deadly volley. They repeated the attack with still greater fury, and dislodged the French from their ambuscade. Then ensued a fight, which Frontenac declares to have been the most hot and stubborn ever known in Canada. The object of Schuyler was to break through the French and reach his canoes: the object of Yalrenne was to drive him back upon the superior force at La Prairie. The cautious tactics of the bush were forgotten. Three times the combatants became mingled together, firing breast to breast, and scorching each other's shirts by the flash of their guns. The Algonquins did themselves no credit; and at first some of the Canadians gave way, but they were rallied by Le Ber Duchesne, their commander, and afterwards showed great bravery. On the side of the English, many of the Mohegan allies ran off. ; but the whites and the Mohawks fought with equal desperation. In the midst of the tumult, Valrenne was perfectly cool, directing his men with admirable vigor and address, and barring Schuyler's Yetreat for more than an hour. At length, the French were driven

from the path. " We broke through the middle of their body," says Schuyler, " until we got into their rear, trampling upon their dead; then faced about upon them, and fought them until we made them give way; then drove them, by strength of arm, four hundred paces before us; and, to say the truth, we were all glad to see them retreat." ! He and his followers continued their march unmolested, carrying their wounded men, and leaving about forty dead behind them, along with one of their flags, and all their knapsacks, which they had thrown off when the fray began. They reached the banks of the Richelieu, found their canoes safe, and, after waiting several hours for stragglers, embarked for Albany.

Nothing saved them from destruction but the failure of the French at La Prairie to follow their retreat, and thus enclose them between two fires. They did so, it is true, at the eleventh hour, but not till the fight was over and the English were gone. The Christian Mohawks of the Saut also appeared in the afternoon, and set out to pursue the enemy, but seem to have taken care not to overtake them; for the English Mohawks were their relatives, and they had no wish for their scalps. Frontenac was angry at their conduct; and, as he rarely lost an opportunity to find fault with the Jesuits, he laid the blame on the fathers in charge of the mission, whom he sharply upbraided for the shortcomings of their flock. 2

1 Major Peter Schuyler's Journal of his Expedition, to Canada, in N. Y. Col. Docs., m. 800. " Les ennemis enfoncerent notre embuscade." Bel-moot. i

2 As this fight under Valrenne has been represented as a French

He was at Three Rivers at a ball when news of the disaster at La Prairie damped the spirits of the company, which, however, were soon revived by tidings of the fight under Yalrenne and the retreat of the English, who were reported to have left two hundred dead on the field. Frontenac wrote an account of the affair to the minister, with high praise of Valrenne and his band, followed by on appeal for help. "What with fighting and hardship, our troops and militia are wasting away." " The enemy is upon us by sea and land." " Send us a thousand men next spring, if you want the colony to be saved." " We are perishing by inches; the people are in the depths of poverty; the war has doubled prices so that nobody can live." " Many families are without bread. The inhabitants desert the country, and crowd into the towns." l A new enemy appeared in the following summer, almost

victory against overwhelming odds, it may be well to observe the evidence as to the numbers engaged. The French party consisted, according to Be'nac, of 160 regulars and Canadians, besides Indians. La Potherie places it at 180 men, and Frontenac at 200 men. These two estimates do not include Indians; for the author of the Relation of 1682-1712, who was an officer on the spot at the time, puts the number at 800 soldiers, Canadians, and savages.

Schuyler's official return shows that his party consisted of 120 whites, 80 Mohawks, and 66 River Indians (Mohegans): 266 in all. The French writer Be'nac places the whole at 280, and the intendant Champigny at 800. The other French estimates of the English force are greatly exaggerated. Schuyler's strength was reduced by 27 men left to guard the canoes, and by a number killed or disabled at La Prairie. The force under Valrenne was additional to the 700 or

800 men at La Prairie (Relation, 1682-1712). Schuyler reported his loss in killed at 21 whites, 16 Mohawks, and 6 Mohegans, besides many wounded. The French Statements of it are enormously in excess of this, and are irreconcilable with each other.

* Lettres de Frontenac et de Champigny, 1691, 1692.

as destructive as the Iroquois. This was an army of caterpillars, which set at naught the maledictions of the clergy, and made great havoc among the crops. It is recorded that along with the caterpillars came an unprecedented multitude of squirrels, which, being industriously trapped or shot, proved a great help to many families.

Alarm followed alarm. It was reported that Phips was bent on revenge for his late discomfiture, that great armaments were afoot, and that a mighty host of " Bostonnais " was preparing another descent. Again and again Frontenac begged that one bold blow should be struck to end these perils and make King Louis master of the continent, by despatching a fleet to seize New York. If this were done, he said, it would be easy to take Boston and the " rebels and old republican leaven of Cromwell " who harbored there; then burn the place, and utterly destroy it. 1 Yillebon, governor of Acadia, was of the same mind. " No town," he told the minister, " could be burned more easily. Most of the houses are covered with shingles, and the streets are very narrow." 2 But the king could not spare a squadron equal to the attempt; and Frontenac was told that he must wait. The troops sent him did not supply his losses. 3 Money came every summer in sums which now seem small, but were far from being so in the eyes of the king

1 Frontenac in N. Y. Col Docs., IX. 496, 506.

2 Villebon in N. Y. Col. Docs., IX. 507.

8 The returns show 1,313 regulars in 1691, and 1,120 in 1692.

who joined to each remittance a lecture on economy and a warning against extravagance.

The intendant received his share of blame on these occasions, and he usually defended himself vigorously. He tells his master that " war-parties are necessary, but very expensive. We rarely pay money; but we must give presents to our Indians, and fit out the Canadians with provisions, arms, ammunition, moccasons, snow-shoes, sledges, canoes, capotes, breeches, stockings, and blankets. This costs a great deal, but without it we should have to abandon Canada." The king complained that, while the great sums he was spending in the colony turned to the profit of the inhabitants, they contributed nothing to their own defence. The complaint was scarcely just; for, if they gave no money, they gave their blood with sufficient readiness. Excepting a few merchants, they had nothing else to give; and, in the years when the fur trade was cut off, they lived chiefly on the pay they received for supplying the troops and other public services. Far from being able to support the war, they looked to the war to support them. 2

1 Lettres du Roy et du Ministre, 1690-1694. In 1691, the amount allowed for extraordinaires de guerre was 99,000 livres (francs). In 1692, it was 193,000 livres, a part of which was for fortifications. In the following year, no less than 760,000 livres were drawn for Canada, " ce qui ne se pourroit pas supporter, si cela continuoit de la mesme force," writes the minister. (Le Ministre a Frontenac, 13 Mars, 1694.) This last sum probably included the pay of the troops.

" Sa Majeste" fait depuis plusieurs anne'es des sacrifices immenses en Canada. L'avantage en demeure presque tout entier au profit des ha-bitans et des marchands qui y resident. Ces defenses se font pour leur Beurete* et pour leur conservation. II est juste que ceux qui sont en estat secourent le public." Mfmoire du fyi/, 1693. " Les habitans de la

The work of fortifying the vital points of the colony, Quebec, Three Rivers, and Montreal, received constant stimulus from the alarms of attack, and, above all, from a groundless report that ten thousand " Bostonnais " had sailed for Quebec. The sessions of the council were suspended, and the councillors seized pick and spade. The old defences of the place were reconstructed on a new plan, made by the great engineer Vauban. The settlers were, mustered together from a distance of twenty leagues, and compelled to labor, with little or no pay, till a line of solid earthworks enclosed Quebec from Cape Diamond to the St. Charles. Three Rivers and Montreal were also strengthened. The cost exceeded the estimates, and drew upon Frontenac and Champigny fresh admonitions from Versailles. 1

colonie ne contribuent en rien a tout ce que Sa Majeste* fait pour leur conservation, pendant que ses sujets du Koyaume donnent tout ce qu'ils ont pour son service." Le Ministre a Frontenac, 13 Mars, 1694.

1 Lettres du Roy et du Ministre, 1693, 1694. Cape Diamond was now for the first time included within the line of circumvallation at Quebec. A strong stone redoubt, with sixteen cannon, was built upon its summit.

In 1854, in demolishing a part of the old wall between the fort of Quebec and the adjacent " Governor's Garden," a plate of copper was found with a Latin inscription, of which the following is a translation:—

"In the year of Grace, 1693, under the reign of the Most August, Most Invincible, and Most Christian King, Louis the Great, Fourteenth of that name, the Most Excellent and Most Illustrious Lord, Louis de Buade, Count of Frontenac, twice Viceroy of all New France, after having three years before repulsed, routed, and completely conquered the rebellious inhabitants of New England, who besieged this town of Quebec, and who threatened to renew their attack this year, constructed, at the charge of the king, this citadel, with the fortifications therewith connected, for the defence of the country and the safety of the people, and for confounding yet again a people perfidious towards God and towards its lawful king. And he has laid this first stone. "

298 THE SCOURGE OF CANADA. 11691-94-

The bounties on scalps and prisoners were another occasion of royal complaint. Twenty crowns had been offered for each male white prisoner, ten crowns for each female, and ten crowns for each scalp, whether Indian or English. 1 The bounty on prisoners produced an excellent result, since instead of killing them the Indian allies learned to bring tfiem to Quebec. If children, they were placed in the convents; and, if adults, they were distributed to labor among the settlers. Thus, though the royal letters show that the measure was one of policy, it acted in the interest of humanity. It was not so with the bounty on scalps. The Abenaki, Huron, and Iroquois converts brought in many of them; but grave doubts arose whether they all came from the heads of enemies. 2 The scalp of a Frenchman was not distinguishable from the scalp of an Englishman, and could be had with less trouble. Partly for this reason, and partly out of economy, the king gave it as his belief that a bounty of one crown was enough; though the governor and the intendant united in declaring that the scalps of the whole Iroquois confederacy would be a good bargain for his Majesty at ten crowns apiece. 3

The river Ottawa was the main artery of Canada, and to stop it was to stop the flow of her life blood. The Iroquois knew this; and their constant effort

1 Champigny au Ministre, 21 Sept., 1692.

3 Relation de 1682-1712.

1 Mtmoiredu Roy aux Sieurs Frontenac et Champigny, 1693; Frontenac Єt Champigny au Ministre, 4 Nov., 1693. The bounty on prisoners was reduced in the same proportion, showing that economy was the chief object of the change.

was to close it so completely that the annual supply of beaver skins would be prevented from passing, and the colony be compelled to live on credit. It was their habit to spend the latter part of the winter in hunting among the forests between the Ottawa and the upper St. Lawrence, and then, when the ice broke up, to move in large bands to the banks of the former stream, and lie in ambush at the Chaudiere, the Long Saut, or other favorable points, to waylay the passing canoes. On the other hand, it was the constant effort of Frontenac to drive them off and keep the river open; an almost impossible task. Many conflicts, great and small, took place with various results; but, in spite of every effort, the Iroquois blockade was maintained more than two years. The story of one of the expeditions made by the French in this quarter will show the hardship of the service, and the moral and physical vigor which it demanded.

Early in February, three hundred men under Dorvilliers were sent by Frontenac to surprise the Iroquois in their hunting-grounds. When they were a few days out, their leader scalded his foot by the upsetting of a kettle at their encampment near Lake St. Francis; and the command fell on a youth named Beaucour, an officer of regulars, accomplished as an engineer, and known for his polished wit. The march through the snow-clogged forest was so terrible that the men lost heart. Hands and feet were frozen; some of the Indiana refused to proceed, and many of the Canadians lagged behind. Shots were heard, showing that

the enemy were not far off ; but cold, hunger, and fatigue had overcome the courage of the pursuers, and the young commander saw his followers on the point of deserting him. He called them together, and harangued them in terms so animating that they caught his spirit, and again pushed on. For four hours more they followed the tracks of the Iroquois snow-shoes, till they found the savages in their bivouac, set upon them, and killed or captured nearly all. There was a French slave among them, scarcely distinguishable from his owners. It was an officer named La Plante, taken at La Chine three years before. " He would have been killed like his masters," says La Hontan, " if he had not cried out with all his might, ' Misericorde, sauvez-moi, je suis Franqais.' " 1 Beaucour brought his prisoners to Quebec, where Frontenac ordered that two of them should be burned. One stabbed himself in prison; the other was tortured by the Christian Hurons on Cape Diamond, defying them to the last. Nor was this the only instance of such fearful reprisal. In the same year, a number of Iroquois captured by Vaudreuil were burned at Montreal at the demand of the Canadians and the mission Indians, who insisted that their cruelties should be paid back in kind. It is said that the purpose was answered, and the Iroquois deterred for a while from torturing their captives. 2

The brunt of the war fell ou the upper half of

1 La Potherie, III. 166; Relation de ce qui s'est passt de plu$ considerable en Canada, 1691, 1692; La Hontan, I 233.

2 Relation, 1682-1712.

the colony. The country about Montreal, and for nearly a hundred miles below it, was easily accessible to the Iroquois by the routes of Lake Champ-lain and the upper St. Lawrence; while below Three Rivers the settlements were tolerably safe from their incursions, and were exposed to attack solely from the English of New England, who could molest them only by sailing up from the Gulf in force. Hence the settlers remained on their farms, and followed their usual occupations, except when Frontenac drafted them for war-parties. Above Three Rivers, their condition was wholly different. A traveller passing through this part of Canada would have found the houses empty. Here and there he would have seen all the inhabitants of a parish laboring in a field together, watched by sentinels, and generally guarded by a squad of regulars. When one field was tilled, they passed to the next; and this communal process was repeated when the harvest was ripe. At night, they took refuge in the fort; that is to say, in a cluster of log cabins, surrounded by a palisade. Sometimes, when long exemption from attack had emboldened them, they ventured back to their farm-houses, an experiment always critical and sometimes fatal. Thus the people of La Chesnaye, forgetting a sharp lesson they had received a year or two before, returned to their homes in fancied security. One evening a bachelor of the parish made a visit to a neighboring widow, bringing with him his gun and a small dog. As he was taking his leave, his hostess, whose husband had

been killed the year before, told him that she was afraid to be left alone, and begged him to remain with her, an invitation which he accepted. Towards morning, the barking of his dog roused him; when, going out, he saw the night lighted up by the blaze of burning houses, and heard the usual firing and screeching of an Iroquois attack. He went back to his frightened companion, who also had a gun. Placing himself at a corner of the house, he told her to stand behind him. A number of Iroquois soon appeared, on which he fired at them, and, taking her gun, repeated the shot, giving her his own to load. The warriors returned his fire from a safe distance, and in the morning withdrew altogether, on which the pair emerged from their shelter, and succeeded in reaching the fort. The other inhabitants were all killed or captured. 1

Many incidents of this troubled time are preserved, but none of them are so well worth the record as the defence of the fort at Vercheres by the young daughter of the seignior. Many years later, the Marquis de Beauharnais, governor of Canada, caused the story to be written down from the recital of the heroine herself. Vercheres was on the south shore of the St. Lawrence, about twenty miles below Montreal. A strong blockhouse stood outside the fort, and was connected with it by a covered way. On the morning of the twenty-second of October, the inhabitants were at work in the fields, and nobody was left in the place but two soldiers, two boys, an old man of eighty,

1 Relation. 1682-1712.

and a number of women and children. The seignior, formerly an officer of the regiment of Carig-nan, was on duty at Quebec; his wife was at Montreal ; and their daughter Madeleine, fourteen years of age, was at the landing-place not far from the gate of the fort, with a hired man named Laviolette. Suddenly she heard firing from the direction where the settlers were at work, and an instant after Laviolette cried out, " Kun, Mademoiselle, run! here come the Iroquois!" She turned and saw forty or fifty of them at the distance of a pistol-shot. " I ran for the fort, commending myself to the Holy Virgin. The Iroquois who chased after me, seeing that they could not catch me alive before I reached the gate, stopped and fired at me. The bullets whistled about my ears, and made the time seem very long. As soon as I was near enough to be heard, I cried out, To arms ! to arms ! hoping that somebody would come out and help me; but it was of no use. The two soldiers i$ the fort were so scared that they had hidden in the blockhouse. At the gate, I found two women crying for their husbands, who had just been killed. I made them go in, and then shut the gate. I next thought what I could do to save myself and the few people with me. I went to inspect the fort, and found that several palisades had fallen down, and left openings by which the enemy could easily get in. I ordered them to be set up again, and helped to carry them myself. When the breaches were stopped, I went to the blockhouse where the ammunition is kept, and

here I found the two soldiers, one hiding in a corner, and the other with a lighted match in his hand. ' What are you going to do with that match ?' I asked. He answered, ' Light the powder, and blow us all up.' (You are a miserable coward/ said I, ' go out of this place/ I spoke so resolutely that he obeyed. I then threw off my bonnet; and, after putting on a hat and taking a gun, I said to my two brothers: ' Let us fight to the death. We are fighting for our country and our religion. Kemember that our father has taught you that gentlemen are born to shed their blood for the service of God and the king/ '

The boys, who were twelve and ten years old, aided by the soldiers, whom her words had inspired with some little courage, began to fire from the loopholes upon the Iroquois, who, ignorant of the weakness of the garrison, showed their usual reluctance to attack a fortified place, and occupied themselves with chasing and butchering the people in the neighboring fields. Madeleine ordered a cannon to be fired, partly to deter the enemy from an assault, and partly to warn some of the soldiers, who were hunting at a distance. The women and children in the fort cried and screamed without ceasing. She ordered them to stop, lest their terror should encourage the Indians. A canoe was presently seen approaching the landing-place. It was a settler named Fontaine, trying to reach the fort with his family. The Iroquois were still near ; and Madeleine feared that the new comers would be killed, if something were not done to aid them.

She appealed to the soldiers, but their courage was not equal to the attempt; on which, as she declares, after leaving Laviolette to keep watch at the gate, she herself went alone to the landing-place. " I thought that the savages would suppose it to be a ruse to draw them towards the fort, in order to make a sortie upon them. They did suppose so, and thus I was able to save the Fontaine family. When they were all landed, I made them march before me in full sight of the enemy. We put so bold a face on it, that they thought they had more to fear than we. Strengthened by this reinforcement, I ordered that the enemy should be fired on whenever they showed themselves. After sunset, a violent north-east wind began to blow, accompanied with snow and hail, which told us that we should have a terrible night. The Iroquois were all this time lurking about us; and I judged by their movements that, instead of being deterred by the storm, they would climb into the fort under cover of the darkness. I assembled all my troops, that is to say, six persons, and spoke to them thus: * God has saved us to-day from the hands of our enemies, but we must take care not to fall into their snares to-night. As for me, I want you to see that I am not afraid. I will take charge of the fort with an old man of eighty and another who never fired a gun; and you, Pierre Fontaine, with La Bonte and Gachet (our two soldiers), will go to the blockhouse with the women and children, because that is the strongest place; and, if I am taken,

don't surrender, even if I am cut to pieces and

20

burned before your eyes. The enemy cannot hurt you in the blockhouse, if you make the least show of fight/ I placed my young brothers on two of the bastions, the old man on the third, and I took the fourth; and all night, in spite of wind, snow, and hail, the cries of ' All's well' were kept up from the blockhouse to the fort, and from the fort to the blockhouse. One would have thought that the place was full of soldiers. The Iroquois thought BO, and were completely deceived, as they confessed afterwards to Monsieur de Callieres, whom they told that they had held a council to make a plan for capturing the fort in the night but had done nothing because such a constant watch was kept.

" About one in the morning, the sentinel on the bastion by the gate called out, ' Mademoiselle, I hear something.' I went to him to find what it was; and by the help of the snow, which covered the ground, I could see through the darkness a number of cattle, the miserable remnant that the Iroquois had left us. The others wanted to open the gate and let them in, but-I answered: ' God forbid. You don't know all the tricks of the savages. They are no doubt following the cattle, covered with skins of beasts, so as to get into the fort, if we are simple enough to open the gate for them/ Nevertheless, after taking every precaution, I thought that we might open it without risk, I made my two brothers stand ready with their guns cocked in case of surprise, and so we let in the cattle.

"At last, the daylight came again; and, as the darkness disappeared, our anxieties seemed to disappear with it. Everybody took courage except Mademoiselle Marguerite, wife of the Sieur Fontaine, who being extremely timid, as all Parisian women are, asked her husband to carry her to another fort. . . He said, ' I will never abandon this fort while Mademoiselle Madelon (Madeleine) is here I answered him that I would never abandon it; that I would rather die than give it up to the enemy; and that it was of the greatest importance that they should never get possession of any French fort, because, if they got one, they would think they could get others, and would grow more bold and presumptuous than ever. I may say with truth that I did not eat or sleep for twice twenty-four hours. I did not go once into my father's house, but kept always on the bastion, or went to the blockhouse to see how the people there were behaving. I always kept a cheerful and smiling face, and encouraged my little company with the hope of speedy succor. " We were a week in constant alarm, with the enemy .always about us. At last Monsieur de la Monnerie, a lieutenant sent by Monsieur de Callieres, arrived in the night with forty men. As he did not know whether the fort was taken or not, he approached as silently as possible. One of our eoiitinels, hearing a slight sound, cried, Qui vive ? I was at the time dozing, with my head on a table and my gun lying across my arms. The sentinel told me that he heard a voice from the river. I went up at once to the bastion to see whether it was Indians or Frenchmen. I asked, ' Who are you ?' One of them answered, ' We are Frenchmen : it is La Monnerie, who comes to bring you help I caused the gate to be opened, placed a sentinel there, and went down to the river to meet them. As soon as I saw Monsieur de la Monnerie, I saluted him, and said, ' Monsieur, I surrender my arms to you He answered gallantly, ' Mademoiselle, they are in good hands (Better than you think I returned. He inspected the fort, and found every thing in order, and a sentinel on each bastion. ' It is time to relieve them, Monsieur,' said I: e we have not been off our bastions for a week"

A band of converts from the Saut St. Louis arrived soon after, followed the trail of their heathen countrymen, overtook them on Lake Champlain, and recovered twenty or more French prisoners. Madeleine de Vercheres was not the only heroine of Jier family. Her father's fort was the Castle Dangerous of Canada; and it was but two years before that her mother, left with three or four

1 Rfcit de Mile. Magdelaine de Vercheres, df/tfe de 14 arts (Collection de TAbW Ferland). It appears from Tanguay, Dictionnaire Ge'ne'alogique, that Marie-Madeleine Jarret de Vercheres was born in April, 1678, which corresponds to the age given in the Pe'cit. She married Thomas Tarieu de la Naudiere in 1706, and M. de la Perrade, or Prade, in 1722. Her brother Louis was born in 1680, and was therefore, as stated in the Rtcit, twelve years old in 1692. The birthday of the other, Alexander, is not given. His baptism was registered in 1682. One of the brothers was killed at the attack of Haverhill, in 1708.

Madame de Poncbartrain, wife of the minister, procured a pension for life to Madeleine de Vercheres. Two versions of her narrative are before me. There are slight variations between them, but in all essential points they are the same. The following note is appended to one of them : "Ce recit fut fait par ordre de M^ de Beauharnois, gouverneur du Canada."

armed men, and beset by the Iroquois, threw herself with her followers into the blockhouse, and held the assailants two days at bay, till the Marquis de Crisasi came with troops to her relief. 1

From the moment when the Canadians found a chief whom they could trust, and the firm old hand of Frontenac grasped the reins of their destiny, a spirit of hardihood and energy grew up in all this rugged population; and they faced their stern fortunes with a stubborn daring and endurance that merit respect and admiration.

Now, as in all their former wars, a great part of their suffering was due to the Mohawks. The Jesuits had spared no pains to convert them, thus changing them from enemies to friends; and their efforts had so far succeeded that the mission colony of Saut St. Louis contained a numerous population of Mohawk Christians. 3 The place was well fortified ; and troops were usually stationed here, partly to defend the converts and partly to ensure their fidelity. They had sometimes done excellent service for the French; but many of them still remembered their old homes on the Mohawk, and their old ties of fellowship and kindred. Their heathen countrymen were jealous of their secession, and spared no pains to reclaim them. Sometimes they tried intrigue, and sometimes force. On one occasion, joined by the Oneidas and Onondagas, they appeared before the palisades of St. Louis, to the

i La Potherie, I. 326.

a This mission was also called Caghnawaga. The village still exists, at the head of the rapid of St. Louis, or La Chine.

number of more than four hundred warriors; but, finding the bastions manned and the gates shut, they withdrew discomfited. It was of great importance to the French to sunder them from their heathen relatives so completely that reconciliation would be impossible, and it was largely to this end that a grand expedition was prepared against the Mohawk towns.

All the mission Indians in the colony were invited to join it, the Iroquois of the Saut and Mountain, Abenakis from the Chaudiere, Hurons from Lorette, and Algonquins from Three Rivers. A hundred picked soldiers were added, and a large band of Canadians. All told, they mustered six hundred and twenty-five men, under three tried leaders, Mantet, Courtemanche, and La Noue. They left Chambly at the end of January, and pushed southward on snow-shoes. Their way waa over the ice of Lake Champlain, for more than a century the great thoroughfare of war-parties. They bivouacked in the forest by squads of twelve or more ; dug away the snow in a circle, covered the bared earth with a bed of spruce boughs, made a fire in the middle, and smoked their pipes around it. Here crouched the Christian savage, muffled in his blanket, his unwashed face still smirched with soot and vermilion, relics of the war-paint he had worn a week before when he danced the war-dance in the square of the mission village; and here sat the Canadians, hooded like Capuchin monks, but irrepressible in loquacity, as the blaze of the camp-fire glowed on their hardy visages and

fell in fainter radiance on the rocks and pines behind them.

Sixteen days brought them to the two lower Mohawk towns. A young Dutchman who had been captured three years before at Schenectady, and whom the Indians of the Saut had imprudently brought with them, ran off in the night, and carried the alarm to the English. - The invaders had no time to lose. The two towns were a quarter of a league apart. They surrounded them both on the night of the sixteenth of February, waited in silence till the voices within were hushed, and then captured them without resistance, as most of the inmates were absent. After burning one of them, and leaving the prisoners well guarded in the other, they marched eight leagues to the third town, reached it at evening, and hid in the neighboring woods. Through all the early night, they heard the whoops and songs of the warriors within, who were dancing the war-dance for an intended expedition. About midnight, all was still. The Mohawks had posted no sentinels; and one of the French Indians, scaling the palisade, opened the gate to his comrades. There was a short but bloody fight. Twenty or thirty Mohawks were killed, and nearly three hundred captured, chiefly women and children. The French commanders now required their allies, the mission Indians, to make good a promise which, at the instance of Frontenac, had been exacted from them by the governor of Montreal. It was that they should kill all their male captives, a proceeding which

would have averted every danger of future reconciliation between the Christian and heathen Mohawks. The converts of the Saut and the Mountain had readily given the pledge, but apparently with no intention to keep it; at least, they now refused to do so. Remonstrance was useless; and, after burning the town, the French and their allies began their retreat, encumbered by a long train of prisoners. They inarched two days, when they were hailed from a distance by Mohawk scouts, who told them that the English were on their track, but that peace had been declared in Europe, and that the pursuers did not mean to fight, but to parley. Hereupon the mission Indians insisted on waiting for them, and no exertion of the French commanders could persuade them to move. Trees were hewn down, and a fort made after the Iro-quois fashion, by encircling the camp with a high and dense abatis of trunks and branches. Here they lay two days more, the French disgusted and uneasy, and their savage allies obstinate and impracticable.

Meanwhile, Major Peter Schuyler was following their trail, with a body of armed settlers hastily mustered. A troop of Oneidas joined him; and the united parties, between five and six hundred in all, at length appeared before the fortified camp of the French. It w r as at once evident that there was to be no parley. The forest rang with war-whoops ; and the English Indians, unmanageable as those of the French, set at work to entrench themselves with felled trees. The French and their

allies sallied to dislodge them. The attack was fierce, "and the resistance equally so. Both sides lost ground by turns. A priest of the mission of the Mountain, named Gay, was in the thick of the fight; and, when he saw his neophytes run, he threw himself before them, crying, " What are you afraid of ? We are fighting with infidels, who have nothing human but the shape. Have you forgotten that the Holy Virgin is our leader and our protector, and that you are subjects of the King of France, whose name makes all Europe tremble ? " 1 Three times the French renewed the attack in vain; then gave over the attempt, and lay quiet behind their barricade of trees. So also did their opponents. The morning was dark and stormy, and the driving snow that filled the air made the position doubly dreary. The English were starving. Their slender stock of provisions had been consumed or shared with the Indians, who, on their part, did not want food, having resources unknown to their white friends. A group of them squatted about a fire invited Schuyler to share their broth; but his appetite was spoiled when he saw a human hand ladled out of the kettle. His hosts were breakfasting on a dead Frenchman.

All night the hostile bands, ensconced behind their sylvan ramparts, watched each other in silence. In the morning, an Indian deserter told the English commander that the French were packing their baggage. Schuyler sent to reconnoitre, and found

1 Journal de Jacques Le Ber, extract in Faillon, Vie de Mile. Le Ber, Appendix.

them gone. They had retreated unseen through the snow-storm. He ordered his men to follow ; but, as most of them had fasted for two days, they refused to do so till an expected convoy of provisions should arrive. They waited till the next morning, when the convoy appeared : five biscuits were served out to each man, and the pursuit began. By great efforts, they nearly overtook the fugitives, who now sent them word that, if they made an attack, all the prisoners should be put to death. On this, Schuyler's Indians refused to continue the chase. The

French, by this time, had reached the Hudson, where to their dismay they found the ice breaking up and drifting down the stream. Happily for them, a large sheet of it had become wedged at a turn of the river, and formed a temporary bridge, by which they crossed, and then pushed on to Lake George. Here the soft and melting ice would not bear them; and they were forced to make their way along the shore, over rocks and mountains, through sodden snow and matted thickets. The provisions, of which they had made a depot on Lake Champlain, were all spoiled. They boiled moccasons for food, and scraped away the snow to find hickory and beech nuts. Several died of famine, and many more, unable to move, lay helpless by the lake; while a few of the strongest toiled on to Montreal to tell Callieres of their plight. Men and food were sent them; and from time to time, as they were able, they journeyed on again, straggling towards their homes, singly or in small parties, feeble, emaciated,

and in many instances with health irreparably broken.

" The expedition," says Frontenac, " was a glorious success." However glorious, it was dearly bought; and a few more such victories would be ruin. The governor presently achieved a success more solid and less costly. The wavering mood of the north-western tribes, always oscillating between the French and the English, had caused him incessant anxiety; and he had lost no time in using the defeat of Phips to confirm them in alliance with Canada. Courtemanche was sent up the Ottawa to carry news of the French triumph, and stimulate the savages of Michillimackinac to lift the hatchet. It was a desperate venture ; for the river was beset, as usual, by the Iroquois. With ten followers, the daring partisan ran the gauntlet of a thousand dangers, and safely reached his destination ; where his gifts and his harangues, joined with the tidings of victory, kindled great excitement among the Ottawas and Hurons. The indispensable but most difficult task remained : that of opening the Ottawa for the descent of the great accumulation of beaver skins, which had been gathering at Michillimackinac for three years, and for the want of which Canada was bankrupt. More than two hundred

1 On this expedition, Narrative of Military Operations in Canada^ ill N. Y. Col. Docs., IX. 550; Relation de ce qui s'est passe' de plus remarquable en Canada, 1692, 1693; Callieres au Ministre, 7 Sept., 1693; La Potherie, HI. 169; Relation de 1682-1712; Faillon, Vie de Mile. Le Ber, 313; Bel-mont, Hist, du Canada; Beyard and Lodowick, Journal of the Late Actions of the French at Canada; Report of Major Peter Schuyler, in N. Y. Col. Docs., IV. 16; Golden, 142.

The minister wrote to Callieres, finding great fault with the conduct of the mission Indians Ponchartrain a Callieres, 8 Mai, 1694.

Frenchmen were known to be at that remote post, or roaming in the wilderness around it; and Fron-tenac resolved on an attempt to muster them together, and employ their united force to protect the Indians and the traders in bringing down this mass of furs to Montreal. A messenger, strongly escorted, was sent with orders to this effect, and succeeded in reaching Michillimackinac, though there was a battle on the way, in which the officer commanding the escort was killed. Frontenac anxiously waited the issue, when after a long delay the tidings reached him of complete success. He hastened to Montreal, and found it swarming with Indians and coureurs de bois. Two hundred canoes had arrived, filled with the coveted beaver skins. " It is impossible," says the chronicle, " to conceive the joy of the people, when they beheld these riches. Canada had awaited them for years. The merchants and the farmers were dying of hunger. Credit was gone, and everybody was afraid that the enemy would waylay and seize this last resource of the country. Therefore it was, that none could find words strong enough to praise and bless him by whose care all this wealth had arrived. Father of the People, Preserver of the Country, seemed terms too weak to express their gratitude." *

While three years of arrested sustenance came down together from the lakes, a fleet sailed up the St. Lawrence, freighted with soldiers and supplies. The horizon of Canada was brightening.

1 Relation de ce qui s'est passé de plus remarquable en Canada, 1692,1693. Compare La Potherie, III. 185.

CHAPTER XV.

1691-1695. AN INTERLUDE.

APPEAL OF FRONTENAC. — His OPPONENTS. — His SERVICES. — RIVALRY AND STRIFE. — BISHOP SAINT-VALLIER. — SOCIETY AT THE CHATEAU. — PRIVATE THEATRICALS. — ALARM OF THE CLERGY. — TARTUFFE. — A SINGULAR BARGAIN. — MAREUIL AND THE BISHOP. — MAREUIL ON TRIAL. — ZEAL OF SAINT-VALLIER. — SCANDALS AT MONTREAL. — APPEAL TO THE KING. — THE STRIFE COMPOSED. — LIBEL AGAINST FRONTENAC.

WIIILE the Canadians hailed Frontenac as a father, he found also some recognition of his services from his masters at the court. The king wrote him a letter with his own hand, to express satisfaction at the defence of Quebec, and sent him a gift of two thousand crowns. He greatly needed the .money, but prized the letter still more, and wrote to his relative, the minister Ponchartrain: " The gift you procured for me, this year, has helped me very much towards paying the great expenses which the crisis of our affairs and the excessive cost of living here have caused me; but, though I receive this mark of his Majesty's goodness with the utmost respect and gratitude, I confess that I feel far more deeply the satisfaction that he has been pleased to express with my services. . The raising of the siege of Quebec did not

deserve all the attention that I hear he has given it in the midst of so many important events, and therefore I must needs ascribe it to your kindness in commending it to his notice. This leads me to hope that whenever some office, or permanent employment, or some mark of dignity or distinction, may offer itself, you will put me on the list as well as others who have the honor to be as closely connected with you as I am; for it would be very hard to find myself forgotten because I am in a remote country, where it is more difficult and dangerous to serve the king than elsewhere. I have consumed all my property. Nothing is left but what the king gives me; and I have reached an age where, though neither strength nor goodwill fail me as yet, and though the latter will last as long as I live, I see myself on the eve of losing the former: so that a post a little more secure and tranquil than the government of Canada will soon suit my time of life; and, if I can be assured of your support, I shall not despair of getting such a one. Please then to permit my wife and my friends to refresh your memory now and then on this point." 1 Again, in the following year: " I have been encouraged to believe that the gift of two thousand crowns, which his Majesty made me last year, would be continued; but apparently you have not been able to obtain it, for I think that you know the difficulty I have in living here on my salary. I hope that, when you find a better opportunity, you will try to procure me this favor. My

1 Frontenac au Ministre, 20 Oct., 1691-

only trust is in your support; and I am persuaded that, having the honor to be so closely connected with you, you would reproach yourself, if you saw me sink into decrepitude, without resources and without honors." 1 And still again he appeals to the minister for " some permanent arid honorable place attended with the marks of distinction, which are more grateful than all the rest to a heart shaped after the right pattern." 2 In return for these sturdy applications, he got nothing for the present but a continuance of the king's gift of two thousand crowns.

Not every voice in the colony sounded the governor's praise. Now, as always, he had enemies in state and Church. It is true that the quarrels and the bursts of passion that marked his first term of government now rarely occurred, but this was not so much due to a change in Frontenac himself as to a change in the conditions around him. The war made him indispensable. He had gained what he wanted, the consciousness of mastexy; and under its soothing influence he was less irritable and exacting. He lived with the bishop on terms of mutual courtesy, while his relations with his colleague, the intendant, were commonly smooth enough on the surface; for Champigny, warned by the court not to offend him, treated him with studied deference, and was usually treated in return with urbane condescension. During all this time, the intendant was complaining of him to the

1 Frontenac au Ministre, 15 Sept., 1692. * Ibid., 25 Oct., 1693.

minister. " He is spending a great deal of money; but he is master, and does what he pleases. I can only keep the peace by yielding every thing." " He wants to reduce me to a nobody." And among other similar charges, he says that the governor receives pay for garrisons that do not exist, and keeps it for himself. " Do not tell that I said so," adds the prudent Champigny, " for it would make great trouble, if he knew it." 2 Frontenac, perfectly aware of these covert attacks, desires the minister not to heed " the falsehoods and impostures uttered against me by persons who meddle with what does not concern them." 3 He alludes to Champigny's allies, the Jesuits, who, as he thought, had also maligned him. " Since I have been here, I have spared no pains to gain the goodwill of Monsieur the intendant, and may God grant that the counsels which he is too ready to receive from certain persons who have never been friends of peace and harmony do not some time make division between us. But I close my eyes to all that, and shall still persevere." 4 In another letter to Pon-chartrain, he says : " I write you this in private, because I have been informed by my wife that charges have been made to you against my conduct since my return to this country. I promise you, Mon-seigneur, that, whatever my accusers do, they will not make me change conduct towards them, and that I shall still treat them with consideration. I

1 Champigny au Ministre, 12 Oct., 1691.
2 Ibid., 4 A T oy., 1693.
8 Frontenac mi Ministre, 15 Sept., 1692. * Ibid., 20 Oct., 1691.

merely ask your leave most humbly to represent that, having maintained this colony in full prosperity during the ten years when I formerly held the government of it, I nevertheless fell a sacrifice to the artifice and fury of those whose encroachments, and whose excessive and unauthorized power, my duty and my passionate affection for the service of the king obliged me in conscience to repress. My recall, which made them masters in the conduct of the government, was followed by all the disasters which overwhelmed this unhappy colony. The millions that the king spent here, the troops that he sent out, and the Canadians that he took into pay, all went for nothing. Most of the soldiers, and 110 small number of brave Canadians, perished in enterprises ill devised and ruinous to the country, which I found on my arrival ravaged with unheard-of cruelty by the Iroquois, without resistance, and in sight of the troops and of the forts. The inhabitants were discouraged, and unnerved by want of confidence in their chiefs; while the friendly Indians, seeing our weakness, were ready to join our enemies. I was fortunate' enough and diligent enough to change this deplorable state of things, and drive away the English, whom my predecessors did not have on their hands, and this too with only half as many troops as they had. I am far from wishing to blame their conduct. I leave you to judge it. But I cannot have the tranquillity and freedom of mind which I need for the work I have to do here, without feeling entire confidence that the cabal which is again

21

forming against me cannot produce impressions which may prevent you from doing me justice. For the rest, if it is thought fit that I should leave the priests to do as they like, I shall he delivered from an infinity of troubles and cares, in which I can have no other interest than the good of the colony, the trade of the kingdom, and the peace of the king's subjects, and of which I alone bear the burden, as well as the jealousy of sundry persons, and the iniquity of the ecclesiastics, who begin to call impious those who are obliged to oppose their passions and their interests." 1

As Champigny always sided with the Jesuits, his relations with Frontenac grew daily more critical. Open rupture at length seemed imminent, and the king interposed to keep the peace. " There has been discord between you under a show of harmony," he wrote to the disputants. 2 Frontenac was exhorted to forbearance and calmness; while the intendant was told that he allowed himself to be made an instrument of others, and that his charges against the governor proved nothing but his own ill-temper. 3 The minister wrote in vain. The bickerings that he reproved were but premonitions of a greater strife.

Bishop Saint-Vallier was a rigid, austere, and contentious prelate, who loved power as much as

1 " L'iniquit£ des eccl&iastiques qui commencent a traiter d'impies ceux qui eont obliges de resister a leurs passions et a leurs interets." Fnmtenfic au Ministre, 20 Oct., 1691.

* Mfnwire du Roy pour Frontenac et Champigny, 1694.

3 Le Ministre a Frontenac, 8 May, 1694; Le Minittre a Champigny, m&me date.

Frontenac himself, and thought that, as the deputy of Christ, it was his duty to exercise it -to the utmost. The governor watched him with a jealous eye, well aware that, though the pretensions of the Church to supremacy over the civil power had suffered a check, Saint-Vallier would revive them the moment he thought he could do so with success. I have shown elsewhere the severity of the ecclesiastical rule at Quebec, where the zealous pastors watched their flock with unrelenting vigilance, and associations of pious women helped them in the work. 1 This naturally produced revolt, and tended to divide the town into two parties, the worldly and the devout. The love of pleasure was not extinguished, and various influences helped to keep it alive. Perhaps none of these was so potent as the presence in winter of a considerable number of officers from France, whose piety was often less conspicuous than their love of enjoyment. At the Chateau St. Louis a circle of young men, more or less brilliant and accomplished, surrounded the governor, and formed a centre of social attraction. Frontenac was not without religion, and he held it becoming a man of his station not to fail in its observances; but he would not have a Jesuit confessor, and placed his conscience in the keeping of the Recollet friars, who were not politically aggressive, and who had been sent to Canada expressly as a foil to the rival order. They found no favor in the eyes of the bishop and his adherents, and the governor found none, for the support he lent them.

1 Old Regime, chap. xix.

The winter that followed the arrival of the fura from the upper lakes was a season of gayety without precedent since the war began. All was harmony at Quebec till the carnival approached, when Fronteriac, whose youthful instincts survived his seventy-four years, introduced a startling novelty which proved the signal of discord. One of his military circle, the sharp-witted La Motte-Cadiliac, thus relates this untoward event in a letter to a friend : " The winter passed very pleasantly, especially to the officers, who lived together like comrades; and, to contribute to their honest enjoyment, the count caused two plays to be acted, (Nicomede ' and ' Mithridate." It was an amateur performance, in which the officers took part along with some of the ladies of Quebec. The success was prodigious, and so was the storm that followed. Half a century before, the Jesuits had grieved over the first ball in Canada. Private theatricals were still more baneful. "The clergy," continues La Motte, " beat their alarm drums, armed cap-a-pie, and snatched their bows and arrows. The Sieur Glandelet was first to begin, and preached two sermons, in which he tried to prove that nobody could go to a play without mortal sin. The bishop issued a mandate, and had it read from the pulpits, in which he speaks of certain impious, impure, and noxious comedies, insinuating that those which had been acted were such. The credulous and infatuated people, seduced by the sermons and the mandate, began already to regard the count as a corrupter of morals and a destroyer of religion.

The numerous party of the pretended devotees mustered in the streets and public places, and presently made their way into the houses, to confirm the weak-minded in their illusion, and tried to make the stronger share it; but, as they failed in this almost completely, they resolved at last to conquer or die, and persuaded the bishop to use a strange device, which was to publish a mandate in the church, whereby the Sieur de Mareuil, a half-pay lieutenant, was interdicted the use of the sacraments."

This story needs explanation. Not only had the amateur actors at the chateau played two pieces inoffensive enough in themselves, but a report had been spread that they meant next to perform the famous " Tartuffe " of Moliere, a satire which, while purporting to be levelled against falsehood, lust, greed, and ambition, covered with a mask of religion, was rightly thought by a portion of the clergy to be levelled against themselves. The friends of Fron-tenac say that the report was a hoax. Be this as it may, the bishop believed it. " This worthy prelate," continues the irreverent La Motte, " was afraid of ' Tartuffe and had got it into his head that the count meant to have it played, though he had never thought of such a thing. Monsieur de Saint-Vallier sweated blood and water to stop a torrent which existed only in his imagination." It was now that he launched his two mandates, both on the same day; one denouncing comedies in general and " Tartuffe " in particular, and the other smiting

* La Motte-Cadillac a , 28 Sept., 1694.

Mareuil, who, he says, " uses language capable of making Heaven blush," and whom he elsewhere stigmatizes as "worse than a Protestant." It was Mareuil who, as reported, was to play the part of Tartuffe ; and on him, therefore, the brunt of episcopal indignation fell. He was not a wholly exemplary person. " I mean," says La Motte, " to show you the truth in all its nakedness. The fact is that, about two years ago, when the Sieur de Mareuil first came to Canada, and was carousing with his friends, he sang some indecent song or other. The count was told of it, and gave him a severe reprimand. This is the charge against him. After a two years' silence, the pastoral zeal has wakened, because a play is to be acted which the clergy mean to stop at any cost."

The bishop found another way of stopping it. He met Frontenac, with the intendant, near the Jesuit chapel, accosted him on the subject which filled his thoughts, and offered him a hundred pistoles if he would prevent the playing of " Tartuffe." Frontenac laughed, and closed the bargain. Saint-Yallier wrote his note on the spot; and the governor took it, apparently well pleased to have made the bishop disburse. " I thought," writes the intendant, " that Monsieur de Frontenac would have given him back the paper." He did no such thing, but drew the money on the next day and gave it to the hospitals. 2

1 Mandement au Sujet des Comedies, 16 Jan., 1694 ; Mandement au Sujet de certaines

Personnes qui tenoient des Discours impies, mSme date; Registre du Conseil Souverain. •

* This incident is mentioned by La Motte-Cadillac; by the intendant,

Mareuil, deprived of the sacraments, and held up to reprobation, went to see the bishop, who refused to receive him; and it is said that he was taken by the shoulders and put out of doors. He now resolved to bring his case before the council; but the bishop was informed of his purpose, and anticipated it. La Motte says " he went before the council on the first of February, and denounced the Sieur de Mareuil, whom he declared guilty of impiety towards God, the Virgin, and the Saints, and made a fine speech in the absence of the count, interrupted by the effusions of a heart which seemed filled with a profound and infinite charity, but which, as he said, was pushed to extremity by the rebellion of an indocile child, who had neglected all his warnings. This was, nevertheless, assumed ; I will not say entirely false."

The bishop did, in fact, make a vehement speech against Mareuil before the council on the day in question; Mareuil stoutly defending himself, and entering his appeal against the episcopal mandate. 1 The battle was now fairly joined. Frontenac stood alone for the accused. The intendant tacitly favored his opponents. Auteuil, the attorney-general, and Villeray, the first councillor, owed the governor an old grudge; and they and their colleagues sided with the bishop, with the outside support of all the clergy, except the Recollets, who, as usual, ranged themselves with their patron. At first,

who reports it to the minister; by the minister Ponchartrain, who asks Frontenae for an explanation ; by Frontenac, who passes it off as a jest ; and by several other contemporary writers.

1 Registre du Conseil Souverain, 1 et 8 F4v., 1694

Frontenac showed great moderation, but grew vehement, and then violent, as the dispute proceeded ; as did also the attorney-general, who seems to have done his best to exasperate him. Frontenac affirmed that, in depriving Mareuil and others of the sacraments, with no proof of guilt and no previous warning, and on allegations which, even if true, could not justify the act, the bishop exceeded his powers, and trenched on those of the king. The point was delicate. The attorney-general avoided the issue, tried to raise others, and revived the old quarrel about Frontenac's place in the council, which had been settled fourteen years before. Other questions were brought up, and angrily debated. The governor demanded that the debates, along with the papers which introduced them, should be entered on the record, that the king might be informed of every thing; but the demand was refused. The discords of the council chamber spread into the town. Quebec was divided against itself. Mareuil insulted the bishop; and some of his scapegrace sympathizers broke the prelate's windows at night, and smashed his chamber-door. 1 Mareuil was at last ordered to prison, and the whole affair was referred to the king. 2

These proceedings consumed the spring, the summer, and a part of the autumn. Meanwhile, an access of zeal appeared to seize the bishop; and he launched interdictions to the right and left.

1 Champigny au Ministry 27 Oct., 1694.

8 Registre du Conseil Souverain ; Requests du Sieur de Mareuil, Nov., 1694,

Even Chainpigny was startled when lie refused the sacraments to all but four or five of the military officers for alleged tampering with the pay of their soldiers, a matter wholly within the province of the temporal authorities. 1 During a recess of the council, he set out on a pastoral tour, and, arriving at Three Rivers, excommunicated an officer named Desjordis for a reputed intrigue with the wife of another officer. He next repaired to Sorel, and, being there on a Sunday, was told that two officers had neglected to go to mass. He wrote to Frontenac, complaining of the offence. Frontenac sent for the culprits, and rebuked them; but retracted his words when they proved by several witnesses that they had been duly present at the rite. 2 The bishop then went up to Montreal, and discord went with him.

Except Frontenac alone, Callieres, the loca, governor, was the man in all Canada to whom the country owed most; but, like his chief, he was a friend of the Recollets, and this did not commend him to the bishop. The friars we*re about to receive two novices into their order, and they invited the bishop to officiate at the ceremony. Callieres was also present, kneeling at a prie-dieu, or prayer-desk, near the middle of the church. Saint-Vallier, having just said mass, was seating himself in his arm-chair, close to the altar, when he saw Callieres

1 Champigny au Ministre, 24 Oct., 1694. Trouble on this matter had begun some time before. Me'moire du Roy pour Frontenac et Champigny, 1694 ; Le Ministre a I'fiveque, 8 Mai, 1694.

a La Motte-Cadillac a , 28 Sept., 1694; Champigny au Ministre , 27 Oct . 1694.

at the prie-dieu, with the position of which he had already found fault as being too honorable for a subordinate governor. He now rose, approached the object of his disapproval, and said, " Monsieur, you are taking a place which belongs only to Monsieur de Frontenac." Callieres replied that the place was that which properly belonged to him. The bishop rejoined that, if he did not leave it, he himself would leave the church. " You can do as you please," said "Callieres; and the prelate withdrew abruptly through the sacristy, refusing any farther part in the ceremony. 1 When the services were over, he ordered the friars to remove the obnoxious prie-dieu. They obeyed; but an officer of Callieres replaced it, and, unwilling to offend him, they allowed it to remain. On this, the bishop laid their church under an interdict; that is, he closed it against the celebration of all the rites of religion. 2 He then issued a pastoral mandate, in which he charged Father Joseph Denys, their superior, with offences which he " dared not name for fear of making the paper blush." 3 His tongue was less bashful than his pen; and he gave out publicly that the father superior had acted as go-between in an intrigue of his sister with the

1 Proems-verbal du Ptre Hyacinthe Perrault, Commissaire Provincial des Recottete (Archives Nationales) • Ml'moire touchant le Dfmeslf entre M. rtfvegque dz Qutbec et le Chevalier de Callieres (Ibid.).

2 Mandement ordonnant defermer l'J$glise des Rfcollets, 13 Mai, 1694.

8 "Le Sup€rieur du dit Convent estant lie avec le Gouverneur de la dtte ville par des interests que tout le monde scait et qu'on n'oseroit ex-primer de peur de faire rougir le papier." Ext'-ait du Mandement de I'tfvesque de Quebec (Archives, Nationales). He had before charged Mareuil with language " capable de faire rougir le ciel."

Chevalier de Calli&res. 1 It is said that the accusation was groundless, and the character of the woman wholly irreproachable. The Re'collets submitted for two months to the bishop's interdict, then refused to obey longer, and opened their church again.

Quebec, Three Rivers, Sorel, and Montreal had all been ruffled by the breeze of these dissensions, and the farthest outposts of the wilderness were not too remote to feel it. La Motte-Cadillac had been sent to replace Louvigny in the command of Michillimackinac, where he had scarcely arrived, when trouble fell upon him. " Poor Monsieur de la Motte-Cadillac/' says Frontenac, " would have sent you a journal to show you the persecutions he has suffered at the post where I placed him, and where he does wonders, having great influence over the Indians, who both love and fear him, but he has had no time to copy it. Means have been found to excite against him three or four officers of the posts dependent on his, who have put upon him such strange and unheard of affronts, that I was obliged to send them to prison when they came down to the colony. A certain Father Carheil, the Jesuit who wrote me such insolent letters a few

i " M* l'Evesque accuse publiquement le Rev. Pere Joseph, sup&ieur des Re'collets de Montreal, d'etre l'entremetteur d'une galanterie entre ga soeur et le Gouverneur. Cependant M.Evesque salt certainement que le Pere Joseph est l'un des meilleurs et des plus saints religieux de son ordre. Ce qu'il allegue du pretendu commerce entre le Gouverneur et la Dame de la Naudiere (sceur du Pere Joseph) est entierement faux, et il l'a public avec scandale, sans preuve et centre toute apparence, la ditte Dame ayant toujours eu une conduite irre'prochable." Me'moire touchant le Dfrneste, etc. Champigny also says that the bishop has brought this charge, and that Callieres declares that he has told a falsehood, Cham pigny au Mmistre, 27 Or.l. t 1694.

years ago has played an amazing part in this affair. I shall write about it to Father La Chaise, that he may set it right. Some remedy must be found ; for, if it continues, none of the officers who were sent to Michillimackinac, the Miamis, the Illinois, and other places, can stay there on account of the persecutions to which they are subjected, and the refusal of absolution as soon as they fail to do what is wanted of them. Joined to all this is a shameful traffic in influence and money. Monsieur de Tonty could have written to you about it, if he had not been obliged to go off to the Assinneboins, to rid himself of all these torments." * In fact, there was a chronic dispute at the forest outposts between the officers and the Jesuits, concerning which matter much might be said on both sides.

The bishop sailed for France. " He has gone," writes Callieres, " after quarrelling with everybody." The various points in dispute were set before the king. An avalanche of memorials, letters, and proces-verbaux, descended upon the unfortunate monarch ; some concerning Mareuil and the quarrels in the council, others on the excommunication of Desjordis, and others on the troubles at Montreal. They were all referred to the king's privy council. 3 An adjustment was effected: order, if not harmony, was restored ; and the usual distribution of advice, exhortation, reproof, and menace, was made to the parties in the strife. Frontenac was commended for defending the royal preroga-

1 Frontenac a M. de Lagny, 2 Nov., 1695.

2 Arrest gui ordonne que les Procedures faites entre le Sicur jZvesque de Qttfbec et les Sieurs Mareuil, Desjordis, etc., seront 6voqmz an Conseil Prive de Sa Majesty 3 Juillet, 1695.

tive, censured for violence, and admonished to avoid future quarrels. 1 Champigny was reproved for not supporting the governor, and told that " his Majesty sees with great pain that, while he is making extraordinary efforts to sustain Canada at a time so critical, all his cares and all his outlays are made useless by your misunderstanding with Monsieur de Frontenac." The attorney-general was sharply reprimanded, told that he must mend his ways or lose his place, and ordered to make an apology to the governor. 3 Villeray was not honored by a letter, but the intendant was directed to tell him that his behavior had greatly displeased the king. Callieres was mildly advised not to take part in the disputes of the bishop and the Kecollets. 4 Thus was conjured down one of the most bitter as well as the most needless, trivial, and untimely, of the quarrels that enliven the annals of New France.

A generation later, when its incidents had faded from memory, a passionate and reckless partisan, Abbe La Tour, published, and probably invented, a story which later writers have copied, till it now forms an accepted episode of Canadian history. According to him, Frontenac, in order to ridicule the clergy, formed an amateur company of comedians expressly to play " Tartuffe;" and, after rehearsing at the chateau during three or four months, they acted the piece before a large audience. " He was not satisfied with having it played at the chateau, but wanted the actors and actresses and the dan-

1 Le Ministre a Frontenac, 4 Jmn, 1695; Ibid., 8 Juin, 1695. a Le Ministre a Champigny, 4 Juin, 1695; Ibid., 8 Juin., 1696. 3 Le Ministre a d'Auteuil, 8 Juin, 1695. * Le Ministre a Callieres. 8 Jvin. 1695.

cers, male and female, to go in full costume, with violins, to play it in all the religious communities, except the K£collets. He took them first to the house of the Jesuits, where the crowd entered with him; then to the Hospital, to the hall of the paupers, whither the nuns were ordered to repair; then he went to the Ursuline Convent, assembled the sisterhood, and had the piece played before them. To crown the insult, he wanted next to go to the seminary, and repeat the spectacle there; but, warning having been given, he was met on the way, and begged to refrain. He dared not persist, and withdrew in very ill-humor." *

Not one of numerous contemporary papers, both official and private, and written in great part by enemies of Frontenac, contains the slightest allusion to any such story, and many of them are wholly inconsistent with it. It may safely be set down as a fabrication to blacken the memory of the governor, and exhibit the bishop and his adherents as victims of persecution. 2

1 La Tour, Vie de Laval, liv. xii.

2 Had an outrage, like that with which Frontenac is here charged, actually taken place, the registers of the council, the letters of the in-tendant and the attorney-general, and the records of the bishopric of Quebec would not have failed to show it. They show nothing beyond a report that " Tartuffe " was to be played, and a payment of money by the bishop in order to prevent it. We are left to infer that it was prevented accordingly. I have the best authority — that of the superior of the convent (1871), herself a diligent investigator into the history of her community— for stating that neither record nor tradition of the occurrence exists among the Ursulines of Quebec; and I have been unable to learn that any such exists among the nuns of the Hospital (Hotel-Dieu). The contemporary Rtcit d'une Rdigieuse Ursuline speaks of Frontenac with gratitude, as a friend and benefactor, as does also Mother Juchereau, superior of the Hotel-Dieu.

CHAPTER XVI.

1690-1694. THE WAR IN ACADIA.

STATE OP THAT COLONY. — THE ABENAKIS. — ACADIA AND NEW ENGLAND. — PIRATES. — BARON DE SAINT-CASTIN. — PENTEGOET — THE ENGLISH FRONTIER. — THE FRENCH AND THE ABENAKIS,

— PLAN OP THE WAR. — CAPTURE OP YORK. — VILLEBON. — GRAND WAR-PARTY. — ATTACK OF WELLS. — PEMAQUID REBUILT — JOHN NELSON. — A BROKEN TREATY. — VILLIEU AND THURY.

— ANOTHER WAR-PARTY, — MASSACRE AT OYSTER RIVER.

AMID domestic strife, the war with England and the Iroquois still went on. The contest for territorial mastery was fourfold : first, for the control of* the west; secondly, for that of Hudson's Bay ; thirdly, for that of Newfoundland; and, lastly, for that of Acadia. All these vast and widely sundered regions were included in the government of Fron-tenac. Each division of the war was distinct from the rest, and each had a character of its own. As the contest for the west was wholly with New York and her Iroquois allies, so the contest for Acadia was wholly with the " Bostonnais," or people of New England.

Acadia, as the French at this time understood the name, included Nova Scotia, New Brunswick, and the greater part of Maine. Sometimes they placed its western boundary at the little River St. George, and sometimes at the

Kennebec. Since the wars of D'Aulnay and La Tour, this wilderness had been a scene of unceasing strife; for the English drew their eastern boundary at the St. Croix, and the claims of the rival nationalities overlapped each other. In the time of Cromwell 1 , Sedgwick, a New England officer, had seized the whole country. The peace of Breda restored it to France: the Chevalier de Grandfontaine was ordered to reoccupy it, and the king sent out a few soldiers, a few settlers, and a few women as their wives. 1 Grand-fontaine held the nominal command for a time, followed by a succession of military chiefs, Chambly, Marson, and La Valliere. Then Perrot, whose malpractices had cost him the government of Montreal, was made governor of Acadia; and, as he did not mend his ways, he was replaced by Meneval. 2

One might have sailed for days along these lonely coasts, and seen no human form. At Can-seau, or Chedabucto, at the eastern end of Nova Scotia, there was a fishing station and a fort; Chi-buctouynow Halifax, was a solitude; at La Heve there were a few fishermen; and thence, as you doubled the rocks of Cape Sable, the ancient haunt of La Tour, you* would have seen four French settlers, and an unlimited number of seals and sea-

1 In 1671, 3Qgar$ons and SQJHles were sent by the king to Acadia, at the cost of 6,000 livres. £tat de Dfpenses, 1671.

2 Grandfontaine, 1670; Chambly, 1673; Marson, 1678; La Valliere, the same year, Marson having died; Perrot, 1684; Meneval, 1687. The last three were commissioned as local governors, in subordination to the governor-general. The others were merely military commandants.

fowl. Ranging the shore by St. Mary's Bay, and entering the Strait of Annapolis Basin, you would have found the fort of Port Royal,, the chief place of all Acadia. It stood at the head of the basin, where De Monts had planted his settlement nearly a century before. Around the fort and along the neighboring river were about ninety-five small houses; and at the head of the Bay of Fundy were two other settlements, Beaubassin and Les Mines, comparatively stable and populous. At the mouth of the St. John were the abandoned ruins of La Tour's old fort; and on a spot less exposed, at some distance up the river, stood the small wooden fort of Jemsec, with a few intervening clearings. Still sailing westward, passing Mount Desert, another scene of ancient settlement, and entering Penobscot Bay, you would have found the Baron de Saint-Castin with his Indian harem at Pente-goet, where the town of Castine now stands. All Acadia was comprised in these various stations, more or less permanent, together with one or two small posts on the Gulf of St Lawrence, and the huts of an errant population of fishermen and fur traders. In the time of Denonville, the colonists numbered less than a thousand souls. The king, busied with nursing Canada, had neglected its less important dependency.

Rude as it was, Acadia had charms, and it has them still: in its wilderness of woods and its

The census taken by order of Meules in 1686 gives a total of 886 persons, of whom 592 were at Port Royal, and 127 at Beaubassin. By the census of 1693, the number had reached 1,009.

22

wilderness of waves; the rocky ramparts that guard its coasts; its deep, still bays and foaming headlands ; the towering cliffs of the Grand Menan ; the innumerable islands that cluster about Penobscot Bay; and the romantic highlands of Mount Desert, down whose gorges the sea-fog rolls like an invading host, while the spires of fir-trees pierce the surging vapors like lances in the smoke of battle.

Leaving Pentegoet, and sailing westward all day along a solitude of woods, one might reach the English outpost of Pemaquid, and thence, still sailing on, might anchor at evening off Casco Bay, and see in the glowing west the distant peaks of the White Mountains, spectral and dim amid the weird and fiery sunset.

Inland Acadia was all forest, and vast tracts of it are a primeval forest still. Here roamed the Abenakis with their kindred tribes, a race wild as their haunts. In habits they were all much alike. Their villages were on the waters of the Andro-scoggin, the Saco, the Kennebec, the Penobscot, the St. Croix, and the St. John; here in spring they planted their corn, beans, and pumpkins, and then, leaving them to grow, went down to the sea in their birch canoes. They returned towards the end of summer, gathered their harvest, and went again to the sea, where they lived in abundance on ducks, geese, and other water-fowl. During winter, most of the women, children, and old men remained in the villages; while the hunters ranged the forest in chase of moose, deer, caribou, beavers, and bears.

Their summer stay at the seashore was perhaps

the most pleasant, and certainly the most picturesque, part of their lives. Bivouacked by some of the innumerable coves and inlets that indent these coasts, they passed their days in that alternation of indolence and action which is a second nature to the Indian. Here in wet weather, while the torpid water was dimpled with rain-drops, and the upturned canoes lay idle on the pebbles, the listless warrior smoked his pipe under his roof of bark, or launched his slender craft at the dawn of the July day, when shores and islands were painted in shadow against the rosy east, and forests, dusky and cool, lay waiting for the sunrise.

The women gathered raspberries or whortleberries in the open places of the woods, or clams and oysters in the sands and shallows, adding their shells as a contribution to the shell-heaps that have accumulated for ages along these shores. The men fished, speared porpoises, or shot seals. A priest was often in the camp watching over his flock, and saying mass every day in a chapel of bark. There was no. lack of altar candles, made by mixing tallow with the wax of the bayberry, which abounded among the rocky hills, and was gathered in profusion by the squaws and children.

The Abenaki missions were a complete success. Not only those of the tribe who had been induced to migrate to the mission villages of Canada, but also those who remained in their native woods, were, or were soon to become, converts to Romanism, and therefore allies of France. Though less ferocious than the Iroquois, they were brave, after

the Indian manner, and they rarely or never practised cannibalism.

Some of the French were as lawless as their Indian friends. Nothing is more strange than the incongruous mixture of the forms of feudalism with the independence of the Acadian woods. Vast grants of land were made to various persons, some of whom are charged with using them for no other purpose than roaming over their domains with Indian women. The only settled agricultural population was at Port Royal, Beaubassin, and the Basin of Minas. The rest were fishermen, fur traders, or rovers of the forest. Repeated orders came from the court to open a communication with Quebec, and even to establish a line of military posts through the intervening wilderness, but the distance and the natural difficulties of the country proved insurmountable obstacles. If communication with Quebec was difficult, that with Boston was easy; and thus Acadia became largely dependent on its New England neighbors, who, says an Acadian officer, " are mostly fugitives from England, guilty of the death of their late king, and accused of conspiracy against their present sovereign ; others of them are pirates, and they are all united in a sort of independent republic." 1 Their relations with the Acadians were of a mixed sort. They continually encroached on Acadian fishing grounds, and we hear at one time of a hundred of their vessels thus engaged. This was not all. The interlopers often landed and traded with the Indians

1 Mtmoire du Sieur Bergier, 1685.

along the coast. Meneval, the governor, complained bitterly of their arrogance. Sometimes, it is said, they pretended to be foreign pirates, and plundered vessels and settlements, while the aggrieved parties could get no redress at Boston. They also carried on a regular trade at Port Royal and Les Mines or Grand Pre, where many of the inhabitants regarded them with a degree of favor which gave great umbrage to the military authorities, who, nevertheless, are themselves accused of seeking their own profit by dealings with the heretics ; and even French priests, including Petit, the cure* of Port Royal, are charged with carrying on this illicit trade in their own behalf, and in that of the seminary of Quebec. The settlers caught from the "Bostonnais" what their governor stigmatizes as English and parliamentary ideas, the chief effect of which was to make them restive under his rule. The Church, moreover, was less successful in excluding heresy from Acadia than from Canada. A number of Huguenots established themselves at Port Royal, and formed sympathetic relations with the Boston Puritans. The bishop at Quebec was much alarmed. " This is dangerous," he writes. " I pray your Majesty to put an end to these disorders." 1 A sort of chronic warfare of aggression and re-

1 L'Eveque au Roy, 10 Nov., 1683. For the preceding pages, the authorities are chiefly the correspondence of Grandfontaine, Marson, La Valliere, Meneval, Bergier, Goutins, Perrot, Talon, Frontenac, and other officials. A large collection of Acadian documents, from the archives of Paris, is in my possession. I have also examined the Acadian collections made for the government of Canada and for that of Massachusetts.

THE WAR IN ACADIA. [1670-90.

prisal, closely akin to piracy, was carried on at intervals in Acadian waters by French private armed vessels on one hand, and New England private armed vessels on the other. Genuine pirates also frequently appeared. They were of various nationality, though usually buccaneers from the West Indies. They preyed on New England trading and fishing craft, and sometimes attacked French settlements. One of their most notorious exploits was the capture of two French vessels and a French fort at Chedabucto by a pirate, manned in part, it is said, from Massachusetts. 1 A similar proceeding of earlier date was the act of Dutchmen from St. Domingo. They made a descent on the French fort of Pentegoet, on Pen-obscot Bay. Chambly, then commanding for the king in Acadia, was in the place. They assaulted his works, wounded him, took him prisoner, and carried him to Boston, where they held him at ransom. His young ensign escaped into the woods, and carried the news to Canada ; but many months elapsed before Chambly was released. 2

This young ensign was Jean Vincent de 1'Abadie, Baron de Saint-Castin, a native of Beam, on the slopes of the Pyrenees, the same rough, strong soil

1 Meneval, Memoire, 1688 ; Denonville, Mtmoire, 18 Oct., 1688 ; Prods-verbal du Pillage de Chedabucto ; Relation de la Boullaye, 1688.

2 Frontenac au Ministre, 14 Nov., 1674 ; Frontenac a Leverett, gouverneur de Boston, 24 Sept., 1674 , Frontenac to the Governor and Council of Massachusetts, 25 May, 1675 (see 3 Mass. Hist. Coll., I. 64) ; Colbert a Frontenac, 16 May, 1675. Frontenac supposed the assailants to be buccaneers. They had, howerer, a commission- from William of Orange. Hutchin-son says that the Dutch again took Pentegoet in 1676, but were driven off by ships from Boston, as the English claimed the place for them selres

that gave to France her Henri IY. When fifteen years of age, he came to Canada with the regiment of Carignan-Salieres, ensign in the company of Chambly; and, when the regiment was disbanded, he followed his natural bent, and betook himself to the Acadian woods. At this time there was a square bastioned fort at Pentegoet, mounted with twelve small cannon; but after the Dutch attack it fell into decay. 1 Saint-Castin, meanwhile, roamed the woods with the Indians, lived like them, formed connections more or less permanent with their women, became himself a chief, and gained such ascendency over his red associates that, according to La Hontan, they looked upon him as their tutelary god. He was bold, hardy, adroit, tenacious ; and, in spite of his erratic habits, had such capacity for business, that, if we may believe the same somewhat doubtful authority, he made a fortune of three or four hundred thousand crowns. His gains came chiefly through his neighbors of New England, whom he hated, but to whom he sold his beaver skins at an ample profit. His trading house was at Pentegoet, now called Castine, in or near the old fort; a perilous spot, which he occupied or abandoned by turns, according to the needs of the time. Being a devout Catholic he wished to add a resident priest to his establishment

1 On its condition in 1670, Estat du Fort et Place de Pentegoet fait en I'annde 1670, lorsque les Anglois I'ont rendu. In 1671, fourteen soldiers and eight laborers were settled near the fort. Talon au Ministre, 2 Nw. t 1671. In the next year, Talon recommends an envoi de filles for the benefit of Pentegoet. Mfmoire sur le Canada, 1672. As late as 1698, we find Acadian officials advising the reconstruction of the fort.

for the conversion of his Indian friends; but, observes Father Petit of Port Royal, who knew him well," he himself has need of spiritual aid to sustain him in the paths of virtue." l He usually made two visits a year to Port Royal, where he gave liberal gifts to the church of which he was the chief patron, attended mass with exemplary devotion, and then, shriven of his sins, returned to his squaws at Pentegoet. Perrot, the governor, maligned him; the motive, as Saint-Castin says, being jealousy of his success in trade, for Perrot himself traded largely with the English and the Indians. This, indeed, seems to have been his chief occupation; and, as Saint-Castin was his principal rival, they were never on good terms. Saint-Castin complained to Denonville. " Monsieur Petit," he writes, " will tell you every thing. I will only say that he (Perrot) kept me under arrest from the twenty-first of April to the ninth of June, on pretence of a little weakness I had for some women, and even told me that he had your orders to do it: but that is not what troubles him; and as I do not believe there is another man under heaven who will do meaner things through love of gain, even to selling brandy by the pint and half-pint before strangers in his own house, because he does not trust a single one of his servants, — I see plainly what is the matter with him. He wants to be the only merchant in Acadia." 2

Perrot was recalled this very year; and his sue-

1 Petit in Saint-Vallier, Estat de I'tfgli'se, 39 (1856).
2 Saint-Castin a Denonville, 2 Juillet, 1687.

cessor, Meneval, received instructions in regard to Saint-Castin, which show that the king or his minister had a clear idea both of the baron's merits and of his failings. The new governor was ordered to require him to abandon " his vagabond life among the Indians/' cease all trade with the English, and establish a permanent settlement, Meneval was farther directed to assure him that, if he conformed to the royal will, and led a life "more becoming a gentleman," he might expect-to receive proofs of his Majesty's approval. 1

In the next year, Meneval reported that he had represented to Saint-Castin the necessity of reform, and that in consequence he had abandoned his trade with the English, given up his squaws, married, and promised to try to make a solid settlement. 2 True he had reformed before, and might need to reform again; but his faults were not of the baser sort: he held his honor high, and was free-handed as he was bold. His wife was what the early chroniclers would call an Indian princess, for she was the daughter of Madockawandb, chief of the Penobscots.

So critical was the position of his post at Pente-goet that a strong fort and a sufficient garrison could alone hope to maintain it against the pirates and the " Bostonnais." Its vicissitudes had been many. Standing on ground claimed by the English, within territory which had been granted to

1 Instruction du Roy au Sieur de Meneval, 5 Avril, 1687.

2 Memoire du Sieur de Meneval sur I'Acadie, 10 Sept., 1688.

the Duke of York, and which, on his accession to the throne, became a part of the royal domain, it was never safe from attack. In 1686, it was plundered by an agent of Dongan. In 1687, it was plundered again; and in the next year Andros, then royal governor, anchored before it in his frigate, the " Rose," landed with his attendants, and stripped the building of all it contained, except a small altar with pictures and ornaments, which they found in the principal room. Saint-Castin escaped to the woods; and Andros sent him word by an Indian that his property would be carried to Pemaquid, and that he could have it again by becoming a British subject. He refused the offer. 1

The rival English post of Pemaq*uid was destroyed, as we have seen, by the Abenakis in 1689; and, in the following year, they and their French allies had made such havoc among the border settlements that nothing was left east of the Piscataqua except the villages of Wells, York, and Kittery. But a change had taken place in the temper of the savages, mainly due to the easy conquest of Port Royal by Phips, and to an expedition of the noted partisan Church by which they had suffered considerable losses. Fear of the English on one hand, and the attraction of their trade on the other, disposed many of them to peace. Six chiefs signed a truce with the commissioners of Massachusetts, and promised to meet them in council to bury the hatchet for ever.

1 Mtmoireprfsenteau Roy d'Angleterre, 1687 ; Saint-Castin a Denonvtlte, 7 JuUlet. 1687; Hutchinson Collection, 662, 568 ; Andros Tracts, I 118.

The French were filled with alarm. Peace between the Abenakis and the " Bostonnais " would be disastrous both to Acadia and to Canada, because these tribes held the passes through the northern wilderness, and, so long as they were in the interest of France, covered the settlements on the St. Lawrence from attack. Moreover, the government relied on them to fight its battles. Therefore, no pains were spared to break off their incipient treaty with the English, and spur them again to war. Yillebon, a Canadian of good birth, one of the brothers of Portneuf, was sent by the king to govern Acadia. Presents for the Abenakis were given him in abundance; and he was ordered to assure them of support, so long as they fought for France. 1 He and his officers were told to join their war-parties; while the Canadians, who followed him to Acadia, were required to leave all other employments and wage incessant war against the English borders. " You yourself," says the minister, " will herein set them so good an example, that they will be animated by no other desire than-that of making profit out of the enemy: there is nothing which I more strongly urge upon you than to put forth all your ability and prudence to prevent the Abenakis from occupying themselves in any thing but war, and by good management of the supplies which you have received for then* use to enable them to live by it more to their advantage than by hunting." 2

1 Memoire pour servir d'Instruction au Sieur de Villebon, 1691.

2 " Comme yostre principal objet doit estre de faire la guerre sans re-l£che aux Anglois, il faut que vostre plus particuliere application soit

Armed with these instructions, Villebon repaired to his post, where he was joined by a body of Canadians under Portneuf. His first step was to reoccupy Port Royal; and, as there was nobody there to oppose him, he easily succeeded. The settlers renounced allegiance to Massachusetts and King William, and swore fidelity to their natural sovereign. 1 The capital of Acadia dropped back quietly into the lap of France; but, as the " Boston-nais" might recapture it at any time, Yillebon crossed to the St. John, and built a fort high up the stream at Naxouat, opposite the present city of Fredericton. Here no " Bostonnais" could reach him, and he could muster war-parties at his leisure.

One thing was indispensable. A blow must be struck that would encourage and excite the Aben-akis. Some of them had had no part in the truce. and were still so keen for English blood that a deputation of their chiefs told Frontenac at Quebec that they would fight, even if they must head their arrows with the bones of beasts. 2 They were under no such necessity. Guns, powder, and lead were given them in abundance; and Thury, the priest

de detourner de tout autre employ les Franpois qui sont avec vous, en leur donnant de vostre part un si bon exemple en cela qu'ils ne soient animez que du desir de chercher k faire du proffit sur les ennemis. Je n'ay aussy rien a vous recommander plus fortement que de mettre en usage tout ce que vous pouvez avoir de capacite et de prudence afin que les Canibas (AbenalciK) ne s'employent qu'k la guerre, et que par l'econo-mie de ce que vous avez a leur fournir ils y puissent trouver leur subsis-tance et plus d'avantage qu'a la chasse." Le Ministre a Villebon, Avril, 1692. Two years before, the king had ordered that the Abenakis should be made to attack the English settlements.

l Proces-verfal de la Prise de Possession du Port Royal, 27 Sept 1691,

* Paroles des Sauvaaes de la Mission de Pentegoet.

on the Penobscot, urged them to strike the English. A hundred and fifty of his converts took the war-path, and were joined by a band from the Ken-nebec. It was January; and they made their way on snow-shoes along the frozen streams, and through the deathly solitudes of the winter forest, till, after marching a month, they neared their destination, the frontier settlement of York. In the afternoon of the fourth of February, they encamped at the foot of a high hill, evidently Mount Agamenticus, from the top of which the English village lay in sight. It was a collection of scattered houses along the banks of the river Agamenticus and the shore of the adjacent sea. Five or more of them were built for defence, though owned and occupied by families like the other houses. Near the sea stood the unprotected house of the chief man of the place, Dummer, the minister. York appears, to have contained from three to four hundred persons of all ages, for the most part rude and ignorant borderers.

The warriors lay shivering ah 1 night in the forest, not daring to make fires. In the morning, a heavy fall of snow began. They moved forward, and soon heard the sound of an axe. It was an English boy chopping wood. They caught him, extorted such information as they needed, then tomahawked him, and moved on, till, hidden by the forest and the thick snow, they reached the outskirts of the village. Here they divided into two parties, and each took its station. A gun was fired as a signal, upon which they all yelled the war-whoop, and dashed

upon their prey. One party mastered the nearest fortified house, which had scarcely a defender but women. The rest burst into the unprotected houses, killing or capturing the astonished inmates. The minister was at his door, in the act of mounting his horse to visit some distant parishioners, when a bullet struck him dead. He was a graduate of Harvard College, a man advanced in life, of some learning, and greatly respected. The French accounts say that about a hundred persons, including women and children, were killed, and about eighty captured. Those who could, ran for the fortified houses of Preble, Harmon, Alcock, and Norton, which were soon filled with the refugees. The Indians did not attack them, but kept well out of gun-shot, and busied themselves in pillaging, killing horses and cattle, and burning the unprotected houses. They then divided themselves into small bands, and destroyed all the outlying farms for four or five miles around.

The wish of King Louis was fulfilled. A good profit had been made out of the enemy. The victors withdrew into the forest with their plunder and their prisoners, among whom were several old women and a number of children from three to seven years old. These, with a forbearance which docs them credit, they permitted to return uninjured to the nearest fortified house, in requital, it is said, for the lives of a number of Indian children spared by the English in a recent attack on the Androscoggin. The wife of the minister was allowed to go with them; but her son remained a

prisoner, and the agonized mother went back to the Indian camp to beg for his release. They again permitted her to return; but, when she came a second time, they told her that, as she wanted to be a prisoner, she should have her wish. She was carried with the rest to their village, where she soon died of exhaustion and distress. One of the warriors arrayed himself in the gown of the slain minister, and preached a mock sermon to the captive parishioners.

Leaving York .in ashes, the victors began their march homeward ; while a body of men from Portsmouth followed on their trail, but soon lost it, and failed to overtake them. There was a season of feasting and scalp-dancing at the Abenaki towns; and then, as spring opened, a hundred of the warriors set out to visit Yillebon, tell him of their triumph, and receive the promised gifts from their great father the king. Villebon and his brothers, Portneuf, Neuvillette, and Desiles, with their Canadian followers, had spent the winter chiefly on the St. John, finishing their fort at Naxouat, and preparing for future operations. The Abenaki visitors

1 The best French account of the capture of York is that of Cham-pigny in a letter to the minister, 6 Oct., 1692. His information came from an Abenaki chief, who was present. The journal of Villebon contains an exaggerated account of the affair, also derived from Indians. Compare the English accounts in Mather, Williamson, and Niles. These writers make the number of slain and captives much less than that given by the French. In the contemporary journal of Rev. John Pike, it is placed at 48 killed and 73 taken.

Two fortified houses of this period are still (1875) standing at York. They are substantial buildings of squared timber, with the upper story projecting over the lower, so as to allow a vertical fire on the heads of assailants. In one of them some of the loopholes for musketry are still left open. They may or may not have been originally enclosed by palisades.

arrived towards the end of April, and were received with all possible distinction. There were speeches, gifts, and feasting; for they had done much, and were expected to do more. Portneuf sang a war-song in their language; then he opened a barrel of wine: the guests emptied it in less than fifteen minutes, sang, whooped, danced, and promised to repair to the rendezvous at Saint-Castin's station of Pentegoet. 1 A grand war-party was afoot; and a new and withering blow was to be struck against the English border. The guests set out for Pentegoet, followed by Portneuf, Desiles, La Brognerie, several other officers, and twenty Canadians. A few days after, a large band of Micmacs arrived; then came the Malicite warriors from their village of Medoctec; and at last Father Baudoin appeared, leading another band of Micmacs from his mission of Beaubassin. Speeches, feasts, and gifts were made to them all; and they all followed the rest to the appointed rendezvous.

At the beginning of June, the site of the town of Castine was covered with wigwams and the beach lined with canoes. Malecites and Micmacs, Abenakis from the Penobscot and Abenakis from the Kennebec, were here, some four hundred warriors in all. 2 Here, too, were Portneuf and his Canadians, the Baron de Saint-Castin and his Indian father-in-law, Madockawando, with Moxus, Egere-met, and other noted chiefs, the terror of the English borders. They crossed Penobscot Bay, and marched upon the frontier village of Wells.

1 Villebon, Journal de ce qui s'est passt a I'Acadie, 1691,1692. 8 Frontenac au Ministre, 15 Sept 1692.

Wells, like York, was a small settlement of scattered houses along the sea-shore. The year before, Moxus had vainly attacked it with two hundred warriors. All the neighboring country had been laid waste by a murderous war of detail, the lonely farm-houses pillaged and burned, and the survivors driven back for refuge to the older settlements. 1 Wells had been crowded with these refugees ; but famine and misery had driven most of them beyond the Piscataqua, and the place was now occupied by a remnant of its own destitute inhabitants, who, warned by the fate of York, had taken refuge in five fortified houses. The largest of these, belonging to Joseph Storer, was surrounded by a palisade, and occupied by fifteen armed men, under Captain Convers, an officer of militia. On the ninth of June, two sloops and a sail-boat ran up the neighboring creek, bringing supplies and fourteen more men. The succor came in the nick of time. The sloops had scarcely anchored, when a number of cattle were seen running frightened and wounded from the*woods. It was plain that an enenr^ was lurking there. All the families of the place now gathered within the palisades of Storer's house, thus increasing his force to about thirty men ; and a close watch was kept throughout the night.

In the morning, no room was left for doubt. One John Diamond, on his way from the house to

1 The ravages committed by the Abenakis in the preceding year among the scattered farms of Maine and New Hampshire are said by Frontenac to have been " impossible to describe." Another FremL, writer says that they burned more than 200 houses.

23

THE WAK IN ACADIA.

the sloops, was seized by Indians and dragged off by the hair. Then the whole body of savages appeared swarming over the fields, so confident of success that they neglected their usual tactics of surprise. A French officer, who, as an old English account says, was " habited like a gentleman/' made them an harangue: they answered with a burst of yells, and then attacked the house, firing, screeching, and calling on Convers and his men to surrender. Others gave their attention to the two sloops, which lay together in the narrow creek, stranded by the ebbing tide. They fired at them for a while from behind a pile of planks on the shore, and threw many fire-arrows without success, the men on board fighting with such cool and dexterous obstinacy that they held them all at bay, and lost but one of their own number. Next, the Canadians made a huge shield of planks, which they fastened vertically to the back of a cart. La Brognerie with twenty-six men, French and Indians, got behind it, and shoved the cart towards the stranded sloops. It was within fifty feet of them, when a wheel sunk in the mud, and the machine stuck fast. La Brognerie tried to lift the wheel, and was shot dead. The tide began to rise. A Canadian tried to escape, and was also shot. The rest then broke away together, some of them, as they ran, dropping under the bullets of the sailors.

The whole force now gathered for a final attack on the garrison house. Their appearance was so frightful, and their clamor so appalling, that one

of the English muttered something about surrender. Convers returned, " If you say that again, you are a dead man." Had the allies made a bold assault, he and his followers must have been overpowered ; but this mode of attack was contrary to Indian maxims. They merely leaped, yelled, fired, and called on the English to yield. They were answered with derision. The women in the house took part in the defence, passed ammunition to the men, and sometimes fired themselves on the enemy. The Indians at length became discouraged, and offered Convers favorable terms. He answered, " I want nothing but men to fight with." An Abenaki who spoke English cried out: " If you are so bold, why do you stay in a garrison house like a squaw ? Come out and fight like a man ! " Convers retorted, " Do you think I am fool enough to come out with thirty men to fight five hundred ? " Another Indian shouted, " Damn you, we'll cut you small as tobacco before morning." Convers returned a contemptuous defiance.

After a while, they ceased firing, and dispersed about the neighborhood, butchering cattle and burning the church and a few empty houses. As the tide began to ebb, they sent a fire-raft in full blaze down the creek to destroy the sloops; but it stranded, and the attempt failed. They now wreaked their fury on the prisoner Diamond, whom they tortured to death, after which they all disappeared. A few resolute men had foiled one of the most formidable bands that ever took the war-path in Acadia. 1

Villebon, Journal de ce gui s'est vassf a I'Acadie, 1601,1692; Mather,

The warriors dispersed to their respective haunts; and, when a band of them reached the St. John, Villebon coolly declares that he gave them a prisoner to burn. They put him to death with all their ingenuity of torture. The act, on the part of the governor, was more atrocious, as it had no motive of reprisal, and as the burning of prisoners was not the common practice of these tribes. 1

The warlike ardor of the Abenakis cooled after the failure at Wells, and events that soon followed nearly extinguished it. Phips had just received his preposterous appointment to the government of Massachusetts. To the disgust of its inhabitants, the stubborn colony was no longer a republic. The new governor, unfit as he was for his office, understood the needs of the eastern frontier, where he had spent his youth; and he brought a royal order

Magnolia, II. 613; Hutchinson, Hist. Mass., II. 67; Williamson, History of Maine, 1. 631; Bourne, History of Wells, 2>3; Niles, Indian and Frenck

Wars, 229. Williamson, like Sylvanus Davis, calls Portneuf Biimeffe or Burniffe. He, and other English writers, call La Brognerie Labocree. The French could not recover his body, on which, according to Niles and others, was found a pouch " stuffed full of relics, pardons, and indulgences." The prisoner Diamond told the captors that there were thirty men in the sloops. They believed him, and were cautious accordingly. There were, in fact, but fourteen. Most of the fighting was on the tenth. On the evening of that day, Convers received a reinforcement of sii men. They were a scouting party, whom he had sent a few days before in the direction of Salmon River. Returning, they were attacked, when near the garrison house, by a party of Portneuf's Indians. The sergeant in command instantly shouted, " Captain Convers, send your men round the hill, and we shall catch these dogs." Thinking that Con-vere had made a sortie, the Indians ran off, and the scouts joined the garrison without loss.

1 "Le 18 m « (Aovt) un sauvage anglois fut pris au bas de la riviere de St. Jean. Je le donnai & nos sauvages pour estre brute, ce qu'ils firent le .endemain. On ne pent rien adjouter aux tourmena qu'ils luy flrent

ouffrir." Villebon, Journal, 1691, 1692.

to rebuild the ruined fort at Pemaquid. The king gave the order, but neither men, money, nor munitions to execute it; and Massachusetts bore all the burden. Phips went to Pemaquid, laid out the work, and left a hundred men to finish it. A strong fort of stone was built, the abandoned cannon of Casco mounted on its walls, and sixty men placed in garrison.

The keen military eye of Frontenac saw the danger involved in the re-establishment of Pemaquid. Lying far in advance of the other English stations, it barred the passage of war-parties along the coast, and was a standing menace to the Abe-nakis. It was resolved to capture it. Two ships of war, lately arrived at Quebec, the " Poli " and the " Envieux," were ordered to sail for Acadia with above four hundred men, take on board two or three hundred Indians at Pentegoet, reduce Pemaquid, and attack Wells, Portsmouth, and the Isles of Shoals; after which, they were to scour the Acadian seas of " Bostonnais " fishermen.

At this time, a gentleman of Boston, John Nelson, captured by Yillebon the year before, was a prisoner at Quebec. Nelson was nephew and heir of Sir Thomas Temple, in whose right he claimed the proprietorship of Acadia, under an old grant of Oliver Cromwell. He was familiar both with that country and with Canada, which he had visited several times before the war. As he was a man of birth and breeding, and a declared enemy of Phips, and as he had befriended French prisoners, and shown especial kindness to Meneval, the

captive governor of Acadia, he was treated with distinction by Frontenac, who, though he knew him to be a determined enemy of the French, lodged him at the chateau, and entertained him at his own table. 1 Madockawando, the father-in-law of Saint-Castin, made a visit to Frontenac; and Nelson, who spoke both French and Indian, contrived to gain from him and from other sources a partial knowledge of the intended expedition. He was not in favor at Boston; for, though one of the foremost in the overthrow of Andros, his creed and his character savored more of the Cavalier than of the Puritan. This did not prevent him from risking his life for the colony. He wrote a letter to the authorities of Massachusetts, and then bribed two soldiers to desert and carry it to them. The deserters were hotly pursued, but reached their destination, and delivered their letter. The two ships sailed from Quebec; but when, after a long delay at Mount Desert, they took on board the Indian allies and sailed onward to Pemaquid, they found an armed ship from Boston anchored in the harbor. Why they did not attack it, is a mystery. The defences of Pemaquid were still unfinished, the French force was far superior to the English, and Iberville, who commanded it, was a leader of unquestionable enterprise and daring. Nevertheless, the French did nothing, and soon after bore away for France. Frontenac was indignant, and eeverely blamed Iberville, whose sister was on

1 Champigny au Ministre, 4 Nov. 1698.

board his ship, and was possibly the occasion of .his inaction.

Thus far successful, the authorities of Boston undertook an enterprise little to their credit. They employed the two deserters, joined with two Acadian prisoners, to kidnap Saint-Castin, whom, next to the priest Thury, they regarded as their most insidious enemy. The Acadians revealed the plot, and the two soldiers were shot at Mount Desert. Nelson was sent to France, imprisoned two years in a dungeon of the Chateau of Angouleme, and then placed in the Bastile. Ten years passed before he was allowed to return to his family at Boston. 2

The French failure at Pemaquid completed the discontent of the Abenakis; and despondency and

1 Frontenac au Ministre, 25 Oct., 1693.

2 Lagny, Me'moire surl'Acadie, 1692 ; Me'moire sur I'Enlevement de Saint-Castin; Frontenac au Ministre, 25 Oct., 1693; Relation de ce gut s'est passt de plus remarquable, 1690, 1691 (capture of Nelson); Frontenac au Min~ istre, 15 Sept., 1692; Champigny au Ministre, 15 Oct., 1692. Champigny here speaks of Nelson as the most audacious of the English, and the most determined on the destruction of the French. Nelson's letter to the authorities of Boston is printed in Hutchinson, I. 338. It does not warn them of an attempt against Pemaquid, of the rebuilding of which he seems not to have heard, but only of a design against the seaboard towns. Compare N. Y. Col. Docs., IX. 555. In the same collection is a Memorial on the Northern Colonies, by Nelson, a paper showing much good sense and penetration. After an imprisonment of four and a half years, he was allowed to go to England on parole; a friend in France giving security of 15,000 livres for his return, in case of his failure to procure from the king an order for the fulfilment of the terms of the capitulation of Port Royal. (Le Ministre a Bfyon, 13 Jan., 1694.) He

did not succeed, and the king forbade him to return. It is characteristic of him that he preferred to disobey the royal order, and thus incur the high displeasure of his sovereign, rather than break his parole and involve his friend in loss. La Hontan calls him a " fort galant homme." There is a portrait of him at Boston, where his descendants are represented by the prom inent families of Winthrop, Derby and Borland.

terror seized them when, in the spring of 1693, Convers, the defender of Wells, ranged the fron-. tier with a strong party of militia, and built another stone fort at the falls of the Saco. In July, they opened a conference at Pemaquid ; and, in August, thirteen of their chiefs, representing, or pretending to represent, all the tribes from the Merrimac to the St. Croix, came again to the same place to conclude a final treaty of peace with the commissioners of Massachusetts. They renounced the French alliance, buried the hatchet, declared themselves British subjects, promised to give up all prisoners, and left five of their chief men as hostages. 1 The frontier breathed again. Security and hope returned to secluded dwellings buried in a treacherous forest, where life had been a nightmare of horror and fear; and the settler could go to his work without dreading to find at evening his cabin burned and his wife and children murdered. He was fatally deceived, for the danger was not past. It is true that some of the Abenakis were sincere in their pledges of peace. A party among them, headed by Madockawando, were dissatisfied with the French, anxious to recover their captive countrymen, and eager to reopen trade with the English. But there was an opposing party, led by the chief Taxous, who still breathed war; while between the two was an unstable mob of warriors, guided by the impulse of the hour. 2 The French

1 For the treaty in full, Mather, Magnaha, II. 625

* The state of feeling among the Abenakis is shown in a letter of Thury to Frontenac, 1] Sept., 1694, and in the journal of Villebon for 1693.

spared no efforts to break off the peace. The two missionaries, Bigot on the Kennebec and Thury on the Penobscot, labored with unwearied energy to urge the savages to war. The governor, Villebon, flattered them, feasted them, adopted Taxous as his brother, and, to honor the occasion, gave him his own best coat. Twenty-five hundred pounds of gunpowder, six thousand pounds of lead, and a multitude of other presents, were given this year to the Indians of Acadia. 1 Two of their chiefs had been sent to Versailles. They now returned, in gay attire, their necks hung with medals, and their minds filled with admiration, wonder, and bewilderment.

The special duty of commanding Indians had fallen to the lot of an officer named Villieu, who had been ordered by the court to raise a war-party and attack the English. He had lately been sent to replace Portneuf, who had been charged with debauchery and peculation. Villebon, angry at his brother's removal, was on ill terms with his successor; and, though he declares that he did his best to ajd in raising the war-party, Villieu says, on the contrary, that he was worse than indifferent. The new lieutenant spent the winter at Naxouat, and on the first of May went up in a canoe to the Mali-cite village of Medoctec, assembled the chiefs, and invited them to war. They accepted the invitation with alacrity. Villieu next made his way through the wilderness to the Indian towns of the Penobscot* On the ninth, he reached the mouth of the Matta*

1 Estat de Munitions, etc., pour ies Sauvages de I'Acadie, 169P

wamkeag, where he found the chief Taxous, paddled with him down the Penobscot, and, at midnight on the tenth, landed at a large Indian village, at or near the place now called Passadumkeag. Here he found a powerful ally in the Jesuit Vincent Bigot, who had come from the Kennebec, with three Abenakis, to urge their brethren of the Pen-obscot to break off the peace. The chief envoy denounced the treaty of Pemaquid as a snare; and Villieu exhorted the assembled warriors to follow him to the English border, where honor and profit awaited them. But first he invited them to go back with him to Naxouat to receive their presents of arms, ammunition, and every thing else that they needed.

They set out with alacrity. Villieu went with them, and they all arrived within a week. They were feasted and gifted to their hearts' content; and then the indefatigable officer led them back by the same long and weary routes which he had passed and repassed before, rocky and shallow streams, chains of wilderness lakes, threads of water writhing through swamps where the canoes could scarcely glide among the water-weeds and alders. Villieu was the only white man. The governor, as he says, would give him but two soldiers, and these had run off. Early in June, the whole flotilla paddled down the Penobscot to Pentegeot. Here the Indians divided their presents, which they found somewhat less ample than they had imagined. In the midst of their discontent, Ma-dockawando came from Pemaquid with news that

the governor of Massachusetts was about to deliver up the Indian prisoners in his hands, as stipulated by the treaty. This completely changed the temper of the warriors. Madockawando declared loudly for peace, and Villieu 'saw all his hopes wrecked. He tried to persuade his disaffected allies that the English only meant to lure them to destruction, and the missionary Thury supported him with his utmost eloquence. The Indians would not be convinced ; and their trust in English good faith was confirmed, when they heard that a minister had just come to Pemaquid to teach their children to read and write. The news grew worse and worse. Villieu was secretly informed that Phips had been off the coast in a frigate, invited Madockawando and other chiefs on board, and feasted them in his cabin, after which they had all thrown their hatchets into the sea, in token of everlasting peace. Villieu now despaired of his enterprise, and prepared to return to the St. John ; when Thury, wise as the serpent, set himself to work on the jealousy of Taxous, took him aside, and persuaded him that his rival, Madockawando, had put a slight upon him in presuming to make peace without his consent. " The effect was marvellous," says Villieu. Taxous, exasperated, declared that he would have nothing to do with Madockawando's treaty. The fickle multitude caught the contagion, and asked for nothing but English scalps; but, before setting out, they must needs go back to Passadumkeag to finish their preparations.

Villieu again went with them, and on the way his enterprise and he nearly perished together. His canoe overset in a rapid at some distance above the site of Bangor : he was swept down the current, his head was dashed against a rock, and his body bruised from head to foot. For five days he lay helpless with fever. He had no sooner recovered than he gave the Indians a war-feast, at which they all sang the war-song, except Madockaw r ando and some thirty of his clansmen, whom the others made the butt of their taunts and ridicule. The chief began to waver. The officer and the missionary beset him with presents and persuasion, till at last he promised to join the rest.

It was the end of June when Villieu and Thury, with one Frenchman and a hundred and five Indians, began their long canoe voyage to the English border. The savages were directed to give no quarter, and told that the prisoners already in their hands would insure the safety of their hostages in the hands of the English. 1 More warriors were to join them from Bigot's mission on the Kennebec. On the ninth of July, they neared Pemaquid ; but it was no part of their plan to attack a garrisoned post. The main body passed on at a safe distance; while Villieu approached the fort, dressed and painted like an Indian, and accompanied by two or three genuine savages, carrying a. packet of furs, as if on a peaceful errand of trade. Such visits from Indians had been common since the treaty ; and, while his companions bartered their beaver

1 Villebon, Mfmoire, Juittet, 1694 ; Instruction du S r . dt ViUcbon au St <U Villieu.

skins with the unsuspecting soldiers, he strolled about the neighborhood and made a plan of the works. The party was soon after joined by Bigot's Indians, and the united force now amounted to two hundred and thirty. They held a council to determine where they should make their attack, but opinions differed. Some were for the places west of Boston, and others for those nearer at hand. Necessity decided them. Their provisions were gone, and Villieu says that he himself was dying of hunger. They therefore resolved to strike at the nearest settlement, that of Oyster Kiver, now Durham, about twelve miles from Portsmouth. They cautiously moved forward, and sent scouts in advance, who reported that the inhabitants kept no watch. In fact, a messenger from Phips had assured them that the war was over, and that they could follow their usual vocations without fear.

Villieu and his band waited till night, and then made their approach. There was a small village; a church ; a mill; twelve fortified houses, occupied in most cases only by families; and many unprotected farm-houses, extending several miles along the stream. The Indians separated into bands, and, stationing themselves for a simultaneous attack at numerous points, lay patiently waiting till towards day. The moon was still bright when the first shot gave the signal, and the slaughter began. The two palisaded houses of Adams and Drew, without garrisons, were taken immediately, and the families butchered. Those of Edgerly, Beard, and Medar were abandoned, and most of the inmates

escaped. The remaining seven were successfully defended, though several of them were occupied only by the families which owned them. One of these, belonging to Thomas Bickford, stood by the river near the lower end of the settlement. Roused by the firing, he placed his wife and children in a boat, sent them down the stream, and then went back alone to defend his dwelling. When the Indians appeared, he fired on them, sometimes from one loophole and sometimes from another, shouting the word of command to an imaginary garrison, and showing himself with a different hat, cap, or coat, at different parts of the building. The Indians were afraid to approach, and he saved both family and home. One Jones, the owner of another of these fortified houses, was wakened by the barking of his dogs, and went out, thinking that his hog-pen was visited by wolves. The flash of a gun in the twilight of the morning showed the true nature of the attack. The shot missed him narrowly ; and, entering the house again, he stood on his defence, when the Indians, after firing for some time from behind a neighboring rock, withdrew and left him in peace. Woodman's garrison house, though occupied by a number of men, was attacked more seriously, the Indians keeping up a long and brisk fire from behind a ridge where they lay sheltered; but they hit nobody, and at length disappeared. 1

Among the unprotected houses, the carnage was

1 Woodman's garrison house is still standing, having been carefully preserved by his descendants.

horrible. A hundred and four persons, chiefly women and children half naked from their beds, were tomahawked, shot, or killed by slower and more painful methods. Some escaped to the fortified houses, and others hid in the woods. Twenty-seven were kept alive as prisoners. Twenty or more houses were burned; but, what is remarkable, the church was spared. Father Thury entered it during the massacre, and wrote with chalk on the pulpit some sentences, of which the purport is not preserved, as they were no doubt in French or Latin.

Thury said mass, and then the victors retreated in a body to the place where they had hidden their canoes. Here Taxous, dissatisfied with the scalps that he and his band had taken, resolved to have more ; and with fifty of his own warriors, joined by others from the Kennebec, set out on a new enterprise. " They mean," writes Villieu in his diary, " to divide into bands of four or five, and knock people in the head by surprise, which cannot fail to produce a good effect." 1 They did in fact fall a few 'days after on the settlements near Groton, and killed some forty persons.

Having heard from one of the prisoners a rumor of ships on the way from England to attack Quebec, Villieu thought it necessary to inform Frontenac at once. Attended by a few Indians, he travelled four days and nights, till he found Bigot at an

1 " Casser des testes a la surprise apres s'estre divises en plusieurs bandes de quatre au cinq, ce qui ne peut manquer de faire un bon effect/' Villieu. Relation,

Abenaki fort on the Kennebec. His Indians were completely exhausted. He took others in their place, pushed forward again, reached Quebec on the twenty-second of August, found that Fronte-nac had gone to Montreal, followed him thither told his story, and presented him with thirteen English scalps. 1 He had displayed in the achievement of his detestable exploit an energy, perseverance, and hardihood rarely equalled; but all would have been vain but for the help of his clerical colleague Father Pierre Thury. a

THE INDIAN TRIBES OF ACADIA. —The name Abenaki is generic, and of very loose application. As employed by the best French writers at the end of the seventeenth century, it may be taken to include the tribes from the Kennebec eastward to the St. John. These again may be sub-divided as follows. First, the Canibas (Kenibas), or tribes of the Kennebec and adjacent waters. These with kindred neighboring tribes on the Saco, the Andro-

1 " Dans cette assemble M. de Villieu avec 4 gauvages qu'il avoit amends de TAccadie pre"senta k Monsieur le Comte de Frontenac 13 chevelures angloises." Callleres au Ministre, 19 Oct., 1694.

2 The principal authority for the above is the very curious Relation du Voyage fait par le Sieur de Villieu . . . pourfaire la Guerre aux Angloit au printemps de Fan 1694. It is the narrative of Villieu himself, written in the form of a journal, with great detail. He also gives a brief summary in a letter to the minister, 7 Sept. The best English account is that of Belknap, in his History of New Hampshire. Cotton Mather tells the story in his usual unsatisfactory and ridiculous manner. Pike, in his journal, gays that ninety-four persons in all were killed or taken. Mather says, " ninety four or a hundred." The Provincial Record of New Hampshire. estimates it at eighty. Charlevoix claims two hundred and thirty, and Villieu himself but a hundred and thirty-one. Champigny, Frontenac, and Callieres, in their reports to the court, adopt Villieu's statements. Frontenac says that the success was due to the assurances of safety which Phips had given the settlers.

In the Massachusetts archives is a letter to Phips, written just after the attack. The devastation extended six or seven miles. There are also a number of depositions from persons present, giving a horrible picture of the cruelties practised.

scoggin, and the Sheepscot, have been held by some writers to be the Abenakis proper, though some of them, such as the Sokokis or Pequawkets of the Saco, spoke a dialect distinct from the rest. Secondly, the tribes of the Penobscot, called Tarratines by early New England writers, who sometimes, however, give this name a more extended application. Thirdly, the Malicites (Marechitos) of the St. Croix and the St. John. These, with the Penobscots or Tarratines, are the Etchemins of early French writers. All these tribes speak dialects of Algonquin, so nearly related that they understand each other with little difficulty. That eminent Indian philologist, Mr. J. Hammond Trumbull, writes to me: " The Malicite, the Penobscot, and the Kennebec, or Caniba, are dialects of the same language, which may as well be called

Abenaki. The first named differs more considerably from the other two than do these from each other. In fact the Caniba and the Penobscot are merely provincial dialects, with no greater difference than is found in two English counties." The case is widely different with the Micmacs, the Souriquois of the French, who occupy portions of Nova Scotia and New Brunswick, and who speak a language which, though of Algonquin origin, differs as much from the Abenaki dialects as Italian differs from French, and was once described to me by a Malicite (Passamaquoddy) Indian as an unintelligible jargon.

CHAPTER XVn.

1690-1697. NEW FRANCE AND NEW ENGLAND.

THI FRONTIER OF NEW ENGLAND. — BORDER WARFARE. — MOTIVES OF THE FRENCH. — NEEDLESS BARBARITY. — WHO WERE ANSWERABLE? — FATHER THURY. — THE ABENAKIS WAVER. — TREACHERY AT PEMAQUID. — CAPTURE OF PEMAQDID. — PROJECTED ATTACK ON BOSTON. — DISAPPOINTMENT. — MISERIES OF THE FRONTIER. — A CAPTIVE AMAZON.

"Tnis stroke," says Villebon, speaking of the success at Oyster River, "is of great advantage, because it breaks off all the talk of peace between our Indians and the English. The English are in despair, for not even infants in the cradle were spared." l

I have given the story in detail, as showing the origin and character of the destructive aids, of which New England annalists show only the results. The borders of New England were peculiarly vulnerable. In Canada, the settlers built their houses in lines, within supporting distance of each other, along the margin of a river which supplied easy transportation for troops; and, in time of danger, they all took refuge in forts under com-

1 "Ce coup est tres-avantageux, parcequ'il rompte tous les pourparlers de paix entre nos sauvages et les Anglois. Les Anglois sont au d&espoir de ce qu'ils ont tue jusqu'aux enfants au berceau." Villeboti au Ministre, 19 Sept., 1694.

mand of the local seigniors, or of officers with detachments of soldiers. The exposed part of the French colony extended along the St. Lawrence about ninety miles. The exposed frontier of New England was between two and three hundred miles long, and consisted of farms and hamlets, loosely scattered through an almost impervious forest. Mutual support was difficult or impossible. A body of Indians and Canadians, approaching secretly and swiftly, dividing into small bands, and falling at once upon the isolated houses of an extensive district, could commit prodigious havoc in a short time, and with little danger. Even in so-called villages, the houses were far apart, because, except on the sea-shore, the people lived by farming. Such as were able to do so fenced their dwellings with palisades, or built them of solid timber, with loopholes, a projecting upper story like a blockhouse, and sometimes a flanker at one or more of the corners. In the more considerable settlements, the largest of these fortified houses was occupied, in time of danger, by armed men, and served as a place of refuge for the neighbors. The palisaded house defended by Convers at Wells was of this sort, and so also was the Woodman house at Oyster River. These were " garrison houses," properly so called, though the name was often given to fortified dwellings occupied only by the family. The French and Indian war-parties commonly avoided the true garrison houses, and very rarely captured them, except unawares for their tactics were essentially Iroquois, and con-

sisted, for the most part, in pouncing upon peaceful settlers by surprise, and generally in the night. Combatants and non-combatants were slaughtered together. By parading the number of slain, without mentioning that most of them were women and children, and by counting as forts mere private houses surrounded with palisades, Charlevoix and later writers have given the air of gallant exploits to acts which deserve a very different name. To attack military posts, like Casco and Pemaquid, was a legitimate act of war; but systematically to butcher helpless farmers and their families can hardly pass as such, except from the Iroquois point of view.

The chief alleged motive for this ruthless warfare was to prevent the people of New England from invading Canada, by giving them employment at home; though, in fact, they had never thought of invading Canada till after these attacks began. But for the intrigues of Denonville, the Bigots, Thury, and Saint-Castin, before war was declared, and the destruction of Salmon Falls after it, Phips's expedition would never have taken place. By successful raids against the borders of New England, Frontenac roused the Canadians from their dejection, and prevented his red allies from deserting him; but, in so doing, he brought upon himself an enemy who, as Charlevoix himself says, asked only to be let alone. If there was a political necessity for butchering women and children on the frontier of New England, it was a necessity created by the French themselves.

There was no such necessity. Massachusetts was
the only one of the New England colonies which took an aggressive part in the contest. Connecticut did little or nothing. Rhode Island was non-combatant through Quaker influence; and New Hampshire was too weak for offensive war. Massachusetts was in no condition to fight, nor was she impelled to do so by the home government. Canada was organized for war, and must fight at the bidding of the king, who made the war and paid for it. Massachusetts was organized for peace ; and, if she chose an aggressive part, it was at her own risk and her own cost. She had had fighting enough already against infuriated savages far more numerous than the Iroquois, and poverty and political revolution made peace a necessity to her. If there was danger of another attack on Quebec, it was not from New England, but from Old; and no amount of frontier butchery could avert it.

Nor, except their inveterate habit of poaching on Acadian fisheries, had the people of New England provoked these barbarous attacks. They never .even attempted to retaliate them, though the settlements of Acadia offered a safe and easy revenge. Once, it is true, they pillaged Beau-bassin; but they killed nobody, though countless butcheries in settlements yet more defenceless were fresh in their memory. 1

1 The people of Beaubassin had taken an oath of allegiance to England in 1690, and pleaded it as a reason for exemption from plunder; but it appears by French authorities that they had violated it (Observations sur les Depeches tonchant I'Acadie, 1695), and their priest Baudoin had led a band of Micmacs to the attack of Wells (Villebon, Journal). When the " Bostonnais " captured Port Royal, they are described by the French as excessively irritated by the recent slaughter at Salmon Falls, yet the only revenge they took was plundering some of the inhabitants.

With New York, a colony separate in government and widely sundered in local position, the case was different. Its rulers had instigated the Iroquois to attack Canada, possibly before the declaration of war, and certainly after it; and they had no right to complain of reprisal. Yet the frontier of New York was less frequently assailed, because it was less exposed; while that of New England was drenched in blood, because it was open to attack, because the Abenakis were convenient instruments for attacking it, because the adhesion of these tribes was necessary to the maintenance of French power in Acadia, and because this adhesion could best be secured by inciting them to constant hostility against the English. They were not only needed as the barrier of Canada against New England, but the French commanders hoped, by means of their tomahawks, to drive the English beyond the Piscataqua, and secure the whole of Maine to the French crown.

Who were answerable for these offences against Christianity and civilization? First, the king; and, next, the governors and military officers who were charged with executing his orders, and who often executed them with needless barbarity. But a far different responsibility rests on the missionary priests, who hounded their converts on the track of innocent blood. The Acadian priests are not all open to this charge. Some of them are even accused of being too favorable to the English; while others gave themselves to their proper work, and neither abused their influence, nor perverted

their teaching to political ends. The most prominent among the apostles of carnage, at this time, are the Jesuit Bigot on the Kennebec, and the seminary priest Thury on the Penobscot. There is little 'doubt that the latter instigated attacks on the English frontier before the war, and there is conclusive evidence that he had a hand in repeated forays after it began. Whether acting from fanaticism, policy, or an odious compound of both, he was found so useful, that the minister Ponchartrain twice wrote him letters of commendation, praising him in the same breath for his care of the souls of the Indians and his zeal in exciting them to war. " There is no better man," says an Acadian official, " to prompt the savages to any enterprise." * The king was begged to reward him with money; and Ponchartrain wrote to the bishop of Quebec to increase his pay out of the allowance furnished by the government to the Acadian clergy, because he, Thury, had persuaded the Abenakis to begin the

war anew. 2

1 Tibierge, Mfmoire sur I'Acadie, 1695.

2 " Les temoignages qu'on a rendu a. Sa Majeste de Taffection et da zele du S* de Thury, missionaire chez les Canibas (Abenakis), pour son service, et particulierement dans 1'engagement ou il a mis les Sauvages de recommencer la guerre centre les Anglois, m'oblige de vous prier de luy faire une plus forte part sur les 1,500 livres de gratification que Sa Maj-este" accorde pour les eccle'siastiques de I'Acadie." Le Ministre a I'lZvesquc de Quebec, 16 Avril, 1695.

" Je suis bien aise de me servir de cette occasion pour vous dire que j'ay este informe, non seulement de vostre zele et de vostre application pour vostre mission, et du progres qu'elle fait pour 1'avancement de la religion avec les sauvages, mais encore de vos soins pour les maintenir dans le service de Sa Majeste et pour les encourager aux expeditions de guerre." Le Ministre a Thury, 23 Avril, 1697. The other letter to Tbury, written two years before, is of the same tenor.

376 NEW FRANCE AND NEW ENGLAND. [1690-97.

The French missionaries are said to have made use of singular methods to excite their flocks against the heretics. The Abenaki chief Bomaseen, when a prisoner at Boston in 1696, declared that they told the Indians that Jesus Christ was a Frenchman, and his mother, the Virgin, a French lady; that the English had murdered him, and that the best way to gain his favor was to revenge his death. 1

Whether or not these articles of faith formed a part of the teachings of Thury and his fellow-apostles, there is no doubt that it was a recognized part of their functions to keep their converts in hostility to the English, and that their credit with the civil powers depended on their success in doing so. The same holds true of the priests of the mission villages in Canada. They avoided all that might impair the warlike spirit of the neophyte, and they were well aware that in savages the warlike spirit is mainly dependent on native ferocity. They taught temperance, conjugal fidelity, devotion to the rites of their religion, and submission to the priest; but they left the savage a savage still. In spite of the remonstrances of the civil authorities, the mission Indian was separated as far as possible from intercourse with the French, and discouraged

1 Mather, Magnolia, II. 629. Compare Dummer, Memorial, 1709, in Mast. Hist. Coll., 3 Ser., I., and the same writer's Letter to a Noble Lord concerning the Late Expedition to Canada, 1712. Dr. Charles T. Jackeon, the geologist, when engaged in the survey of Maine in 1836, mentions, as an example of the simplicity of the Acadians of Madawaska, that one of them asked him " if Bethlehem, where Christ was born, was not a town In France." First Report on the Geology of Maine, 72. Here, perhaps, is a tradition from early missionary teaching.

from learning the French tongue. He wore a crucifix, hung wampum on the shrine of the Virgin, told his beads, prayed three times a day, knelt for hours before the Host, invoked the saints, and confessed to the priest; but, with rare exceptions, he murdered, scalped, and tortured like his heathen countrymen. 1

The picture has another side, which must not pass unnoticed. Early in the war, the French of Canada began the merciful practice of buying English prisoners, and especially children, from their Indian allies. After the first fury of attack, many

1 The famous Ourehaoue, who had been for years under the influence of the priests, and who, as Charlevoix says, died " un vrai Chretien," being told on his death-bed how Christ was crucified by the Jews, exclaimed with fervor: " Ah! why was not I there ? I would have revenged him : I would have had their scalps." La Potherie, IV 91. Charlevoix, after his fashion on such occasions, suppresses the revenge and the scalping, and instead makes the dying Christian say, " I would have prevented them from so treating my God."

The savage custom of forcing prisoners to run the gauntlet, and sometimes beating them to death as they did so, was continued at two, if not all, of the mission villages down to the end of the French domination. General Stark of the Revolution, when a young man, was subjected to this kind of torture at St. Francis, but saved himself by snatching a club from one of the savages, and knocking the rest to the right and left as he ran. The practice was common, and must have had the consent of the priests of the mission.

At the Sulpitian mission of the Mountain of Montreal, unlike the rest, the converts were taught to speak French and practise mechanical arts. The absence of such teaching in other missions was the subject of frequent complaint, not only from Frontenac, but from other officers. La Motte-Cadillac writes bitterly on the subject, and contrasts the conduct of the French priests with that of the English ministers, vfho have taught many Indians to read and write, and reward them for teaching others in turn, which they do, he says, with great success. Mtfmoire con-tenant une Description de'taillee de I'Acadie, etc., 1693. In fact, Eliot and his co-workers took great pains in this respect. There were at this time thirty Indian churches in New England, according to the Diary of President Stiles, cited bv Holmes.

lives were spared for the sake of this ransom, Sometimes, but not always, the redeemed captives were made to work for their benefactors. They were uniformly treated well, and often with such kindness that they would not be exchanged, and became Canadians by adoption.

Villebon was still full of anxiety as to the adhesion of the Abenakis. Thury saw the danger still more clearly, and told Frontenac that their late attack at Oyster River was due more to levity than to any other cause; that they were greatly alarmed, wavering, half stupefied, afraid of the English, and distrustful of the French, whom they accused of using them as tools. 1 It was clear that something must be done; and nothing could answer the purpose so well as the capture of Pemaquid, that English stronghold which held them in constant menace, and at the same time tempted them by offers of goods at a low rate. To the capture of Pemaquid, therefore, the French government turned its thoughts.

One Pascho Chubb, of Andover, commanded the post, with a garrison of ninety-five militiamen. Stoughton, governor of Massachusetts, had written to the Abenakis, upbraiding them for breaking the peace, and ordering them to bring in their prisoners without delay. The Indians of Bigot's mission, that is to say, Bigot in their name, retorted by a letter to the last degree haughty and abusive. Those of Thury's mission, however, were so anxious to recover their friends held in prison

Thury a Frontenac, 11 Sept. 1694.

at Boston that they came to Pemaquid, and opened a conference with Chubb. The French say that they meant only to deceive him. 1 This does not justify the Massachusetts officer, who, by an act of odious treachery, killed several of them, and captured the chief, Egeremet. Nor was this the only occasion on which the English had acted in bad faith It was but playing into the hands of the French, who saw with delight that the folly of their enemies had aided their own intrigues. 2

Early in 1696, two ships of war, the " Envieux " and the " Profond," one commanded by Iberville and the other by Bonaventure, sailed from Roche-fort to Quebec, where they took on board eighty troops and Canadians; then proceeded to Cape Breton, embarked thirty Micmac Indians, and steered for the St. John. Here they met two British frigates and a provincial tender belonging to Massachusetts. A fight ensued. The forces were very unequal. The " Newport," of twenty-four guns, was dismasted and taken; but her companion frigate along with the tender escaped in the fog. The French then anchored at the mouth of the St, John, where Villebon and the priest Simon were waiting for them, with fifty more Micmacs. Simon and the Indians went on board; and they all sailed for Pentegoet, where Villieu, with twenty-five soldiers, and Thury and Saint-Castin, with some

1 Villebon, Journal, 1694-1696.

2 N. Y. Col Docs., IX. 613, 616,642, 643 ; La Potherie, III. 258; Col-tires au Ministre, 25 Oct., 1695; Rev. John Pike to Governor and Council, 7

Jan., 1694 (1695), in Johnston, Hist, of Bristol and Bremen; Hutchinson, Hist. Mass., H. 81. 90.

three hundred Abenakis, were ready to join them, After the usual feasting, these new allies paddled for Pemaquid; the ships followed; and on the next day, the fourteenth of August, they all reached their destination.

The fort of Pemaquid stood at the west side of the promontory of the same name, on a rocky point at the mouth of Pemaquid River. It was a quadrangle, with ramparts of rough stone, built at great pains and cost, but exposed to artillery, and incapable of resisting heavy shot. The government of Massachusetts, with its usual military fatuity, had placed it in the keeping of an unfit commander, and permitted some of the yeoman garrison to bring their wives and children to this dangerous and important post.

Saint-Castin and his Indians landed at New Harbor, half a league from the fort. Troops and cannon were sent ashore ; and, at five o'clock in the afternoon, Chubb was summoned to surrender. He replied that he would fight, " even if the sea were covered with French ships and the land with Indians." The firing then began ; and the Indian marksmen, favored by the nature of the ground, ensconced themselves near the fort, well covered from its cannon. During the night, mortars and heavy ships' guns were landed, and by great exertion were got into position, the two priests working lustily with the rest. They opened fire at three o'clock on the next day. Saint-Castin had just before sent Chubb a letter, telling him that, if the garrison were obstinate, they would get no quarter.

and would be butchered by the Indians. Close upon this message followed four or five bomb-shells. Chubb succumbed immediately, sounded a parley, and gave up the fort, on condition that he and his men should be protected from the Indians, sent to Boston, and exchanged for French and Abenaki prisoners. They all marched out without arms; and Iberville, true to his pledge, sent them to an island in the bay, beyond the reach of his red allies. Villieu took possession of the fort, where an Indian prisoner was found in irons, half dead from long confinement. This so enraged his countrymen that a massacre would infallibly have taken place but for the precaution of Iberville.

The cannon of Pemaquid were carried on board the ships, and the small arms and ammunition given to the Indians. Two days were spent in destroying the works, and then the victors withdrew in triumph. Disgraceful as was the prompt surrender of the fort, it may be doubted if, even with the best defence, it could have held out many days; for it had no casemates, and its occupants were defenceless against the explosion of shells. Chubb was arrested for cowardice on his return, and remained some months in prison. After his release, he,returned to his family at Andover, twenty miles from Boston; and here, in the year following, he and his wife were killed by Indians, who seem to have pursued him to this apparently safe asylum to take revenge for his treachery toward their countrymen. 1

1 Baudoin, Journal d'un Voyage fait avec M. d'lberville. Baudoia

The people of Massachusetts, compelled by a royal order to build and maintain Pemaquid, had no love for it, and underrated its importance. Having been accustomed to spend their money as they themselves saw fit, they revolted at compulsion, though exercised for their good. Pemaquid was nevertheless of the utmost value for the preservation of their hold on Maine, and its conquest was a crowning triumph to the French.

The conquerors now projected a greater exploit. The Marquis de Nesmond, with a powerful squadron of fifteen ships, including some of the best in the royal navy, sailed for Newfoundland, with orders to defeat an. English squadron supposed to be there, and then to proceed to the mouth of the Penobscot, where he was to be joined by the Abenaki warriors and fifteen hundred troops from Canada. The whole united force was then to fall upon Boston. The French had an exact knowledge of the place. Meneval, when a prisoner there, lodged in the house of John Nelson, had carefully examined it; and so also had the Chevalier d'Aux; while La Motte-Cadillac had reconnoitred the town and harbor before the war began. An accurate map of them was made for the use of the expedition, and the plan of operations was arranged with great care. Twelve hundred troops and Canadians

was an Acadian priest, who accompanied the expedition, which he describes in detail, delation de ce qui s'est passe", etc., 1696, 1696; Des Goutim au Mini&tre, 23 Sept., 1696; Hutchinson, Hist. Mass., II. 89; Mather, Magnolia, H. 633. A letter from Chubb, asking to be released from prison, is preserved in the archives of Massachusetts. I have examined the site of the fort, the remains of which are still distinct.

were to land with artillery at Dorchester, and march at once to force the barricade across the neck of the peninsula on which the town stood. At the same time, Saint-Castin was to land at Noddle's Island, with a troop of Canadians and all the Indians ; pass over in canoes to Charlestown; and, after mastering it, cross to the north point of Boston, which would thus be attacked at both ends. During these movements, two hundred soldiers were to seize the battery on Castle Island, and then land in front of the town near Long Wharf, under the guns of the fleet.

Boston had about seven thousand inhabitants, but, owing to the seafaring habits of the people, many of its best men were generally absent; and, in the belief of the French, its available force did not much exceed eight hundred. " There are no soldiers in the place/' say the directions for attack, " at least there were none last September, except the garrison from Pemaquid, who do not deserve the name." An easy victory was expected. After Boston was taken, the land forces, French and Indian, were to march on Salem, and thence northward to Portsmouth, conquering as they went; while the ships followed along the coast to lend aid, when necessary. All captured places were to be completely destroyed after removing all valuable property. A portion of this plunder was to be abandoned to the officers and men, in order to encourage them, and the rest stowed in the ships for transportation to France. 1

1 Mfrnmre sur I'Entreprise de Baston, pour M. le Marquis de Nesmond t Versailles, 21 Avril, 1697; Instruction a M. le Marquis de Desmond, mem*

Notice of the proposed expedition had reached Frontenac in the spring; and he began at once to collect men, canoes, and supplies for the long and arduous march to the rendezvous. He saw clearly the uncertainties of the attempt; but, in spite of his seventy-seven years, he resolved to command the land force in person. He was ready in June, and waited only to hear from Nesmond. The summer passed ; and it was not till September that a ship reached Quebec with a letter from the marquis, telling him that head winds had detained the fleet till only fifty days' provision remained, and it was too late for action. The enterprise had completely failed, and even at Newfoundland nothing was ac-

date; Le Roy a Frontenac, meme date; Le Roy a Frontenac et Champigny t 27 Avril, 1697; Le Ministre a Nesmond, 28 Avril, 1697; Ibid., 16 Juin, 1697; Frontenac au Ministre, 15 Oct., 1697; Carte tfe Baston, par le S r . Franquelin, 1697. This is the map made for the use of the expedition. A fac-simile of it is before me. The conquest of New York had originally formed part of the plan. Lagny au, Ministre, 20 Jan., 1696. Even as it was, too much was attempted, and the scheme was fatally complicated by the operations at Newfoundland. Four years before, a projected attack on Quebec by a British fleet, under Admiral Wheeler, had come to nought from analogous causes.

The French spared no pains to gain accurate information as to the strength of the English settlements. Among other reports on this subject there is a curious Me'moire sitr les fitablissements anglois au dela de Pemaquid, jusqu'a Baston. It was made just after the capture of Pemaquid, with a view to farther operations. Saco is described as a small fort a league above the mouth of the river Saco, with four cannon, but fit only to resist Indians. At Wells, it says, all the settlers have sought refuge in four petits forts, of which the largest holds perhaps 20 men, besides women and children. At York, all the people have gathered into one fort, where there are about 40 men. At Portsmouth there is a fort, of slight account, and about a hundred houses. This neighborhood, no doubt including Kittery, can furnish at most about 300 men. At the Isles of Shoals there are some 280 fishermen, who are absent, except on Sundays. In the same manner, estimates are made for every village and district as far as Boston.

complished. It proved a positive advantage to New England, since a host of Indians, who would otherwise have been turned loose upon the borders, were gathered by Saint-Castin at the Penobscot to wait for the fleet, and kept there idle all summer.

It is needless to dwell farther on the war in Acadia. There were petty combats by land and sea; Yillieu was captured and carried to Boston; a band of New England rustics made a futile attempt to dislodge Yillebon from his fort at Nax-ouat; while, throughout the contest, rivalry and jealousy rankled among the French officials, who continually maligned each other in tell-tale letters to the court. Their hope that the Abenakis would force back the English boundary to the Piscataqua was never fulfilled. At Kittery, at Wells, and even among the ashes of York, the stubborn settlers held their ground, while war-parties prowled along the whole frontier, from the Connecticut. A single incide^iwifrsliow the nature of the situation, and the qualities which it sometimes called forth.

Early in the spring that followed the capture of Pemaquid, a band of Indians fell, after daybreak, on a number of farm-houses near the village of Haverhill. One of them belonged to a settler named Dustan, whose wife Hannah had borne a child a week before, and lay in the house, nursed by Mary Neff, one of her neighbors. Dustan had gone to his work ii* a neighboring field, taking with him his seven children, of whom the youngest was two years old. Hearing the noise of the attack,

25

he told them to run to the nearest fortified house, a mile or more distant, and, snatching up his gun, threw himself on one of his horses and galloped towards his own house to save his wife. It wa§ too late : the Indians were already there. He now thought only of saving his children; and, keeping behind them as they ran, he fired on the pursuing savages, and held them at bay till he and his flock reached a place of safety. Meanwhile, the house was set on fire, and his wife and the nurse carried off. Her husband, no doubt, had given her up as lost, when, weeks after, she reappeared, accompanied by Mary Neff and a boy, and bringing ten Indian scalps. Her story was to the following effect.

The Indians had killed the new-born child by dashing it against a tree, after which the mother and the nurse were dragged into the forest, where they found a number of friends and neighbors, their fellows in misery. Some of these were presently tomahawked, and the rest divided among their captors. Hannah Dustan and the nurse fell to the share of a family consisting of two warriors, three squaws, and seven children, who separated from the rest, and, hunting as they went, moved northward towards an Abenaki village, two hundred and fifty miles distant, probably that of the mission on the Chaudiere. Every morning, noon, and evening, they told their beads, and repeated their prayers. An English boy captured at Worcester, was also of the party. After a while, the Indians began to amuse themselves by telling the

women that, when they reached the village, they would be stripped, made to run the gauntlet, and severely beaten, according to custom.

Hannah Dustan now resolved on a desperate effort to escape, and Mary Neff and the boy agreed to join in it. They were in the depths of the forest, half way on their journey, and the Indians, who had no distrust of them, were all asleep about their camp fire, when, late in the night, the two women and the boy took each a hatchet, and crouched silently by the bare heads of the unconscious savages. Then they all struck at once, with blows so rapid and true that ten of the twelve were killed before they were well awake. One old squaw sprang up wounded, and ran screeching into the forest, followed by a small boy whom they had purposely left unharmed. Hannah Dustan and her companions watched by the corpses till daylight ; then the Amazon scalped them all, and the three made their way back to the settlements, with the trophies of their exploit. 1

1 This story is told by Mather, who had it from the women themselves, and by Niles, Hutchinson, and others. An entry in the contemporary journal of Rer. John Pike fully confirms it. The facts were notorious at the time. Hannah Dustan and her companions received a bounty of £60 for their ten scalps; and the governor of Maryland, hearing of what they had done, sent them

a present.

CHAPTER XVm.

1693-1697. FRENCH AND ENGLISH RIVALRY

LE MOTNB D'IBERVILLE. — His EXPLOITS IN NEWFOUNDLAND. —IiJ HUDSON'S BAT. — THE GREAT PRIZE. — THE COMPETITORS. — FATAL POLICY OP THE KINO. — THE IROQUOIS QUESTION. — NEGOTIATION. — FIRMNESS OF FRONTENAC. — ENGLISH INTERVENTION. — WAR RB-NEWED. — STATE OF THE WEST. — INDIAN DIPLOMACY. — CRUEL MEASURES. —A PERILOUS CRISIS. — AUDACITY OF FRONTENAC.

No Canadian, under the French rule, stands in a more conspicuous or more deserved eminence than Pierre Le Moyne d'Iberville. In the seventeenth century, most of those who acted a prominent part in the colony were born in Old France; but Iber-ville was a true son of the soil. He and his brothers, Longueuil, Serigny, Assigny, Maricourt, Sainte-Helene, the two Chateauguays, and the two Bien-villes, were, one and all, children worthy of their father, Charles Le Moyne of Montreal, and favorable types of that Canadian noblesse, to whose adventurous hardihood half the continent bears witness. Iberville was trained Jn the French navy, and was already among its most able commanders. The capture of Pemaquid was, for him, but the beginning of greater things; and, though the exploits that followed were outside the main theatre of action, they were too remarkable to be passed in silence.

The French had but one post of any consequence on the Island of Newfoundland, the fort and village at Placentia Bay; while the English fishermen had formed a line of settlements two or three hundred miles along the eastern coast. Iberville had represented to the court the necessity of checking their growth, and to that end a plan was settled, in connection with the expedition against Pemaquid. The ships of the king were to transport the men; while Iberville and others associated with him were to pay them, and divide the plunder as their compensation. The chronicles of the time show various similar bargains between the great king and his subjects.

Pemaquid was no sooner destroyed, than Iberville sailed for Newfoundland, with the eighty men he had taken at Quebec; and, on arriving, he was joined by as many more, sent him from the same place. He found Brouillan, governor of Placentia, with a squadron formed largely of privateers from St. Malo, engaged in a vain attempt to seize St. John, the chief post of the English. Brouillan was a man of harsh, jealous, and impracticable temper; and it was with the utmost difficulty that he and Iberville could act in concert They came at last to an agreement, made a combined attack on St. John, took it, and burned it to the ground. Then followed a new dispute about the division of the spoils. At length it was settled. Brouillan went back to Placentia, and Iberville and his men were left to pursue their conquests alone.

There were no British soldiers on the island. The settlers were rude fishermen without commanders, and, according to the French accounts, without religion or morals. In fact, they are described as " worse than Indians." Iberville now had with him a hundred and twenty-five soldiers and Canadians, besides a few Abenakis from Aea-dia. 1 It was mid-winter when he began his march. For two months he led his hardy band through frost and snow, from hamlet to hamlet, along those forlorn and desolate coasts, attacking each in turn and carrying havoc everywhere. Nothing could exceed the hardships of the way, or the vigor with which they were met and conquered. The chaplain Baudoin gives an example of them in his diary. "January 18th. The roads are so bad that we can find only twelve men strong enough to beat the path. Our snow-shoes break on the crust, and against the rocks and fallen trees hidden under the snow, which catch and trip us; but, for all that, we cannot help laughing to see now one, and now another, fall headlong. The Sieur de Martigny fell into a river, and left his gun and his sword there to save his life."

A panic seized the settlers, many of whom were without arms as well as without leaders. They imagined the Canadians to be savages, who scalped and butchered like the Iroquois. Their resistance was feeble and incoherent, and Iberville carried all before him. Every hamlet was pillaged and burned;

1 The reinforcement sent him from Quebec consisted of fifty soldiers thirty Canadians, and three officers Frontenac au Ministre, 28 Oct., 1696

and, according to the incredible report of the French writers, two hundred persons were killed and seven hundred captured, though it is admitted that most of the prisoners escaped. When spring opened, all the English settlements were destro\'7d*ed, except the post of Bonavista and the Island of Car-bonniere, a natural fortress in the sea. Iberville returned to Placentia, to prepare for completing his conquest, when his plans were broken by the arrival of his brother Serigny, with orders to proceed at once against the English at Hudson's BayJ It was the nineteenth of May, when Serigny appeared with five ships of war, the " Pelican," the " Palmier," the « Wesp," the « Profond," and the "Violent." The important trading-post of Fort Nelson, called Fort Bourbon by the French, was the destined object of attack. Iberville and Serigny had captured it three years before, but the English had retaken it during the past summer, and, as it commanded the fur-trade of a vast inte-

1 On the Newfoundland expedition, the best authority is the long iiary of the chaplain Baudoin, Journal du Voyage que fai /ait avec M* d'Iberville; also, Me"moire sur l'Entreprise de Terreneuve, 1696. Compare La Potherie, I. 24-52. A deposition of one Phillips, one Roberts, and several others, preserved in the Public Record Office of London, and quoted by Brown in his History of Cape Breton, makes the French force much greater than the statements of the French writers. The deposition also says that at the attack of St. John's " the French took one William Brew, an inhabitant, a prisoner, and cut all round his scalp, and then, by strength of hands, stript his skin from the forehead to the crown, and so sent him into the fortifications, assuring the inhabitants that they would serve them all in like manner if they did not surrender."

St. John's was soon after reoccupied by the English.

Baudoin was one of those Acadian priests who are praised for services " en empeschant les sauvages de faire la paix avec les Anglois, ayant mesme este* en guerre avec eux," Champigny au Ministre, 24 Oct.,,

rior region, a strong effort was now to be made for its recovery. Iberville took command of the " Pelican," and his brother of the " Palmier." They sailed from Placentia early in July, followed by two other ships of the squadron, and a vessel carrying stores. Before the end of the month they entered the bay, where they were soon caught among masses of floating ice. The store-ship was crushed and lost, and the rest were in extreme danger. The " Pelican " at last extricated herself, and sailed into the open sea; but her three consorts were nowhere to be seen. Iberville steered for Fort Nelson, which was several hundred miles distant, on the western shore of this dismal inland sea. He had nearly reached it, when three sail hove in sight; and he did not doubt that they were his missing ships. They proved, however, to be English armed merchantmen : the " Hampshire " of fifty-two guns, and the " Daring " and the " Hudson's Bay" of thirty-six and thirty-two. The " Pelican" carried but forty-four, and she was alone. A desperate battle followed, and from half past nine to one o'clock the cannonade was incessant. Iberville kept the advantage of the wind, and, coming at length to close quarters with the "Hampshire," gave her repeated broadsides between wind and water, with such effect that she sank with all on board. He next closed with the " Hudson's Bay," which soon struck her flag; while the " Daring " made sail, and escaped. The " Pelican " was badly damaged in hull, masts, and rigging : and the increasing fury of a gale from the

east made her position more critical every hour, She anchored, to escape being driven ashore; but the cables parted, and she was stranded about two leagues from the fort. Here, racked by the waves and the tide, she split amidships; but most of the crew reached land with their weapons and ammunition. The northern winter had already begun, and the snow lay a foot deep in the forest. Some of them died from cold and exhaustion, and the rest built huts and kindled fires to warm and dry themselves. Food was so scarce that their only hope of escape from famishing seemed to lie in a desperate effort to carry the fort by storm, but now fortune interposed. The three ships they had left behind in the ice arrived with all the needed succors. Men, cannon, and mortars were sent ashore, and the attack began.

Fort Nelson was a palisade work, garrisoned by traders and other civilians in the employ of the English fur company, and commanded by one of its agents, named Bailey. Though it had a considerable number of small cannon, it was incapable of defence against any thing but musketry; and the French bombs soon made it untenable. After being three times summoned, Bailey lowered his flag, though not till he had obtained honorable terms; and he and his men marched out with arms and baggage, drums beating and colors flying.

Iberville had triumphed over the storms, the icebergs, and the English. The north had seen his prowess, and another fame awaited him in the regions of the sun; for he became the father of

Louisiana, and his brother Bienville founded New Orleans. 1

These northern conflicts were but episodes. In Hudson's Bay, Newfoundland, and Acadia, the issues of the war were unimportant, compared with the momentous question whether France or England should be mistress of the west; that is to say, of the whole interior of the continent. There was a strange contrast in the attitude of the rival colonies towards this supreme prize : the one was inert, and seemingly indifferent; the other, intensely active. The reason is obvious enough. The English colonies were separate, jealous of the crown and of each other, and incapable as yet of acting in concert. Living by agriculture and trade, they could prosper within limited areas, and had no present need of spreading beyond the Alleghanies. Each of them was an aggregate of persons, busied with their own affairs, and giving little heed to matters which did not immediately concern them. Their rulers, whether chosen by themselves or appointed in England, could not compel them to become the instruments of enterprises in which the sacrifice was present, and the advantage remote. The neglect in which the English court left them, though wholesome in most respects, made them unfit for aggressive action; for they had neither troops, commanders, political union, military organization, nor military habits. In

1 On the capture of Fort Nelson, Iberville au Ministre, 8 AW-., 1607; Jere'mie, Relation de la Baye de Hudson; La Potherie, I. 86-109. AU these writers were present at the attack.

communities so busy, and governments so popular, much could not be done, in war, till the people were roused to the necessity of doing it; and that awakening was still far distant. Even New York, the only exposed colony, except Massachusetts and New Hampshire, regarded the war merely as a nuisance to be held at arm's length. 1

In Canada, all was different. Living by the fur trade, she needed free range and indefinite space. Her geographical position determined the nature of her pursuits; and her pursuits developed the roving and adventurous character of her people, who, living under a military rule, could be directed at will to such ends as their rulers saw fit. The grand French scheme of territorial extension was not born at court, but sprang from Canadian soil, and was developed by the chiefs of the colony, who, being on the ground, saw the possibilities and requirements of the situation, and generally had a personal interest in realizing them. The rival colonies had two different laws of growth. The one increased by slow extension, rooting firmly as it spread; the other shot offshoots, with few or no roots, far out into the wilderness. It was the nature of French colonization to seize upon detached strategic points, and hold them by the bayonet, forming no agricultural basis, but attracting the Indians by trade, and holding them by conversion. A musket, a rosary, and a pack of beaver skins may serve to represent it, and in fact it consisted of little else.

1 See note at the end of the chapter.

Whence came the numerical weakness of New France, and the real though latent strength of her rivals ? Because, it is answered, the French were not an emigrating people ; but, at the end of the seventeenth century, this was only half true. The French people were divided into two parts, one eager to emigrate, and the other reluctant. The one consisted of the persecuted Huguenots, the other of the favored Catholics. The government chose to construct its colonies, not of those who wished to go, but of those who wished to stay at home. From the hour when the edict of Nantes was revoked, hundreds of thousands of Frenchmen would have hailed as a boon the permission to transport themselves, their families, and their property to the New World. The permission was fiercely refused, and the persecuted sect was denied even a refuge in the wilderness. Had it been granted them, the valleys of the west would have swarmed with a laborious and virtuous population, trained in adversity, and possessing the essential qualities of self-government. Another France would have grown beyond the Alleghanies, strong with the same kind of strength that made the future greatness of the British colonies. British America was (an asylum for the oppressed and the suffering of all creeds and nations, and population poured into her by the force of a natural tendency. France, like England, might have been great in two hemispheres, if she had placed herself in accord with this tendency, instead of opposing it; but despotism was consistent with itself, and a mighty opportunity was for ever lost.

As soon could the Ethiopian change his skin as the priest-ridden king change his fatal policy of exclusion. Canada must be bound to the papacy, even if it blasted her. The contest for the west must be waged by the means which Bourbon policy ordained, and which, it must be admitted, had some great advantages of their own, when controlled by a man like Frontenac. The result hung, for the present, on the relations of the French with the Iroquois and the tribes of the lakes, the Illinois, and the valley of the Ohio, but, above all, on their relations with the Iroquois; for, could they be conquered or won over, it would be easy to deal with the rest.

Frontenac was meditating a grand effort to inflict such castigation as would bring them to reason, when one of their chiefs, named Tareha, came to Quebec with overtures of peace. The Iroquois had lost many of their best warriors. The arrival of troops from France had discouraged them; the war had interrupted their hunting ; and, having no furs to barter with the English, they were in want of arms, ammunition, and all the necessaries of life. Moreover, Father Milet, nominally a prisoner among them, but really an adopted chief, had used all his influence to bring about a peace; and the mission of Tareha was the result. Frontenac received him kindly. " My Iroquois children have been drunk; but I will give them an opportunity to repent. Let each of your five nations send me two deputies, and I will listen to what they have to say." They would not come, but sent him in-

stead an invitation to meet them and their friends, the English, in a general council at

Albany ; a proposal which he rejected with contempt. Then they sent another deputation, partly to him and partly to their Christian countrymen of the Saut and the Mountain, inviting all alike to come and treat with them at Onondaga. Frontenac, adopting the Indian fashion, kicked away their wampum belts, rebuked them for tampering with the mission Indians, and told them that they were rebels, bribed by the English; adding that, if a suitable deputation should be sent to Quebec to treat squarely of peace, he still would listen, but that, if they came back with any more such proposals as they had just made, they should be roasted alive.

A few weeks later, the deputation appeared. It consisted of two chiefs of each nation, headed by the renowned orator Decanisora, or, as the French wrote the name, Tegannisorens. The council was held in the hall of the supreme council at Quebec. The dignitaries of the colony were present, with priests, Jesuits, Re'collets, officers, and the Christian chiefs of the Saut and the Mountain. The appearance of the ambassadors bespoke their destitute plight; for they were all dressed in shabby deerskins and old blankets, except Decanisora, who was attired in a scarlet coat laced with gold, given him by the governor of New York. Golden, who knew him in his old age, describes him as a tall, well-formed man, with a face not unlike the busts of Cicero. " He spoke," says the French reporter, 46 with as perfect a grace as is vouchsafed to an

uncivilized people;" buried the hatchet, covered the blood that had been spilled, opened the roads, and cleared the clouds from the sun. In other words, he offered peace; but he demanded at the same time that it should include the English. Frontenac replied, in substance: " My children are right to come submissive and repentant. I ain ready to forgive the past, and hang up the hatchet; but the peace must include all my other children, far and near. Shut your ears to English poison. The war with the English has nothing to do with you, and only the great kings across the sea have power to stop it. You must give up all your prisoners, both French and Indian, without one exception. I will then return mine, and make peace with you, but not before." He then entertained them at his own table, gave them a feast described as " magnificent," and bestowed gifts so liberally, that the tattered ambassadors went home in embroidered coats, laced shirts, and plumed hats. They were pledged to return with the prisoners before the end of the season, and they left two hostages as security. 1

Meanwhile, the authorities of New York tried to prevent the threatened peace. First, Major Peter Schuyler convoked the chiefs at Albany, and told them that, if they went to ask peace in Canada, they would be slaves for ever. The Iroquois declared that they loved the English, but they repelled

1 Oil these negotiations, and their antecedents, Callieres, Relation de ce qui s'est passe' de plus remarquable en Canada depuis Sept., 1692, jusqu'au Depart des Vaisseaux en 1693 ; La Motte-Cadillac, Memoire des Negociations avec les Iroquois, 1694; Callieres au Ministre, 19 Oct., 1694; La Potherie, III. 200-220; Golden, Five Nations, chap. x.: N. Y. Col. Docs., IV. 85,

every attempt to control their action. Then Fletcher, the governor, called a general council at the same place, and told them that they should not hold councils with the French, or that, if they did so, they should hold them at Albany in presence of the English. Again they asserted their rights as an independent people. " Corlaer," said their speaker, " has held councils with our enemies, and why should not we hold councils with his?" Yet they were strong in assurances of friendship, and declared themselves " one head, one heart, one blood, and one soul, with the English." Their speaker continued: " Our only reason for sending deputies to the French is that we are brought so low, and none of our neighbors help us, but leave us to bear all the burden of the war. Our brothers of New England, Pennsylvania, Maryland, and Virginia, all of their own accord took hold of the covenant chain, and called themselves- our allies; but they have done nothing to help us, and we cannot fight the French alone, because they are always receiving soldiers from beyond the Great Lake. Speak from your heart, brother: will you and your neighbors join with us, and make strong war against the French ? If you will, we will break off all treaties, and fight them as hotly as ever; but, if you will not help us, we must make peace."

Nothing could be more just than these reproaches; and, if the English governor had answered by a vigorous attack on the French forts south of the St. Lawrence, the Iroquois warriors would have raised the hatchet again with one accord. But

Fletcher was busy with other matters; and he had besides no force at his disposal but four companies, the only British regulars on the continent, defective in numbers, ill-appointed, and mutinous. 1 Therefore he answered not with acts, but with words. The negotiation with the French went on, and Fletcher called another council. It left him in a worse position than before. The Iroquois again asked for help : he could not promise it, but was forced to yield the point, and tell them that he consented to their making peace with Onontio.

It is certain that they wanted peace, but equally certain that they did not want it to be lasting, and sought nothing more than a breathing time to regain their strength. Even now some of them were for continuing the war; and at the great council at Onondaga, where the matter was debated, the Onondagas, Oneidas, and Mohawks spurned the French proposals, and refused to give up their prisoners. The Cayugas and some of the Senecas were of another mind, and agreed to a partial compliance, with Frontenac's demands. The rest seem to have stood passive in the hope of gaining time.

They were disappointed. In vain the Seneca and Cayuga deputies buried the hatchet at Montreal, and promised that the other nations would soon do likewise. Frontenac was not to be deceived. He would accept nothing but the frank fulfilment of his conditions, refused the proffered

1 Fletcher is, however, charged with gross misconduct in regard to the four companies, which he is said to have kept at about half their complement, in order to keep the balance of their pay for himself.

26

peace, and told his Indian allies to wage war to the knife. There was a dog-feast and a war-dance, and the strife began anew.

In all these conferences, the Iroquois had stood by their English allies, with a fidelity not too well merited. But, though they were loyal towards the English, they had acted with duplicity towards the French, and, while treating of peace with them, had attacked some of their Indian allies, and intrigued with others. They pursued with more persistency than ever the policy they had adopted in the time of La Barre, that is, to persuade or frighten the tribes of the west to abandon the French, join hands with them and the English, and send their furs to Albany instead of Montreal; for the sagacious confederates knew well that, if the trade were turned into this new channel, their local position would enable them to control it. The scheme was good; but, with whatever consistency their chiefs and elders might pursue it, the wayward ferocity of their young warriors crossed it incessantly, and murders alternated with intrigues. On the other hand, the western tribes, who since the war had been but ill supplied with French goods and French brandy, knew that they could have English goods and English rum in great abundance, and at far less cost; and thus, in spite of hate and fear, the intrigue went on. Michilli-mackinac was the focus of it, but it pervaded all the west. The position of Frontenac was one of great difficulty, and the more so that the intestine quarrels of his allies excessively complicated the

mazes of forest diplomacy. This heterogeneous multitude, scattered in tribes and groups of tribes over two thousand miles of wilderness, was like a vast menagerie of wild animals; and the lynx bristled at the wolf, and the panther grinned fury at the bear, in spite of all his efforts to form them into a happy family under his paternal rule.

La Motte-Cadillac commanded at Michillimacki-iiac, Courtemanche was stationed at Fort Miamis, and Tonty and La Foret at the fortified rock of St. Louis on the Illinois; while Nicolas Perrot roamed among the tribes of the Mississippi, striving at the risk of his life to keep them at peace with each other, and in alliance with the French. Yet a plot presently came to light, by which the Foxes, Mas-con tins, and Kickapoos were to join hands, renounce the French, and cast their fortunes with the Iroquois and the English. There was still more anxiety for the tribes of Michillimackinac, because the results of their defection would be more immediate. This important post had at the time an Indian population of six or seven thousand souls, a Jesuit mission, a fort with two hundred soldiers, and a village of about sixty houses, occupied by traders and coureurs de bois. The Indians of the place were in relations more or less close with all the tribes of the lakes. The Huron village was divided between two rival chiefs: the Baron, who was deep in Iroquois and English intrigue; and the Rat, who, though once the worst enemy of the French, now stood their friend. The Ottawas and other Algonquins of the adjacent villages were

savages of a lower grade, tossed continually between hatred of the Iroquois, distrust of the French, and love of English goods and English rum, 1

La Motte-Cadillac found that the Hurons of the Baron's band were receiving messengers and peace belts from New York and her red allies, that the English had promised to build a trading house on Lake Erie, and that the Iroquois had invited the lake tribes to a grand convention at Detroit. These belts and messages were sent, in the Indian expression, " underground," that is, secretly; and the envoys who brought them came in the disguise of prisoners taken by the Hurons. On one occasion, seven Iroquois were brought in; and some of the French, suspecting them to be agents of the negotiation, stabbed two of them as they landed. There was a great tumult. The Hurons took arms to defend the remaining five; but at length suffered themselves to be appeased, and even gave one of the Iroquois, a chief, into the hands of the French, who, says La Potherie, determined to "make an example of him." They invited the Ottawas to " drink the broth of an Iroquois." The wretch was made fast to a stake, and a Frenchman began the torture by burning him with a red-hot gun-barrel. The mob of savages was soon wrought

1 "Si les Outaouacs (Ottawas) et Hurons concluent la paix avec ITroquois sans nostre participation, et donnent chez eux l'entree a 1 An glois pour le commerce, la Colonie est entierement ruinee, puiique c'est le seul (moyen) par lequel ce pays-cy puisse subsister, et Ton peut as-eeurer que si les sauvages goustent une fois du commerce de 1'Anglois, Us rompront pour toujours arec les Francois, parcequ'ils ne peuvent donner les marchandises qu'a un prix beaucoup plus hault." FranteruK av Afinistre, 25 Oct., 1696,

up to the required pitch of ferocity; and, after atrociously tormenting him, they cut him to pieces, and ate him. 1 It was clear that the more Iroquois the allies of France could be persuaded to burn, the less would be the danger that they would make peace with the confederacy. On another occasion, four were tortured at once; and La Motte-Cadillac writes, " If any more prisoners are brought me, 1 promise you that their fate will be no sweeter." 2

The same cruel measures were practised when the Ottawas came to trade at Montreal. Fronte-nac once invited a band of them to " roast an Iroquois," newly caught by the soldiers; but as they had hamstrung him, to prevent his escape, he bled to death before the torture began. 3 In the next spring, the revolting tragedy of Michillimackinac was repeated at Montreal, where four more Iroquois were burned by the soldiers, inhabitants, and Indian allies. " It was the mission of Canada/] says a Canadian writer, " to propagate Christianity and civilization." 4

Every effort was vain. La Motte-Cadillac wrote that matters grew worse and worse, and that the

1 La Potherie, II. 298.

2 La Motte-Cadillac a , 3 Aug., 1695. A translation of this letter will be found in Sheldon, Early History of Michigan.

3 Relation de ce qui s'est passt de plus remarquable entre les Francois et les Iroquois durant la pr&ente annfe, 1695. There is a translation in N Y Cci. Docs., IX. Compare La Potherie, who misplaces the incident as to date.

4 This last execution was an act of reprisal: " J'abandonnay les 4 prisonniers aux soldats, habitants, et sauvages, qui les bruslerent par represailles de deux du Sault que cette nation avoit traitte de la mesme maniere." Callieres au Ministre, 20 Oct.. 1696.

Ottawas had been made to believe that the French neither would nor could protect them, but meant to leave them to their fate. They thought that they had no hope except in peace with the Iroquois, and had actually gone to meet them at an appointed rendezvous. One course alone was now left to Frontenac, and this was to strike the Iroquois with a blow heavy enough to humble them, and teach the wavering hordes of the west that he was, in truth, their father and their defender. Nobody knew so well as he the difficulties of the attempt; and, deceived perhaps by his own energy, he feared that, in his absence on -a distant expedition, the governor of New York would attack Montreal. Therefore, he had begged for more troops. About three hundred were sent him, and with these he was forced to content himself.

He had waited, also, for another reason. In his belief, the re-establishment of Fort Frontenac, abandoned in a panic by Denonville, was necessary to the success of a campaign against the Iroquois. A party in the colony vehemently opposed the measure, on the ground that the fort would be used by the friends of Frontenac for purposes of trade. It was, nevertheless, very important, if not essential, for holding the Iroquois in check. They themselves felt it to be so; and, when they heard that the French intended to occupy it again, they appealed to the governor of New York, who told them that, if the plan were carried into effect, he would march to their aid with all the power of

his government. He did not, and perhaps could not, keep his word.

In the question of Fort Frontenac, as in every thing else, the opposition to the governor, always busy and vehement, found its chief representative in the in tend ant, who told the minister that the policy of Frontenac was all wrong ; that the public good was not its object; that he disobeyed or evaded the orders of the king; and that he had suffered the Iroquois to delude him by false overtures of peace. The representations of the intendant and his faction had such effect, that Ponchartrain wrote to the governor that the plan of re-establishing Fort Frontenac " must absolutely be abandoned." Frontenac, bent on accomplishing his purpose, and doubly so because his enemies opposed it, had anticipated the orders of the minister, and sent seven hundred men to Lake Ontario to repair the fort. The day after they left Montreal, the letter of Ponchartrain arrived. The intendant demanded their recall. Frontenac refused. The fort was repaired, garrisoned, and victualled for a year.

A successful campaign was now doubly necessary to the governor, for by this alone could he hope to avert the consequences of his audacity. He waited no longer, but mustered troops, militia, and Indians, and marched to attack the Iroquois. 2

1 Golden, 178. Fletcher could get no men from his own or neighboring governments. See note, at the end of the chapter.

2 The above is drawn from the correspondence of Frontenac, Cham-pigny, La Motte-Cadillac, and Callieres, on one hand, and the king and the minister on the other. The letters are too numerous to specify. Also, from the official Relation de ce qui s'est passé de plus remarquable en Canada, 1694 1695, and Ibid., 1695 1696; Mtmoire soumis au Mwistre de ce qui re-

MILITARY INEFFICIENCY OF THE BRITISH COLONIES. — u His Majesty has subjects enough in those parts of America to drive out the French from Canada; but they are so crumbled into little governments, and so disunited, that they have hitherto afforded little assistance to each other, and now seem in a much worse disposition to do it for the future." This is the complaint of the Lords of Trade. Governor Fletcher writes bitterly : " Here every little government sets up for despotic power, and allows no appeal to the Crown, but, by a little juggling, defeats all commands and injunctions from the King." Fletcher's complaint was not unprovoked. The Queen had named him commander-in-chief, during the war, of the militia of several of the colonies, and empowered him to call on them for contingents of men, not above 350 from Massachusetts, 250 from Virginia, 160 from Maryland, 120 from Connecticut, 48 from Rhode Island, and 80 from Pennsylvania. This measure excited the jealousy of the colonies, and several of them remonstrated on constitutional grounds; but the attorney-general, to whom the question was referred, reported that the crown had power, under certain limitations, to appoint a commander-in-chief. Fletcher, therefore, in his character as such, called fora portion of the men; but scarcely one could he get. He was met by excuses and evasions, which, especially in the case of Connecticut, were of a most vexatious character. At last, that colony, tired by his importunities, condescended to furnish him with twenty-five men. With the others, he was less fortunate, though Virginia and Maryland compounded with a sum of money. Each colony claimed the control of its own militia, and was anxious to avoid the establishment of any precedent which might deprive it of the right. Even in the military management of each separate colony, there was scarcely less difficulty. A requisition for troops from a royal governor was always regarded with jealousy, and the provincial assemblies were slow to grant money for their support. In 1692, when Fletcher came to New York, the assembly gave him 300 men, for a year; in 1693, they gave him an equal number; in 1694, they allowed him but 170, he being accused, apparently with truth, of not having made good use of the former levies. He afterwards asked that the force at his disposal should be increased to 500 men, to guard the frontier; and the request was not granted. In 1697 he was recalled; and the Earl of Bellomont was commis-

sulte des Avis re$us du Canada en 1695; Clmmpigny, Mtmoire concernant le Fm-t de Cataracouy; La Potherie, II. 284-302 IV. 1-80; Colden, chaps x. xi

sioned governor of New York, Massachusetts, and New Hampshire, and captain-general, during the war, of all the forces of those colonies, as well as of Connecticut, Rhode Island, and New Jersey. The close of the war quickly ended this military authority; but there is no reason to believe that, had it continued, the earl's requisitions for men, in his character of captain-general, would have had more success than those of Fletcher. The whole affair is a striking illustration of the original isolation of communities, which afterwards became welded into a nation. It involved a military paralysis almost complete. Sixty years later, under the sense of a great danger, the British colonies were ready enough to receive a commander-in-chief, and answer his requisitions.

A great number of documents bearing upon the above subject will be found in the New York Colonial Documents, IT-

CHAPTER XIX.

1696-1698. FEONTENAC ATTACKS THE ONONDAGAS.

MABCH OF FRONTENAC. — FLIGHT OF THE ENEMY. — AN IROQUOIS STOIC. — RELIEF FOR THE ONONDAGAS. — BOASTS OF FRONTENAC. — His COMPLAINTS. — His ENEMIES. — PARTIES IN CANADA.— VIEWS OF FRONTENAC AND THE KING. — FRONTENAC PREVAILS. — PEACE OF RYBWICK. — FRONTENAC AND BELLOMONT. — SCHUYLEB AT QUEBEC. — FESTIVITIES. —A LAST DEFIANCE.

ON the fourth of July, Frontenac left Montreal, at the head of about twenty-two hundred men. On the nineteenth he reached Fort Frontenac, and on the twenty-sixth he crossed to the southern shore of Lake Ontario. A swarm of Indian canoes led the way; next followed two battalions of regulars, in bateaux, commanded by Callieres; then more bateaux, laden with cannon, mortars, and rockets; then Frontenac himself, surrounded by the canoes of his staff and his guard ; then eight hundred Canadians, under Ramesay ; while more regulars and more Indians, all commanded by Yaudreuil, brought up the rear. In two days they reached the mouth of the Oswego ; strong scouting-parties were sent out to scour the forests in front; while the expedition slowly and painfully worked its way up the stream. Most of the troops and Canadians marched through the matted woods along the banks ; while the bateaux and canoes were pushed, rowed, paddled, or dragged forward against the current. On the evening of the thirtieth, they reached the falls, where the river plunged over ledges of rock which completely stopped the way. The work of " carrying " was begun at once. The Indians and Canadians carried the canoes to the navigable water above, and gangs of men dragged the bateaux up the portage-path on rollers. Night soon came, and the work was continued till ten o'clock by torchlight. Frontenac would have passed on foot like the rest, but the Indians would not have it so. They lifted him in his canoe upon their shoulders, and bore him in triumph, singing and yelling, through the forest and along the margin of the rapids, the blaze of the torches lighting the strange procession, where plumes of officers and uniforms of the governor's guard mingled with the feathers and scalp-locks of naked savages.

When the falls were passed, the troops pushed on as before along the narrow stream, and through the tangled labyrinths on either side; till, on the first of August, they reached Lake Onondaga, and, with sails set, the whole flotilla glided before the wind, and landed the motley army on a rising ground half a league from the salt springs of Salina. The next day was spent in building a fort to protect the canoes, bateaux, and stores; and, as evening closed, a ruddy glow above the southern forest told them that the town of Onondaga was on fire.

412 FRONTENAC ATTACKS THE ONONDAGAS. [1696.

The Marquis de Crisasy was left, with a detachment, to hold the fort; and, at sunrise on the fourth, the army moved forward in order of battle. It was formed in two lines, regulars on the right and left, and Canadians in the centre. Callieres commanded the first line, and Vaudreuil the second. Frontenac was between them, surrounded by his staff officers and his guard, and followed by the artillery, which relays of Canadians dragged and lifted forward with inconceivable labor. The governor, enfeebled by age, was carried in an arm-chair; while Callieres, disabled by gout, was mounted on a horse, brought for the purpose in one of the bateaux. To Subercase fell the hard task of directing the march among the dense columns of the primeval forest, by hill and hollow, over rocks and fallen trees, through swamps, brooks, and gullies, among thickets, brambles, and vines. It was but eight or nine miles to Onondaga; but they were all day in reaching it, and evening was near when they emerged from the shadows of the forest into the broad light of the Indian clearing. The maize-fields stretched before them for miles, and in the midst lay the charred and smoking ruins of the Iroquois capital. Not an enemy was to be seen, but they found the dead bodies of two murdered French prisoners. Scouts were sent out, guards were set, and the disappointed troops encamped on the maize-fields.

Onondaga, formerly an open town, had been fortified by the English, who had enclosed it with a double range of strong palisades, forming a rect-
angle, flanked by bastions at the four coiners, and surrounded by an outer fence of tall poles. The place was not defensible against cannon and mortars; and the four hundred warriors belonging to it had been but slightly reinforced from the other tribes of the confederacy, each of which feared that the French attack might be directed against itself. On the approach of an enemy of five times their number, they had burned their town, and retreated southward into distant forests.

The troops were busied for two days in hacking down the maize, digging up the caches, or hidden stores of food, and destroying their contents. The neighboring tribe of the Oneidas sent a messenger to beg peace. Frontenac replied that he would grant it, on condition that they all should migrate to Canada, and settle there ; and Vaudreuil, with seven hundred men, was sent to enforce the demand. Meanwhile, a few Onondaga stragglers had been found; and among them, hidden in a hollow tree, a withered warrior, eighty years old, and nearly blind. Frontenac would have spared him; but the Indian allies, Christians from the mission villages, were so eager to burn him that it was thought inexpedient to refuse them. They tied him to the stake, and tried to shake his constancy by every torture that fire could inflict; but not a cry nor a murmur escaped him. He defied them to do their worst, till, enraged at his taunts, one of them gave him a mortal stab. " I thank you," said the old Stoic, with his last breath; " but you ought to have finished as you began, and killed me by fire. Learn from me,

you dogs of Frenchmen, how to endure pain : and you, dogs of dogs, their Indian allies, think what you will do when you are burned like me."

Vaudreuil and his detachment returned within three days, after destroying Oneida, with all the growing corn, and seizing a number of chiefs as hostages for the fulfilment of the demands of Frontenac. There was some thought of marching on Cayuga, but the governor judged it to be inexpedient ; and, as it would be useless to chase the fugitive Onondagas, nothing remained but to return home. 3

While Frontenac was on his march, Governor

1 Relation de ce qui s'est pass?, etc., 1695, 1696; La Potherie, III. 279. Callieres and the author of the Relation of 1682-1712 also speak of the extraordinary fortitude of the victim. The Jesuits say that it was not the Christian Indians who insisted on burning him, but the French themselves, " qui voulurent absolument qu'il fut brute & petit feu, ce qu'ils executerent eux-m€mes. Un Jesuite le confessa et l'assista a la mort, l'encourageant a souffrir courageusement et ckr&iennement les tour-mens." Relation de 1696 (Shea), 10. This writer adds that, when Frontenac heard of it, he ordered him to be spared; but it was too late. Charlevoix misquotes the old Stoic's last words, which were, according to the official Relation of 1696-6: " Je te remercie mais tu aurais bien du achever de me faire mourir par le feu. Apprenez, chiens de Francois, a Bouffrir, et vous sauvages leurs allies, qui etes les chiens des chiensi souvenez vous de ce que vous devez faire quand vous serez en pareil £tat que moi."

2 On the expedition against the Onondagas, Callieres au Ministre, 20 Oct., 1696; Frontenac au Ministre, 26 Oct., 1696 ; Frontenac et Champigny au Ministre (lettre commune) 26 Oct., 1696; Relation dece qui s'est passt, etc., 1696,1696; Relation, 1682-1712; Relation des Jesuites, 1696 (Shea); Doc. Hist. N. Y., I 323-366; La Potherie, III. 270-282; N..Y. Col. Docs., IV. 242.

Charlevoix charges Frontenac on this occasion with failing to pursue his advantage, lest others, and especially Callieres, should get more honor than he. The accusation seems absolutely groundless. His many enemies were silent about it at the time; for the king warmly commends his conduct on the expedition, and Callieres himself, writing immediately after, gives him nothing but praise.

Fletcher liad heard of his approach, and called the council at New York to consider what should be done. They resolved that " it will be very grievous to take the people from their labour; and there is likewise no money to answer the charge thereof." Money was, however, advanced by Colonel Cort-landt and others; and the governor wrote to Connecticut and New Jersey for their contingents of men; but they thought the matter no concern of theirs, and did not respond. Fletcher went to Albany with the few men he could gather at the moment, and heard on his arrival that the French were gone. Then he convoked the chiefs, condoled with them, and made them presents. Corn w r as sent to the Onondagas and Oneidas to support them through the winter, and prevent the famine which the French hoped would prove their destruction.

What Frontenac feared had come to pass. The enemy had saved themselves by flight; and his expedition, like that of Denonville, was but half successful. He took care, however, to announce it to the king as a triumph.

" Sire, the benedictions which Heaven has ever showered upon your Majesty's arms have extended even to this New World; whereof we have had visible proof in the expedition I have just made against the Onondagas, the principal nation of the Iroquois. I had long projected this enterprise, but the difficulties and risks which attended it made me regard it as imprudent; and I should never have resolved to undertake it, if I had not last, year es-

416 FEONTENAC ATTACKS THE ONONDAGAS. [1696

tablished an entrepot (Fort Frontenac), which made my communications more easy, and if I had not known, beyond all doubt, that this was absolutely the only means to prevent our allies from making peace with the Iroquois, and introducing the English into their country, by which the colony would infallibly be ruined. Nevertheless, by unexpected good fortune, the Onondagas, who pass for masters *of the other Iroquois, and the terror of all the Indians of this country, fell into a sort of bewilderment, which could only have come from on High; and were so terrified to see me march against them in person, and cover their lakes and rivers with nearly four hundred sail, that, without availing themselves of passes where a hundred men might easily hold four thousand in check, they did not dare to lay a single ambuscade, but, after waiting till I was five leagues from their fort, they set it on fire with all their dwellings, and fled, with their families, twenty leagues into the depths of the forest. It could have been wished, to make the affair more brilliant, that they had tried to hold their fort against us, for we were prepared to force it and kill a great many of them; but their ruin is not the less sure, because the famine, to which they are reduced, will destroy more than we could have killed by sword and gun.

" All the officers and men have done their duty admirably; and especially M. de Callieres, who has been a great help to me. I know not if your Majesty will think that I have tried to do mine, and will hold me worthy of some mark of honor that

may enable me to pass the short remainder of my life in some little distinction; but, whether this be so or not, I most humbly pray your Majesty to believe that I will sacrifice the rest of my days to your Majesty's service with the same ardor I have always felt." l

The king highly commended him, and sent him the cross of the Military Order of St. Louis. Cal-lieres, who had deserved it less, had received it several years before; but he had not found or provoked so many defamers. Frontenac complained to the minister that his services had been slightly and tardily requited. This was true, and it was due largely to the complaints excited by his own perversity and violence. These complaints still continued; but the fault was not all on one side, and Frontenac himself had often just reason to retort them. He wrote to Ponchartrain : " If you will not be so good as to look closely into the true state of things here, I shall always be exposed to detraction, and forced to make new apologies, which is very hard for a person so full of zeal and uprightness as I am. My secretary, who is going to France, will tell you all the ugly intrigues used to defeat my plans for the service of the king, and the growth of the colony. I have long tried to combat these artifices, but I confess that I no longer feel strength to resist them, and must succumb at last, if you will not have the goodness to give me strong support." 2

1 Frontenac au Roy, 25 Oct., 1696.

2 Frontenac au Ministre, 25 Oct., 1696.

27

FKONTENAC ATTACKS THE ONONDAGAS. [169&-9&

He still continued to provoke the detraction which he deprecated, till he drew, at last, a sharp remonstrance from the minister. " The dispute you have had with M. de Champigny is without cause, and I confess I cannot comprehend how you could have acted as you have done. If you do things of this sort, you must expect disagreeable consequences, which all the desire I have to oblige you cannot prevent. It is deplorable, both for you and for me, that, instead of using my good-will to gain favors from his Majesty, you compel me to make excuses for a violence which answers no purpose, and in which you indulge wantonly, nobody can tell why." 1

Most of these quarrels, however trivial in themselves, had a solid foundation, and were closely connected with the great question of the control of the west. As to the measures to be taken, two parties divided the colony; one consisting of the governor and his friends, and the other of the in-tendant, the Jesuits, and such of the merchants as were not in favor with Frontenac. His policy was to protect the Indian allies at all risks, to repel by force, if necessary, every attempt of the English to encroach on the territory in dispute, and to occupy it by forts which should be at once posts of war and commerce and places of rendezvous for traders and voyageurs. Champigny and his party denounced this system; urged that the forest posts should be abandoned, that both garrisons and traders should be recalled, that the French should

1690-98.] PARTIES IN CANADA.

not go to the Indians, but that the Indians should come to the French, that the fur trade of the interior should be carried on at Montreal, and that no Frenchman should be allowed to leave the settled limits of the colony, except the Jesuits and persons in their service, who, as Champigny insisted, would be able to keep the Indians in the French interest without the help of soldiers.

Strong personal interests were active on both sides, and gave bitterness to the strife. Frontenac, who always stood by his friends, had placed Tonty, La Foret, La Motte-Cadillac, and others of their number, in charge of the forest posts, where they made good profit by trade. Moreover, the licenses for trading expeditions into the interior were now, as before, used largely for the benefit of his favorites. The Jesuits also declared, and with some truth, that the forest posts were centres of debauchery, and that the licenses for the western trade were the ruin of innumerable young men. All these reasons were laid before the king. In vain Frontenac represented that to abandon the forest posts would be to resign to the English the trade of the interior country, and at last the country itself. The royal ear was open to his opponents, and the royal instincts reinforced their arguments. The king, enamoured of subordination and order, wished to govern Canada as he governed a province of France; and this could be done only by keeping the population within prescribed bounds. Therefore, he commanded that licenses for the forest trade should cease, that the

NAG ATTACKS THE ONONDAGAS, [1696-98

>osts should be abandoned and destroyed, Frenchmen should be ordered .back to the lements, and that none should return under pain of the galleys. An exception was made in favor of the Jesuits, who were allowed to continue their western missions, subject to restrictions designed to prevent them from becoming a cover to illicit fur trade. Frontenac was also directed to make peace with the Iroquois, even, if necessary, without including the western allies of France; that is, he was authorized by Louis XIY. to pursue the course which had discredited and imperilled the colony under the rule of Denonville. 1

The intentions of the king did not take effect. The policy of Frontenac was the true one, whatever motives may have entered into his advocacy of it. In view of the geographical, social, political, and commercial conditions of Canada, the policy of his opponents was impracticable, and nothing less than a perpetual cordon of troops could have prevented the Canadians from escaping to the backwoods. In spite of all the evils that attended the forest posts, it would have been a blunder to abandon them. This quickly became apparent.

1 M^moire du Eoy pour Frontenac et Champigny, 26 Mai, 1696; Ibid., 27 Avril, 1697; Registres du Conseil Supfrieur, Edit du 21 Mai, 1696.

" Ce qui vous avez mande' de raccommodement des Sauvages allies avec les Irocois n'a pas permis a Sa Majestd d'entrer dans la discutiou de la maniere de faire Fabandonnement des postes des Francis daiis la profondeur des terres, particulierement a Missilimackinac. . . En tout cas vous ne devez pas manquer de donner ordre pour ruiner les forts et tous les edifices qui pourront y avoir este' faits." Le Ministre a Fronte-nac, 26 Mai, 1696.

Besides the above, many other letters and despatches on both sides have been examined in relation to these questions.

Champigny himself saw the necessity of compromise. The instructions of the king were scarcely given before they were partially withdrawn, and they soon became a dead letter. Even Fort Frontenac was retained after repeated directions to abandon it. The policy of the governor prevailed; the colony returned to its normal methods of growth, and so continued to the end.

Now came the question of peace with the Iroquois, to whose mercy Frontenac was authorized to leave his western allies. He was the last man to accept such permission. Since the burning of Onondaga, the Iroquois negotiations with the western tribes had been broken off, and several fights had occurred, in which the confederates had suffered loss and been roused to vengeance. This was what Frontenac wanted, but at the same time it promised him fresh trouble ; for, while he was determined to prevent the Iroquois from making peace with the allies without his authority, he was equally determined to compel them to do so with it. There must be peace, though not till he could control its conditions.

The Onondaga campaign, unsatisfactory as it was, had had its effect. Several Iroquois chiefs came to Quebec with overtures of peace. They brought no prisoners, but promised to bring them in the spring; and one of them remained as a hostage that the promise should be kept. It was nevertheless broken under English influence ; and, instead of a solemn embassy, the council of

Onoii-daga sent a messenger with a wampum belt to tell

Frontenac that they were all so engrossed in bewailing the recent death of Black Kettle, a famous war chief, that they had no strength to travel; and they begged that Onontio would return the hostage, and send to them for the French prisoners. The messenger farther declared that, though they would make peace with Onontio, they would not make it with his allies. Frontenac threw back the peace-belt into his face. " Tell the chiefs that, if they must needs stay at home to cry about a trifle, I will give them something to cry for. Let them bring me every prisoner, French and Indian, and make a treaty that shall include all my children, or they shall feel my tomahawk again." Then, turning to a number of Ottawas who were present: " You see that I can make peace for myself when I please. If I continue the war, it is only for your sake. I will never make a treaty without including you, and recovering your prisoners like my own."

Thus the matter stood, when a great event took place. Early in February, a party of Dutch and Indians came to Montreal with news that peace had been signed in Europe; and, at the end of May, Major Peter Schuyler, accompanied by Del-lius, the minister of Albany, arrived with copies of the treaty in French and Latin. The scratch of a pen at Ryswick had ended the conflict in America, so far at least as concerned the civilized combatants. It was not till July that Frontenac received the official announcement from Versailles, coupled with an address from the king to the people of Canada.

OUR FAITHFUL AND BELOVED, — The moment has arrived ordained by Heaven to reconcile the nations. The ratification of the treaty concluded some time ago by our ambassadors with those of the Emperor and the Empire, after having made peace with Spain, England, and Holland, has everywhere restored the tranquillity so much desired. Strasbourg, one of the chief ramparts of the empire of heresy, united for ever to the Church and to our Crown ; the Rhine established as the barrier between France and Germany; and, what touches us even more, the worship of the True Faith authorized by a solemn engagement with sovereigns of another religion, are the advantages secured by this last treaty. The Author of so many blessings manifests Himself so clearly that we cannot but recognize His goodness; and the visible impress of His all-powerful hand is as it were the seal He has affixed to justify our intent to cause all our realm to serve and obey Him, and to make our people happy. We have begun by the fulfilment of our duty in offering Him the thanks which are His due ; and we have ordered the archbishops and bishops of our kingdom to cause Te Deum to be sung in the cathedrals of their dioceses. It is our will and our command that you be present at that which will be sung in the cathedral of our city of Quebec, on the day appointed by the Count of Frontenac, our governor and lieutenant-general in New France. Herein fail not, for such is our pleasure.

Louis. 1

There was peace between the two crowns; but a serious question still remained between Frontenac and the new governor of New York, the Earl of Bellomont. When Schuyler and Dellius came to Quebec, they brought with them all the French prisoners in the hands of the English of New York, together with a promise from Bellomont that he would order the Iroquois, subjects of the British crown, to deliver to him all those in their possession, and that he would then send them to Canada under

1 Lettre du Roy pour faire chanter le Te Deum, 12 Mars, 1698.

a safe escort. The two envoys demanded of Froii-tenac, at the same time, that he should deliver to them all the Iroquois in his hands. To give up Iroquois prisoners to Bellomont, or to receive through him French prisoners whom the Iroquois had captured, would have been an acknowledgment of British sovereignty over the five confederate tribes. Frontenac replied that the earl need give himself no trouble in the matter, as the Iroquois were rebellious subjects of King Louis; that they had already repented and begged peace ; and that, if they did not soon come to conclude it, he should use force to compel them.

Bellomont wrote, in return, that he had sent arms to the Iroquois, with orders to defend themselves if attacked by the French, and to give no quarter to them or their allies; and he added that, if necessary, he would send soldiers to their aid. A few days after, he received fresh news of Fron-tenac's warlike intentions, and wrote in wrath as follows: —

SIB, — Two of our Indians, of the Nation called Onondages, came yesterday to advise me that you had sent two renegades of their Nation to them, to tell them and the other tribes, except the Mohawks, that, in case they did not come to Canada within forty days to solicit peace from you, they may expect your marching into their country at the head of an army to constrain them thereunto by force. I, on my side, do this very day send my lieutenant-governor with the king's troops to join the Indians, and to oppose any hostilities you will attempt; and, if needs be, I will arm every man in the Provinces under my government to repel you, and to make reprisals for the damage which you will commit on our Indians. This, in a few words, is the part I will take, and the resolution I have adopted, whereof I have thought it proper by these presents to give you notice. I am, Sir, yours, &c.,

EARL OF BELLOMONT. NBW YOHK, 22d August, 1698.

To arm every man in his government would have been difficult. He did, however, what he could, and ordered Captain Nanfan, the lieutenant-governor, to repair to Albany; whence, on the first news that the French were approaching, he was to march to the relief of. the Iroquois with the four shattered companies of regulars and as many of the militia of Albany and Ulster as he could muster. Then the earl sent Wessels, mayor of Albany, to persuade the Iroquois to deliver their prisoners to him, and make no treaty with Frontenac. On the same day, he despatched Captain John Schuyler to carry his letters to the French governor. When Schuyler reached Quebec, and -delivered the letters, Frontenac read them with marks of great displeasure. " My Lord Bellomont threatens me," he said. " Does he think that I am afraid of him ? He claims the Iroquois, but they are none of his. They call me father, and they call him brother; and shall not a father chastise his children when he sees fit ? " A conversation followed, in which Frontenac asked the envoy what was the strength of Bellomont's government. Schuyler parried the question by a grotesque exaggeration, and answered that the earl could bring about a hundred thousand men into the field. Frontenac pretended to believe him, and returned with careless gravity that he had always heard so.

426 FRONTENAC ATTACKS THE ONONDAGAS.

The following Sunday was the day appointed for the Te Deum ordered by the king; and all the dignitaries of the colony, with a crowd of lesser note, filled the cathedral. There was a dinner of ceremony at the chateau, to which Schuyler was invited ; and he found the table of the governor thronged with officers. Frontenac called on his guests to drink the health of King William. Schuyler replied by a toast in honor of King Louis; and the governor next gave the health of the Earl of Bello-mont. The peace was then solemnly proclaimed, amid the firing of cannon from the batteries and ships; and the day closed with a bonfire and a general illumination. On the next evening, Frontenac gave Schuyler a letter in answer to the threats of the earl. He had written with trembling hand, .but unshaken will and unbending pride: —

" I am determined to pursue my course without flinching; and I request you not to try to thwart me by efforts which will prove useless. All the protection and aid you tell me that you have given, and will continue to give, the Iroquois, against the terms of the treaty, will not cause me much alarm, nor make me change my plans, but rather, on the contrary, engage me to pursue them still more." 1

1 On the questions between Bellomont and Frontenac, Relation de ce qui s'est passe", etc., 1697, 1698; Champigny au Ministre, 12 Juittet, 1698; Frontenac au Ministre, 18 Oct., 1698; Frontenac et Champigny au Ministre (lettre commune), 16 Oct., 1698; Callieres au Ministre, metne date, etc. The correspondence of Frontenac and Belloraont, the report of Peter Schuyler and Dellius, the journal of John Schuyler, and other papers on the same subjects, will be found in N. Y. Col. Docs., IV. John Schuyler was grandfather of General Schuyler of the American Revolution. Peter Schuyler and his colleague Dellius brought to Canada all the French prisoners in the hands of the English of New York, and asked for English

All
,il more
The Dinner of Ceremony at the Chateau

As the old soldier traced these lines, the shadow of death was upon him. Toils and years, passions and cares, had wasted Ins strength at last, and his fiery soul could bear him up no longer. A few weeks later he was lying calmly on his deathbed.

prisoners in return; but nearly all of these preferred to remain, a remarkable proof \f the kindness with which the Canadians treated their civilized captives.

CHAPTER XX.

1698. DEATH OF FRONTENAC.

His LAST HOURS. — His WILL. — His FUNERAL. — His EULOGIST AND HIS CRITIC. — His DISPUTES WITH THE CLERGY. — ^Bi» CHARACTER.

IN November, when the last ship had gone, and Canada was sealed from the world for half a year, a mortal illness fell upon the governor. On the twenty-second, he had strength enough to dictate his will, seated in an easy-chair in his chamber at the chateau. His colleague and adversary, Cham-pigny, often came to visit him, and did all in his power to soothe his last moments. The reconciliation between them was complete. One of his Recollet friends, Father Olivier Goyer, administered extreme unction; and, on the afternoon of the twenty-eighth, he died, in perfect composure and full possession of his faculties. He was in his seventy-eighth year.

He was greatly beloved by the humbler classes, who, days before his death, beset the chateau, praising and lamenting him. Many of higher station shared the popular grief. " He was the love and delight of New France," says one of

them: " churchmen honored him for his piety? nobles esteemed him for his valor, merchants respected him for his equity, and the people loved him for his kindness. " He was the father of the poor says another, " the protector of the oppressed, and a perfect model of virtue and piety." 3 An Ursuline nun regrets him as the friend and patron of her sisterhood, and so also does the superior of the Hotel-Dieu. 3 His most conspicuous though not his bitterest opponent, the intendant Champigny, thus announced his death to the court: " I venture to send this letter by way of New England to tell you that Monsieur le Comte de Frontenac died on the twenty-eighth of last month, with the sentiments of a true Christian. After all the disputes we have had together, you will hardly believe, Monseigneur, how truly and deeply I am touched by his death. He treated me during his illness in a manner so obliging, that I should be utterly void of gratitude if I did not feel thankful to him." 4

As a mark of kind feeling, Frontenac had bequeathed to the intendant a valuable crucifix, and to Madame de Champigny a reliquary which he had long been accustomed to wear. For the rest, he gave fifteen hundred livres to the Recollets, to be expended in masses for his soul, and that of his wife after her death. To her he bequeathed all the remainder of

1 La Potherie, I. 244, 246.

2 Hennepin, 41 (1704). Le Clerc speaks to the same effect

3 Histoire des Ursuiines de Quebec, I. 508; Juchereau, 378. * Champigny au Ministre, 22 Dec., 1698.

his small property, and he also directed that his heart should be sent her in a case of lead or silver. 1 His enemies reported that she refused to accept it, saying that she had never had it when he was living, and did not want it when he was dead.

On the Friday after his death, he was buried as lie had directed, not in the cathedral, but in the church of the Recollets, a preference deeply offensive to many of the clergy. The bishop officiated; and then the Re'collet, Father Goyer, who had attended his death-bed, and seems to have been his confessor, mounted the pulpit, and delivered his funeral oration. " This funeral pageantry," exclaimed the orator, " this temple draped in mourning, these dim lights, this sad and solemn music, this great assembly bowed in sorrow, and all this pomp and circumstance of death, may well penetrate your hearts. I will not seek to dry your tears, for I cannot contain my own. After all, this is a time to weep, and never did people weep for a better governor."

A copy of this eulogy fell into the hands of an enemy of Frontenac, who wrote a running commentary upon it. The copy thus annotated is still preserved at Quebec. A few passages from the orator and his critic will show the violent conflict of opinion concerning the governor, and illustrate in some sort, though with more force than fairness, the contradictions of his character :
—

1 Testament du Comte de Frontenac. I am indebted to Abbe* Bois of Maskinongd for a copy of this will. Frontenac expresses a wish that the heart should be placed in the family tomb

at the Church of St. Nicolas des Champs.

The Orator. " This wise man, to whom the Senate of Venice listened with respectful attention, because he spoke before them with all the force of that eloquence which you, Messieurs, have so often admired, — l

The Critic. "It was not his eloquence that they admired, but his extravagant pretensions, his bursts of rage, and his uu-worthy treatment of those who did not agree with him."

The Orator. " This disinterested man, more busied with duty than with gain,—

The Critic. " The less said about that the better."

The Orator. " Who made the fortune of others, but did not increase his own, —

The Critic. " Not for want of trying, and that very often in spite of his conscience and the king's orders."

The Orator. "Devoted to the service of his king, whose majesty he represented, and whose person he loved, —

The Critic. "Not at all. How often has he opposed his orders, even with force and violence, to the great scandal of everybody 1"

The Orator. " Great in the midst of difficulties, by that consummate prudence, that solid judgment, that presence of mind, that breadth and elevation of thought, which he retained to the last moment of his life, —

Tie Critic. " He had in fact a great capacity for political manoeuvres and tricks ; but as for the solid judgment ascribed to

Alluding to an incident that occurred when Frontenac commanded a Venetian force for the defence of Candia against the Turks.

him, his conduct gives it the lie, or else, if he had it, the vehemence of his passions often unsettled it. It is much to be feared that his presence of mind was the effect of an obstinate and hardened self-confidence by which he put himself above everybody and every thing, since he never used it to repair, so far as in him lay, the public and private wrongs he caused. What ought he not to have done here, in this temple, to ask pardon for the obstinate and furious heat with which he so long persecuted the Church; upheld and even instigated rebellion against her; protected libertines, scandal-mongers, and creatures of evil life against the ministers of Heaven; molested, persecuted, vexed persons most eminent in virtue, nay, even the priests and magistrates, who defended the cause of God; sustained in all sorts of ways the wrongful and scandalous traffic in brandy with the Indians ; permitted, approved, and supported the license and abuse of taverns; authorized and even introduced, in spite of the remonstrances of the servants of God, criminal and dangerous diversions ; tried to decry the bishop and the clergy, the missionaries, and other persons of virtue, and to injure them, both here and in France, by libels and calumnies; caused, in fine, either by himself or through others, a multitude of disorders, under which this infant church has groaned for many years ! What, I say, ought he not to have done before dying to atone for these scandals, and give proof of sincere penitence and compunction ? God gave him full time to recognize his errors, and yet to the last he showed a great indifference in all these matters. When, in presence of the Holy Sacrament, he was asked according to the ritual, Do you not beg pardon for all the ill examples you may have given ?' he answered, ' Yes,' but did not confess that he had ever given any. In a word, he behaved during the few days before his death like one who had led an irreproachable life, and had nothing to fear. And this is the presence of mind that he retained to his last moment!"

The Orator. " Great in dangers by his courage, he always came off with honor, and never was reproached with rashness, —

The Critic. " True ; he was not rash, as was seen when the Bostonnais besieged Quebec."

The Orator. " Great in religion by his piety, he practised its good works in spirit and in truth, —

The Critic. " Say rather that he practised its forms with parade and ostentation: witness the inordinate ambition with which he always claimed honors in the Church, to which he had no right; outrageously affronted intendants, who opposed his pretensions ; required priests to address him when preaching, and in their intercourse with him demanded from them humiliations which he did not exact from the meanest military officer. This was his way of making himself great in religion and piety, or, more truly, in vanity and hypocrisy. How can a man be called great in religion, when he openly holds opinions entirely opposed to the True Faith, such as, that all men are predestined, that Hell will not last for ever, and the like ? "

The Orator. " His very look inspired esteem and confidence, —

The Critic. " Then one must have taken him at exactly the right moment, and not when he was foaming at the mouth with rage."

The Orator. " A mingled air of nobility and gentleness; a countenance that bespoke the probity that appeared in all his acts, and a sincerity that could not dissimulate, —

The Critic. " The eulogist did not know the old fox."

The Orator. " An inviolable fidelity to friends, —

The Critic. " What friends ? Was it persons of the other sex ? Of these he was always fond, and too much for the honor of some of them."

The Orator. " Disinterested for himself, ardent for others, he used his credit at court only to recommend their services, excuse their faults, and obtain favors for them,

28

The Critic. "True; but it was for his creatures and for nobody else."

The Orator. " I pass in silence that reading of spiritual books which he practised as an indispensable duty more than forty years; that holy avidity with which he listened to the word of God, —

The Critic. " Only if the preacher addressed the sermon to him, and called him Monseigneur. As for his reading, it was often Jansenist books, of which he had a great many, and which he greatly praised and lent freely to others."

The Orator. " He prepared for the sacraments by meditation and retreat, —

The Critic. " And generally came out of his retreat more excited than ever against the Church."

The Orator. " Let us not recall his ancient and noble descent, his family connected with all that is greatest in the army, the magistracy, and the government; Knights, Marshals of France, Governors of Provinces, Judges, Councillors, and Ministers of State : let us not, I say, recall all these without remembering that their examples roused this generous heart to noble emulation ; and, as an expiring flame grows brighter as it dies, so did all the virtues of his race unite at last in him to end with glory a long line of great men, that shall be no more except in history."

The Critic. " Well laid on, and too well for his hearers to believe him. Far from agreeing that all these virtues were collected in the person of his pretended hero, they would find it very hard to admit that he had even one of them." 1

1 Oraison Funebre du tres-haut et tres-puissant Seigneur Louis de Buade, Comte de Frontenac et de Palluau, etc,, avec des remarques critiques, 169&

It is clear enough from what quiver these arrows came. From the first, Frontenac had set himself in opposition to the most influential of the Canadian clergy. When he came to the colony, their power in the government was still enormous, and even the most devout of his predecessors had been forced into conflict with them to defend the civil authority; but, when Frontenac entered the strife, he brought into it an irritability, a jealous and exacting vanity, a love of rule, and a passion for having his own way, even in trifles, which made him the most exasperating of adversaries. Hence it was that many of the clerical party felt towards him a bitterness that was far from ending with his life.

The sentiment of a religion often survives its convictions. However heterodox in doctrine, he was still wedded to the observances of the Church, and practised them, under the ministration of the R^collets, with an assiduity that made full amends to his conscience for the vivacity with which he opposed the rest of the clergy. To the R6collets their patron was the most devout of men; to his ultramontane adversaries, he was an impious persecutor.

His own acts and words best paint his character, and it is needless to enlarge upon it. What per-

That indefatigable investigator of Canadian history, the late M. Jacques Viger, to whom I am indebted for a copy of this eulogy, suggested that the anonymous critic may have been Abbe la Tour, author of the Vie do Laval. If so, his statements need the support of more trustworthy evidence. The above extracts are not consecutive, but are taken from vari ous parts of the manuscript.

haps may be least forgiven him is the barbarity of the warfare that he waged, and the cruelties that he permitted. He had seen too. many towns sacked to be much subject to the scruples of modern humanitarianism; yet he was no whit more ruthless than his times and his surroundings, and some of his contemporaries find fault with him for not allowing more Indian captives to be tortured. Many surpassed him in cruelty, none equalled him in capacity and vigor. When civilized enemies were once within his power, he treated them, according to their degree, with a chivalrous courtesy, or a generous kindness. If he was a hot and pertinacious foe, he was also a fast friend; and he excited love and hatred in about equal measure. His attitude towards public enemies was always proud and peremptory, yet his courage was guided by so clear a sagacity that he never was forced to recede from the position he had taken. Towards Indians, he was an admirable compound of sternness and conciliation. Of the immensity of his services to the colony there can be no doubt. He found it, under Denonville, in humiliation and terror; and he left it in honor, and almost in triumph.

In spite of Father Goyer, greatness must be denied him; but a more remarkable figure, in its bold and salient individuality and sharply marked light and shadow, is nowhere seen in American history.

There is no need to exaggerate the services of Frontenac. Nothing could be more fallacious than the assertion, often repeated, that in

his time Canada withstood the united force of all the British colonies. Most of these colonies took no part whatever in the war. Only two of them took an aggressive part, New York and Massachusetts. New York attacked Canada twice, with the two inconsiderable war-parties of John Schuyler in 1690 and of Peter Schuyler in the next year. The feeble expedition under Winthrop did not get beyond Lake George. Massachusetts, or rather her seaboard towns, attacked Canada once. Quebec, it is true, was kept in alarm during several years by rumors of another attack from the same quarter; but no such danger existed, as Massachusetts was exhausted by her first effort. The real scourge of Canada was the Iroquois, supplied with arms and ammunition from Albany

CHAPTEK XXI.

1699-1701. CONCLUSION.

Tun NEW GOVERNOR. — ATTITUDE OP THE IROQUOIS. — NEGOTIATIONS. — EMBASSY TO ONONDAGA. — PEACE. — THE IROQUOIS AND THE ALLIES. — DIFFICULTIES. — DEATH OF THE GREAT HURON. — FUNERAL RITES. — THE GRAND COUNCIL. — THE WORK OF FRON TENAC FINISHED. — RESULTS.

IT did not need the presence of Frontenac to cause snappings and sparks in the highly electrical atmosphere of New France. Callieres took his place as governor ad interim, and in due time received a formal appointment to the office. Apart from the wretched state of his health, undermined by gout and dropsy, he was in most respects well fitted for it; but his deportment at once gave umbrage to the excitable Champigny, who declared that he had never seen such hauteur since he came to the colony. Another official was still more offended. "Monsieur de Frontenac," he says, " was no sooner dead than trouble began. Monsieur de Callieres, puffed up by his new authority, claims honors due only to a marshal of France. It would be a different matter if he, like his predecessor, were regarded as the father of the country, and the love and delight of the Indian allies. At

the review at Montreal, he sat in his carriage, and received the incense offered him with as much composure and coolness as if he had been some divinity of this New World." In spite of these complaints, the court sustained Callieres, and authorized him to enjoy the honors that he had assumed. 1

His first and chief task was to finish the work that Frontenac had shaped out, and bring the Iro-quois to such submission as the interests of the colony and its allies demanded. The fierce confederates admired the late governor, and, if they themselves are to be believed, could not help lamenting him; but they were emboldened by his death, and the difficulty of dealing with them was increased by it. Had they been sure of effectual support from the English, there can be little doubt that they would have refused to treat with the French, of whom their distrust was extreme. The treachery of Denonville at Fort Frontenac still rankled in their hearts, and the English had made them believe that some of their best men had lately been poisoned by agents from Montreal. The French assured them, on the other hand, that the English meant to poison them, refuse to sell them powder and lead, and then, when they were helpless, fall upon and destroy them. At Montreal, they were told that the English called them their negroes ; and, at Albany, that if they made peace with Onontio, they would sink into " perpetual in-

1 Champigny au Ministre, 20 Mai, 1699; La Potherie au Ministre, 2 Mi'n, 1699 ; TT vdreuil et La P&herie au Ministre. meme. date.

famy and slavery." Still, in spite of their perplexity, they persisted in asserting their independence of each of the rival powers, and played the one against the other, in order to strengthen their position with both. When Bellomont required them to surrender their French prisoners to him, they answered : " We are the masters; our prisoners are our own. We will keep them or give them to the French, if we choose/ ' At the same time, they told Callieres that they would bring them to the English at Albany, and invited him to send thither his agents to receive them. They were much disconcerted, however, when letters were read to them which showed that, pending the action of commissioners to settle the dispute, the two kings had ordered their respective governors to refrain from all acts of hostility, and join forces, if necessary, to compel the Iroquois to keep quiet. 1 This, with their enormous losses, and their desire to recover their people held captive in Canada, led them at last to serious thoughts of peace. Eesolving at the same time to try the temper of the new Onon-tio, and yield no more than was absolutely necessary, they sent him but six ambassadors, and no prisoners. The ambassadors marched in single file to the place of council; while their chief, who led the way, sang a dismal song of lamentation for the French slain in the war, calling on them to thrust their heads above ground, behold the good work

1 Le Roy a Frontenac, 25 Mars, 1699. Frontenac's death was not known at Versailles till April. Le Roy d'Angleterre 0 Bellomont, 2 Avril, 1699 : La Potherie, IV. 128 ; Callieres 'a Bellomont, 7 Aa&t, 1699.

of peace, and banish every thought of vengeance. Callieres proved, as they had hoped, less inexorable than Frontenac. He accepted their promises, and consented to send for the prisoners in their hands, on condition that within thirty-six days a full deputation of their principal men should come to Montreal. The Jesuit Bruyas, the Canadian Mari-court, and a French officer named Joncaire went back with them to receive the prisoners.

The history of Joncaire was a noteworthy one. The Senecas had captured him some time before, tortured his companions to death, and doomed him to the same fate. As a preliminary torment, an old chief tried to burn a finger of the captive in the bowl of his pipe, on which Joncaire knocked him down. If he had begged for mercy, their hearts would have been flint; but the warrior crowd were so pleased with this proof of courage that they adopted him as one of their tribe, and gave him an Iroquois wife. He lived among them for many years, and gained a commanding influence, which proved very useful to the French. When he, with Bruyas and Maricourt, approached Onon-daga, which had long before risen from its ashes, they were greeted with a fusillade of joy, and regaled with the sweet stalks of young maize, followed by the more substantial refreshment of venison and corn beaten together into a pulp and boiled. The chiefs and elders seemed well inclined to peace; and, though an envoy came from Albany; to prevent it, he behaved with such arrogance that, far from dissuading his auditors, he confirmed

them in their resolve to meet Onontio at Montreal. They seemed willing enough to give up their French prisoners, but an unexpected difficulty arose from the prisoners themselves. They had been adopted into Iroquois families; and, having become attached to the Indian life, they would not leave it. Some of them hid in the woods to escape their deliverers, who, with their best efforts, could collect but thirteen, all women, children, and boys. With these, they returned to Montreal, accompanied by a peace embassy of nineteen Iroquois.

Peace, then, was made. " I bury the hatchet," said Callieres, " in a deep hole, and over the hole I place a gieat rock, and over the rock I turn a river, that the hatchet may never be dug up again." The famous Huron, Kondiaronk, or the Rat, was present, as were also a few Ottawas, Abenakis, and converts of the Saut and the Mountain. Sharp words passed between them and the ambassadors; but at last they all laid down their hatchets at the feet of Onontio, and signed the treaty together. It was but a truce, and a doubtful one. More was needed to confirm it, and the following August was named for a solemn act of ratification. 1

Father Engelran was sent to Michillimackinac, while Courtemanche spent the winter and spring in toilsome journey ings among the tribes of the

1 On these negotiations, La Potherie, IV. lettrexi.; N. Y. Col. Docs., IX. 708,711,716; Colden, 200; Callieres au Ministre, 16 Oct., 1700; Champigny au Ministre, 22 Juillet, 1700; La Potherie au Ministre, 11 Aout, 1700; Ibid., 16 Oct., 1700; Callieres et Champigny au Ministre, 18 Oct., 1700. See also N. Y. Col. Docs., IV., for a great number of English documents bearing on the subject

west. Such was his influence over them that he persuaded them all to give up their Iroquois prisoners, and send deputies to the grand council. Engelran had had scarcely less success among the northern tribes; and early in July a great fleet of canoes, conducted by Courtemanche, and filled with chiefs, warriors, and Iroquois prisoners, paddled down the lakes for Montreal. Meanwhile Bruyas, Maricourt, and Joncaire had returned on the same errand to the Iroquois towns; but, so far as concerned prisoners, their success was no greater than before. Whether French or Indian, the chiefs were slow to give them up, saying that they had all been adopted into families who would not part with them unless consoled for the loss by gifts. This was true; but it was equally true of the other tribes, whose chiefs had made the necessary gifts, and recovered the captive Iroquois. Joncaire and his colleagues succeeded, however, in leading a large deputation of chiefs and elders to Montreal. Courtemanche with his canoe fleet from the lakes was not .far behind ; and when their approach was announced, the chronicler, La Potherie, full of curiosity, went to meet them at the mission village' of the Saut. First appeared the Iroquois, two hundred in all, firing their guns as their canoes drew near, while the mission Indians, ranged along the shore, returned the salute. The ambassadors were conducted to a capacious lodge, where for a quarter of an hour they sat smoking with immovable composure. Then a chief of the mission made a speech, and then followed a feast of boiled dogs

In the morning they descended the rapids to Mont real, and in due time the distant roar of the Baluting cannon told of their arrival.

They had scarcely left the village, when the river was covered with the canoes of the western and northern allies. There was another fusillade of welcome as the heterogeneous company landed, and marched to the great council-house. The calumet was produced, and twelve of the assembled chiefs sang a song, each rattling at the same time a dried gourd half full of peas.

Six large kettles were next brought in, containing several dogs and a bear suitably chopped to pieces, which being ladled out to the guests were despatched in an instant, and a solemn dance and a supper of boiled corn closed the festivity.

The strangers embarked again on the next day, and the cannon of Montreal greeted them as they landed before the town. A great quantity of evergreen boughs had been gathered for their use, and of these they made their wigwams outside the palisades. Before the opening of the grand council, a multitude of questions must be settled, jealousies soothed, and complaints answered. Callieres had no peace. He was busied for a week in giving audience to the deputies. There was one question which agitated them all, and threatened to rekindle the war. Kondiaronk, the Rat, the foremost man among all the allied tribes, gave utterance to the general feeling : " My father, you told us last autumn to bring you all the Iroquois prisoners in our hands. We have obeyed, and

brought them. Now let us see if the Iroquois have also obeyed, and brought you our people whom they captured during the war. If they have done so, they are sincere; if not, they are false. But I know that they have not brought them. I told you last year that it was better that they should bring their prisoners first. You see now how it is, and how they have deceived us."

The complaint was just, and the situation became critical. The Iroquois deputies were invited to explain themselves. They stalked into the council-room with their usual haughty composure, and readily promised to surrender the prisoners in future, but offered no hostages for their good faith. The Rat, who had counselled his own and other tribes to bring their Iroquois captives to Montreal, was excessively mortified at finding himself duped. He came to a later meeting, when this and other matters were to be discussed; but he was so weakened by fever that he could not stand. An armchair was brought him; and, seated in it, he harangued the assembly for two hours, amid a deep silence, broken only by ejaculations of approval from his Indian hearers. When the meeting ended, he was completely exhausted; and, being carried in his chair to the hospital, he died about midnight. He was a great loss to the French; for, though he had caused the massacre of La Chine, his services of late years had been invaluable. In spite of his unlucky name, he was one of the ablest North American Indians on record, as appears by his remarkable influence over many tribes, and by

the respect, not to say admiration, of his French contemporaries.

The French charged themselves with the funeral rites, carried the dead chief to his wigwam, stretched him on a robe of beaver skin, and left him there lying in state, swathed in a scarlet blanket, with a kettle, a gun, and a sword at his side, for his use in the world of spirits. This was a concession to the superstition of his countrymen ; for the Rat was a convert, and went regularly to mass. 1 Even the Iroquois, his deadliest foes, paid tribute to his memory. Sixty of them came in solemn procession, and ranged themselves around the bier; while one of their principal chiefs pronounced a-n harangue, in which he declared that the sun had covered his face that day in grief for the loss of the great Huron. 3 He was buried on the next morning. Saint-Ours, senior captain, led the funeral train with an escort of troops, followed by sixteen Huron warriors in robes of beaver skin, marching four and four, with faces painted black and guns reversed. Then came the clergy, and then six war-chiefs carrying the coffin. It was decorated with flowers, and on it lay a plumed hat, a sword, and a gorget. Behind it were the brother

1 La Potherie, IV. 229. Charlevoix suppresses the kettle and gun, and says that the dead chief wore a sword and a uniform, like a French officer. In fact, he wore Indian leggins and a capote under his scarlet blanket.

2 Charlevoix says that these were Christian Iroquois of the missions. Potherie, his only authority, proves them to have been heathen, as their chief mourner was a noted Seneca, and

their spokesman, Avenano, was the accredited orator of the Oneidas, Onondagas, Cayugas, and Senecas in whose name he made the funeral harangue.

and sons of the dead chief, and files of Huron and Ottawa warriors; while Madame de Champigny, attended by Vaudreuil and all the military officers, closed the procession. After the service, the soldiers fired three volleys over the grave; and a tablet was placed upon it, carved with the words, —

GIT LE RAT, CHEF DBS HURONS.

All this ceremony pleased the allied tribes, and helped to calm their irritation. Every obstacle being at length removed or smoothed over, the fourth of August was named for the grand council. A vast, oblong space was marked out on a plain near the town, and enclosed with a fence of branches. At one end was a canopy of boughs and leaves, under which were seats for the spectators Troops were drawn up in line along the sides; the seats under the canopy were filled by ladies, officials, and the chief inhabitants of Montreal; Callieres sat in front, surrounded by interpreters; and the Indians were seated on the grass around the open space. There were more than thirteen hundred of them; gathered from a distance of full two thousand miles, Hurons and Ottawas from Michilli-mackinac, Ojibwas from Lake Superior, Crees from the remote north, Pottawatamies from Lake Michigan, Mascontins, Sacs, Foxes, "Winnebagoes, and Menominies from Wisconsin, Miamis from the St. Joseph, Illinois from the river Illinois, Abenakis from Acadia, and many allied hordes of less account ; each savage painted with diverse hues and patterns, and each in his dress of ceremony,

leathern shirts fringed with scalp-locks, colored blankets or robes of bison hide and beaver skin, bristling crests of hair or long lank tresses, eagle feathers or horns of beasts. Pre-eminent among them all sat their valiant and terrible foes, the warriors of the confederacy. " Strange,'* exclaims La Potherie, " that four or five thousand should make a whole new world tremble. New England is but too happy to gain their good graces ; New France is often wasted by their wars, and our allies dread them over an extent of more than fifteen hundred leagues." It was more a marvel than he knew, for he greatly overrates their number.

Callieres opened the council with a speech, in which he told the assembly that, since but few tribes were represented at the treaty of the year before, he had sent for them all to ratify it; that he now threw their hatchets and his own into a pit so deep that nobody could find them; that henceforth they must live like brethren; and, if by chance one should strike another, the injured brother must not revenge the blow, but come for redress to him, Onontio, their common father. Nicolas Perrot and the Jesuits who acted as interpreters repeated the speech in five different languages ; and, to confirm it, thirty-one wampum belts were given to the thirty-one tribes present. Then each tribe answered in turn. First came Hassaki, chief of an Ottawa band known as Cut Tails. He approached with a majestic air, his long robe of beaver skin trailing on the grass behind him. Four Iroquois captives followed, with eyes bent on the

ground; and, when he stopped before the governor, they seated themselves at his feet. " You asked us for our prisoners/' he said, " and here they are. I set them free because you wish it, and I regard them as my brothers." Then turning to the Iro-quois deputies: " Know that if I pleased I might have eaten them; but I have not done as you would have done. Eemember this when we meet, and let us be friends." The Iroquois ejaculated their approval.

Next came a Huron chief, followed by eight Iroquois prisoners, who, as he declared, had been bought at great cost, in kettles, guns, and blankets, from the families who had adopted them. "We thought that the Iroquois would have done by us as we have done by them; and we were astonished to see that they had not brought us our prisoners. Listen to me, my father, and you, Iroquois, listen. I am not sorry to make peace, since my father wishes it, and I will live in peace with him and with you." Thus, in turn, came the spokesmen of all the tribes, delivering their prisoners and making their speeches. The Miami orator said: " I am very angry with the Iroquois, who burned my son some years ago; but to-day I forget all that. My father's will is mine. I will not be like the Iroquois, who have disobeyed his voice." The orator of the Mississagas came forward, crowned with the head and horns of a young bison bull, and, presenting his prisoners, said: " I place them in your hands. Do with them as you like. I am only too proud that you count me among your allies."

29

The chief of the Foxes now rose from his seat at the farther end of the enclosure, and walked sedately across the whole open space towards the stand of spectators. His face was painted red, and he wore an old French wig, with its abundant curls in a state of complete entanglement. When he reached the chair of the governor, he bowed, and lifted the wig like a hat, to show that he was perfect in French politeness. There was a burst of laughter from the spectators; but Callieres, with ceremonious gravity, begged him to put it on again, which he did, and proceeded with his speech, the pith of which was briefly as follows: "The darkness is gone, the sun shines bright again, and now the Iroquois is my brother."

Then came a young Algonquin war-chief, dressed like a Canadian, but adorned with a drooping red feather and a tall ridge of hair like the crest of a cock. It was he who slew Black Kettle, that redoubted Iroquois whose loss filled the confederacy with mourning, and who exclaimed as he fell, " Must I, who have made the whole earth tremble, now die by the hand of a child!" The young chief spoke concisely and to the purpose: "I am not a man of counsel: it -is for me to listen to your words. Peace has come, and now let us forget the past."

When he and all the rest had ended, the orator of the Iroquois strode to the front, and in brief words gave in their adhesion to the treaty. " Onontio, we are pleased with all you have done, and we have listened to all you have said. We assure you by

these four belts of wampum that we will stand fast in our obedience. As for the prisoners whom we have not brought you, we place them at your disposal, and you will send and fetch them."

The calumet was lighted. Callieres, Champigny, and Vaudreuil drew the first smoke, then the Iro-quois deputies, and then all the tribes in turn. The treaty was duly signed, the representative of each tribe affixing his mark, in the shape of some bird, beast, fish, reptile, insect, plant, or nondescript object.

u Thus," says La Potherie, " the labors of the late Count Frontenac were brought to a happy consummation." The work of Frontenac was indeed finished, though not as he would have finished it. Callieres had told the Troquois that till they surrendered their Indian prisoners he would keep in his own hands the Iroquois prisoners surrendered by the allied tribes. To this the spokesman of the confederacy coolly replied : " Such a proposal was never made since the world began. Keep them, if you like. We will go home, and think no more about them; but, if you gave them to us without making trouble, and gave us our son Joncaire at the same time, we should have no reason to distrust your sincerity, and should all be glad to send you back the prisoners we took from your allies." Callieres yielded, persuaded the allies to agree to the conditions, gave up the prisoners, and took an empty promise in return. It was a triumph for the Iroquois, who meant to keep their Indian captives, and did in fact keep nearly all of them. 1

1 The council at Montreal is described at great length by La Potherie,

The chief objects of the late governor were gained. The power of the Iroquois was so far broken that they were never again very formidable to the French. Canada had confirmed her Indian alliances, and rebutted the English claim to sovereignty over the five tribes, with all the consequences that hung upon it. By the treaty of Ryswick, the great questions at issue in America were left to the arbitrament of future wars ; and meanwhile, as time went on, the policy of Frontenac developed and ripened. Detroit was occupied by the French, the passes of the west were guarded by forts, another New France grew up at the mouth of the Mississippi, and lines of military communication joined the Gulf of Mexico with the Gulf of St. Lawrence; while the colonies of England lay passive between the Alleghanies and the sea till roused by the trumpet that sounded with wavering notes on many a bloody field to peal at last in triumph from the Heights of Abraham.

a spectator. There is a short official report of the various speeches, of which a translation will be found in N. Y. Col. Docs., IX. 722. Callieres himself gives interesting details. (Callieres au Ministre, 4 Oct., 1701.) A great number of papers on Indian affairs at this time will be found in N. Y. Col. Docs., IV.

Joncaire went for the prisoners whom the Iroquois had promised to give up, and could get but six of them. Callieres au Ministre, 81 Oct., 1701. The rest were made Iroquois by adoption.

According to an English official estimate made at the end of the war, the Iroquois numbered 2,650 warriors in 1689, and only 1,230 in 1698. N. Y. Col. Docs., IV. 420. In 1701, a French writer estimates them at only 1,200 warriors. In other words, their strength was reduced at least one half. They afterwards partially recovered it by the adoption of prisoners, and still more by the adoption of an entire kindred tribe, the Tuscaroras. In 1720, the English reckon them at 2,000 warriors. N. Y. Col. Docs., V 557

APPENDIX.

THE FAMILY OF FKONTENAC.

COUNT FKONTENAC'S grandfather was

ANTOINE DE BUADE, Seigneur de Frontenac, Baron de Pal-iuau, Conseiller d'Etat, Chevalier des Ordres du Roy, son premier maitre d'hotel, et gouverneur de St. Germain-en-Laye. By Jeanne Secontat, his wife, he had, among other children,

HENRI DE BUADE, Chevalier, Baron de Palluau et mestre de camp (colonel) du regiment de Navarre, who, by his wife Anne Phelippeaux, daughter of Raymond Phelippeaux, Secretary of State, had, among other children,

Louis DE BUADE, Comte de Palluau et Frontenac, Seigneur de Flsle-Savary, mestre de camp du regiment de Normandie, mare'chal de camp dans les armies du Roy, et gouverneur et lieutenant general en Canada, Acadie, Isle de Terreneuve, et autres pays de la France septentrionale. Louis de Buade had by his wife, Anne de La Grange-Trianon, one son, Franyois Louis, killed in Germany, while in the service of the king, and leaving no issue.

The foregoing is drawn from a comparison of the following authorities, all of which will be found in the Bibliotheque Nationale of Paris, where the examination was made: Memoires de Marolles, abbe de Vitteloin, II. 201; L'Hermite-Souliers, Histoire Genealogique de la Noblesse de Touraine; Du Chesne, Recherches Historiques de I'Ordre du Saint-Esprit; Morin, Statute de r Ordre du Saint-Esprit; Marolles de Villeloin, Histoire des Anciens Gomtes tfAnjou ; Pere Anselme, Grands Officiers de la Oouronne; Pinard, Chronologic Historique-militaire ; Table de la Gazette de France. In this matter of the Frontenac geneal-

ogy, I am much indebted to the kind offices of my friend, James Gordon Clarke, Esq.

When, in 1600, Henry IV. was betrothed to Marie de Medicis, Frontenac, grandfather of the governor of Canada, described as " ung des plus antiens serviteurs du roy," was sent to

Florence by the king to carry his portrait to his affianced bride. Memoires de Philippe Hurault, 448 (Petitot).

The appointment of Frontenac to the post, esteemed as highly honorable, of maitre (f hotel in the royal household, immediately followed. There is a very curious book, the journal of Jean He*roard, a physician charged with the care of the infant Dauphin, afterwards Louis XIII., born in 1601. It records every act of the future monarch: his screaming and kicking in the arms of his nurses, his refusals to be washed and dressed, his resistance when his hair was combed; how he scratched his governess, and called her names; how he quarrelled with the children of his father's mistresses, and at the age of four declined to accept them as brothers and sisters; how his mother slighted him; and how his father sometimes caressed, sometimes teased, and sometimes corrected him with his own hand. The details of the royal nursery are, we may add, astounding for their grossness; and the language and the manners amid which the infant monarch grew up were worthy of the days of Rabelais.

Frontenac and his children appear frequently, and not unfavorably, on the pages of this singular diary. Thus, when the Dauphin was three years old, the king, being in bed, took him and a young Frontenac of about the same age, set them before him, and amused himself by making them rally each other in their infantile language. The infant Frontenac had a trick of stuttering, which the Dauphin caught from him, and retained for a long time. Again, at the age of five, the Dauphin, armed with a little gun, played at soldier with two of the Frontenac children in the hall at St. Germain. They assaulted a town, the rampart being represented by a balustrade before the fireplace. "The Dauphin," writes the journalist, "said that he would be a musketeer, and yet he spoke sharply to the others

who would not do as he wished. The king said to him, My boy, you are a musketeer, but you speak like a general/ " Long after, when the Dauphin was in his fourteenth year, the following entry occurs in the physician's diary : —

St. Germain, Sunday, 22d (July, 1614). He (the Dauphin) goes to the chapel of the terrace, then mounts his horse and goes to find M. de Souvre and M. de Frontenac, whom he surprises as they were at breakfast at the small house near the quarries. At half past one, he mounts again, in hunting boots ; goes to the park with M. de Frontenac as a guide, chases a stag, and catches him. It was his first stag-hunt."

Of Henri de Buade, father of the governor of Canada, but little is recorded. When in Paris, he lived, like his son after him, on the Quai des Celestins, in the parish of St. Paul. His Bon, Count Frontenac, was born in 1620, seven years after his father's marriage. Apparently his birth took place elsewhere than in Paris, for it is not recorded with those of Henri de Buade's other children, on the register of St. Paul (Jal, Diction-naire Critique, Biographique, et d'Histoire). The story told by Tallemant des Reaux concerning his marriage (see page 6) seems to be mainly true. Colonel Jal says : " On congoit que j'ai pu §tre tente de connattre ce qu'il y a de vrai dans les remits de Saint-Simon et de Tallemant des Reaux; voici ce qu'apr&s bien des recherches, j'ai pu apprendre. M". e La Grange fit, en effet, un mariage a demi secret. Ce ne fut point a sa paroisse que fut benie son union avec M. de Frontenac, mais dans une des petites eglises de la Cite" qui avaient le privilege de recevoir les amants qui s'unissaient malgre' leurs parents, et ceux qui regularisaient leur position et s'e"pousaient un peu avant — quel-quefois apres —la naissance d'un enfant. Ce fut a St. Pierre-aux-Bceufs que, le mercredy, 28 Octobre, 1648, Messire Louis de Buade, Chevalier, comte de Frontenac, conseiller du Roy en ses conseils, mareschal des camps et armees de S. M., et maistre de camp du regiment du Normandie epousa ' demoiselle Anne de La Grange, fille de Messire Charles de La Grange, conseiller du

Roy et maistre des comptes' de la paroisse de St. Paul comme M. de Frontenac, en vertu de la dispense . obtenue

de M. Pofficial de Paris par laquelle il est permis au Sf de Buade et demoiselle de La Grange de celebrer leur marriage suyvant et conforme'nient a la permission qu'ils en ont obtenue du Sf Coquerel, vicaire de St. Paul, devant le premier cure oil vicaire sur ce requis, en gardant les solennite's en ce cas requises et ac-coutumees.'" Jal then gives the signatures to the act of marriage, which, except that of the bride, are aU of the Frontenac family.

THE END

Made in the USA
Coppell, TX
29 January 2022

72605042R00114